A Dual
Affair

A Dual
Affair

Ria Bonneamie

REGENT PRESS
Berkeley, California

[Paperback]
ISBN 10: 1-58790-570-1
ISBN 13: 978-1-58790-570-4

[E-Book]
ISBN 10: 1-58790-572-8
ISBN 13: 978-1-58790-572-8

Library of Congress Control Number: 2021933390

The persons and events in this book are fictional. Names and places have no relevance to any real facts. Any coincidence should be examined thoroughly for cosmic consequences. Canines and other domesticated creatures must be respected, for initially they are innocent, until transformed by humans.

Manufactured in the U.S.A.
REGENT PRESS
Berkeley, California
www.regentpress.net

This book is dedicated to Michel B. Kamara,
for stimulating my artistic potential.

Much praise to all my helpers, family and friends,
for their patience with my unconventional locution.

"So we grew together, like to a double cherry,
seeming parted,
but yet a union in partition, two lovely berries
moulded in one stem"
— WILLIAM SHAKESPEARE

"You were born together,
and together you shall be forevermore
but let there be spaces in your togetherness.
And let the winds of heaven dance between you."
— KHALIL GIBRAN

Table of Contents

Chapter 1
A Peculiar Dog

THERE WAS THAT DOG AGAIN, SITTING ON THE sidewalk across the street, perfectly framed in front of the green chile field. With an elegant, pointed face, a white stripe along its muzzle and dark mascara around the eyes, the dog had a long, curled tail, and all over its coat of satin white, large chocolate-brown and small tan spots. It resembled a prize-winning Australian Shepherd the twins had been hired to locate a few years ago. Its fine features looked female, a young one, maybe a year old. She had been showing up every day, usually mid-morning, and staying put for a couple of hours before disappearing again. Each day she would sit absolutely still, a behavior somewhat unusual for that extremely active breed of dog. Once in a while, she would turn her head one way and then the other, as if getting ready to cross the road.

Antonia reminded her brother that shortly after starting their business, seven years ago, they had investigated the disappearance of such a dog, an Aussie that looked a lot like the one across from their office, minus its tail. As detectives, most of their prior cases had consisted of tracking cheating spouses. They had welcomed a different kind of inquiry.

A wealthy woman from El Paso — Rebecca something, she could not remember her last name — had hired them to look for Leduc, her three-year-old Australian Shepherd male, who had won the Texas State Championship the previous year. The dog was to be entered in that year's national dog show in Dallas, but had been stolen from Rebecca's car while she was registering in the hotel lobby.

Antonia had flown in to meet Rebecca. After looking at hundreds of pictures of Leduc, she discovered much about the woman's friends, enemies, and Richard, the soon-to-be ex-husband. Her husband was demanding a divorce, as their marriage had been on the rocks ever since his wife had started showing the dog.

Tony thought the spouse the most likely suspect, as the car had been locked and alarmed, with the rear windows slightly cracked open. It was still locked when Rebecca discovered the dog missing.

Antonia met Richard at his mansion. He told her that he had bought the dog for both of them and that he had the dog with him in the backyard. He complained that his wife had turned this smart animal into a vain, selfish toy that only answered to her, and asked his housekeeper to bring him inside the living room. The beautiful Aussie was very well trained, obediently sitting down as soon as his master commanded, staying right by his side, looking up at him, begging for attention or for a treat. Richard had explained that he was going to keep him and try to bring him back to the original purpose he had bought him for: a companion, a protector, and a natural shepherd who should learn to work sheep on his ranch in northern New Mexico. He told Tony that if Rebecca wanted to show Leduc one last time, she should come see him, sign the divorce papers, and the dog would be returned to him after the show.

Antonia helped mediate the conflict between the two of them. She wished she could have communicated freely with her twin brother, Antonio, for advice, or that he had been the one present for this confrontation, instead of her. He did not get upset as fast as she did. She did her best to mitigate a sane solution for the estranged couple. After a heated time of much squabbling, the couple decided to sign the divorce papers, dividing their possessions equally, but the dog would come back to Richard temporarily after the show, with the condition that the first male pup Leduc sired, would belong to him.

On the flight home, Antonia had conveyed to her brother that in the future they should stay away from splitting couples. They both agreed that other people's marital problems were just too messy and unpleasant. Already they were beginning to get calls for more varied cases. They looked forward to being able to pick and choose their own clients.

Sis, we didn't know in advance that there was a divorce in the middle of this case. Besides, you might have discreetly tried to get my opinion.

Yeah, Tone, but it's harder for me to be seen as the detective. Needed to assert myself in this male-dominated profession.

~ ~ ~

The three, large windows of their agency, the Two Tonys Search Engine, peer right on the sunny side of West Amador Avenue, on the edge of Las Cruces. Deep in the southern half of New Mexico, the city is rapidly growing, ever sprawling between the slow, meandering Rio Grande and the sharp-jutting Organ Mountains. The building is surrounded by an old storefront for antiques and recycled goods, a brand-new lamp and lighting warehouse, and a decrepit motel. Across the street, chile fields bloom, then fruit in the fall, later red on green, like small Christmas trees until harvested. Past these, a trendy café stands next to a traditional Mexican restaurant. After a stretch of empty lots and scattered, dusty antique stores on either side of the road, two truck stops compete with garish advertisements, just before the entrance to the interstate.

Despite the vertical prison bars on the windows to deter vandals, the agency looks stylish and well kept. Red flowering bushes in the yard surround the earth- colored adobe building, complete with a flat roof over vigas sticking outside of the walls, dark-turquoise doors and window shutters, as if springing from Santa Fe. Only a small, black, hanging sign with white lettering adorns the front porch, bearing the establishment's name and two cupped hands under a watchful eye.

The interior is modern, done in dark-red, tan, and light-gray tones. The office in the front room offers a relaxing setting, with a slick, half-circle, stainless-steel desk surrounded by padded, cherrywood armchairs. Contemporary Navajo Indian prints hang on sand-colored walls, while in the far corner a single red-and-white blooming orchid stands on a hammered-copper table.

~~~

In the early afternoon, Antonio noticed that the Aussie was still there, on the sidewalk, across the busy road. After sitting still for a few hours she would disappear, trotting to a dirt road that crossed a wide ditch, winding toward the river. What was she waiting for? The return of her owner? Who would leave such a beautiful dog behind? His sister thought the dog lived nearby. He was tempted to go follow it to prove her right, but each time he started getting ready for it, the phone would ring. It did not seem meant to be.

The Tonys' fifteen-year-old Border Collie had died of old age the previous year, and with their grief finally over, they wondered if they could find the owner to purchase this bitch or one of her pups. It was time to find out. They have a friend who is a gifted clairvoyant, and who had helped them discover details they had missed or overlooked in previous cases. Maybe she could help them find out who the dog belonged to. She considered them as friends rather than clients as they had helped each other many times before.

~~~

Tony sat down in the flowery, upholstered chair in the windowless room, thinking once again, *This must be what her place looked like in Louisiana.* Ceramic saints, silk flow-ers, and shiny bead necklaces profusely covered a small altar with a backdrop of pictures of white and black Ma-donnas. Scented candles were lit and scattered among miniature plastic skeletons. Small toy animals sat on two narrow, high tables, while chicken feet, dried herbs, roots, and odd-looking fungi hung from the ceiling.

Madame Rosetta LaFleur was perched on a tall, red-velvet padded stool, as she was never able to sit still for very long. A big, dark-skinned woman somewhere over fifty, she runs the Seeing-eye Cave, built into the north side of the locally known Tres Chichis — a set of three pyramidal peaks, shown on official maps as the "Three Sisters" — just south of Deming. Madame Rosetta was originally from New Orleans, but she was called to the area when one of her friends had asked her for protection from a Mexican warlock.

Deming, the home of cattle ranchers, used to have a livestock auction barn years before. A few farmers still raise hay and chile. Lured by the constant sunshine and the Florida Mountains that tower over the eastern edge of the city, many retired people live there now. After help-ing her friend, Rosetta had decided to stay in the sand-blown area where much black sorcery still thrive. She felt she was needed as a healer, with many alternative talents. She had never bothered to advertise her skills, as word of mouth has kept her busy the three days a week she is open for business.

"So, which of the twins is here today?"

"Both of us are involved this time."

Although only a few people knew about their dual nature, Rosetta had assessed Antonio and Antonia as Siamese twins, the very first time she saw them, five years earlier. Outwardly they looked like one person: two arms, two legs, one torso. But the Tonys were two individual beings, slim, almost six foot tall, with dark-brown hair, blue and green eyes, beautiful Italian facial features, with an elongated skull and a large heart inside a single body. When the masculine side of them spoke, he would use a deeper voice than his sister. From their different intonations, Rosetta had also guessed that they were a hermaphrodite entity with the genitalia of both genders. When people first saw them, they were convinced by the displayed gender, due to the twins careful selection of outfits to project a male or a female persona, according to which they felt was needed at the time. After a few sessions together, Rosetta had deduced that Antonio was the practical, reasoning, methodical half, while Antonia remained the artist, the dreamer, the storyteller of the two. Both got along very well in a single body, while being quite aware of the other at all time.

Antonia spoke first. "It's about this dog, and maybe this little girl the dog belongs to. A few days ago, the nine or ten-year-old child was walking her dog, right across from our agency. A car stopped by and picked up the girl, but left the dog behind. That dog is a red merle Australian Shepherd, so well-bred she could be a show winner. No one leaves a dog like that behind, and she's shown up each day since, as though waiting for the child to return. So we were wondering if you could help us remember the make and license-plate number of the car, or anything else we might have missed that would help us find the owner of that dog?"

Rosetta knew the twins were receptive to hypnosis, having used it on them many times before. They also knew what to expect from her sessions and were easy to plunge back into the subconscious realm each time they saw her. She slowly counted to ten, every number making them go deeper into the desired state. As usual, she reminded them how she was going to wake them up later by counting backward from five to one. Once relaxed, the Tonys' body sunk into the chair, shoulders and head slackened, eyes closed.

"Let's talk about the car. What color was it?" asked Rosetta.

"It was a brown van, with darkened windows and a side door," she said.

"Yeah, it was an old Chevy Astro, looked like late nineties," he said in a deeper voice.

"Which way was it traveling?"

"Going east, toward the center of town."

"Did it have a New Mexico license plate?"

There was a long pause. Rosetta wondered if they would be able to recall what they saw or if they would wake up from the stress of the memory. "Yes! Old plates.

Yellow color, numbers four, five, two."

Another pause. "H-G-B", they both warbled.

"Thank you. What was the little girl doing before she was picked up?"

"She was walking her dog. I've seen her a couple of times before, walking her dog when she should be in school. That's all I see." Antonia said.

"Do not give up so easily. Describe the child."

After a couple of minutes of silence, in a slow faint voice as if coming from a deep well, Antonia said: "The child is nine, ten or maybe eleven with a café-au-lait complexion. She has light-colored eyes, could be green, that seem to carry a great burden in them. That day, she wore a thin, embroidered shirt, faded blue jeans, and worn-out tennis shoes. All of her clothes look like hand-me-downs."

"Tell me about the van."

Antonio took over in a faster voice, as if worried his sister would get all the credit. "The van stopped next to her, across from our shop. The windows were dark. When the passenger in the back opened the sliding door, we only saw dark pants and his or her hand, a very white hand, maybe wearing a glove. We could see a tall driver, probably a man, wearing a jacket with the hood over his head. The girl seemed to smile at the person with the white hand, and got in the van. After a couple of minutes, she threw the leash on the dog's back before the door closed. Then the van made a U-turn and pulled away, leaving the dog in the middle of the road."

The air in the stuffy little room was suddenly electrically charged. Restlessly, Tony shifted in the seat, from one butt cheek to the other, the long head shaking back and forth. Rosetta got off her stool and stiffly walked over to their chair. Towering over the twins, she extended her left hand over their head and in a commanding voice, she boomed: "Speak now, child! "

They heard a tiny voice. "He lied to me. He's hurting me. I wanna go home." There was a sharp crack, as if lightning hit nearby. The room went quiet. The seer pulled them out of their trance. They could not remember what the girl had said, so she told them as she handed them the recording of their session. She recorded all her sessions; they were as important as vivid dreams and, like dreams, could be forgotten without a verbal or written reminder.

On the hour-long drive back home, they replayed the girl's voice a few times. Antonia said aloud as if convincing herself, "It did not sound like me at all. More like a five year old child."

Her brother reflected. *Why would it be someone else?*

They bantered internally whenever they disagreed. She was fast to reply. *Why can't we remember what the child had said, before we got the recording?*

Sis, how did it come through?

Why was she wearing cheap clothing when the fancy looking dog must have cost a pretty penny?

They needed to follow the dog. But no one had hired them to find the girl.

Sis, what if she is not missing? What if she just walks the dog for someone else?

Then, Tone, who was hurting her and keeping her away from home?

Their curiosity deepened and as they had no paying clients at the moment, they decided to look more closely into the case of the abandoned dog.

~~~

Chapter 2
Old Man Walking

THE NEXT DAY A GENTLE RAIN FELL FOR HOURS. A hurricane had torn through the East Coast a couple of days before. In the desert rain means floods, yet people smile, mushrooms surge into life, cacti bloom. But no dog in sight.

The phone rang. "Two Tonys," Antonio responded in his deepest voice. He liked to sound very masculine on the phone. Once, when Antonia had answered a call in her melodious tone, the male solicitor had taken her for a secretary and asked to speak to her boss. When she said she was it, he had hung up on her. Their inside joke was: *When they are looking for a private dick, they don't want to hire a private vagina.*

"Do you search for people?" A male voice asked on the other end of the phone.

"We sure do, but only after the local Search and Rescue teams have done their job."

The caller drew a deep breath before saying, "My father has Alzheimer's and has been missing for five days now. The SAR teams have already searched the whole area but cancelled today, due to the rain and lack of tracks. They think he may have hitched a ride with someone. I'm very worried that he could be lying in a ditch somewhere nearby."

This was the sort of case the Tonys preferred. They felt gratified when they could locate the missing person. They had helped a family or a friend. Or, if the person was found deceased, at least it gave closure to their loved ones. Only once, they had failed to find a man, who had vanished, leaving behind his sports car with keys, wallet and laptop on the front seat. After searching for many days, they deduced that the man had probably staged his disappearance, as he left huge debts behind. They gave up, feeling remorse for not being able to fulfill their contract, and did not charge the client for all the work they had done.

"May I have your name, please?"

"Jim Overmyer. My father's name is Jack, Jack Overmyer."

"Okay Jim. Let me tell you a little about us and how we operate."

"It's all right. I know about you two. Your sheriff's department recommended you to me."

Usually the police liked to keep cases for themselves, but the local law agencies, like all police departments in New Mexico, were overstretched and understaffed at the moment, besides the twins had worked many times with the Doña Ana sheriff.

"Okay then, let me give you my quick spiel about rates."

Tony read off the paragraph in their brochure detailing their daily and hourly rates, mileage, and other expenses.

Jim responded in a tense voice. "It's all right, it's all right. I just need to get my father back quickly. Well, you see, I'm very worried."

"Give me your address and I'll be right over."

~ ~ ~

The beginning of any case was usually a time of anticipation and dressing up for the part was always enjoyable, like putting on a costume for a theater performance. They had to make it look genuine enough for anyone to not have any doubts about their gender, whether male or female. They called it play-acting, because although they were of two separate genders, they also knew they would be regarded as freaks should anyone find out. Over the years, they had learned to adapt quickly to their circumstances and behave according to what people expected from them.

While still very young they learned to use the royal "we" as twins will do, so no mistakes would be made. At first, they were home-schooled, until their mother decided she should no longer shelter them. They were clever and strong enough to start high school. Alternating schools each year, when in public they took turns being one twin or the other, immersed into that specific gender to perfect it. They were not able to make friends outside the school for fear of being found out, of being ridiculed, despised, or hated. Their doctor was the only one who knew their predicament. He had two children, and the younger one became their main playmate through-out their childhood.

Once in college, they had perfected their distinctive roles, playing each to the point where they could have cautious relationships with a few selected friends.

Now as adults, they truly enjoyed their work, especially helping others with what could not be easily found, and getting paid for it. They knew that two heads were better than one, but never mentioned to anyone that both were in the same body.

~~~

Antonio was the single actor that day, wearing cowboy boots with riding heels, to look a little taller, and a turquoise bolo tie on a light gray shirt over a tight fitting T-shirt that flattened their small, feminine breasts. A tan denim jacket with padded shoulders over the shirt, loose, black jeans, and a cowboy hat completed the outfit. Tony felt confident in his male garb, as he drove to the small village below the Organ Mountains on the other side of Las Cruces.

At the end of a quarter-mile dirt road, he spotted the open iron gate that revealed a wide path leading to a century-old adobe house. The front door was adorned on each side with horse and cow skulls painted with scenery in the style of Georgia O'Keefe. At the front of the house stood a portal with a couple of old wooden wagon wheels built into its rails. On a sun-bleached bench behind a row of tall, blue sage bushes, sat a middle-aged, handsome, but stern-looking man.

Easing himself from his truck, Antonio walked up to the man, extending his hand as he introduced himself. The man shook it and nodded, giving Tony a slow, appraising stare. This was obviously someone used to sizing up others. It was hard to tell if he trusted what he saw. For a brief moment, Antonia wondered if her brother appeared a little too flamboyant for this sullen-looking man.

After another few seconds' delay, the man seemed to make a decision. He stood up and, looking Antonio in the eye, said, "Jim Overmyer, I'm a detective in Albuquerque. My dad lives here by himself with his caretaker, José, who called me last week, well, five days ago, saying that Dad had gone for his usual morning walk toward the highway, around nine, and had not come back. I called State Police and they called the search teams. They came right away. They found his tracks going north to the pavement. They went door to door. They canvassed the neighborhood, they called the hospitals and local cops. Finally they told me they were suspending the search and would reopen it when new clues or new information showed up. The sheriff's department put out a BOLO — Be On the Look-Out, you know — and a Silver Alert for him, but they are not looking actively. I came over day before yesterday, and talked with many of the neighbors. Nothing. It's like he's vanished. I have to go back to work Monday. I've taken the last four days off already, but we're overwhelmed with two waring street gangs right now. The state has cut our budget again, and we don't have enough officers as it is. Well, I can't abandon him laying who knows where like that. I really fear the worst."

"Okay, let's start at the beginning," said Antonio. "Give me your dad's full name, age, and physical description."

Jim paused, then sighing he continued. "His name is Jack Gordon Overmyer, seventy-eight years old, tall and skinny."

"Was your dad the same Jack Overmyer who busted that Mexican ring of cocaine traffickers about twenty years ago?"

"Yes, that's him."

"Can you give me a recent picture? And I would also like a record of his past arrests."

He pulled a picture of his father out of his shirt pocket and continued. "I'll see what I can get you locally, if it's no longer confidential. I'd thought of that angle, but Dad has been retired for a while. Well, it seemed unlikely."

Antonio nodded. "I'd like to follow up on it, all the same. How is his health?"

"He's starting to have some bouts of dementia. Nothing too serious, just not his usual sharp self. You'd be better off asking his caretaker, José, about that."

Jim ran his hands through his hair. He seemed to shrink in his chair. "Well actually, José tells me he's been getting much worse, fast! I guess I don't want to hear that."

Jim's face crumpled a bit more. Seconds later, Antonio watched him pulling himself together, glancing furtively at his head to see if he had noticed that fleeting weakness.

Acting as if he had not spotted it, Tony asked: "Where was the caretaker when your father disappeared?"

"Well, I think recently Dad has taken to wandering off,

especially in the early morning. José was fixing breakfast when Dad left. Dad always comes back in time for breakfast, but that morning he didn't."

Tony inquired about Jack's current friends and about his life before his mind started drifting. Where did he live before? Where was he raised? Where did he go to school? Where would he often go with his wife? Where did their best friends live? Where was his wife buried? Where does he shop? Does he go out to eat? To drink? To hang out with friends? What is his favorite pastime? And so on.

Jim answered by rote. He had already told all he knew to the police and the Incident Commanders of the search teams. The teams had looked at the cemetery, his childhood house, his schools, the old tennis court where he used to play years before. They had also talked to his friends, old and new. Jim mentioned that it was interesting being on the other side, being the one answering the questions, not asking them.

Antonio knew that all the obvious places would have already been searched, all the obvious questions answered. He changed tack. "Is José available? I'd like to talk to him."

"He is very upset right now. You see, they've lived together here for twenty years, even before my dad retired. José takes care of him and feels he has failed him. Anyway, he's visiting a few friends, trying to find out if anyone has seen him. At six-three, well, maybe just six foot tall now, and wearing a big cowboy hat, my dad stands out around here. I'll let José know tonight that you'll be here tomorrow."

Antonio thought for a minute, then said, "My sister has to be on the East side tomorrow. She'll be the one coming in. Can she talk to him in the early afternoon?"

"Only if she speaks Spanish, that's what he prefers."

Antonio smiled. "She does, fluently. You'll recognize her, we're twins."

~~~

The Tonys took time to familiarize themselves with the area. They looked all around the property, inside and out, checking under thick growth and in arroyos, looking over backyards fences — the ones without dogs. They found remnants of the searchers tracks where the rain had not obliterated them. The teams had been thorough, but there were no signs of Jack. The highway was a busy one, he could have hitched a ride.

The owner of the small bar across the pavement had seen Jack many times, mainly walking just to the highway before turning around, but he did not remember seeing him recently.

"He used to come in for an afternoon beer once in a while, until about three years ago. The old guy was a little off then, you know. He's probably completely batty by now! A few times I saw his Mexican friend come and get him if he took too long, just standing on the other side of the road. If I were his kid, I'd put him in the nut house. That's what I told that search commander when he came looking for him. Look in the loony bin!"

Tony thanked the man, left and then walked behind the building in a small expanding fan, through the sandy brush and scattered trash of bottles and beer cans. But once again, the search teams had thought of that, too, and all he found were some hiking boot tracks, all most likely from the searchers.

The twins' thoughts moved at full speed, firing back and forth inside their shared brain.

Not here! Tone

He could have kept on walking, Sis. What do you think of Jim?

He's delusional about his dad's mental state. Seems like he doesn't spend much time with him.

He's busy, lives three hours away, but he cares about him.

Not enough to take more than four days off, Tone!

The rival gangs in Albuquerque are going at it right now. It's all over the news.

Yeah, Tone, but you only get one father, if you're lucky.

~ ~ ~

Antonia usually liked to wear a little bit of makeup: a dark-rose lipstick, a little eye liner, and a well-blended spot of color to highlight her cheekbones. She would often spray washable auburn color on her dark hair, although it would be mostly covered with a colorful silk scarf, so her long skull would not be as noticeable. Flat heels hidden under comfortable loose slacks, made her look shorter than her brother in his cowboy boots. That day, a billowing, midnight-blue linen shirt mostly hid her compact breasts. A pair of discreet earrings matched an elegant, small necklace, both turquoise on silver. She felt these accessories accented her feminine side, providing the subtle touches that helped define their physiological differences. Another distinguishing aspect between the two was that he drove a full-size, white pick-up truck, while her car was a sensible and discreet, all-wheel drive, dark-green Subaru station wagon.

She had an appointment to check a "For Sale" ad for a red merle Aussie on the other side of the sprawled city. She had picked up the flyer at the local grocery store. When she had called the number, a man told her that he and his wife had bought the dog a few months before, but that they could not cope with his hyper-active manners. "Too much of a dog for us old fogies," they said.

After she found their place, she let herself into their neat but tiny front yard. The pair, in their late seventies, lived in a small house of cement bricks, in a freshly established suburb. They both looked frail and tired. Inside were dark brown and tan curtains, the same colors as the plaid cushions of the couch. Through a window facing the backyard, Antonia watched a dog run circles, confined in his ten-by-ten, chain-linked pen. They told her they would sell him for half of what they paid. They had not neutered him yet, but if he did not sell fast, they would take him to the vet. Maybe that would settle him down.

"It may help. Do you know the owners of the sire and dam?" She was hoping the owners were local. No, it turned out they got him in California, while visiting their grandkids. They did not have a phone number for the dam's owners but could find out if she needed it. They could make her a copy of his registration.

She replied, "No thanks, I am looking for a female anyhow." She did not tell them she was really looking for a link to Calico, the name she had given the dog who stood still for hours across the shop.

This venture had not been productive. She felt sorry for the couple and more for their dog, but there were only so many problems she could solve in one day.

"If I can make a suggestion, I'd go ahead and neuter him and find some young person to take him for long walks. That should help settle him down."

~~~

Antonia was frustrated. The dog and girl issue was not going anywhere. And now they had this new investigation into the disappearance of the Alzheimer's case to focus on. She was also worried about the child, who had mentioned someone hurting her, but was more curious about the beautiful Aussie, as was Antonio. They had made a few calls. There were no missing children with her description in Las Cruces. The dog pound did not have anyone looking for a missing Australian Shepherd either.

The girl was not worried about the dog, Sis.

Tone, we need to get info on the brown van. That might lead us to a friend or a relative.

OK, I'll call Jim Overmyer. See if he can get that info from the MVD for us.

She laughed inwardly at that.

Tone, how is he gonna feel about us working on another case, while he is paying us to find his father?

We're only charging him for the time on his search. It won't be the first time we've worked multiple cases at once. Shall I try it?

Sure, Tone. Go for it.

"Jim. Hi, Tony here. Hey, my sister should be at your dad's shortly. Anything new on your side?"

The man sounded as tired as the day before. "No, nothing! I spoke with José last night. He's out in the garden right now. He's eager to meet your sister. I'm trying to get some time off, but I'm up to my eyeballs in one criminal case after the other. Well, you know how it goes…" He trailed off.

Sounds like he's accepted our knowhow. Perfect opening! Go for it, Tone.

"Yes, I do, as a matter of fact. Jim, my sister has been working on another case for a while. This one has gotten cold, but she'd like to nudge it along a little when she has time. I was wondering if you could help her and check a license plate number for us."

"Sure, what is it?" He relented.

Tony gave him the number of the van the little girl had gone in. He could have used his friend Sunny Villegas for that, but Sunny was a local city cop and would have asked too many questions, maybe even start looking into it. There was probably no call for an investigation as the girl had been smiling when she climbed into the van. It was only one of Antonia's hunches, he thought. Of course her intuition was usually right on.

Antonia butted in. *You bet it is, Tone!*

Yeah, but she could have just been taking care of the dog for someone else.

And leave it behind? Come on! Not good enough.

Sis, it's not her dog. She doesn't look wealthy!

Then, whose little girl's voice is it that reached us, the one that wants to go home?

Your enormous imagination!

Get lost! Let me focus on this Jack person.

~ ~ ~

Disappointed the old couple had been no help, she drove to Jack's remote adobe and was greeted by the missing man's son at the wide open front gate.

"Come in. You can park just past the long porch. José is watering out back. Your brother did not lie. You two do look alike. Well, you are much prettier than he is."

She smiled, glad that once again, a little bit of jewelry and makeup had made such a difference.

People see what they expect to see, Sis.

Even cops!

Jim led her to the house through a heavy double door

to a clean, wide mudroom and into a generous living room that looked over a small, well-kept courtyard. Dark, hefty but artfully carved Mexican furniture covered an old pine plank floor but for a large, well-worn Navajo rug in the middle of the sitting area. He offered her a glass of iced tea, already set on an antique coffee table next to a long, comfortable-looking couch, and went out to find José. The room smelled of old leather, dried herbs and oiled wood. Everything was spotless, except for a circle of dried blooms that had fallen off forgotten flowers, sticking out of a black-and-white pottery vase on top of a big chest of drawers. She went to look at the pictures hanging on one wall, depicting the same man at different stages of life: shaking hands with officials or receiving medals and certificates.

Must be Jack in his younger days! She thought.

His son looked like him. Only one woman appeared amongst all these men. She wore a long, white wedding dress next to a young and tall dashing Jack, dressed in black. In another picture, she held hands with two young children, on each side. There was also one of a young student in graduation clothes and another of a heavily decorated military man shaking Jim's hand, who looked to be in his forties then.

Only child? She wondered.

Jim returned a few minutes later followed by a short but stocky man with salt-and-pepper hair above dark eyes sunken in a leathery face.

"José, this is Antonia, a private detective" Jim said in perfect Spanish.

"¡Hola, señor! ¿Como esta?" Antonia replied as she shook hands with the man who was looking sharply into her eyes.

Jim begged off saying he had a meeting with the local sheriff. "The one who had recommended the Two Tonys as being very thorough detectives," he added with a smile in her direction.

After nodding her head at him, Antonia then turned to José giving him her full attention.

They first made small talk about the garden, then the weather, like two sniffing dogs checking each other out. Finally José relaxed his stare and began to tell her how Jack had been sinking into dementia at what he felt was a rapid pace.

"Such a smart man, but now he acts and talks like a little kid some of the time. We have known each other for more than forty years, and I have taken care of him for the last fifteen, since his wife died. Some mornings he does not know who he is."

He told her how he had always fixed him his favorite breakfast, *huevos rancheros.* "But now, most of the time, he wants milk and cereals, like a child. He is a different person, almost a stranger".

Antonia asked a few more questions about his regular habits, his moods, how he dealt with the dementia.

"He does not seem to realize that he is mostly living in the past. He lives from day to day. No plans for the future as if he does not care anymore about anything but his basic needs. He is content with just staying here as long as his routine does not change. He spends his time outside, sitting on the bench, just staring ahead. He eats well, sleeps on and off during the night. But he does not do much else. He used to be so active."

He stopped and waited for more questions.

She told him that she was curious about the house. Who built it, when?

"It was started in the mid 1800s, and belonged to a Spanish family. It's all adobe, strong, thick adobe, cool in the summer daytime, and warm in the winter nights. Jack's grandfather had a big store in Las Cruces, and with the money he made he bought the house from the Parra's. Then it was handed down from father to son."

With a sly grin, as if he had correctly read where she was going with her inquiry, he said, "When Jack sold me the little casita on a half acre down the lane about fifteen years ago, he told me that Jim would inherit this mansion when he passes away. That way Jim can't get rid of me."

She laughed at that and asked if Jim was a single child.

"His sister passed away when she was ten. A horse accident, I think."

A long silence followed. José was watching her, inspecting her in a way that was starting to make her tense. But she waited. This was why they had chosen her feminine persona for this meeting. Some men are more willing to open up to a woman, to a sister or a mother figure, than to another man. She sensed that he wanted to tell her something important.

"You like women, yes?" He blurted out.

She managed to hide her surprise at the way the conversation had shifted. "I do, I also like men, I don't care what color, shape or religion people are, I am not... ¿Como se dice, perjudicada? In English, not prejudiced, right?"

Now looking directly into her eyes. "Yes, but you are a woman who likes women like a man does."

"Yes, I am!" she said, holding his gaze. Then ensued another long silence. Was that all he wanted to know? No, there had to be more to it. She waited.

Then as if she had answered his question correctly, a torrent came pouring out of him in flawless English. "Jack and I have a very close connection. We have known each other for many, many years. I helped him on numerous cases involving people from across the border. We saved each other's lives at different times. Once he saved me from drowning in the Elephant Butte Lake, while he was chasing criminals who damaged young girls. Another time, across the border, I saved him from being shot down by a drug cartel king. I shot this man myself. I had to. He was going to kill Jack. I almost lost my mind, but Jack, he pulled me out of my sadness and made me whole again. That is why we are connected. I cannot see where he is now, but he is alive. I know it. I think he is many miles from here. I think his life is in danger. None of the neighbors have seen him since that day. I'm worried that Jack walked to the highway and was picked up and disposed of by one of the Mexican drug lords. He busted a lot of people when he was one of the big narcos."

There it was. The admission of subliminal cognition that most people cannot accept for fear of being wrong or ridiculed. Over the years, some clients had told her their hunches, their gut feelings, what their intuition had revealed to them. She found that they were often correct. Being close to someone seemed to connect people on more than a physical level, adding an emotional and sometimes psychic level, especially within a long lasting relationship.

Your antennas are up, Sis!

Shush, he might be able to hear us.

She asked, "Can you be more specific, José. Can you give me a direction of travel?"

"Not now, but I can take seeing herbs from a *curandera* who lives near here. Maybe my dreams will show me where he went."

She reached out to him with her left hand, the one closest to where he was sitting. As he took it in both of his, she felt an electric tingle rushing through her arm. He held on, looking into her eyes.

"Yes, I think you can find him, if anyone can. There is more to you than one can see."

~~~

Chapter 3
Search Engines

THE NEXT MORNING JIM DROPPED OFF A STACK OF documents at their office. He explained to Antonia that these were all the local files he could get, and he needed to return them the next day before he left the city. "Lots of black marker on them, probably mostly names". With a smile he added, "But that was only to protect the guilty." He was afraid it would be a waste of their time to look through this mess. Everybody loved his dad.

"Even the ones he put in jail?" Tony said softly.

He ignored her remark. With his thumb and index finger combing his mustache while his eyebrows rose up, he suddenly said, "What's a pretty girl like you doing being a detective in a place like this?"

Not very original, Antonia thought, pretending not to hear. In a way, she was flattered by the compliment, but she hated that any man would expect a favorable reaction to his clumsy flirting.

And I hate it when they sweet-talk you for sexual favors.

OK, Tone, but you like it when someone pays special attention to you. Shut up now and let's keep listening.

Jim could see he'd been rebuffed and swiftly moved on. "Oh, and here is the info on the vehicle your brother said you needed"

"Thank you for all the data on your dad. We'll get on it right away and see what we can turn up. And I'll look into this when I have a minute," she replied, pointing to the info on the van with just a hint of annoyance, so he would understand that although he did her a favor by getting that information, she did not care for his flirting. It took a lot to discourage some of the good-looking, middle-aged men who thought no woman could resist them. She didn't want to lose a client but she also was not attracted to him at all, and it was important that he knew it. She sensed he did, as he looked a little dejected when he left the office.

~~~

Searching through records, poring over every scrap of paper in order not to miss any possible clues, that was the part that took most of their time on any case. Jack Overmyer had clearly been busy during his eighteen years as a narcotics cop. Many were petty busts, mostly small crooks caught by their own stupidity, breaking and entering, leaving fingerprints everywhere, and selling stolen goods so they could buy drugs. Sometimes he worked with undercover partners whose names were blacked out. Two were male, one of which was most likely Hispanic.

Sis, José must have been his main partner while working narcotics.

Is there more to him than meets the eye? May confirm it, next time we see him.

Three of the most significant cases stood out. First the

bust of a ring of Mexican drug and flesh peddlers that used teenage girls to move cocaine across the border, then sell them to bordellos catering to the wealthy. These lowlifes were apprehended near a large lake. Only two large lakes on the southern side of the Rio Grande. Unfortunately much of the narrative about the Elephant Butte Lake incident was blacked out. The end of the report mentioned that three men had died that day from .40 caliber bullets, from two different guns. Those fit the Glock 22 pistol, the kind favored by the police force at the time. Besides lead slugs, one of the dead also had water in his lungs. That case was probably the one José had referred to.

Then there was an unsolved case of two meth brewers that got away from the police, twice, before disappearing permanently, probably put out of their profitable miseries by another manufacturer. The only significant factor in this one was that the perps had told Jack that they would come back to kill him, on both occasions.

Antonia liked the third and most recent one: his last big case involving Southern European mafia. They read how a tip had been given to the El Paso narcotics division, then later to the New Mexico State Police in Las Cruces, Deming, and Kingsburg. That tip was that every hundredth gallon tin can of olive oil actually contained pure heroine destined for the West Coast. A friend of Jack Overmyer with state police had ticketed a speeding semi going to California, and seeing from the truck's records that it was delivering olive oil, had told him of the truck.

Jack knew then that he had stumbled across one of the biggest European heroine busts of his career.

With a partner, he had caught the truck at the main filling station in Kingsburg, just before the Arizona border. He told the driver he needed to take a look inside the trailer, but as soon as he climbed in, he was pushed in and the doors were locked behind him. A small fume-oozing canister was tossed in through a tiny door up high. According to the record, Jack's partner had tried to intervene and been shot. These shots were the last sounds Jack heard before he lost consciousness in that trailer.

A week later he awoke in a hospital in the state of Georgia. From there he had called his boss, the chief of the narcotics division in New Mexico. But the whole thing was a blur, and no amount of therapy had ever helped him recover the memories of that week. The doctors had found a lot of heroine in his system. This explained his lack of recollection and also put him in rehab for a full month. Finally, the report also mentioned how he quit the force shortly after, blaming himself for the death of his partner.

Tone, that one is the most promising! Am certain this is the one to follow.

Antonio had his doubts. *Nah, Sis! He walked in a straight line behind the café and never turned back. Statistics show this happens with ninety-seven percent of lost Alzheimer's patients.*

Wrong! This is revenge from that Southern Euro family, who shipped Italian olive oil to Brownsville by sea, then moved it to California by trucks.

~ ~ ~

When there were multiple possibilities in a case, the Tonys liked to brainstorm different scenarios. For Jack Overmyer, they came up with four.

1) Check on the heroin available locally. Jack may have somehow gotten back on the dope without José being aware of it. Unlikely but possible. They would need to get one of their informers to find out if, when, and where heroin had been available lately.

2) The old man just walked away from a familiar place, got more confused after running into obstacles, got himself hopelessly lost, and is still in the vicinity.

Still my favorite, Sis.

Three percent don't fit in your category!

3) He could had been picked up on the highway, an innocent ride for an innocent hitchhiker, in which case he could be anywhere, in or out of the state, dead or alive. The Silver Alert would need to be placed in Arizona, California, and Texas too. An extensive search of more hospitals and morgues in these three states would also be needed. They had already called all the ones in New Mexico.

My second favorite scenario, Sis!

You do the rest of the calling then!

4) One of his busted criminals had picked him up and disposed of him. That one would be the hardest to figure out, but the more she worked with it, the more Antonia's intuition pointed to the European Mafiosi. Had they had exacted their revenge?

Sis, wouldn't they kill him then?

No, they know he is a cop who has survived the first hurdle. He should have died from the overdose, the report said. Killing him later may leave traces.

Right, and killing a cop would be a lot harder to do in his home base.

Besides, José thinks he is still alive!

Yeah, you always believe the psychics. Just because you have a lot of intuition doesn't mean others do too.

Tone, even if he is dead, we still need to find out what happened to him.

OK, but still think he is lost somewhere near his home.

Then with this summer heat and no water, he is most certainly dead. Which means he is not going anywhere! It's no longer a priority.

There were other possibilities, but those were less plausible and would have to wait until they checked these four more thoroughly.

~~~

They followed up on their first line of inquiry: could Jack have started using drugs again? Tony got in touch with Janos, a young man covered in tattoos. They had rescued him from near death in a back alley a few years back, and helped him into rehab. Since then, he had been sticking to the Narcotics Anonymous program. To repay the Tonys and the cop who had also helped him, he had become an informant for them, pretending to go back to drugs whenever he was asked to help. It was a dangerous game he played, but he understood the rules and stuck to them, staying clean despite the odds. Janos agreed to check if there was any heroin available at the moment.

Scenario two: he walked away, disoriented.

We've already looked. The SAR teams too. Let's put this one on the back burner, Tone.

The third possibility also presented few leads. Unless his description and location were reported, then looking for an elderly hitchhiker would be nearly impossible. It took Antonio four hours to make calls to the hospitals, the morgues, and the city's and sheriffs' offices throughout the southern halves of Arizona, California and Texas.

Their fourth theory was also convoluted. They would need to ask all their cop friends what they knew about the Mediterranean Mafiosi in the import business.

That could prove to be nearly impossible because it had happened so many years before. Maybe José would be willing to share more info?

Will get in touch with him again. Maybe, you could talk to Jim? His dad may have talked about that case.

You talk to him, Sis. You're better at reading people than I am.

He respects you more than me. Am just a woman.

Antonio laughed aloud. *Right! Sis.*

~ ~ ~

Antonio called Jim Overmyer. "Jim? Tony here. Hey, I was wondering if your dad ever talked about his cases with you. Like I mentioned before, we're looking into the possibility that his disappearance could be linked to a grudge. We know it's a long shot but we'd like to turn every stone as it comes up."

"Thanks for that. Well, I would visit him every other week while he was still working. We'd talk professionally when something bothered one of us. I don't know if I can help. Do you have one case in mind?"

"Actually, my sister is interested in his last big one, when he was kidnapped and drugged by the olive oil and heroine dealers. Did he talk about that one?"

Thanks, Tone, now he'll want to talk to me!

No problem, Sis, it was your idea anyhow!

"Sure enough. Is Antonia around? I'll talk to her if she is, if you don't mind."

At least, he is asking for your permission!

"Let me check if she's available, Jim."

Covering the phone's mouthpiece, the Tonys took time to clear their throat to help change the timbre of their voice.

"Hi, Jim. It's the other Tony! We're following up on the olive oil traffickers, but the file stops when your dad came back from Georgia and quit the force. It does not give us any info about what happened to the perps. If you know and can talk about it, can you tell us if they were busted, or if they got away?"

"Sure, would you like to meet for dinner? I am making my mean, green, cheese enchilada tonight, and I've got a bottle of this great local Cabernet."

"Thanks, Jim, but I've been working on this for the last eight hours today and still got a ton of work in front of me. So if you don't mind, let's do this over the phone for now."

Sis, he likes you!

And how do you think he'd react if he knew what we really are?

"Well, actually Antonia, my dad's partner had called in the make and license of the truck before he got shot. So later that day, the truck was apprehended in Arizona. They had gotten off the interstate and were taking smaller roads. An Arizona State Police helicopter spotted them, and they had roadblocks all over Safford and Highway 70. By the time the truck was apprehended, only the driver was in it. The accomplice was gone, and so was Dad. Probably the other guy, the one who shot our officer, switched vehicles in Kingsburg and transported Dad to Georgia. They must have taken off right away in another car going east. Dad did not remember anything. Well, you know, this was a big operation. They confiscated twelve kilos of pure heroine. Of course, the Graham County cops got all the glory."

"So do you think your dad could have identified the co-pilot?"

"He did, yes, and with his help they made a composite picture of him, but they could not find a match on any of the police records. He was still fairly out of it when they questioned him. They never found the other guy. You know, he probably went back overseas. The driver had a really strong, foreign accent. He went straight to jail without bail. A week later, he got a bullet in the center of his forehead while exercising in the yard. They said that bullet traveled a long ways."

"Thanks, Jim. I have another question, one I hope

won't offend you."

"Antonia, I'm a cop! I've heard and seen it all. Nothing you say can offend me!"

The Tonys smirked inwardly. They knew the one thing that would really shock him.

"Do you think your dad could have taken heroin again after his rehab?" she asked.

"That one I know the answer for sure. When I was a kid, in high school, I tried marijuana. Well, he found out. He said he smelled it on me. He took out his belt and I got a good lashing. He said he would put me in a pension for juvenile delinquents if I ever did it again. He was very strict. He was so ashamed about them doping him up like that, he could hardly talk about it. So no, there is no way he could have gone back on it. But I appreciate your looking at that possibility."

The Tonys hung up the phone, disappointed that this case was not moving very fast. *Hard to figure anything out on such an old case, Tone.*

So many dead ends.

Hey, don't use that word, the old man may still be alive.

Whatever, Sis. Am tired, tired and bored from reading all these transcripts!

~~~

Chapter 4
A Tiger and a Girl

THE TONYS SAW THE AUSTRALIAN SHEPHERD sitting across the street. It was almost five o'clock, unlikely that new clients would call this late. They were both exhausted from reading all the sanitized police reports. They decided to close early, go out, and walk over to her. Antonio called out, "Come Calico, come girl!" as he walked toward her.

She doesn't know that's the name we gave her, Tone!

She doesn't, but she'll respond to my tone of voice.

The dog looked at them. As they got close to her, she started moving slowly across the chile field. It seemed as if she was waiting for them, her long tail wagging up high, like a flag. They followed her next through a cotton field, then to a couple of alleys bordering what looked like housing for farm hands. Finally she turned toward a well-kept modest house, with brightly colored zinnias and marigolds planted around it. She sat down by the front door, giving one short yelp.

The door opened and a pretty dark-haired woman called out, "*¿Hola?* "

"Hi, sorry to bother you. I'm just looking for the owner

of this dog."

"She's not here," she said. "Can I help you?"

The Tonys had to think quickly. Had the dog been living here all along? They were startled to see how easy this was. They should have taken the time previously to follow the dog. Instantly, they regretted not wearing their feminine persona.

"Please, if you can. We saw a young girl with this dog early last week..."

He didn't have to think of what to say next because the woman immediately interjected, "I think she went with her father," she replied. "I have not seen either of them for a while. Are you with the police?"

He reassured her that he was not and continued. "I'm just curious about the dog. Some days, most days for the last week, she hangs out across from our office as if waiting for the young girl to come back."

"Yes, Tiger waits for her when she runs away. But I think she went with her father this time."

"Runs away? At her age! How old is she? Nine? Ten?" Antonio was incredulous, and then introduced himself. "I'm Antonio with Two Tony's Search Engine Detective Agency. My sister and I are private detectives. We were wondering about the girl when we saw her get in the van."

The woman tilted her head to the side, raised her eyebrows and asked about the van.

"It was an older brown van, it happened about a week ago."

She flinched and looked worried, as she exclaimed, "A brown van! That is not her father's car!" She looked up at

Antonio as if she had just understood what he was saying, then her sentences tumbled together. "I do not have any money left to find her. The police will not look for her anymore. She has run away too many times. She hides and then she comes back."

Bending down toward her and offering his most reassuring face, Antonio replied, "Ma'am, if you want us to try to find her, we can work out a deal. We like your dog."

"Tiger belongs to my daughter. I cannot sell her."

"What I meant was if the dog is not fixed, we would love a pup from her, in trade."

"Is that why you came here?" shouted Maria, with tears in her eyes. "To try and win some business?"

Antonia hissed internally at Antonio. *Tell her we did not know the girl was abducted or we would have reported it ourselves. She got in willingly. Tell her we were just following the dog.*

Antonio stood up straighter as he addressed the woman. "No! No, ma'am, that was not what I came here for. The girl. What is her name?"

"Mora", said the woman more quietly. "And I am Maria."

"Well, Maria, your daughter seemed to climb into the van willingly. We thought she must have known the people in it. She dropped the dog's leash. We like the look of the dog, so we've kept an eye out for Mora, just to ask her about puppies. We see Calico, I mean Tiger, we see her often, always in the same place, but we've not seen your daughter again."

At once the pretty black-eyed woman broke down and started to cry.

Antonio stepped forward and gently put a hand on her arm. "When did you last see Mora?"

Maria started in a hesitant voice. "It was six days ago. When she left, she was upset with me. She is always upset with me." She hiccuped and choked back a sob.

Over the next fifteen minutes, a sad tale unfolded. She explained how Mora ran away regularly. Maria's husband, Andrés, married her months after she got pregnant, but a DNA test showed that Mora was not his child. Being very religious, he did not want a divorce. He only came home every now and then, paid some of the bills, but never wanted to stay more than a couple of days. Sometimes Andrés would pick Mora up at school and take her out for an ice cream. She would eat it and leave soon after being driven home, after checking up on Tiger. Maria's husband did not have a phone, and she had not seen him since Mora left. She had hoped he had taken her to his own casita.

Maria cleaned houses and also worked at a beauty shop. She bought the dog for Mora with the promise that she would not run away anymore. But the girl would still disappear every time Andrés came home, usually for the duration of his stay, and sometimes for many days in a row. Mora always called home after two or three days to find out if he was gone and to see how her dog fared, but she hadn't this time. Maria did not know where she went while she was gone. She had not made any friends in school. When Mora ran away, she also skipped her classes. The school was calling all the time to let her know when she had missed another day, but her counselor seemed to understand that Maria was doing her best to keep her in school, and had not yet reported her to the authorities.

"Does your daughter hate your husband?" said Antonio.

"No, I don't think she hates him. She just doesn't like him to be here, at home. She thinks he does not like her. Last week she was angry with me, because I had told her I wanted us to be a family living together again." Maria dabbed her eyes.

The poor girl clearly does not like her stepfather!

I agree, Sis. Be quiet and let me concentrate on Maria's story.

Antonio listened and waited for the woman to finish. When he could see she had nothing else to say, he spoke. "I would like to try and help you find your daughter. Will you let my sister and me do that for you?"

Maria nodded and said, "But I have no money."

"Until this afternoon we were really just interested in getting a puppy from Tiger. Now that we know Mora is missing, we want to help you find her. How about this, we will help you find Mora in exchange for a puppy if and when Tiger has some. Would that work for you?"

We want to take the dog now, Tone. She might help us find the girl.

Yes, yes, okay!

"Maria, would you mind if I took Tiger back to our

office with me? We will take very good care of her. I think she might help lead us to Mora."

"I don't think Mora will mind if you borrowed her while she's gone," said Maria as she began to weep again. She looked at Tiger as if evaluating her, and then at Antonio and shrugged. "I don't see how that will help but sure, take her. She's a good dog, but I worry that she is always wandering off. Maybe she'd be happier since you're near the place where she last saw my daughter."

Antonio found out where Andrés worked and what kind of car he drove. Then Tony asked for a picture of Mora, which school the girl went to, if she had other relatives or close friends nearby, how old she was, and what she was wearing the last day she saw her.

Maria gave him a lot of details. Mora was eleven years old, small for her age but never sick, except for the measles when she first started school. She did very well in school, always an A student, despite missing some of her classes. She liked to be by herself and did not make any friends at school. She only had one friend, Omar, a boy two years younger, who lived nearby. She babysat him now and then. Maria described the clothes Mora wore the day she left, the same ones Tony had remembered with Rosetta's help. Then she went into a back room, and returned with a school picture from the prior year. It showed a confident face, fine features, with cocoa-colored skin, almond-shaped hazel eyes, and full lips. The little girl would surely grow into a stunningly beautiful adult.

Antonio was given contact info for Andrés, Omar, and

the school counselor. He told Maria that he and his sister would start looking into Mora's disappearance right away, that her dog would be well cared for, and that they would phone her with any progress they made. Then he called Tiger, who followed him without any prompting all the way home. The twins reflected that they would be busy now with two intriguing missing-persons cases.

~~~

Early the next morning, using one of the addresses Maria had given him, Antonio found Andrés working at a pecan farm just off the Rio Grande. A short, black-haired man with the rugged hands and face of someone who worked outside all the time, he told Tony he had not seen the girl and had no idea where she went when she left home. Suddenly, seeming nervous, looking down at the ground in front of him, he said, "She comes and goes when and where she wants. She does not like me. Me, I always tries to be nice to her. I take her to the movies. She loves the movies! I buy her clothes and ice cream. But she does not talk to me."

Looking up at Antonio straight into his eyes as if to convince him of his innocence, Andrés spat out in a louder voice, "I have given her my family name when I married Maria, but the girl is not mine. She is a black man's child, not mine. She was conceived before I married her mother. I love Maria. I wish the girl would like me. I am an honest man, Mister Tony."

Hoping for a reaction from this man, Tony then

mentioned the brown Chevy van.

Andrés thought about it for a minute as if hesitating, then shook his head. "No, I do not know anyone with a van like this."

"It would help us find your adopted daughter if we knew who that van belonged to. She might be in trouble. She did get inside a van like that."

Andrés took his time before answering. "Sometimes I pick her up at the school when I finish work early. I think I have seen a van like that at the school a couple of times. It is not a new van. It is a little bit dented, I think. Maybe that is the same van."

Then as if defending himself, he quickly added, "My truck is a Ford Ranger pickup. It is not new and has many colors on it, but the engine is very strong. I take good care of it."

Tony had seen it parked by the ditch, on the edge of the field where Andrés was working. A small truck, an older model with a brown hood, one red door and one white door, and a black bed filled with shovels and other farm tools.

Tony gave him his business card before he left.

As an afterthought, Andrés said: "I like this girl. I will call you if I see her. You call me for the same."

He seems pretty nervous, yet old-fashioned!

I agree, Tone, but he has his heart in the right place. He adopted her!

Yeah, but he can't even say her name!

Together, they thought, *Ulterior nasty motives?* Then together again, *Let's get Lou to run a background check on him!* Their friend Lou, the local sheriff, was always willing to help them.

~~~

They researched Jack's files again but nothing new came up. The Silver Alerts had not borne fruit either. Deciding to let that pursuit rest for now, Tony had just enough time to visit the school before it closed for the day. The counselor had already left, so he went back to his pick-up and watched as children filed out to buses or idling cars. Quite a few of the kids walked home. No brown van.

After a quick change of attire, Antonia, followed by Tiger, walked the few blocks from the office to see Mora's young friend Omar. A small adobe with white shutters sat at the end of a dirt road, surrounded by similar houses. No cars were parked in front of it, but the barren ground had been raked clean recently. She pulled the string on a large brass bell hanging next to the white front door. As she was getting ready to ring the bell again, a slim brown-skinned child appeared. He first recoiled at the sight of the dog, but then brightened up when he recognized her. "Tiger?" He asked.

"*¡Sí! Hola. Me llamo Antonia, soy una amiga de Mora.*" She introduced herself as a friend of Mora. "*¿Es usted Omar?* "

"I am not Mexican, I am Pakistani, I don't want to speak Mexican!" He replied in an annoyed tone.

In English now, she said, "Hi, Omar. I'm looking for Mora. She's been gone for a few days. I was wondering if you knew where she was."

Antonia left Tiger outside, asking her to wait, when the boy invited her into his house. Omar, barefoot, wearing shorts and a T-shirt, limped all the way to a small desk with a lit laptop on it. He noticed her glance at his skinny legs, one of which looked twisted and much shorter than the other. He went on to explain that he had contracted polio when he was three years old, when he went with his parents to visit his family in Pakistan. He continued, as if rehashing a story he had told many times. "My older brother also contracted polio, but he died from it. I'm the lucky one."

Antonia murmured that she was sorry, as she recalled that polio had been eradicated in the United States in the middle of the last century.

It is still prevalent in some countries, in Asia and Africa, Sis. Remember reading about it in school?

You're right, remember reading it now. But we've never seen someone who has suffered from it before.

On the opposite side of the room, a quiet very old woman was sitting still, curled up on a coach, and covered with a blanket, despite the heat. In Pakistani, Omar explained to his grandmother who Antonia was. The old woman nodded her head before lowering it down and falling back to sleep.

The boy talked about Mora, who used to babysit him, before his grandmother had to move in with them. Mora was his friend. They shared everything. "We are like brother and sister. Even our names have the same letters."

59

Don't even start with your coincidences, Tone.

OK, Sis, but only because you know this time I'm right.

Most likely intuitive causality, Tone

Omar continued explaining. "When Baba moved in with us, my parents did not need Mora to watch me anymore. Now, I'm old enough to take care of myself and of my Baba too. But Mora still come and visits me almost every week, but not last week."

Antonia asked: "What do you do together when she visits?"

"Most times she helps me with my homework. I don't go to school anymore because the kids were mean to me, making fun of my weird leg. So now I am taking classes on my computer. Mora is really smart. Sometimes we take Tiger for a walk when she brings her. She doesn't bring her very often because my dad doesn't want Tiger in the house. A lot of dogs like to bark at me, and some dogs will chase me. But when we walk together with Tiger, the other dogs don't bother me. That's why she calls her Tiger. She is our protector. Mora also protects me when she comes by herself. And she rubs my leg to make it stronger. She has made it straighter already."

"Has Mora been here since your grandmother moved in?"

"Oh yes. Baba likes her, too. Sometimes she brings movies. Baba does not sleep as much when she comes, because we watch the movies together," he said, as he pointed to a TV monitor in a corner of the room. "You see, she is going to be an actress in the movies when she is older."

He went on naming some of the movies she had brought over. Her favorite films were all about young romance. "The one she likes best is 'West Side Story'. I like it too, but it is a very old movie. The woman is named Maria, like her mother. I think that is one of the reasons she likes it so much. Another one of her favorites is 'Dirty Dancing'. She knows a lot of the dancing moves in it, and she dances along when we watch it. Baba likes this one a lot. But my father does not, so we cannot watch it when he is home. He says that it is a movie for adults and that Mora should be married before she watches it again. My parents are old-fashioned."

After Antonia got him back on track, Omar told her he had no idea where she could be if she was not at her mom's, and that she never spent time at her dad's house. A few times she had stayed here, in the garage, when her dad was visiting her mother. Omar took Antonia to the garage, where she saw a small loft above tool benches, with a thin mattress covered by a colorful, Indian paisley print. It did not look like anyone had slept there for a while.

Another dead end, Sis.

Let's think positively about this. We did get more info about her.

~ ~ ~

The Tonys' office was in the front room of their home, their private quarters behind it. There was a large enclosure around the back, with a six foot wooden fence

61

for privacy. This was her first time there, yet Tiger acted as if she knew the place already. Once in the private yard, she barked once, as if asking to have the gate opened, but Antonio did not know if she would come back.

She will, she knows where we live, she'll be back.

The dog did not show up that evening but then was back the next day, with one short yelp at the backyard gate.

What did I tell you, Tone?

Not fair, easier for you to read her.

As soon as she was done greeting them, Tiger asked for the front door and sat in the front yard by the low open gate, looking both ways for cars to come. Antonia had a strong feeling Tiger could lead her to Mora.

~~~

The next morning, as the school bell rang for the students to come in, Mora's guidance counselor made herself available for Antonia. A small, plump woman with rouged cheeks and blue eyeliner to complement her watery blue eyes, she had clamped her graying brown hair with a gold-colored barrette at the back of her head.

With a practiced, but seemingly sincere smile, she extended her hand. "Hi, I'm Mrs. Pendleton. You want to talk about Mora. Her mother called me yesterday. She is willing to have her file released. Which agency are you with?"

"Mrs. Pendleton, my name is Tony Urbani, with Two

Tonys' Search Engine. Maria has hired our agency to help find her daughter, who has been missing for nine days now. Any information you may have that would help us would be greatly appreciated."

After a short pause, with a look of concern, the counselor said, "I will have to report this to the authorities, if she is truly missing. I have sent a letter to her mother, as Mora had not been in school for a week. I wish this was unusual but it's not, which is why I was not really worried. I certainly have no idea where she went. She does not open up to anyone very fast. I don't think she has made any friends at this school. Every time she misses a day at school, she must come see me first thing in the morning. I get to see her a lot, as Maria has probably told you. It usually takes her at least ten minutes before she'll start talking to me. She is a gifted but troubled child. All A's, even though she misses so many days. I don't know how she does it. The principal wants to hold her back this year. I think it would be a mistake. She'd never come in then. She'd be so bored."

"Did she make any friends at the school, even in the past?"

"None that I know of. She did mention a young neighbor by the name of Omar, but I know very little about him, except for what she has told me. I understand he is handicapped, which could explain why he is not registered in this school. I do know she talks to the school secretary and the librarian, too. I hope you can find her. She is a sweet kid. I do wish she would not miss classes all the time."

Mrs. Pendleton looked very upset, her light-blue eyes seemed to be misting. "I'm sorry, this is a shock. This is very disturbing. I thought this was only one of her short fugues. I like Mora very much and don't want any harm coming to her."

Antonia waited, letting the silence grow. Finally, she thanked her for the information she had offered and went to look for the other two women the counselor had mentioned.

The librarian, Mrs. Montoya, revealed that Mora thought the school's collection of books were all for babies. "She's bright, maybe too bright for this school, you see?" She gave Antonia an inquiring look. "I have tried to get her some young mysteries with female heroines, but after reading a couple, she returned them, saying that these were not what she wanted. So I thought that she'd like some adult historical novels and I had offered to take her to the public library and get her a library card. But Mora has not yet taken me up on that offer."

Antonia was glad she had found other women concerned about the young girl, but disappointed that she was not discovering any new, useful information.

Finally Tony found and met with Mrs. Castillo, the school secretary. A very pretty brunette, in her late thirties, who obviously shopped the more elegant clothing stores, she was standing tall on her four-inch heels. Antonia introduced herself and asked if she had heard about Mora's disappearance.

As Mrs. Castillo trotted through the large hallway, a

cloud of exotic flowers mixed with vanilla wafted from her. "I have very little to do with the child. She is always missing classes, so I am not surprised that she has been gone for a while."

"Mrs. Pendleton told me that the two of you talk quite a bit."

"True, when she attends school. She does not talk to the other kids here. I think she prefers the company of adults," she replied with a knowing tone while raising her eyebrows.

She stared at Antonia up and down, as if appraising her. "I love your linen pants suit," she remarked, staring at the soft lavender jacket Tony wore that day. "Where did you find it?"

Nice and shallow. Clothing is more important than a missing child.

She's just changing the subject, Tone.

"I got it at the mall. I forget which store. Could you help me locate Mora? You seem to have a better judgment than the other women I met here.

Oh, Sis, flattery will probably get you somewhere.

"Yes, as a matter of fact, I personally know all the kids here. I greet them in the morning and send them home every day. I could tell you countless sordid tales about these kids and their parents." She almost chuckled but quickly recovered her countenance, trying to sound sincere. "Of course, I won't. I do respect their privacy. And yes, Mora likes to come see me during recess. She's one of the more intelligent kids here, that must be why she likes to talk to me."

Antonia nodded her head as if in approval. "Mrs Castillo, can you share what may trouble her?"

"I don't know how much her mother has told you?"

"Maria has shared quite a bit to help us find her. Any information would be helpful. We know about her stepfather, Andrés, and how she does not care for him."

Mrs. Castillo let out a small unladylike snort and looked around for movement.   The hallway was empty. She blurted out, "You mean she hates him! He tries to buy her love with ice cream and movies, but she's not fooled. She only consents to go with him for her mother's sake. Between you and me, I would look into a possible abduction by this man, should anyone ask for a ransom."

An abduction, interesting! A ransom! How did she come up with these ideas?

She's been watching too many cop shows.

No, Sis! What's her angle?

Mrs. Castillo continued, "From what she has told me, he is not the most sound person around her. He never calls ahead of time when he picks her up after school. She said that she doesn't want him to give her hugs, because he smells like sweat and his clothes are dirty. And his house is small. She hates going there. I hope that no inappropriate business goes on at his house, if you know what I mean. Yet, she has not mentioned anything like that to me. Now if you'll excuse me, I have work to do."

Ah, yes. The working poor must always be guilty before considering anyone else.

Especially when they have agricultural jobs, working in the

66

dirt: how gross!

Tony thanked the secretary for her input and quickly left, feeling slimed by the last comments of this narrow-minded woman. Andrés did not seem like a child molester, but rather a caring person trying to do the right thing for his adopted child.

You know, Sis, that one of the parents is always first considered as a suspect in abductions.

Yes, but her father seems honest, unlike that horrid woman.

Before they left, they looked for a brown van in the school parking lot. Except for a fairly new van with gray and tan stripes, nothing remotely matched the abducting vehicle.

~ ~ ~

From the information Jim had given them, they knew that the license plate did not belong to any brown van but to a black Nissan pickup, and that its registration had not been renewed. They were able to track down the owner of the black truck, a young man from Albuquerque. When they called him, he told them that his pickup had been stolen the previous year and was never recovered. He thought his truck had gone across the border. His insurance company had not given him a penny for it. So now, he rode his bicycle to work.

The Tonys were unhappy about their findings. As the

black pick-up had been reported stolen, it could not be registered again in the US, thanks to VIN numbers. No sense in looking for it here, but maybe they could ask various friends on the other side of the border whether they had seen such a truck. However, it may not be relevant at all to this case. Instead, they decided to concentrate on getting information on Andrés and on the school secretary.

Sis, now I'm really worried about Mora.

I don't think we should tell Maria about the stolen license plate until we have more positive info.

We can let her know that she still helps Omar on occasion.

And that it's where she stays when her dad is at home.

That should make her feel better.

Yeah! Omar is a nice kid.

Where do we look next?

~~~

Chapter 5
Across the Border

JANOS, ONE OF THEIR INFORMERS, GOT BACK TO
the Tonys early the next morning. His wavy brown hair,
always ratty, hung down his forehead, almost hiding his
light-blue eyes. His lanky body sported an endless neck
and lengthy arms that stuck out of his long-sleeve shirts.
"Always hide possible track marks if you're an abuser,"
he had once explained to them, when the heat was un-
bearable and they could not fathom how he could stand
anything but short sleeves.

Janos had gone to see the only current heroin dealer
in the area: DD, whose street name was Demon Dog.
In the past, Janos had told them how DD was a sleazy
looking white man, with dirty-blond dreadlocks, giving
true Rastafarians a bad reputation by being lazy about
his matted hair, holding no spiritual beliefs whatsoever.
Drugs were his god of choice. The only other major dealer
Janos knew had been killed recently, leaving DD the main
game in town. After offering the young man an array of
different pills, rocks, liquids, and powders, the dealer had
said, "There has not been any horse in town for the last
two months. Should be some in next month from China."

Janos continued, "DD did mention some scary Italian guys that were in town just last week, who had bought some meth from him. Later, they returned and wanted to kick his ass 'cause they thought he had cheated them. DD had to pull a gun on them, he was proud to tell me, and then they bought more meth. Crazy!"

The dealer did not think they were still around. As Janos could not leave without buying something from him, he bought a quarter ounce of tax-free, primo weed, so the Tonys paid him back with interest. If Janos smoked the grass, it did not bother them. He had proven to them before that he could stay off the heavy drugs, but they always feared that he might have to go back to shooting up again, should a dealer ever ask him to prove that he was still using.

Let's not mention what we just bought with Jim's money on his bill.

You bet, Sis, that's just miscellaneous supplies.

~ ~ ~

Meanwhile, José had gone to see his healer friend and then had called Antonia to ask her to come by. As soon as she arrived, he told her that after taking the curandera's herbs, he had dreamt of Jack walking by La Ultima Vez, a cantina he knew to be just south of Gallina Blanca, a small border town on the Mexican side. In the dream, two rough-looking men were on each side of Jack, holding him up by his arms, but he was not using his legs. He could see that they were dragging him, his feet dangling in the dirt.

The stocky men looked like brothers, but were not Hispanic. Both had thick eyebrows, the bushy, continuous kind with no middle over dark, sunken eyes. It looked like Jack had lost a lot of weight and could not focus his eyes. His mouth was puckered up, as if he was not wearing his dentures.

As he finished narrating his dream, he took Antonia's hand in his and held it tight. He looked into her eyes for any reaction.

"I know that visions are not solid facts. But Jack is like a brother to me. We have worked and lived side by side for many years. I really feel that he is in Mexico, that he is in deep trouble right now, and that he is alive. I hope that you can believe me."

"Thank you for sharing your dream, José. I too have visions at times. I try not to rely on them entirely, but they have rarely proven wrong."

She removed her hand from his grasp, and patted his arm. "My brother will go to check out La Ultima Vez tomorrow."

"I can ride along, if that would help?"

"Thank you for the offer, but I would rather you stayed here. Should you find out anything else, please give us a call.

~~~

Antonio decided to enlist the help of their friend Sunny Villegas, a city cop for Las Cruces, in their quest for the missing man. A short but broad-shouldered Hispanic man, he knew the Mexican town well and would fit in better than a too-well groomed Anglo detective who would attract attention and be seen as a tourist.

They had first met at the University of New Mexico, in Albuquerque. Sunny was on his last year before graduating at UNM and Antonia had just enrolled for her first year. Both were studying criminal justice, but had only one class together. Sunny was immediately attracted to the statuesque Antonia, and they were often seen in the library together, poring over textbooks. He had asked her out on multiple occasions. Once in a while, away from the school, she would hang out with him at local events. Usually she would beg off due to her part-time job that helped pay for her tuition, but mostly she was shy about dating someone she liked but felt would not understand her hermaphroditic characteristics.

They lost touch with each other for a few years, until one day, Sunny came knocking on the office door to ask if this was the same Tony he had met at school. Antonio had answered, and, trying to show no surprise, pretended not to know him. Sunny shook his hand as he introduced himself, mentioning that he knew his twin sister, and was pleased to meet him. Tony, in his male form, was a much easier persona for Sunny to relate to.

~~~

They left for the border early in the morning, feeling naked without any weapons. Crossing with a gun would only land them in jail on either side of the line, should they be discovered. Both wore well-worn blue-jean jackets and pants, old cowboy boots and slightly crushed cowboy hats, the dress of local workingmen looking for cheap deals across the border. Tiger had no intention of going with them, and jumped the low fence in the front yard when she saw them packing the truck with blankets, towels, food, and water.

They drove into the sleepy town immediately past the frontier, with its main street still unpaved, its booming liquor, trinkets, and pharmaceuticals sales belying an ever expending drug trade. The year before, one of the local dentists, frequented by many New Mexicans and Texans looking for a good but cheap dental expert, had been murdered by Mexican drug lords. His son had thought he could transport and sell with impunity large amounts of Columbian cocaine to the other side of the border, being related to a prominent local health practitioner and holding an American passport, as he was born in the US. But the drug Mafia had made an example of him in that little town, brutally killing him and all his immediate family: father, mother, younger siblings and grandparents included. The sins of the children are sometimes just as, if not more, perilous than those of the parents. The whole town mourned them for weeks, as the dentist and his wife had been very generous and helped many destitute families.

Sunny and Tony went into La Tienda Azul, the principal store in Gallina Blanca, whose outside walls were painted a bright, cerulean blue. Inside, its narrow crowded aisles were filled with vibrant, almost lurid, ceramic, plastic, or wood trinkets, colorful cloth scarves and pot holders, beaded jewelry, jazzy glassware, brass knickknacks and other inexpensive gifts. One long aisle was reserved for Mexican alcohol, tax-free and half the cost of the booze on the other side of the border. The tourists spent most of their money there, never venturing into the no-man's land just outside of town, where anyone looking wealthy could lose money easily.

Talking with the Mexican-American owner who knew Tony well, they discovered that an old *gringo loco* had gotten there three days before, looking destitute and out of his mind, surrounded by a couple of tough-looking but well-dressed English-speaking gentlemen who, after buying some tequila, had kept on driving to the south side of town.

After parking the car in front of the old bar called La Ultima Vez, they walked to the southern end of town, the fine dirt of the road lifting around them with every step. They stopped at another little store, someone's house with a few items on an outside table under a small canopy. After Sunny purchased another bottle of tequila, they were told that three American men had come by a few days before, buying bottled water and cheap whisky. Their old father, the small vendor said, looked half asleep and could not stand up on his own. "That gringo had drunk too much whisky!"

Soon enough, the houses dwindled, opening to a barren desert, but for scattered shrubs covered in dust. They came across three young boys who were tossing rocks into a rusty tin can, laughing and counting points when one stone would go in. They quieted down when they saw the two approaching men and stared at them, as if observing an incongruous scene on their side of town.

"*¡Hola, niños!* Did you see an older man come by here a few days ago, accompanied by two other men?" Sunny asked while handing them a few pesos.

"No, señor. We haven't seen anyone," the oldest one answered. The smallest of the three made a small hand gesture as if wanting to talk. Sunny turned to him and gave him a few more coins. "*¿Y tu?*"

He looked at his friends, then at Sunny, completely ignoring Tony. After checking for movement all around and giving a questioning look at his young friends, he motioned for the men to follow. The boy ran barefoot on the hot sand by the side of the road, and Tony and Sunny in their cowboy boots had a hard time keeping up. After a couple of kilometers, he veered off to the left, away from the road, toward a bunch of scrubby mesquite trees on the edge of a gully.

There was a body at the bottom of the arroyo, curled up in a fetal position, immobile and not responding to their calls. He was naked, his exposed side gravely sunburned, his face covered with dried blood, his eyes closed. It was Jack, but he looked either dead or unconscious. Tony bent next to him, calling his name. No response. He checked him for a pulse. The man jerked his arm away, grunted and opened one of his blood-caked eyes with difficulty.

"Mr. Overmyer! Jack! Jack! We have come on behalf of your son, Jim, and your friend José. We would like you to come back with us, back to the United States."

He did not seem to follow anything they said. His only opened eye was vacant and unfocused. He laid his head down in the dirt again. Despite the sweltering heat, his skin was clammy. Sunny took off his jacket and covered his shivering body.

"Let's get him out of here before he passes out."

It's a miracle he is still alive!

Barely alive. Let's get moving.

"You go, Tony. I'll stay. But don't be too long! I'm not comfortable here. I don't have my gun!"

Antonio quickly walked back to the car, with the young boy in tow, while Sunny waited with the old man.

Even after gaining a few more hundred pesos, which translated only into a couple of dollars, the small boy did not want to talk about the men who brought Jack there. He did not want any trouble, and he soon left to rejoin his bunch of friends on the edge of town. The little ragtag group seemed worried for him when he had not returned right away. Tony tossed them another couple of small bills as he drove past them on his way back to Sunny and the old man.

~~~

Jack did not put up a fight when Sunny and Antonio wrapped him in a blanket, carried him, and finally laid him down in the back of the car. The old man reeked of sweat, urine, and cheap whisky. They drove with all the windows open. They knew that US Immigration would not let him go through their post without papers. So they took him to a three-room out-of-the-way hotel on the west side of town, paying the owner extra to keep his mouth shut. Antonio had called Jim as soon as they had found him. They bathed Jack, treated his burns, clothed him, gave him plenty of water, and spoon-fed him soft foods before he fell asleep on the bed.

While Sunny was out purchasing more baby food and fruit juices, Antonia called José and appraised him of Jack's situation. He let her know that Jim had just updated him, and that he was going to travel south to bring his friend back across the border.

~~~

As soon as Jack was sleeping, Antonio called Jim back. "To protect his life, you will have to pretend Jack is dead. He should not go back to his home, but instead you may want to move him to Albuquerque or even out of state. The last thing you want is for someone to tell the perps where to find him, even if inadvertently."

Jim replied that just last month he had found a nursing home near his place, one which would be able to take him in on short notice. He'd call them on the way down, to let them know.

"He's going to need some medical care first," Antonio added.

They discussed how to proceed and Jim told him how, with José's help, he had found his dad's current ID, some clothes and a set of spare dentures. They were just leaving Las Cruces.

~~~

According to the plan, Antonio hired a private ambulance and had the medics wait on the American side of the border.

It took Jim less than two hours to drive his black SUV to the Mexican hotel. After looking at his father, who did not seem to recognize him, he went to see the hotel owner and gave him a generous tip, asking him to tell anyone who asked that his father had died.

José, with tears in his eyes, attended to Jack, rubbing more ointment on his wounds while softly talking to him, recounting some of the work they had done together, how beautiful his wife had been, how his garden was full of flowers right now. The old man turned his head and looked at him with his one good eye. He smiled and then laid his head back on the pillow, without uttering a word. Then with Jim's help and with difficulty due to the sunburns, José dressed him in his own clothes.

~~~

After clearing the border, Jack was placed on a gurney, in the waiting ambulance. Jim asked the driver to speed with lights and sirens on, all the way to the first large town. The paramedic on board shot the old man full of saline fluid to rehydrate him. Tony and José followed in Jim's car, while Sunny drove his pickup back to Las Cruces.

Inside the vehicle, Jim kept talking to his father. "I apologize for not taking better care of you, Dad. I was not a good son, thinking my life was more important than yours. Thank you for all you've done for me. You made me a good man, a good cop." Jim could not tell if his father could hear him, as his eyes were closed and his breathing seemed very shallow.

Once on the interstate, the ambulance turned off the sirens. Antonio had suggested that they pretend he had passed away while going through town, just in case someone had followed his journey and would talk about it. Jim had agreed that his father should be enrolled under a different name at the rest home.

Jim asked the paramedic whether it would make a difference in his father's life to drive another three hours to Albuquerque. The medic called his advisor and explaining the situation, mentioned that Jack had a Do-Not-Resuscitate notice inside his passport. After the medical director cleared it, Jim instructed them to take him to the closest Albuquerque hospital from the interstate.

But Jack never regained consciousness. He passed away less than an hour from the city. Jim felt guilty. Guilty that he had pretended that he was dead from the time they picked him up. Guilty that he had let his father down when he needed help. Guilty that José, in the last twenty years, had been closer to Jack than he, his only son.

Once Antonio arrived back in Las Cruces, Sunny picked him up at the Overmyer's mansion. As they were traveling back to the station, Tony recounted how Jack's last big bust had gone awry. Sunny savored the story. He felt both respect and sorrow for the old cop. He told Tony he'd keep an eye out for the Greeks, if they ever showed up in town, but agreed with him that without concrete proof, these guys were too dangerous to pursue at the moment.

Shortly after, Antonia went to see José. He invited her to Jack's wake. He told her that Jim would pay him to keep taking care of the homestead and its grounds for as long as he wanted, adding that eventually Jim wanted to retire in this home his great-grandparents had settled. Winking at her, he also said that Jim had his eyes on a young lady he thought he could woo in a few years, if she wasn't married by then. When she got ready to leave, Antonia shook his hand, but he reached up and gave her a hug, thanking her again for believing in him.

~~~

Chapter 6
Sirena's Story

THE TONYS WENT TO VISIT THEIR MOTHER WHEN-
ever they felt stymied by a difficult case. She was their
anchor, their means of regaining their unique mental
faculties — maybe their sanity as well — when getting
sidetracked. She completely understood their dual per-
sonalities and did not try to change them, but had always
accepted and supported their peculiarity from the time
they were born. They had quickly discovered that she
would offer them a certain clarity of mind by just being
in her presence, benefiting from a symbiotic mental boost
conveyed through her calm aura. They would not even
need to tell her what they were working on.

Sirena was nearing sixty years of age but looked ten
years younger. Of Italian descent, tall with violet-blue eyes
and wavy salt-and-pepper hair, more black than white, to
the observant eye she conveyed a hidden sadness under
her cheerful appearance. She always dressed well, despite
making a meager living as a cook for a nearby bed and
breakfast. Starting at four in the morning, her job freed up
most of her daytime, so the twins could see her any day
after noon. They helped her with unexpected expenses,

but also respected her wish to keep on working. On Sunday mornings, she donated her time to a soup kitchen for the needy and then helped handicapped children learn to read in the afternoon. Their respect and affection for her were unbounded and reciprocated. Whenever they visited her, she would fix them a delicious meal which they could never resist. If they could stay a while, they sat at the dining table, talking for a couple of hours as Europeans like to do.

~~~

Bothered by the lack of clues for Mora's whereabouts, after a quick phone call to their mother, the Tonys went to see her. Aromatic smells wafted from her kitchen. Sirena was preparing fettuccine with scallops a la puttanesca, one of their favorite dishes. After exchanging news about their respective health and what was happening around them, the steaming dish was ready and they sat down at her kitchen table.

When done with the excellent feast, they asked her to recount their birth. She told them that this would make the sixth or seventh time, but chuckling, she relented. The twins, being her first and only children, won any and all contests with her in the long run. And as many firstborns realize, they got away with most of their whims.

"Alright, one more time just for you. When your dad and I went to see the midwife, three month after you were conceived, she told us that she could hear two heartbeats, or maybe more like a strong beat and an echo, through her stethoscope. Your father at first rejoiced at the prospect of twins: "Two for one!" he shouted. A month passed before the midwife said that she feared that one of the twins was fading, getting absorbed by the other, although I stayed healthy. Your father did not like that. He said that the midwife did not know what she was talking about, and a few days later, he blurted out to me, for the first time, that there had been a set of Siamese twins birthed by a great aunt on the Urbani's side of his family.

"What was born from that women was an evil thing that had to be killed right away. It had extra legs and arms growing out of its stomach. If this abomination was to happen again, this monster would have to be killed too."

Sirena stopped, took a few deep breaths, and a sip of water.

No matter how often she had told the story, the emotional charge was present every time. She wiped her forehead, pushed away her plate and now with anger in her eyes, she continued. "You were a couple of weeks early when the contractions began. I had wanted to have you at home, with the help of a midwife. After about six hours of rapid contractions, your father insisted that we go to the big hospital in Albuquerque, in case of complications. A few hours after we got there, and a couple of hours more of pushing, your head first appeared. Your beautiful, long head. Much longer and pointier than any other babies. Your eyes were just showing, tightly closed.

But when your father saw your very long cranium, he screamed, 'Abominazione!' He tried to grab you while you were just emerging, despite the doctor's warning. Two nurses forcefully yanked him out of the delivery room, as he kept screaming 'Abominazione!' The pain was such that I did not think your shoulders would come out, I was too small. I too feared that you may be joined to another. I told the doctor to cut me open and pull you out right away. To save your life, at any cost. He did not hesitate once I told him that the baby could be part of a set of Siamese twins and pushed you back in while I was getting a shot to numb me for the surgery. The doctor worked fast and the beautiful you came out, screaming your little lungs out."

Her hands slightly trembling, she went on once again with her eyes looking downward, as if in shame. "I tried to have a nurse call your father back so he could see how perfect you were. But he had run out and could not be found. What I did not know then, was that before he ran away, Tonino had told the first doctor that he should have the baby killed and perform a hysterectomy on the spot so that I would not have any more evil children. He had always led a spiritual life before. But at that moment, I no longer understood him. Since he was the head of the family at the time, I did not know if I had any say so in the decision about my body. I was lucky that the doctor who performed the C-section cared about his oath to help people before all else, respected women, and had also called one of his colleagues who specialized in difficult neonatal medicine."

She took a few more sips of water, but the anger was gone from her voice, now replaced with a smile. "Doctor Carrel was wonderful. He happened to be at the hospital that day and dropped everything and came right away. The other doctor stitched me up and later told me that it would have been too dangerous to remove my ovaries at that time. I could have bled out, and besides, he would not have done it without a medical reason and my permission. Your father thought that the old ways from his foreign origins would work here, but the doctors were wonderful and protected us."

She was smiling still, remembering the easier time once their father had left.

"After the hospital's nursery had checked you out, Doctor Carrel came in and told me his specialty was conjoined and non-identical twins. As soon as the local anesthetic wore off, he showed you to me, although I was too groggy to hold you. Then he asked me if I was conscious enough to make a decision. Did I want to decide which sex you would be? As you both know, one in every many thousands of babies is born a hermaphrodite. A couple of days later, after getting the DNA tests results that showed you had both male and female sets of chromosomes, he said that you were a medical miracle, a one in a billion being, non-identical twins in one body. He called you a real and live Tetragametic Chimera. He warned me, as I have warned you, about possible hormonal disturbances, as well as all the myriad of other potential problems you could encounter in your lifetime. He also said that your head would shrink back to a more reasonable size, and that the extreme point was because I had to push for so long before you started coming out. And as you know, we are so lucky that you were and still are the most healthy people I know. God has always watched over both of you."

In the past she had mentioned that when Tonino left her and her babies, she had held doubts about their common faith, eventually going back to it a year later. She had not raised them as Catholics, as she had been by her Italian family, but decided to educate them in all the major religions of this world. As children they were neither baptized nor circumcised. The Tonys had told her many times how glad they were that she had such a broad-minded awareness.

She took a deep breath followed by a sip of water. With tears still in her eyes, she went back to her story. "Later I realized that it was best that Tonino left, so I could make the proper decisions by myself. When you were born, I was able to keep you the beautiful way God made you. I declared you as conjoined twins, male and female. Doctor Carrel told me that it was the right choice, and that he would like to be the one to provide medical care for the two of you, while you were growing up. And so he did. He came at first every month to check on you, then, as you know, we went to see him four times a year, every year, or when you would get the least little sneeze, as he had asked. He eventually wrote a thesis about you, not mentioning any names or dates, of course."

Sirena next talked about how, while they still lived in Albuquerque, she had not liked the hospital interns to come just to gawk at the odd children. She did not want their life to turn into a circus show. That was why they moved to Socorro for the first few years of their life. She also decided not to have any more children, as she knew that the twins would be enough for her.

"I had hoped and waited for Tonino to return, but he never did. As you know, I never saw him again, and never heard what happened to him until you found him that year after you graduated."

They thanked her for the meal and for sharing again the story of their birth. While their mother was talking, Antonia got a strong feeling that she needed to find Mora soon, or she would be lost to a greater evil. It was time to get more involved. While clearing up the table, they decided to use Sirena as a sounding board, telling her about the young girl and her dog.

"You have made the right choice. Look for her, let your spiritual guides help you. You don't need money. You have plenty to live on for now, but the girl may not have much time left."

As they drove home, Antonia thought: *There is something different, something special about the dog. She really cares about Mora.*

You're right! The key is no longer the van with the stolen plate. It is Tiger.

Am always right, haven't you learned that yet?

Oh, shut up, you would not be half of what you are without me!

They decided to try to reach Mora again with the help of Rosetta. It had worked before, and as controversial as the method was, it had given them some results.

~~~

Chapter 7
Looking for a Pearl

SINCE FORMALLY STARTING AS PRIVATE EYES
seven years before, the Tonys used a professional internet company to do background checks. Trying to get more
information about the people Mora knew, they looked up
both of her parents, as well as the school's secretary.

Maria Martinez, Mora's mother, was born and raised
in Garfield, New Mexico, on a chile and pecan farm, the
youngest of a family of seven children. She had been a
cheerleader for her high-school football team, studied
education for two years at the New Mexico State University,
worked first as a hair dresser, then moved back to Las
Cruces to become a prep cook for an elementary school
cafeteria. Eleven years ago, she married Andrés Aguirre
and, four years after having a single child, she went to
work part-time at the Bellisima beauty salon.

Mora's father, Andrés Aguirre was born in Hatch, a few
miles from Maria's birthplace. The eldest of two children,
he went to a high-school in Truth or Consequences but quit
the school at sixteen to spend a full year in Mexico City
as an exchange student. His paternal great-grandparents

were from Mexico and he still had distant family in the capital. Thirteen years later, he returned to the U.S., became a full-time farmhand, first in Hatch, then in Las Cruces. As an adult, his travels outside the U.S. included two-week-long trips to Mexico every four years.

Very little was known of Hope Esperanza Castillo, the school secretary, before she turned eighteen in a juvenile correctional facility. She had been adopted as a baby by Jennie and Armando Castillo, after being abandoned as a newborn on the steps of an El Paso hospital. The report only mentioned that Hope had a difficult childhood and that her adoptive mother died when Hope was fourteen years old, shortly before entering the juvenile jail. No records were available but for her release on parole on her eighteenth birthday. She received her high-school diploma while in prison and was admitted to the Doña Anna College for a two-year associate degree in Early Childhood Education. She worked at a daycare center for six months before getting fired. No records of employment were available for the next thirteen months. Her adoptive father had died a week before she disappeared. She resurfaced in Brownsville, Texas, after failing a drug test for a UPS driving job. Another undocumented year passed before she married a New Mexico school district superintendent named Ernest Castillo. She applied for a secretarial position at the Western Hills High School in town, on the recommendation of her husband, and has been working there for the last four years.

She is creepy, Sis!

She could have killed both her parents!

You think Lou could get the lowdown on her?

Don't know. They keep those juvie records locked up tight.

Told you, had a bad feeling about her. Am getting to be as much an empath as you.

As long as your emotions don't get in the way.

Am the man, therefore never get emotional.

Stop raising your mental tone, can hear you fine.

~ ~ ~

Later that day, they went with Tiger to see Madame LaFleur. Not knowing how well the dog would fare in a moving vehicle for a long drive, they took the precaution of having a large towel on hand. Less than twenty minutes after they started moving, Tiger who was sitting in the back seat with the window cracked open, was panting heavily, and soon she started drooling. They stopped on an exit ramp and walked her on a leash. It did not take long for Tiger to learn to whimper a little when she needed to get out. She made the most of her new skill, and they had to stop every fifteen minutes or so, to let her recover from the ride.

That's going to take a lot of time!

Yes, but it might be worth it. She'll get better at it, if we respect her motion sickness.

Rosetta's camouflaged house always made them smile. Dug into the hillside facing the graveled road, at a distance, it just seemed like a hole in the bottom of the most eastern of the small peaks. The stuccoed walls had been naively but realistically painted with pictures of local trees and shrubs, the background matching the color of the surrounding sand, but for a large bluish-white moon crescent adorning the top of the wall, in contrast to the rounded, dark frame of the door. Serving as windows, two dusky-brown portholes stood to one side, while underneath one of them, a spotted jaguar hid behind the painted bushes.

She took a couple of minutes to answer their knock, until finally Rosetta opened the door, looking a little drawn, with sunken circles under her eyes. She took an instant liking to the dog, who also acted pleased to see her, frantically wagging her long tail and telling Rosetta, in a high-pitched song, all about the long ride to her place.

"How are you doing, Rosetta? You look tired."

"I'm fine. Just not getting enough sleep lately, that's all. I have a couple of clients with big problems. So what are we looking for today, with this lovely dog? Is this Calico?"

"Tiger! We found out her real name."

"Ha, yes, Tiger, that is definitely your name." She went in the back room, came back with a jar of herbs, and placed a few spoonfuls in a baggie.

"For Tiger, before the rides. She just told me she gets carsick."

They told Rosetta what they had learned about Mora.

How the van's plates were from a stolen vehicle. Antonia wanted to get in touch with the girl and thought Tiger might be helpful in the process.

The woman leaned back into her armchair, closed her eyes for a minute, and asked them if they would like some herbal tea. The twins nodded affirmatively, while silently considering their dilemma. When Rosetta went to her backroom, they heard the rattle of metal pans, silverware and china cups. A few minutes later, she returned with a large, brass tray filled with a couple of steaming mugs, a bottle of honey, and a small plate of ginger cookies. She set the tray on a low table in front of them.

"Help yourselves," she said, sinking back into her own comfortable chair. "While listening to you, I must tell you I do not get a good feeling about Mora's fate." She lit a candle and, with its flame, heated some amber globs till they glowed red, before placing them in a silver tray. The strong scent of myrrh invaded the room.

The Tonys looked at her inquiringly. "Can you tell us more? What did you see?"

"What I saw while you were talking will not mean the same to you. My tiny fugues, the fleeting images I receive now and then, come loaded with symbols I have developed for myself since I started seeing, or divining, if you wish. What I saw while you were talking about Mora was a light-green pearl surrounded by a dark-red aura rolling toward a large stone well. I don't want to cloud your session. We'll talk afterward, if your subconscious does not give you an answer soon."

Swinging a crystal pendulum in front of them, Rosetta asked them to relax, sink into the chair, look inward, let the mind bring thoughts up without direction, as if they were getting ready to fall asleep.

She had barely put them under hypnosis, when Antonia, with her eyes closed, started talking in a little girl's voice. The words seemed to resonate from inside a long tunnel.

"Hi Tiger! How are you my beauty? I miss you. You're looking so good. Mama is taking good care of you." Tiger let out a short yelp and began licking Antonia's hand.

The seer hissed, "Engage her! Talk to her. Tell her who you are."

"Hi, Mora. My name is Antonia. I really like Tiger. I'm helping your mom take care of her. She is a beautiful dog."

"Right, and she is my dog!"

"Yes, but you're not here to take care of her, so I'm trying to do that until you come back."

"She won't like you like she likes me!" A sharp crack resounded. The connection was broken. Tiger laid down at Antonia's feet, cradling her head between her paws, whimpering.

Rosetta asked Antonia again to call Mora. "Tell her again you're only taking care of her dog. You're only keeping her till she gets back."

But they were not able to re-connect with the girl.

Then the seer asked Antonio to get in touch with Mora. He only replied, "Nothing. I cannot feel anything. I can barely feel my sister and could not find her when the girl was talking. That's never happened before. We're always in contact with each other, even if one of us is quiet for a while. We even dream in tandem. Right now, I just feel nauseous, as if we are no longer one, no longer united."

Rosetta told Antonia to try one more time to get inside that state when Mora had reached her. She tried, but the child's voice did not come back.

"Did you see where Mora is?"

"No. Not really."

"Look back," Rosetta insisted. "Go back to that space and look again. Look at the child, where she stood, what she was doing. Tell me what you see."

"Everything is fuzzy, as if behind a veil or a layer of thin smoke. The girl seems to be in a room with a few beds, a little like a dormitory. Cracked paint on the walls. Small high windows. It does not seem very friendly. It feels sad, lonely, filled with despair. I could not really see Mora. She is almost transparent, like a... a little like a ghost. There is something different about her. Different from her mom's pictures of her, but I'm not sure what."

"What is different?"

"I don't know!"

Rosetta kept insisting. "Was she standing still or moving?"

"I think she was standing very still, until something or

someone got a hold of her before she disappeared."

"What about sounds in that room?"

"It was very quiet, then she got upset about who Tiger likes. She was almost screaming at me."

"We heard. What about smells?"

Her nostrils flaring, she answered, "Maybe cooking smells? Distant but strong. Like onions and beans."

"Was it humid, dry, hot or cold"

"I don't know. It's all fading now. I can't see her anymore. I don't know."

"It's alright. Next time, if there is a next time, it should be easier to connect with her. Eventually, if the girl is responsive enough, you may be able to converse as if you were in the same room, face-to-face. You are very receptive to others, you are also an empath, you can reach into the emotional realm of other people, and I think the girl can as well. I also believe that our lovely Tiger is a receptive being, helping with the connection between the two of you."

While Antonia was recovering from her trance, Madame LaFleur prepared some tea. She cooled it down with cold water and, pouring it in a stainless-steel bowl on the floor, she offered it to Tiger who lapped it all up.

All of a sudden, Antonia sat up in the chair. "It's her eyebrows! She looks different from the picture her mother gave us. I tried to imagine how she looked while she talked to me, and I saw her, faintly, but I did see her. It looks like there is more space between her eyebrows which are thinner. I think it makes her look older, more sophisticated. She must have plucked her eyebrows. And her dark, curly hair has bleached highlights in it, on both sides of her face."

It seemed like a dream where little bits are pinpointed as one thinks about it, but can't quite remember the whole thing for certain.

Antonio said that he had not been able to see the child while she was communicating with his sister. Then he asked Rosetta if she would explain the meaning of her earlier vision.

"When my guide sends me an image, it is like a colored snapshot. I do not see the actual persons or places, although sometimes I do see inert objects. The colors in the picture help me gage the importance of the situation. The objects in it show me the spirit, the quality or the essence, if you will, of the subjects involved. The main entity was a green pearl. To me, a pearl is young and moving; light green is for innocence; but the dark red surrounding it is for lies, mistaken beliefs, and of course blood. The pearl seemed to be rolling, moving toward a stone well, which represents an old association, light at the top, but dark inside, with water someone could drink or drown in, therefore posing multiple dangers."

"Thank you for sharing, Rosetta. If you ever need an apprentice..." Antonio trailed off, smiling.

"You're welcome. And actually I am looking for an apprentice, but you are not the one. Instead you are my friend, my friends, I mean," she added, correcting herself.

Rosetta then mentioned that she would like them to come by when they had more time on their hands. She also said that Antonio should visualize a green pearl when his sister starts communicating with Mora; it could help him be present in the conversation. The ride home was uneventful, except that Tiger did not get sick once during the long hour back to Las Cruces.

Antonia was exhausted, so her brother drove while telling her how he thought he had lost her for a while. She had separated from him. She had left him to go to this child, and during that time, he had sensed she was no longer linked to him.

Sis, don't leave me anymore! Can't remember ever loosing contact with you. Didn't know if you would come back. Am afraid for us. Can't accept the emptiness, the loss, the chasm that had opened during those few minutes.

Don't know what happened. Can't talk about it right now. Too tired. Rosetta was tired too! Wasn't just me.

You left me. Never want to feel that again!

Tone, just want to sleep for a while. Are you sure you were not the one who left me? You never truly accept my empathy. You don't understand it, so you pretend it's just some temporary intuition. You let me go into that foreign space by myself. Could have used your strength. That is one powerful child. Let's talk in the morning, after we sleep. You're exhausted, too. We both need to recharge our batteries.

After they had arrived home, they noticed the light blinking on the office phone. The callers had waited a few hours already; they could wait until morning. After brushing their teeth, sprawling on their king-sized bed, they saw that Tiger had laid down on the rug beside them, instead of asking to be out in the backyard, as she had done previously. She was already dreaming, her legs furiously kicking up invisible trail dirt as she ran and ran. They joined her quickly in sleep.

~~~

Chapter 8
Insult to Injury

"You HAVE FOUR MESSAGES," THE ROBOTIC female voice of the answering machine told them the next morning, as they sipped their coffee: black, fragrant, hold the sugar.

Jim Overmyer was the first caller. "Hi Tony and Antonia. Just wanted to thank you for finding my dad so fast. A preliminary autopsy was done, showing that he had suffered multiple internal injuries. His abdomen was deformed and his liver and kidneys were heavily bruised. The doctors were surprised he had lasted that long after the beating. And with the severe dehydration, his kidneys had shut down. I'll let you know what else they find out."

After a short pause, he resumed, "My father never recognized me during the trip up. Well, I think I may have jinxed him pretending to have him dead before his time. Anyway, the wake will be on Saturday in the afternoon, at the homestead as originally planned. I hope you can both make it."

The second message was so garbled that the Tonys could not figure out what it was about. A woman's voice, crying maybe? They played the message a couple more times but still could not decipher what was being conveyed. This morning was not starting well.

Next, their friend, Sheriff Lou Graves had called. Something about his ex-father-in-law. Nothing pressing, he had said.

The last message was from the woman who had called earlier, or at least it was the same caller ID, a motel in Las Cruces. With tears in her voice, she said that she did not know her own name. "But could you call back and ask for JD Levi, that's what I am registered as, at the Roadrunner Motel. It is urgent! Please, get back to me as soon as possible."

The twins thought they would try to connect again with Mora in the afternoon, if Rosetta was available. The morning was young still, and rarely wanting to turn business down, they decided to see if they could help this JD woman.

~ ~ ~

Antonia drove to the Roadrunner on the edge of Motel Drive. A traditional Western row of single-floor rooms, arranged in a horseshoe, with a center aisle where desert willows, yuccas with tall flower heads, and blue sagebrush gave a semblance of privacy from the opposite side. Just a basic clean-looking, old-fashioned motel, it stood apart from the bigger, flashier lodging chains. A couple of cars were parked by the distant rooms. Antonia displayed her detective badge, which could easily pass for a police identity, at the East Indian concierge who told her in his lilting accent, "Room 106, a few doors down this side. Good luck!"

"What do you mean?"

"She will not answer the door or let the maid clean the room. I doubt if she'll answer the door for the police. Even for a policewoman."

She knocked on the door, announcing herself. "Antonia Urbani, with Two Tonys' Search Engine."

The woman who greeted her was disfigured, both raccoon-like black eyes were swollen and tearful, the lower half of one of her cheeks had turned a sickening mustard-and-purple color, her nose seemed off-kilter, bulging on one side, her mouth a fat yellowish bruise, which she covered with her hand, but not fast enough before Tony saw a couple of front teeth missing. All these injuries made it hard to tell her age: she appeared to be between thirty and forty years old. She had combed her hair and was wearing clean clothes, but at first glance her face looked like that of a street person.

"Thank you for coming so quickly. Please don't stare at me. I'll explain. Call me JD."

"OK, JD. And you can call me Tony. I'm going to take notes, if you don't mind. How can we help?" she replied, as she pulled an electronic pad from her pocket, trying hard not to look at the woman's ravaged face.

"I woke up in a hospital in El Paso ten days ago. I can't... I don't know who I am. I don't remember anything before that day. Nothing looks familiar, not even my ugly face in the mirror. I don't know if I should stay here. I don't know what I've done to deserve what has happened to me. The cops said they would keep looking into it, but I don't think they cared, since I am alive. They asked me who I was working for, as if I were a whore. Please, help me find out who I am and what happened to me."

Antonia motioned for both of them to sit down at the tiny table on one side of the room. "Alright, let's start from when you woke up in the hospital. What did the doctor say?"

"She said I had been raped many times through both orifices. She thinks the bruises on my face and on my breasts were from multiple beatings, probably over the course of many hours. My neck and both wrists showed signs of ligatures by nylon ropes. In my left arm, the os pisiforme and the triquetrum — two small bones in the wrist — were dislocated. The doctor reset them."

JD took a deep breath. "The police took some samples and scrapings but have not found anything yet. They said that no foreign DNA was present. Nothing under my fingernails. Nothing inside my vagina. The police thought I had been scrubbed clean before the medics found me outside the entrance of the hospital, in the middle of the night."

"A psychiatrist came to see me but offered no help at all. He showed me many pictures of places, people and various objects, but nothing looked familiar. He also said that my memories would most likely start to come back in a few days, but they have not. I'm worried it could be permanent."

"How did you get to Las Cruces?"

"Someone signed me out. He said he was my brother, James Levi. He said my name is Jane Levi. But it does not ring a bell. I think I would remember my name if I heard it."

Prompted for more details, she continued. "I was so medicated, I can't really recall his face, only his profile. Dark, curly hair. Not too tall. He was wearing dark glasses and a big mustache I thought was fake. He did not say much. I thought I had heard his voice before, but it was not as familiar as that of a family member. No particular accent, but well educated. He put me in a cab, paid the fare in advance, and told the cabbie to drive me here, to room 106, and he gave me the key card. When I got here, I went straight to the room, and I have not left this motel since then."

"So you have not used the room key this whole time?"

"Just to come back in from breakfast, early after Gopal, the motel owner, puts it out. The man was wearing leather gloves, so I don't think you'll find any fingerprints on this card other than mine."

"Can you describe him again?"

She did and gave her the name of the hospital and her attending doctor in El Paso.

"How do you survive without going out of your room?"

"When I got inside, there was a sealed envelope with the name Jane Levi typed on it, on this night table. It contained twenty one-hundred dollar bills. Then last Sunday, an envelope was slid under the door during the night with the same amount in it. I order meals from local restaurants that deliver. I called the closest department store for clean clothes and had Gopal pick them up. He also picked up toiletries, pain pills and ointments for my face. He's very helpful. He said that the room has already been paid for by my brother, for two months."

"Do you know about what time the envelope showed up?"

"No, it was there in the morning, when I woke up."

"Could I have these envelopes if you still have them?"

JD gave her two empty envelopes. Not wanting to handle them, Antonia had her put them in a plastic bag she carried in her purse.

"Would you mind if I took pictures of your face? I have a friend who can reconstruct it according to your bone structure. Maybe we can find out who you are that way."

"I don't know if I want my picture going on milk cartons. I am very ashamed of what happened to me, whatever it was."

"Your picture would not have any trace of the bruises or other damage done to your face. Your nose would be straightened, too. It would only be available to a select few people. Maybe at first, with your permission, just to a group of private detectives from El Paso. How about hair and spit samples, too, in order to determine your genetic background?"

JD relented and agreed to the pictures and to having Antonia come by with a kit to take a saliva sample the next day. After opening the curtains and turning the lights on, Tony took two full-length pictures of her, front and back. She also took a dozen close-ups of her face.

Interesting case, Sis!
Educated, maybe in the medical field.
Or she listened well to her doc.
She knew the Latin names of those wrist bones, Tone.
OK, so educated, let's see what's up with this James Levi.

On her way out, Antonia stopped by the motel reception desk. She thanked Gopal for taking care of Jane. Then she asked if he had seen anyone stop by her room, besides the food deliveries. He did not think so, except for the first policeman that came the day after she arrived. He mentioned that there were no surveillance cameras outside.

"Can you describe the person who paid for her room?"

"Yes, I can. It was a man. He paid in cash with hundred-dollar bills. He had a big black mustache and dark wrap-around sunglasses, although it was already evening when he came. He said he had light-sensitive eyes. He was wearing a cap low on his forehead. The cap had a rock pick on it, and it said "Miners". This man was not very tall, just a little taller than me, but he looked Mediterranean, like you. He was wearing a brown, argyle vest over a white shirt, tan chino pants, and brown, fine-leather loafers. His car was a small, white foreign car, with a four circles symbol, and Utah plates. I always look at the plates, you know, for security, but now I can't remember the numbers."

"Is there a camera inside your office?"

"Unfortunately there isn't."

"That's alright. You're very observant. Thank you Gopal. Could you give me a call if you see this car again or someone not delivering food going into her room, please," she said as she handed him her business card with a hundred-dollar bill folded in three underneath, a part of the down payment from JD.

"Thank you, also. I thought you were a policewoman, now I see you are a detective. I will call you with anything new, but I cannot take your money. I saw her face the first time she came for breakfast. That poor lady suffered a lot. She is always the first one for the free continental breakfast, before anybody else shows up. After that one time, now she always wears a veil, like a Muslim woman. I hope you find out who did this to her."

A strange reflection on the office bay window caught Tony's eyes.

Tone, do you see that image of three bones hanging down?

Yeah! Spooky, Sis! But I think it's outside the window.

As they looked past the other side of the doubled-pane window, the ghostly arrangement faded.

Just an illusion? Trick of the light?

The projection of someone's gruesome mobile hanging from another room?

The motel manager had tilted his head to one side and was looking at her with concern. *Can he hear us?*

Antonia thanked him again before quickly leaving.

As they got in the Subaru, they saw the same three

bones dangling from the rearview mirror, three vertebras, suspended in mid-air, as if they were strung together with a transparent fishing line, one above the other. The image faded again and they heard Rosetta's voice in an urgent timbre, "Come! Come quick!"

The bones were replaced by a large rattlesnake, followed by a half dozen metal knitting needles floating over a sink filled with boiling gray fumes.

Whoa! Sis, I see it, too. What does it mean?

Rosetta is in trouble. Let's go!

~ ~ ~

Chapter 9
A Mojave Viper

ONE OF THE TONYS' FRIENDS, ERIC "THE SNAKE man," bred venomous snakes from rattler to bushmaster. He had taught the twins how to respect and properly handle any snake. The serpent should be lifted from underneath with a long stick, at a spot one-third of its length from the head, thereby making it go limp, like a kitten picked up by the scruff of the neck. They had done it before and succeeded in relocating many a snake that way, especially the ones that liked to sun themselves in the middle of the pavement. Antonio did not care for the sport.

When they stopped at the house to pick up tools, Tiger was waiting in the front yard, sitting on a short, wide tree stump among flowering geraniums in clay pots. She yapped mournfully as Tony approached her.

She wants to come with us.

OK, let's give her a little of Rosetta's magic potion before we go.

They retrieved a bottle of her car sickness preventive tea from the fridge. They loaded the pickup truck with a long, fiberglass pole and a bucket with a lid, just in case they had to move snakes. Not knowing what was really needed, they were relying on intuition. Tone went to get industrial rubber gloves and bleach. He also strapped his nine-millimeter Smith and Wesson into an ankle holster, while Antonia wondered where she had left the strong magnets they used to own. Moving fast, they added a bottle of bleach, a roll of masking tape, some string, the lost magnets found in an odds-and-ends drawer, and long-handled pincers. Not wanting to be left behind, Tiger jumped in the back seat of the truck as soon as Tony opened the door.

As they were driving west toward Deming, they could see a wide dark band ahead of them, across the horizon like a tornado sky. Still ten miles away, the wind was picking up furiously, sandblasting the front of the truck and slowing it down. The closer they got to town, the worse it became. It almost felt as if they were going backward. They traveled to the other side of the town without seeing a single car in the streets.

We're the only fools out today.

When they pulled up to the Seeing-eye Cave, they saw that the front door was open, banging on its hinges, back and forth. Tiger whimpered as they held her back. "Wait girl! Stay! Stay by the truck!"

Tony removed the pistol from its holster, pulled back the slide to load a bullet into the chamber, and moved toward the door. The sky was dark as night and the wind was still trying to push them backwards. They asked Tiger again to wait outside, and then entered the main room.

The scene was that of a cheap thriller movie. Rosetta, in an electric red velvet dress, was sitting on her high stool, her feet firmly perched on the top rung, her hands frozen up in the air, both index fingers pointing down at a deadly Mojave viper coiled in strike position just below her legs. She was muttering something that sounded like Swahili mixed with French. A dead tortoise-shell cat lay on its side by a reed basket in the middle of the room. A few small saint figurines and unlit candles were scattered on the floor amongst hundreds of loose multicolored beads, all of it partly covered by fine swirling sand.

Unable to shoot at the snake without risking hitting Rosetta, Antonio grabbed the dead cat. The small rattlesnake turned around, faced them, and immediately got hit in the head by the cat. While the viper had its fangs in the poor beast, Tony quickly lifted it with the long stick, about one third down from the head. The snake went limp, let go of its already-dead victim, was shoved into the bucket, the lid quickly slammed shut over it.

Slowly Rosetta lowered her arms but seemed to have trouble talking. Without moving her head, she slurred, "La Vibora caught me by surprise and planted two long fangs into my skull. Can you put on thick gloves and spin my stool around to face that mirror behind me?"

The Tonys could not see anything coming out of her head, besides her wild hair. While looking at the mirror, she directed them to a point four inches above the left side of her head and had them place a magnet at that spot. Suddenly, the magnet stuck to some invisible piece of metal, hanging in mid-air.

"You found it. Now, grab what is just below that magnet with both hands and pull upward, pull hard."

It felt as if they were holding a long, thick, curved nail. She screamed in pain, as they pulled what seemed to be a giant transparent needle out of her head.

Once out, the weight vanished, the magnet fell to the ground, their hands now empty. She told them that one fang was out. They repeated the process on the other side, still unable to see anything but the floating magnet, still feeling that strong resistance as if pulling something out of sticky mud.

The rattler chose this time to shake its tail inside the plastic bucket. They took the bucket outside and put a large rock over the lid. Rosetta had them place the magnets and the gloves into the reed basket and put these by the sealed bucket next to the bleach. Then, being quiet for a while, she ran her fingers through her hair, scratching her scalp hard in the two places where the fangs had seemed to be. Her eyes were tightly closed. Finally, after a few deep breaths, she opened her eyes. The pain seemed to have vanished from her face. At the foot of her stool, Tiger was holding the poor cat between her front paws, licking it clean.

"She's going to get sick!" Antonia exclaimed.

With a tremolo in her voice, Rosetta said, "All the venom went inside Layla. She should not have any on her hair."

~ ~ ~

The wind had died down and the skies were clearing up, except for a few drops of rain coming down from a long cloud. Typical New Mexico weather, capable of completely switching around in five minutes. Only here could the sun be shinning on one side, a double rainbow flying high above, rain coming down on the other side. They were able to close the front door and have it stay shut.

While Rosetta straightened the crystals and figurines on her tables, Tony picked up all the spilled bits and pieces off the floor. Wiping away the sand and handing Rosetta the little saints one at a time, she put them in their proper places, as obviously there were specific locations for each. All the beads went into glass jars for a later restringing.

When done straightening up, she poured the Tonys and herself a couple of glasses of fine, aged tequila. She thanked them profusely, begging forgiveness for calling them to danger, but her local friend was out of town. They were the only ones nearby who could hear her and help her. Then she proceeded to tell them how she happened to have a deadly snake inside her house.

~~~

A few days before, Roberto, a local man, had gone with his wife to identify their teenage daughter at the morgue. He wanted Rosetta to find out who had strangled and cut up his child, as the police had not discovered anything yet. She knew of an evil sorcerer, La Vibora, who was reputed to possess young girls and then harvest their eyes and kidneys. She thought that miserable man lived just outside of Deming, not too far from Roberto's. She sent the bereaved man home after placing many protective spells on him, as well as in and around her home. She then called her guardian spirit.

"My protector is Laytwazoss. She was a Congolese woman, who looked after many babies and women, many centuries ago. She was attacked by a cannibal devil who killed her, cut her up, and ate most of her body. But a leopard grabbed part of her spine and disappeared. Later, three vertebrae were seen attacking any man who hurt an innocent person, rendering him completely mad, or making him disappear forever."

One of Rosetta's distant ancestors had shown her daughter how to call for this tremendous guardian spirit, then that women to her daughter, on and on, until her own mother taught her about the magic protector, when the need arose.

"The very first day I called Laytwazoss for my practice, a spotted house cat, a tortoise-shell, had shown up. When that cat got old, a new one appeared on the day of her death. The one laying on the floor between Tiger's legs was my fourth. She was an old cat who gave up her life to protect me. She attacked the snake when it crawled out of the basket, but the snake was faster and got her in the throat."

Rosetta's eyes were shedding tears as she resumed. "Looking into my mirror, I called again and again for the evil creature that killed and stole the life of Roberto's young girl. At first I could not see anything, my vision was blurred. Suddenly, I had a feeling of cold, slithering worms crawling up my back. Then I knew for sure that it was La Vibora. I called him a coward, a monster, one who killed helpless children, one who could not even face me. At that moment, the door flew open, and I saw a giant snake in the mirror. It was right behind me, like those giant boas in the Amazon River, but that snake looked mean, as if he was going to eat me whole. Before I could turn around, he had planted two long fangs into my head, paralyzing me down to my neck. I was able to spin my seat around, cursing him and his, but he was gone, and all that was left was this basket on the floor. Layla, my cat, went to it, and out came that small snake. After he killed her, he came toward me and for what seemed an eternity, I was able to hold him at bay with spells until you arrived. You know the rest."

~~~

They helped her bury the cat in the back of the house before going home. They told her about their friend Eric, who milked snakes to make anti-venom, and would be glad to have a Mojave in his collection. Rosetta declined and said that this particular snake had been a tool of black magic and had to be destroyed. She would take care of it.

Will have to go look for a new cat at the shelter.

Still spooked, Sis. Maybe we should let her find her own cat.

Right. Can't pick her pet. Just freaked out by the fact that there are still such evildoers out there today.

This black magic shit is sinister. Did an actual anaconda attack her?

Come on, Tone, there are no anaconda in New Mexico. That's just her vision, her interpretation of what happened. She believes in these surreal beings, and therefore they can damage her. Maybe they are real, wouldn't know. But the Mojave rattler was definitely real.

If I had not felt them, I would never have believed these magnets held these giant fangs!

They sparred all the way home.

As soon as they were back at the house, Tiger jumped out of the car and disappeared. *Guess she's freaked out, too.*

Darkness had fallen before they could fully digest what had happened that day. An hour later, they heard Tiger asking to be let into the backyard. In a muffled voice, she was singing her happy song, as when they came home and she had been waiting for them. They opened the wooden gate and let her in. She had a dark rag in her mouth. No, it was not a rag. It was a small, tortoise-shell kitten, all wet, that she gently but proudly carried by the scruff of the neck and dropped in the middle of the living room floor.

~~~

A bath was the Tonys' special time, when nothing else came between them. Naked, by themselves, they felt no inhibition, no need to hide from society's discrimination, they felt free at last. Tiger came in the bathroom, with one paw she tested the bath's temperature and decided it was too warm. Then she brought her kitten in and laid down on the bath mat, protecting her new pet between her front paws. They had recently deduced that she loved water, never missed a chance to swim, but preferred it cold.

While taking a long hot soak that night to wash off the stress of the day, they sang a duet made up on the spur of the moment. A song about loss and friendship, evil and decency. Antonia's mezzo-soprano alternating with his lyric tenor, they sang at a high volume. Raising her head high, Tiger sang too, for a couple of minutes, in harmony with them. Eventually exhausted, they laughed and laughed, their tensions released. After they got out and the water had cooled down, the dog jumped in leaving the cat on the mat. Then, shaking off the water all over the bathroom floor, she brought her wet kitten and laid with her tenderly on the rug beside their bed.

~~~

Chapter 10
Reaching Mora

Rosetta DID NOT WORK EVERY DAY, BUT THE twins felt certain that she would not be too far from her home after all the commotion of the previous day. They called her and she said that of course they could come anytime.

"And bring that dog of yours, if she wants to come."

"We will, and she has a present for you that she picked out on her own. See you soon."

What if she's already found another cat?

Simple: if she already has a kitten, then Tiger will get to keep this one.

Sure, Sis. But unconnected events may happen at the same time for us to understand what we're doing here in the first place.

No, Tone. Those events are connected, even if we don't know how. We really are on the same page. You see chance occurrence, where I see links.

Tiger remembered Layla, then found a cat that looked like her. Coincidence!

No! Tiger went specifically to find this kitten, she must have seen it somewhere before. And she is taking it to Rosetta. At least three links: dog, cat, Rosetta.

Chances are Rosetta already found another cat.

Once in the car, Tiger insisted on holding the kitten between her paws, giving her maternal licks all the way to the Cave. They weren't sure if she would relinquish the cat or if she'd want to keep it.

When the truck pulled in at Rosetta's place, she came out to greet them with a pronounced limp. Not quite as glamorous as the day before, she was dressed entirely in black.

She is mourning for Layla

Yes, and for being unable to fight off the evil Deming warlock on her own.

Her eyes lit up when she saw Tiger and what she was carrying in her mouth. The dog placed the wet kitten into her extended hands.

"*Mon 'ti Tigre,* you brought me back my Layla! Thank you girl."

No comments, Bro?

"Welcome home, Layla," Rosetta said, setting the little feline down on the floor of the living room. The kitten slowly went around the room, checking everything in her path, while Tiger followed her every move intently.

"See, she's settling in already," she told them.

Rosetta mentioned that she had killed the snake. It was not its fault, but it could have become the instrument for another misdeed, if she had let it live.

"I used up all your bleach. He didn't last very long with those fumes. And Laytwazoss has been with me all night. I feel a lot stronger today."

Leading them to the armchair, she continued, "By the way, last night, La Vibora's barn burned up. An electrical fire, according to the local news. His immediate neighbor, one of my clients, said that it may have started with an electrocuted squirrel chewing on rubber-coated wires. A rodent setting the snake on fire: now, that's justice! Truth be known, I don't care for these bushy-tailed rats, although that one died a hero. The neighbor is saying that the owner had left for Mexico, just before it started. You know he'll blame me for the fire when he gets back, but I was right here all night."

"Can you verify that, Rosetta, if the authorities come asking?"

She waved a hand dismissively. "What will they think I did? Trained a squirrel to chew plastic and turned it loose in his barn? There are limits to my powers, you know." Her eyes twinkled, as she picked up the kitten and held her tight against her chest.

"So now, let's get down to business." Rosetta lit a couple of candles, took her place in a big, easy chair across from the soft, enveloping armchair they sat in, while she sprayed her blend of sweet, woodsy essential oils around them and herself. "A blend of cardamom, ginger and fennel, with a hint of cedar in a base of sweet almond oil, all to help center the awareness," she had once told Antonio, when he asked what she had used to scent the room. The kitten left her lap and went to sit on an almost-empty shelf which held only a plush, blue pillow. Tiger laid down below her.

"That's where my Laylas have always napped," Rosetta answered their inquiring eyes in a soft voice. Then gently swirling a many-faceted crystal in front of them, she continued, "Now focus on this crystal pendant and relax every muscle in your body, while I count to ten."

"Call her name, so she can hear you."
"Mora, are you here today?"

As if she had been waiting for them, she whispered in her little-girl voice. "Hi Tiger. Hi Tonia. We must be very quiet or they won't let us talk anymore. I'm sorry I wasn't very nice to you yesterday. Don't be mad at me. You're the only one I can really talk to. You want to know where I am, right? I don't know, but I saw some wolves yesterday through one of the dining room windows. They were skinny and all gray. Last night they howled during the night. That was really scary. Papa Patron, the boss man said if I run away again — I did run away but they caught me pretty fast — if I try to run away again, he will let the wolves catch me and eat me. The other girls are scared, too. I gotta go. They're coming." And she was gone.

Antonio proudly mentioned that he had visualized a green pearl the whole time his sister talked with Mora. He had been present inside Antonia while the girl talked, and he had heard the whole conversation, although it sounded faint, as if it came from a deep well. "It worked. I was there with my sister. I could have talked to the girl." He also said that he was not going to interfere as he was afraid that the young girl would not understand his intrusion.

You're not leaving me behind anymore, Sis.

Never intended to. You were just scared to follow me.

Rosetta replied, "Good! I could also hear the two-way conversation. The connection is getting stronger with your help, Antonio. And you do help, but you're not the only one who's helping with this communication. I hate to rain on your parade, but Tiger is the link between you and Mora. You must bring Tiger every time you try to contact her. I only help with the transport. So let's do this more often and see what we can gather from these exchanges."

"Thank you, Rosetta. We'll be here tomorrow. All three of us!" They exchanged hugs while Tiger walked back from underneath Layla's hiding spot.

Tiger sat very still on the ride home. Was she dreaming about the kitten, or thinking about Mora, or maybe listening to their incessant inner chatter?

It sounded like Mexican wolves.

Yeah, all thin and gray. That could put her in Arizona or in Mexico.

Or near the border. They've been seen as far up as Silver City

That doesn't help.

Could she have seen coyotes?

Nah, she's local. She knows the difference.

Most likely she's near the border, one side or the other. Where the wolves are less likely to get shot.

She got away once. She's brave.

And not alone.

Why are they holding the girls?

Trafficking?

Am thinking that, too.

Any new market for virgins?

Or more Internet child porn?

Is that why they plucked her eyebrows and dyed her hair?

How can we find her?

Mornings seem to be the best time to reach her with Rosetta's help. Let's try it everyday

Let's, as in we?

That's right. Try and leave me behind again!

~ ~ ~

"Hey, Tony!" Sheriff Graves answered when Antonio called him. "I heard about you guys finding Jim's father. I'm glad you found him so fast, even if you never asked for my help. The Mexican cops are looking into it, but I doubt if anything will come of it. Whoever did this is long gone and far away. You know how these border crimes go. Anyway, how are you guys doing?"

Louis Graves, a tall big-boned blond with baby-blue eyes, had run the Doña Anna County Police Department for the last six years. His wife, a newspaper editor, left him the year after he got elected. He then took over the full care of his two kids, who were nineteen and sixteen. Despite the unwelcome media coverage the divorce brought him, he remained well liked and respected.

Lou was already known for not shying away from busting men in power, such as the assistant to the mayor driving drunk again, on a suspended license, no less, this last time plowing into a store's display window. He also recently uncovered one of his own deputies asking for special favors from the young women he arrested for speeding. That one was kicked off the force and later sent to jail, after two more young females came forward and testified against him. Lou was tough and didn't make exceptions, but the people from Las Cruces also knew that he would give the little guys a break, as long as it was only a misdemeanor, or that he would go out of his way to help a needy family find a new apartment. All this had helped get him elected for another four years.

The twins considered themselves his friends, and the feeling was mutual. They admired his courage in upholding the law, and supported his understanding that not everyone was a criminal, especially those who were not given a choice. They had helped him find one of his kids when he first became sheriff, and that had definitely reinforced their friendship.

Five years before, after an intense twenty-four hours, the twins had searched for and found his daughter, Nicole, who had disappeared for a couple of days while attending UNM in Albuquerque. The perfect student, well-behaved, never missing classes and working part-time for her tuition, she had been raped by a fraternity boy, who was often in some sort of trouble or scandal. He had been arrested and dismissed from the school. The frat house was closed for a couple of years afterwards.

Nicole had switched majors and schools, continuing

her studies at the University of Arizona in Tucson, and eventually getting her law degree. She returned to Las Cruces to work part-time with a firm that specialized in immigration and naturalization. When the Tonys needed help, especially with written or internet research, she was always glad to pitch in. Her former tragedy was never spoken of, but she and her father had not forgotten the help the twins had provided her, during that dreadful time.

The Tonys were always glad to hear from Lou. "We're doing fine on this side of town, Lou. Keeping busy with a couple of puzzling cases right now. What are you up to?"

"There have been a series of robberies on your side of town, on your street and all the way to the intersection. Keep your doors locked. You have an alarm system, don't you?"

"Yeah, we do, but half the time, we don't turn it on. We'll be more diligent. Thanks for the heads-up. Are you getting close to catching them?"

The sheriff quickly responded. "We got a lead on this nasty bunch of punks. They'll make a mistake sooner or later. But the reason I called is this: I've got a big problem with my ex-wife's father. He's probably embezzled half of his company's assets so far. Tania is trying to get me to drop it. Let the lawyers take care of it, she says. Of course, it's her father she's protecting! She said that if I meddled into it, she'll write about my sexual inclinations in her newspaper. So I though we could trade a little."

The Tonys knew the big guy was gay. He had never

hid it from them, showing up at their place once, right after his divorce, with an obvious queen who could not keep his hands off him. This was how much he trusted them both. But at work and in public, he had to maintain a conventional profile, as the town was not enlightened enough to accept homosexual sheriffs. Three years back, he had asked Antonia to help and they went out on a date after a negative rumor had started. They were seen dining, dancing, and going to movies for a couple of weekends in a row. Enough to squelch the gossip.

"How urgent is this? I guess you can't use Nicole on this one. We're pretty busy right now with two separate cases, but one of us could do some research if you need it right away," Antonio replied.

"No, I can't use my daughter to research her grandfather. Actually, if you can wait a little, that would be best. Then Tania will get off my back. So, anything you guys need?"

"As a matter of fact, we were going to call you for a few favors."

"A few, hey! OK. What do you need?"

"The Western Hills High School secretary seems to have had quite a shady past. Her name is Hope Esperanza Castillo. She was in juvie until she turned eighteen, but we're unable to find out what she did to get there. Then she hung out in south-east Texas, in Brownsville, by the border, and failed a piss test with UPS."

Lou interrupted. "Whoa! And she got hired at Western Hills, watching over kids! Somebody did not do their homework."

"Exactly. Nothing like knowing the school super with the same last name and then marrying him!"

"OK. You got my interest! What else?"

"You heard about this woman who got dropped off at the El Paso hospital, raped and beat-up, a couple of weeks ago?"

"Yeah, El Paso's finest called me on it. I sent an officer over to her motel room in town, but she would not even open the door, said she didn't want to press charges at the moment."

"Right. She asked us for help. She's suffered total amnesia since the beating. The shrink didn't get too far on her case. He just said her memory would come back eventually. So we're trying to speed up that process. We may have her fingerprints on a piece of paper. Would you mind checking them? If her prints are not on record, we'll have to run a DNA sample, but that probably won't tell us much unless she had it done before. Also, I don't know if El Paso city would release the hospital parking-lot tapes, but we'd love to get a look at those."

"OK. Let me look into this, too. I'll get back to you as soon as I find something. Say "Hi" to Antonia. Tell her we need to go dancing sometime soon."

"Are you in trouble again?" Antonio laughed.

"Nah! Just a little preemptive action. Besides your sister's a great dancer."

See! He likes me too.

"How about dinner tomorrow night, right here? Are you free tomorrow? Antonia should be home. I'll ask her."

"Now you're talking!"

"Bring Nicole. Tell her we've got some research work for her, if she has time."

~~~

Chapter 11
Finding Father

THE TONYS WENT TO THEIR ROOM TO GET dressed for the day.

We're going to see Rosetta this morning, what should we dress up as?

How about unisex? We can always change later if needed.

Right, then we're ready to run should another snake show up!

Not funny, Tone!

Donning a pair of blue jeans and a loose T-shirt, they were surprised by a knock on the bedroom door.

Mom? At this time of the day?

It's not Tiger! Who else has a key and knocks once inside the house!

When they were twelve years old, Sirena, hearing them moaning loudly, had barged into their room thinking them hurt. Instead, she found that they had discovered the joy of masturbation. She retreated rapidly and since then always knocked on their bedroom door, asking for an invitation before coming in.

While the family was having breakfast in the kitchen, Sirena explained that she had only worked a couple of hours this morning, as there was just one customer at the B&B. She had been troubled by an awful dream the night before and could not stay focused.

"Tell us your dream, Mom."

"When it started, I was on a sailboat near some tropical islands. Blue sky, turquoise sea, the water shimmering above coral reefs, the sun hot on my back. I looked around to see who else was in the boat, but could not tell who the other people were. Then someone came toward me. He was very dark, as if in deep shadows, and he was brandishing a large, white cross. The other two men had disappeared below deck. The dark man took out a big knife and sharpened the tip of the cross. The cross started bleeding as he was coming toward me. He raised the cross above his head as if to stab me, but at that time the boat was transformed into the *Titanic*. Everything turned black and white. No colors left but the bright-red blood on the tip of the cross. The ship was now deserted and sinking. There was no one else but him and me. The sky and the sea had gone dark too, by then, and large waves lapped the ship. We started to sink, the dark man fell backward into the roiling sea, and I woke up right then."

Antonia replied, "That's an easy one to read, Mom! We had a long day yesterday. So last night, we slept deeply but in our last dream, we saw Tonino falling off his boat and disappearing into the sea. We think he's gone, Mom."

As Sirena started to sob quietly, Antonio took over and said, "We never knew him as a parent, Mom. He did not raise us, you did. So don't feel bad if it does not seem to affect us. To both of us, he was a stranger who never treated you right."

"I am so sorry to saddle you with this terrible dream, right after your birthday. Will you still be coming by on Sunday for cake and ice cream?"

Now do you believe in coincidences?

No, Tone! Only in direct causation!

"OK, you two. You know I like you to share your inner dialogues when I'm with you. What's going on?"

"Mom, this is no coincidence. Let's say, yesterday Tonino drank more than his usual because we turned thirty on that day. In his stupor, he remembered ordering us to be killed, a cardinal sin in his religious belief. To this day he must have thought he had committed the crime and he could no longer live with it."

Sirena stopped sobbing and looked at them with understanding.

"So Mom, will you be fixing us sweet-potato pie topped with your homemade raspberry ice cream this week-end?"

"Only if you can forgive him for his sins."

"You know," Antonio said, "we forgave him when we found him at his fishing shack. He was only human. We have always thought of him as a confused priest, driven by his unfortunate family history."

Antonia added. "And Mom, thank you for teaching us about all the major religions on this planet. We both hope he will be reborn a person with less suffering."

~~~

After graduating with honors in Criminal Justice, the Tonys thought their first assignment as detectives should be to find out what had happened to the father they had never met. To satisfy their curiosity, Sirena had recounted the story of how she met their father on the *Princesa Isabella*, a large cruise ship going from Miami to Venezuela, by way of the Virgin Islands. Sirena, a native Floridian, was one of the many cooks on the big liner. She loved her job, the traveling on the beautiful clear waters, the opulence of the ship, which even had a swimming pool, a ballroom, and a theater. She was supposed to stay away from the wealthy patrons, but a couple of them had approached her, and they had become friends. Notably an older lady who stayed at sea all the time, claiming that it was cheaper and much more fun for her riding the waves over and over, having a chef and a maid as part of the deal, rather than staying in her boring apartment in a fancy part of Houston.

One day, while having her special-diet breakfast, prepared and served by Sirena, she asked her if she knew of a chaplain on board. Sirena inquired about it and found Tonino Urbani, a Venezuelan of Italian origin. The man was tall, very attractive, and emanated an air of regal knowledge. After guiding him to the older woman, he turned his attention to Sirena and started courting her. They would be seen in the evening, after their shifts had ended, walking the decks, talking about food, about religion, and what the future could hold for everyone on this earth.

They both worked on the *Isabella* for another year and a half before he proposed marriage to her. Neither had family left in North America, so on the following trip, barely outside of Miami, they were married on the liner by the new chaplain. The captain and the head chef were their witnesses. It was the most romantic cruise the two of them ever attended.

After coming back from their honeymoon, they stayed in Miami for a few years. Tonino obtained his American citizenship. He took seasonal jobs working for fishing charters and would sport a deep tan when exposed to the sun. Sirena waitressed in the nearby restaurants. Sooner than later, Tonino would get angry with the fleet owner for not listening to him, or with the customers for drinking heavily while at sea. Then someone inevitably complained to Tonino's boss about his occasional preaching, in his strong South American accent. He would get fired, but being good at piloting the boats and excellent at finding the best fishing spots, he remained in big demand at other marinas.

Finally, after losing yet another job for lecturing his customers, the couple decided it was time to conceive children. They moved to Albuquerque, New Mexico, where a childhood friend of Tonino, also a Venezuelan expat, had extolled the merits of the fast-growing city, its mountains, mild weather, and its lack of discrimination toward people with semi-dark complexions. They lived in New Mexico, until Tonino disappeared on the day of the twins' birth.

~~~

The Tonys had been unable to find their father's childhood friend; there was no one by that name in Albuquerque or anywhere in New Mexico. Hoping Tonino had stayed in the U.S. and not gone back to Venezuela, they traveled to Miami first, but only found older reports of his fishing days. One charter owner remembered him because of the beautiful Sirena, who would wait for him by the docks. He recounted how Tonino got upset with people for looking at his skin and his origins, rather than his skills, but he also thought the constant references to God was what really bothered people around him. People came to have fun, not to be reminded of their weaknesses. He also told them he had heard a rumor that Tonino had his own shop, somewhere on the Gulf of Mexico.

The Tonys drove around the point of Florida, and started probing the various marinas on the gulf, from Key West to Pensacola. They heard another rumor of a South American preacher working a short while with an old sailor, before going west into Louisiana. After a few days, stopping at every marina west of Pensacola, they finally landed in New Iberia. There they met the Cypremort Point Charter Services owner, who shaking his large belly with laughter, told them about his so called competition, the small Pesci Rosso Enterprise, and advised them that it would be much safer going fishing in one of his boats.

Obtaining good verbal directions, they found the shop at the end of a marshy dirt road on the edge of Vermilion Bay. The building had been neglected, the paint eaten by too much salt, its lower edge mud colored. Hugging its wall, stinking trash cans overfilled with empty bottles of rum and dried-up fish guts were prowled by skinny cats and a mangy, yellow dog. The large red letters of the Pesci Rosso were edged with blue-green mold; newer, slipshod, dark-blue script underneath proclaimed *World-Class Salt Water Fishing*. A dilapidated trawler was bobbing gently, tied to a narrow pier. The peeling paint on the back of the boat spelled *La Sirena*.

A tall Choctaw Indian, with a weathered face and impressively large hands and forearms, greeted them at the open garage door.

"Welcome to our fisherman's paradise. First-quarter moon tonight. Quiet seas and redfish near the surface. Fishing will be best between six and eight."

"How many people do you take at once?"

"As many as six or as few as you want. The fish should really be biting tonight."

"Good! It will just be me. Will you be my captain this evening?"

"Oh no! I'm just the mate. Captain Urbani will pilot you to the best schools."

Captain Urbani came out of the shop when he heard his name. The pictures Sirena had on one of her shelves did not resemble anything this man had become. His nose was red, puffy, and streaked with blue veins, his black eyes were bloodshot and dull, his skin was sallow, and a long, deep scar crossed over one of his eyes, from his forehead to his cheek. His dark, curly hair was peppered with white. He held himself hunched over. As he got closer, Tony could smell the fruity rum permeating his whole body.

The tall mate saw Antonio recoil and step back a pace. He knew they had just lost another sale.

He's an alcoholic!

Yeah, Sis, we're not going sailing with him.

"So you're wanting to go out tonight?"

"Yes, sir. I'm interested. What's in season right now?"

"Well, son, we've been catching some four-foot bull reds in the bay every week lately. God willing, there will be many more. Do I know you? You've gone out with us before?"

"No sir, this is my first time here. Someone told me you were the best at finding the fish."

Straightening up, the captain said: "That's right, son! The Lord helps me find them every time! Chucky here, can help you if you want to make an appointment. I better get back to my nets right now. You have a good day, son, and may God bless you." Even through his drunken fog, the captain had also sensed that he had lost the sale.

Tone, don't freak out on me. He did not recognize us. That's just how he talks.

Just wish we had some better news to take back to Mom.

Chucky motioned them near the boat. "The fish are really jumping. You should go out with the Cypremort Point crew before you leave here."

"Thanks Chucky. I may try them. Does the captain have any family, he seems lonely."

136

The gaunt man looked pensive for a while.

"You know, you do look a little like him when he was younger, when I first came here."

"Is that right? How long have you known him?"

Nice redirecting, Tone!

"It's been more than fifteen years now."

Wait. Don't say anything.

After a minute he continued in a slow deep tone.

"I was guiding for fresh water fish in the bayou, took my little boy with me. He'd be about your age now. My son got away from me and a big gator got him. I went to drinking, big-time drinking! Then nobody wanted to hire me. I was bad juju. Then Captain Urbani came by. He said he needed someone to help him, but only if I quit the drinking and went to the Lord. He told me he almost had a son, but that the devil got to him first. He understood my loss, and only the Lord had saved him. I quit drinking and let Jesus in. Is that what you wanted to hear?"

"Thank you for sharing, Chucky. That must be tough, you not drinking, and him drinking himself to hell and back."

"He did not use to drink until the accident."

Wait, Tone! He's going to tell us more.

Don't like it. It feels like cheating on this poor man.

Tony waited.

Chucky took a few deep breaths and lowered his voice although there was no one else nearby. "I don't know why I'm telling you this. I guess I miss my kid."

After another pause, looking Antonio straight into his eyes, his voice still low and slow like a soft growl, he continued, "We had been working together for about three years, neither of us drinking, praying to the Lord every time before going out. One day we had a family come on board. A man, his wife, and their child. There was something wrong with the little girl's face, her hands were always waving, she swayed when she walked. I guess she was retarded. The captain did not want to have her on board. Too dangerous, he said. But the couple insisted, she loved the sea, it did her good to be sailing, she would wear her safety vest on the whole time. So finally we took them out. That day he forgot to pray. I prayed to the Lord myself, but it was not enough. The little girl was laughing, shaking her head and her hands, stomping her feet the whole time. You could tell she really loved being on the water. Soon after we got in the deep, a strong wind picked up. Part of the rigging tore loose, and a steel cable hit the captain in the face and then hit the lady's back. She fell overboard. I dove in, and we were able to get her back on board. We got back to shore and took her to the hospital. She was fine, just had a couple of bruises, but the captain was never the same after that. The next day when I arrived at the shop, you could tell he had not slept at all, but he had been drinking all night. He kept saying that the child had been staring at him, staring at his soul, and that the devil was tormenting him again. He don't pray no more before we go out, but I do. We're safe if you change your mind. God watches over us all."

"Thank you, Chucky. You're a good man. May God keep watching over you."

The Tonys left, having their cup full for a while and were mostly quiet during the return trip. They appreciated knowing what had happened to their father, but were saddened that he had never found peace after leaving their mother and had, instead chosen to reject his beliefs for the bottle.

~~~

After comforting their mother, who had to finish her work at the B & B, they headed out to see Rosetta. On the way, Tony called Henry Carrel, the son of the physician who had helped Sirena and the twins while growing up. Also a pediatrician, his dad had told him about the Siamese oddity he had helped deliver, strictly for his professional enlightenment. The Tonys had visited their childhood doctor many times at his house, even after growing up, and they had met and played with his two children. Henry had grasped right away who the special conjoined twins were, and had remained friends with them after his dad had passed.

Tony asked Henry if he still dabbled in facial recognition technology, and explained that they needed to improve the pictures of a disfigured woman. Henry replied that he had given all his programs to his sister Claire when she joined a criminal investigation team in Santa Fe. It took a lot of time and much study to keep on top of the new scientific development, time he no longer had since he had started his own practice. He could forward the data to her or give them her contact numbers.

"Why don't you give her our number, please. That way we can relay the info directly. Our client wants to remain anonymous."

"Certainly. You haven't seen her in a couple of years, but I know she will be thrilled to help you. Since we're talking about staying anonymous, I do have a confession to make. While Claire and I were both students at Arizona U — her first year and my last — we would compare notes and I mentioned you and your sister as the exceptional case that you are. I did not reveal any names, but she figured it out right away. She even said that it made sense, that she had always thought there were two of you in one shell. No one else knows about it from us, I swear, but I did let it slip then, only to her."

"We appreciate your discretion. We have no interest in being a circus act. We cherish our anonymity."

~ ~ ~

When they arrived at the Seeing Eye, they realized they were much later than they had hoped, but there was no choice in the matter. Sirena was and would always be their first priority. They wondered if they should try to call the fishing shack to inquire about their father.

Let's wait and see what Rosetta can pull out of us.

"Rosetta, would you have time for us to see what may have happened to our father?"

"Sure, I have and you know I will always have time for you, but I think you already know what happened to him."

"Then afterward, if you're not too busy, let's see if we can reach Mora." Soon they were breathing softly in the plushy armchair. The vision came in fast, as if waiting to be revealed right away.

The Pesci Rosso came into view. It looked deserted. Shouting was heard from the inside of the building. Tonino walked out, looking much older than when they had seen him seven years before. His eyes and his skin had turned a dull grayish yellow. He was holding a bottle of rum in each hand and screaming at the top of his lungs: "Come take me Satan! I am your biggest sinner today!" They watched him, barely able to climb into his boat, struggling to start the engine, and leave the marina. They watched him raising both fists to the sky, before falling backwards and sinking into the sea. They watched the boat moving away from him, in large expanding circles, with no one left on board.

Rosetta woke them out of their trance and let them cry silently for this man they did not and would never understand, for all the children who would never know their father, for all the people who perished from the power of their beliefs. When they finally opened their eyes, she easily pushed them back into their subconscious mind.

"Mora, where are you? Mora, I want to talk to you. Tiger is here. Can you feel her here? Mora, can you talk this morning? Mora, please answer."

The silence lingered on. There would be no contact that morning. Seeing the worry on their face, Rosetta suggested:

"How about coming in an hour earlier tomorrow? She's probably busy having breakfast or doing her morning ablutions. I'll be available as early as seven if you care to come in."

"What if she will no longer answer? What if it was a fluke, a serendipity of sorts?"

"It is not. She reached you first. You can reach each other."

Antonio took over. "Only twice. And she got upset the first time, when she thought we were taking her dog. Maybe she ran away and got out this time!"

Rosetta raised her tone of voice, as if scolding a child. "Three times actually! The first time you were only interested in the dog. You were trying to remember what she looked like, but only so you could buy her dog. She has a very strong tie to Tiger. And I think from what you told me, that her mother got her the dog on the condition that she not run away. Yet she did, and I believe that she wants to be with her dog and her mother, where it's safer than where she is now. Her guilt about leaving her dog is what drove her to reach out to you. Now, is there anything else I can help you with?"

"Actually, there is. We'd like to find out more about this amnesiac woman we are working with right now."

"Do you have any personal belongings from this woman?"

Antonio blurted: "Yeah! We took a hair sample from

her. It's in the glove box."

"You stay right there. I'll get it, so I won't have to hypnotize you again. Focus on what you already know of her, while I get it."

While Rosetta ambled to their truck, Tiger, taking advantage of the situation, delicately placed the kitten between her paws and licked her clean.

Holding the plastic bag with blond hair, the twins concentrated on JD. Antonia was drawing a blank. All she could see was the disfigured face, the bruises, the pain still apparent in her whole demeanor.

"Think of her name! What is her name?"

"JD. Jane Doe. JD. That's what she wants to be called, not Jane Levi. D. D. D. Her name starts with D. Dana, Diana, Doreen, Donna? I don't know. DeeDee, Darlene, Danish. That's not a name! I don't know. Pull me out. I'm exhausted."

"Before I do, would you like to try Mora again?"

She did. But there was only silence, no exchange available.

"I will now count from five backward. When I reach the number one, you will feel refreshed and energized. Five. You have learned the fate of your father, may he rest in peace. You have made an indent into the memories of the blond woman. You have realized that this time of the morning is not the right time to reach the young girl. Four. You are fully relaxed and ready to continue your day in a positive manner. Three..."

Rosetta invited them again to come the next day. She explained that today the moon's aspect was void-of-course, coming out of the feet, meaning lost grounding, a lack of roots. Tomorrow morning, the moon would be back in the head, more conducive to learning and understanding.

~~~

Chapter 12

The Road Runner Motel

On the way back home, Antonia stopped by the Road Runner Motel to try some names on JD. The awful hues that had covered the woman's face two days before were starting to marble, letting some of her naturally pale skin tone show through a little more. Her lips were not as swollen as when they'd first met. She had put on a little makeup to cover her injuries. The Tonys thought that was a good sign. The sun shone inside the room, alighting dancing dust motes. JD smiled when she saw Antonia.

We're the only ones she sees, besides Gopal. She's lonely, used to having people around her.

All at once, Antonia knew her name. "Hi Danielle, you're looking much better today."

"Hi, Tony, call me Danny. Everybody does. Wait! How do you know my name?"

"My brother and I have been seeing this woman with amazing clairvoyant abilities. She helped us deduce that your first name starts with a D. When I saw you just now, your name came to me. Kind of eerie, isn't it?"

Antonia was laughing, just as surprised as Danielle was.

"Eerie or not, this is fantastic! I am Danny! I can't tell you my last name though. Can you guess it?"

"I'm afraid not. I'm still shocked that I was able to guess your first name. So, how did you come to use the initials JD?"

"Oh. That was my idea of a joke. Jane Levi did not fit me, so Jane Doe seemed more suitable. Maybe my last name starts with a J. I can tell you for sure it's not Danny Levi."

Coincidence, Sis?

Shush!

"We could not find anyone by the name of James Levi that fit your alleged brother's profile, except maybe, an eighty-year-old man and his teenaged grandson out in New York City," Tony teased. "Seriously, we'll be giving the envelopes with your fingerprints and hopefully Levi's, too, to a friend of ours in the police force. He can find out if they are registered anywhere. Are you remembering anything else?"

This doesn't seem to bother her. If she has anything to hide, she's forgotten it.

Right, Sis! Most people are usually nervous about having their fingerprints checked, guilty or not.

Thereby confirming this is a genuine case of amnesia.

"Not a thing. But I'll work on my last name, see if anything else comes up."

Antonia removed a sheaf of paper from a folder under her arm, and handed them to Danny. "Here is our service contract. Would you read it and sign it, please?"

"Of course," she replied and proceeded to read the document. She took the pen Tony handed her and signed by jotting down a straight up and down line, wrapping it with a large circle, and finishing with a long tail to the right. More like a large D but with no details. Tony asked her to sign again at the bottom of the paper. Another large D.

So much for finding out her last name.

Danny understood what Antonia was trying to accomplish and smiled peevishly. "That did not help, did it?"

"No, it did not. It was worth a try. Do you have enough to purchase an electronic tablet? It could help you search for various places, people, events — anything that might seem familiar to you."

"Could you pick one out for me, please. The motel has free internet service. Here is some extra money."

Antonia agreed to get one and told her she'd be back the next day. "Will you need anything else?"

"Not a thing. The tablet will be a nice addition. This little motel is fantastic. It's not fancy, but Gopal is a treasure. He's always asking me if I'm needing other foods or drinks, more clothes, books to read. He is even the one who chose and picked up my makeup. Sort of the opposite of a woman purchasing condoms! He also fixed me some delicious East Indian dishes. And I think he keeps an eye on my door. He calls the room and lets me know who's coming to the door, when he's not busy."

Certainly in better spirits since you found her name!

"I'm so glad he is helping you. I'll see you tomorrow then. Maybe your last name will appear magically in my dreams! I may have to take a course in divination, add that to my job qualifications!" Tony jokingly finished while closing the door.

~~~

In the evening, Claire called. "I'm so glad you called. I was wondering what you two were up to."

"We're working on a couple of cases, one of which is about a woman who lost her identity. She woke up in an El Paso hospital, unable to remember her name, her past, or what happened to her before she woke up."

"Sounds intriguing! For you, I guess, not for her."

"It's been challenging. We're trying to use different methods. The ones the docs used in the hospital did not help at all. But it may have been too soon after her trauma. Your brother said he gave you all his facial recognition programs?"

"Yes, it's part of what I work with here in Santa Fe. What do you need?"

"The woman's face was badly beaten. It's still swollen. We were wondering if you could tweak some of her pictures. Reduce the swelling here and there, straighten her nose, that sort of things?"

"Most likely! Email me these pics. I'll see what I can do."

"That would be so helpful. Who do you work for?"

"I have to be in Las Cruces for business in a couple of days. I would love to come by and visit. I should have some results by then. I'm really looking forward to working with you. I've missed you two."

Can't wait to see her!

Me too!

She didn't say who she was working for.

Noticed that, too.

She was even mysterious when she was a kid.

~~~

Early the next morning before going to Rosetta's, the twins stopped at the B&B to see their mother. After sharing a hug, Sirena brewed them a cup of strong, black, unsweetened coffee, the way they liked it. They wanted her to call New Iberia, to see if there was any news about the whereabouts of Tonino, but she wasn't ready to accept his demise. Although he had abandoned her when she was in the throws of labor, she was still fond of him; still loved him for who he was when they had first met.

They held her tight, letting her tears soothe her pain. She calmed down and told them that after finishing work, she would make calls to find out what may have happened to her husband. The twins could be wrong. He could be alright. The Tonys left and rushed to the Cave, aiming to get there by seven-thirty. Not much traffic on the wide road, mostly semis and a few cars also in a hurry, the sun climbing high behind them, promising another warm day.

~~~

Appearing full of energy, in a long mumu with soft-pink

roses on a bright-blue background, Rosetta served them a cup of hot, overly sweetened black coffee as soon as they came through the door.

"Let's hope we're not too late," she said, as if to reassure them that they were welcome this early in the day, yet her tone sounded worried. It was obvious that she, too, felt involved in the fate of the young girl and was eager to get started.

Mora answered immediately when Antonia called her. She was whispering, yet it sounded much clearer than before. "Hi, Tonia! Hi, Tiger. Now's a good time to talk! No one is awake yet. I don't trust Imelda, she's one of the girls here. I don't want her to hear me. I think she would tell on me if she heard me."

"Can you see any mountains outside the windows?" Antonia whispered back.

"How's Tiger doing?"

"She is doing well. Did you know she gets carsick?"

"Yes, I do. She was a puppy when we went to buy her. On the way home, she threw up all over the blanket in her basket. Mom was mad. I had to clean everything up. It was gross."

"Rosetta, that's the lady that's helping me talk to you, Rosetta gave me a carsickness magic potion for Tiger. It works great! Tell me, can you see any mountains where you are?"

"Tell Rosa hi, and thank you for Tiger's magic potion. Yeah, there are some mountains, far away."

"Can you describe these mountains? How many peaks

do you see?"

"There are two pointy peaks, with like, some low rocks on one side."

"Good observation. Which side of the mountains are the low rocks on?"

"I think they're on the left-hand side."

"Any mountains on the other side?"

"I think it's pretty flat on the other side."

"In the morning, where is the sun shining on these mountains: left, right, behind them, or in front?"

"I don't know. I'll look again if that's important."

"It is, please. Are there any rivers or lakes?"

"I can't tell, but there is a fountain in the courtyard. The water is kind of slimy and green."

"OK! That will help me find you! Are there a lot of green trees and plants inside and outside the courtyard?"

"There are some weeds in the courtyard. Everything is pretty dried up. When I escaped before, when I was outside, I could see some dark-green plants on the other side of the gate."

"Do you remember where you went when they kidnapped you?"

"They did not kidnap me, 'cause I wanted to go with them."

"OK. But they won't let you out or go back to your mom, will they?"

"No, but I'm going to be an actress, and they don't want anybody to know in advance, 'cause they might steal the writing — I mean, the script about the film."

"So, when they took you into the van, do you remember

which way you were going?"

"No, I didn't look. I just felt bad about not taking Tiger back home. But she found her way back, all by herself."

"How long did it take you to get there?"

"I don't know. They stopped a couple of times. They got me some lunch, a burger. So maybe two or three hours, I don't know. It seemed like a long time."

"You told me they hurt you. What did they do?"

"Oh right! The first day, these two guys grabbed me out of the car, and they were kind of mean, like really rough. They hurt my wrist when they shoved me into their house."

"Are there any other people with you, I mean, in the dorm?"

"Yes. There are seven other girls that are the same age as me, but they are kind of weird. And then there is Imelda, she's older."

"What makes the young girls weird? Can you tell me a little about them?"

"I don't know. They're just different. Like three of them, they only talk Spanish, not like Mexican Spanish, and really fast. I can talk a little with them but they have a weird accent. They said that's because they are from a town called Goatmala. They're like Indians or something. They said that Papa Patron told them he would help them find their family."

"They are from Guatemala?"

"Yes. That's the name. They just hang out by themselves. They talk to me, but not to the others, 'cause the others don't speak Spanish."

"Tell me about the others, please."

"There is big Imelda. She bosses everybody around. She's not nice. She always says that she's gonna report us to Papa Patron. Then there is — Uh-oh! She's waking up. Hi Imelda! No, I'm just talking to my invisible bear again."

The connection was severed. That had been the longest they had spent together. The Tonys thought they had made huge progress, although there were lots of mountains on this side of the Mexican border. Lots of barren flats, too. Then to find out about the other children was another big step. They had something tangible to work with now, and they were thrilled to have connected with Mora again. They would have to get in touch with Maria and let her know.

How do we do that, Sis?

Maybe we could fib a little. Tell her we're making contact through notes?

How do we get the notes?

They're slipped under the door at night.

She may find that hard to believe.

You're the rationalizing one! Am a woman, just going with the flow!

You're crazy. Good thing I like you, Sis.

~~~

They spent most of the afternoon doing research on the internet. They waded through Guatemalan newspapers, old news clips of Central American abductions. So many children of Guatemala had disappeared and were never found again. Some were captured, many had lost one or more family members, most were surely killed. It sadly seemed commonplace.

Then they looked at landmarks on their topographical map program and on satellite maps on the internet. It was difficult to tell how many peaks were on all the chunks of hills scattered in the flat lands between the Arizona and the Texas border. It would take them days to inspect every hillock in that large area north of the border. They were not even certain which side Mora was on. She could be in Mexico or in Arizona. They would need to enlist a small army of people.

They called the two Search and Rescue teams of Las Cruces, asking for help. Both team leaders had the same answer: too big an area. About three hours away from Las Cruces was not a starting point. They would help as soon as they could get more information to narrow the search area. They lacked the manpower to search in what amounted to hundreds of thousands of acres of land, even combining all the teams in the southern half of the state. One of the team members offered some help with mapping. He had an excellent topographic program that he would be glad to share. They accepted his help, exchanged contact emails and thanked him.

After taking Tiger for a walk, they researched the media for any information about Danny in the previous weeks. All they had to go on was the police blotter in one El Paso newspaper, and on the internet's local news, a couple of lines mentioning an amnesiac woman being dropped off at the hospital. "Anyone with information regarding this woman, please call the El Paso police." No picture, no contact number. It certainly would not make it easy for anyone to report anything important. Sitting on the border, El Paso was probably overwhelmed with missing persons and unknown identity cases.

According to Gopal, the motel owner, the cap James Levi had worn, bore the name of the University of Texas-El Paso basketball team, the Miners. Danny showing up at a hospital in El Paso might indicate that she lived there.

They looked through yearbook photos of the last few years of UTEP graduates and of the last ten years of all the city's high schools, until they could no longer see any difference between the many Caucasian, blond, blue-eyed female students. They also looked at faculty members in that university and found a few women named Danielle or Daniella, half of them Hispanic, none remotely looking like Danny. But then they had a find! While coursing through names, they discovered a professor of genetics named Gunter Levi-Schmidt.

Don't start, Tone. Not a coincidence, that's him!

No glasses, no mustache, but dark, curly hair. Can't tell how tall he is.

Yeah, that's him.

We need to go visit this Mr. Schmidt!

Soon!

They enlarged and printed his picture.

~~~

Chapter 13
Asking for Help

NO TIME TO COOK THAT EVENING, AS NICOLE
and Lou would arrive shortly. Tony ordered Thai food
from a nearby restaurant. They delivered the food half an
hour later to a waiting Antonia. Best to be female when
Nicole was there, as her ordeal a few years back had made
it more comfortable for the young woman to relate to Antonia than to her brother, but also because of Lou, who
sometimes stared at Antonio with longing eyes.

They arrived precisely on time. Nicole's hair was cut
very short, a boyish style that suited her well. She wore a
striped gray modern pantsuit over high heels. She hugged
Antonia and mentioned that she was just coming from
work, did not have time to change.
"I brought a change of clothes, if you don't mind."
Antonia pointed to the bathroom with a smile as she
went to hug Lou.

Moving to the dining room, Antonia set the table for
three, with the steaming, spicy food in the center. The
reddish-brown oak table was a piece of art. It had been
given to the Tonys a couple of years back by a client who

was a talented woodworker, so thankful that he wanted to give them more than what they had charged him. Long and heavy, it was made the old-fashioned way of three-inch thick, ten-inch wide boards fitted by tongue and groove, wooden joints, bone glue, and not a single piece of metal. Two long benches matched the table. At an estate sale, they had found a couple of captain's chairs, removed the shiny finish, then stained and oiled them to the same rich brown. The dining table was their favorite place to entertain.

Of course, Lou was disappointed that Tony was away, meeting a contact. He wanted to let him know about Josephine, his sister-in-law, who worked as a nurse in El Paso.

"Tell him that she wasn't working at that hospital but one of her friends, another nurse, works at the University Medical Center and had a lot of info about a woman who was dropped off at the emergency door ten days ago. He was working the night she was admitted."

Antonia's eyebrows raised up as she told Lou. "I'll let him know. I'm sure he'd love to talk to that nurse. Do you think he'd talk to us? Of course, we would not want any confidential medical info, but just anything that might help."

Lou continued. "I did get some information from him, although he did not seem to know too much. Maybe I could interview him again. I mean, I'm sure you two could, but if you need my help..." he stammered, his cheeks glowing red.

Swiftly changing the subject, as Nicole was coming

back in the room, Antonia asked, "So, tell me! When are we going dancing?"

"Antonio told you. I forget that you two don't keep any secrets from each other. Look, I don't need an alibi, just want to have fun. I haven't had much fun lately. Thanks for having us tonight, by the way!"

"Of course, you two are always welcome here. You know you are family."

Pointing to the other end of the table from where they sat, Tony said, "Getting back to business, that plastic bag contains two envelopes, one of which has a crisp, hundred-dollar bill in it. The money and the envelopes should have fingerprints on them. One set will be from the woman; we know she handled the papers. Her first name is probably Danielle or Danny. Hopefully the man who gave her the money will have touched that new bill or the envelopes before putting on his gloves. His name could be Gunter Levi-Schmidt. And by the way, we'll take that hundred bucks back when you're done." Antonia winked at Nicole, who, smiling back at her, almost choked on her glass of white wine.

Lou said, "OK! You've got my curiosity aroused. Can you tell me a little more?"

"As long as you let us handle this."

"Don't worry. We are stretched so thin right now, no one is even allowed to take their overdue vacation time."

She went on telling him a few details about Danny's predicaments.

Nicole looked very uncomfortable. She blurted out,

"This is outrageous! Isn't there anyone who can help her? I mean, besides you. How can someone get beat-up like that today and no one notices? Is she an American?"

Lou got up, went to his daughter and massaged her shoulders to comfort her.

"We think so. She certainly is fluent in English, although she has a slight Texan twang. She seems well educated."

Nicole calmed down at her father's touch and said, "The firm is fairly quiet right now. Just a few cases going. So if you need my help with research, please just ask. You know I'll always help you. I owe you and your brother big time."

Smiling again, Antonia gave her a long stare. "Nicole, you owe us nothing. Really. We are your friends. But I'll take you up on that. We have some dry and boring documents for you to read. We both find that doing dishes or cleaning house is much more enticing than this tedious stuff," she joked.

Nicole grinned in return and agreed to help on Saturday. "I can work from eight till noon."

"Great! Here is a key to the front door. We'll leave you a note as to what and where you should research. Thanks."

~~~

Filled with the tasty red curry, a sweet coconut desert that Antonio had whipped up in the half hour just before they showed up, and plenty of wine — red Zinfandel for Tony, Pinot Grigio for Lou and Nicole — they moved to the living room and visited a while longer. Soon enough they went back to talking shop.

"Can the El Paso EMT tell us anything about her condition before she was admitted?" Antonia asked.

"I might as well let you know. You guys share everything anyhow," he told them.

You don't know half of it, big boy!

Down, Tone! Let me finish this.

So you are interested! He could wear his uniform in bed?

No, thanks! That's one we won't share, you've seen his shiny puppy eyes when he looks at you, but not when he looks at me. We do not want to lose him as a friend.

Just joking, Sis. Like him too much to risk loosing him.

Lou continued, sipping on his wine, unaware of what was transpiring right in front of him. "So, they've got cameras in the parking lot and by the emergency door. In a dark part of the parking lot, two guys were seen dragging the victim out of their car. It looked like a ten-year-old Chevy sedan according to Joe. Joe is my sister-in-law's nurse friend. They must have dropped her just to the side of that door, where the camera did not reach. He just happened to look, because it was middle of the night, and he saw movement on the parking lot camera. By the time Joe figured it out and ran outside, they were long gone. I talked to the El Paso city police. They got the ER door tape but could not make out anything on it. No good shots of the perps. So one possibility is that they knew about the cameras and could be working there."

"I don't know, Lou. Maybe they were just expecting cameras by that door anyway, but did not see the ones for the parking lot, as those were probably up high."

"Yeah, could be. Joe said she was all torn up but most of the blood had been washed off her face, except for some of her own blood, her nose was still bleeding."

"Danny told me that the receiving nurse had said that her body had been scrubbed clean before she was admitted. They probably did not want anybody finding other people's blood or semen."

Antonia stopped herself and looked over at Nicole, who had blanched at the description. She reached out to the young woman and put her hand over hers.

Nicole seemed calm and confident, but she was firmly squeezing Tony's hand as she spoke. "It's all right. I can deal with it. It's been more than five years now. You know back then, I was terrified. I did not even fight back. How do you do it, looking for trouble all the time?"

"We both took martial arts. It helps us be more observant of people's intentions by reading their body. After a few years, it became instinctive. Then you know when to be ready for action in a split second." Antonia replied as she took another sip of wine.

While Nicole was using the bathroom, Antonia wanted to know if Lou had found out anything about the secretary from Mora's high school.

"As a matter of fact, I did. Not an easy task. A lot of her info is not easily accessible. I had to dig deep." He was quiet, looked up, and rolled his eyes.

"Thanks, Lou. You know we really appreciate all you

do for us." She continued smiling, "Should I ply you with another glass of wine for more details?"

"You also owe me a meal and a dance for this," he finally said, his face opening up into a wide smile.

"I sure do!"

"Actually, I was really curious about her. An old guard at the juvie prison where she was incarcerated, said she was extremely violent with the other inmates. The rumor there was that she had bragged about strangling her adoptive mother. Later, as an adult in Brownsville, she tested positive for cocaine twice while trying to get various desk jobs. She may have been a high-class call-girl, according to the Brownsville City Chief. Now that's hearsay, you understand."

He paused and winked at her. "He also told me that the DA there at the time made her clean up and then hooked her up with one of his relatives, Ernest Castillo, from our own Las Cruces. Castillo was a sixty-five-year-old, straight arrow, freshly retired school super, and old money, if you get my drift. He just passed away last year."

Nicole came back in the room as Antonia exclaimed, "She certainly was a busy young woman. I'm amazed at what the right connections can do for some people." She smiled at Lou and added, "I'm grateful for having you as my connection to the police world. Thank you again for your help."

Before they left, Antonia asked Lou if he had contacts with any Customs and Border Protection officers.

"Nah! You know feds and counties don't get along. You

should ask Sunny Villegas. He has a brother or a cousin with CBP. You think Danny came across the border?

"No, this is for another case. How far north have you seen the Mexican wolves? The four legged ones, I mean."

"Just right by the border. Did a rancher lose some calves to them? That's why you want CBP!" He added, fishing as to why she was asking for *La Migra*.

She did not confirm or deny his train of thought. He knew too much about Danny as it was, and she was not about to let him take Mora's case from them. Of course, she would call on him if and when she needed help busting the probable ring of child traffickers. The Tonys did to want anything to happen to Mora. This Papa Patron seemed to be a ruthless criminal. If they shared Mora's fate with the police before they located her whereabouts, they were afraid the job would be botched or put on the back burner without sufficient information.

~~~

Chapter 14
The Dire Wolf

THE NEXT DAY WHILE STILL DARK, THE TONYS started for Deming. It was going to be a scorcher in this western side of the Southwest. At least the wind had stopped, no sandblasting on the horizon. With a lot to accomplish in one day, they needed to see Rosetta as early as possible. She was waiting for them, with the kitten sitting on her lap. Tiger plopped herself down nearby and stared eagerly at Layla the whole time, as if asking her to play.

Seven in the morning seemed a good time to reach Mora. She answered right away. "Hi, Tiger. Hi, Tonia. Hi, Rosa."

Antonia had just looked at the photo the girl's mother had given her. Her brother was contemplating a green pearl. Both actions seemed to make the communication clearer.

"How are you this morning?"

"I'm fine, but I got scared yesterday."

"Why is that? What happened?"

In a tiny little-girl voice, she whispered rapidly, "Yesterday afternoon, Papa Patron — that's the big boss man here — Papa Patron came in with his wolf on a leash.

He calls him Lobo — that's wolf in Mexican, you know. Lobo looks mean when he looks at you. He has a collar with a black box with a green light in it. He said that Lobo can tell if I am lying, the light will go red on the box, and that if I lie to him, Papa Patron will cut me up and feed me to Lobo."

"Does he think you are lying because you talk to us?"

"No, they think I talk to my invisible teddy bear. Imelda tells him everything. She's the biggest girl here. She's old, like eighteen, and she's fat. Papa Patron always tells her not to eat so much. That makes her scared that she won't be an actress. That's why she doesn't like me!"

"Are you really going to be an actress?"

"I am. One of the teachers here said I was going to be famous, 'cause I show a lot of potential."

"Can you tell me what the buildings look like, the room where you practice for the movies?"

"Here it's not like that Hollywood place at all," Mora interjected, then was silent.

"Do you go to any other places?"

"We don't go anywhere! I never go anywhere, only Imelda leaves and comes back. Two girls left and never came back! Imelda says that Lobo ate them because they had lied! I think she is lying, because Lobo could not eat two at the same time, and I would have heard them screaming."

She voiced a loud sigh before continuing, "This house is really long. We stay mostly in the bedroom and during the day we go to the school. The bedroom is long and has many beds on one side, like a ... like a dormitory and there are some tables and some chairs on the other side. The windows have bars on the outside like a jail, and they are high up. I have to climb on a table to look out of them. Then there are the bathrooms and the dining room. Then the school is right next to it. It's kind of the same as the bedroom, but it has all kinds of neat things in it, like tape players and TVs and guitars and drums and weird games and lots of fancy clothes, and a makeup table. I'm learning to play the uke something, it's a tiny guitar."

"The ukulele?"

"Yes, that's it."

"Any computers?"

"No. They don't want us to contact our parents. They said it's gonna distract us too much during the movies."

"Did you go into any other buildings?"

"A couple of times. Another part of the school is around the corner. There is a dancing room in it. The windows are high in there, too."

Lowering her voice even more, she continued: "That's how I got out once. The lady that brings our food had forgotten to lock the door to that room, one time. I think I got her in trouble when I ran away, 'cause the next day, after they caught me, she had a lot of puffy spots on her face and a big nose. She looked like she had cried a lot."

"Where did you go and what did you see when you ran away?"

"I could not get out of the big square yard in the middle. There is some tall, rolled-up, sharp wire all around on top of the buildings. I tried to get inside the next house, but it was locked. Then I hid inside the fountain, with all the

166

nasty water and the old weeds. Bye."

She was gone.

As soon as Rosetta woke them up from their trance, she gushed with admiration for their abilities. "You are amazing! Your connection with this young girl is better than many I have seen. I think Mora must be very gifted psychically. And not to forget our dear Tiger! I don't think we could have reached her without this wonderful dog. And Antonio, you were afraid that your sister was not including you in her channeling connections, but it takes two to tango. Your dancing is matched by your sister, step by step, now that you've accepted your remarkable talent. I think the two of you together really augment the connection."

Antonio was beaming, speechless, in agreement with her, shaking his head up and down.

Antonia spoke in turn. "I still don't believe I can — that we can hear her so clearly. But you are right! As soon as my brother merged with me during that third time with Mora, we were able to truly communicate with her."

When visualizing the green pearl, Sis! Rosetta was the one that helped me.

They thanked the obliging woman again before getting on their way. They had much to do, with the two cases in hand. Tiger looked sad to leave Layla behind as she got in the car.

That was a good session. They had learned a lot. A pet wolf. At least three adults there. Other children. Only

girls? A large, square courtyard with tall fencing and razor
wire. Four long buildings in a square? They already knew
about the central fountain. Two high peaks on one side.
Desert landscape all around. High windows with bars.
A music school? A movie set? It was sounding more and
more like child porn. Time to see if Border Patrol knew of
such a place.

~~~

They called Claire back to see what time she would
be in town. She told them she would only be able to stay
for a few hours tomorrow, but she had results and could
meet them for lunch. Tony invited her to come over for
an Italian meal. She said she would like that, especially if
they were as good a cook as their mom. She remembered
the great dishes Sirena would bring to her father's when
the twins were teenagers and either of the two came to see
him every month.

Then Antonio called Sunny to find out about his
Customs and Border Protection cousin.

"Hey, you guys! A Duke City cop told me that the old
narc cop did not make it long, after we put him in the
ambulance. That's too bad. He seemed like a nice old guy.
Que tal with you guys?"

"We're doing OK, Sunny. Lots of work right now. Jack
lived long enough to hear his friend, but his body gave up
about the time Jim was speaking to him in the ambulance.
I don't know, maybe he heard some of it. I hope so. It was
good for Jim to be able to talk to his dad, to let it out. I

guess they weren't seeing much of each other anymore, since Jack had started losing it."

After a deep breath, Antonio continued, "On another matter, we need to find out a couple of things from one of your cousins. Lou told us that you have one that works for Border Patrol."

"I've got two *primos* working for La Migra. One, Ruben, is a big wig in El Paso. I'll have him give you a call, but he is mostly a higher-up desk jockey and won't be able to help you until Monday. And he is pretty strict, pretty serious about giving classified info. And he doesn't like his agency to be called by its old name. When you deal with him, it's Customs and Border Protection. My other primo is Carlos. Now he's Mister Mellow. He works out of Kingsburg. I think between you and me, all the *motta* that comes over the border, he confiscates and smokes it! *¡Pandejo!* I'll get him in touch with you too. You know, they don't like us to give out their numbers. So, what's going on?"

"A couple of things, Sunny. We're looking for someone who saw gray wolves near the border, but we don't know on which side."

"Hey, there are Mexican wolves on both sides. They don't care about green cards! I've even seen them south of Cruces, near Mesilla Park. Where did he see them?"

"Not sure. Somewhere south of I-10."

"Oh yeah, they're there. I hope they don't cross with those released northern timber wolves in the Gila forest. That will be trouble. They'll breed like mice and have no fear of people. Man, that spells trouble."

Antonio did not want to express his opinion either

way. This was a sore subject between ranchers and hunters on one side and urban environmentalists on the other. Besides, it was not relevant to the problem at hand.

The Tonys thanked Sunny and left to go see Danny that afternoon. On the way, they picked up fresh, homemade linguine from Sirena, who could never resist preparing Italian dishes anytime they asked. Then they stopped at a little Mediterranean deli that had fancy antipasto for the next day's lunch. Antonio would prepare his, he claimed, most-famous marinara with capers and olives.

~~~

Antonia brought pictures of many high-school and university buildings in El Paso to show Danny. She also dropped off the electronic tablet, so the woman could start doing her own research. Danny did not recognize any of the schools, except for UTEP, with its unusual Buddhist-monastery architectural style. She was certain that she had been there before. Then Antonia showed her the picture of Gunter Levi-Schmidt. Danny stared at it.

"He's a professor of genetics, teaching at UTEP. Does he look familiar to you?"

Danny had tears in her eyes as she said, "Yeah! I know him. I think he's the guy that brought me here, without the mustache."

"Could you have known him before?"

"I think so. I'm not sure. Let me digest this. Can I keep his picture?"

Antonia handed her the picture, letting her stare at it for a few minutes.

Next, Danny set up the tablet with the motel's network, and immediately registered a new email address for herself. It started with "jdlostinxxx". She was swiftly typing the letters. She obviously had used a computer before, but then there were few city people her age who had not. She said that she would be able to research more about the university on the internet.

Tony added, "In addition to UTEP, please, look at various other places in El Paso and also in Las Cruces, parks, restaurants, stores, whatever grabs your interest. See if anything rings a bell."

Danny typed up "Used Book Stores" in El Paso.

"I don't know why I typed that. Maybe my fingers have a memory of their own?"

"Perfect! Don't think too hard. Let your fingers remember. Let your subconscious work for you. Call me if anything comes up. I'll come by tomorrow afternoon. I may have more pictures for you to look at."

As they left, Antonio could not stop his suspicious mind from searching for answers. *Something big is missing in this picture.*

Yes, her memories!

What if she has committed a crime and was punished for it?

She's obviously well educated.

The learned ones also break the law.

Let me finish, Tone. She's educated, but in which field?

Accounting, as in money laundering, embezzlement, extortion?

No, don't see her in that role.

Wonder if Lou has come up with anything with her fingerprints?

Yeah, but then why haven't the El Paso police come up with anything?

Too busy, would be my guess, Sis.

Not fascinating enough, is my guess, especially if they thought her a prostitute.

Is an ugly discrimination head rearing up?

We would not know anything about discrimination ourselves, now would we?

Let's hope for the best and see what she can bring up with her tablet.

~~~

That evening, Antonio went to Jack's wake. The job of being a detective also carried the burden of following up, at times long after the find, when everything seemed finished. Tony was the one who had found him. He felt obligated to attend. After having met José, Antonia had instantly liked him and his subtle way, but this wake was mostly for Jim's benefit. She was an empath and would be hard-pressed to stay unresponsive should anyone be extremely sad. Funerals and wakes were challenging for her, as she felt other people's pain and grief; she might even start crying, even if she barely knew the deceased.

When Jim opened the door, it was easy to tell that he

was mourning. His nose was red and swollen. Clearing his throat, he invited Antonio in, muttering softly, "Thanks for coming."

Tony shook his hand and quietly responded, "I'm so sorry for your loss."

See, Sis, he's human after all.

Never doubted it. Did we do everything we could for this man?

We did! We found his dad.

Then Antonio handed him a condolence card from Antonia, while mentioning that she was not able to come. Jim did not seem to hear his words. Barely looking at the envelope, he placed it among many others on a table in the hallway.

The large living room was bustling with thirty or more people, mostly older men. Some in police uniforms, some in suits with well-dressed older women on their arms, while a few of the younger men wore casual clothes. Tony wore his favorite gray, western, three-piece suit, with a turquoise-on-silver bolo tie over a soft, yellow shirt, his smoke-colored, shark-hide cowboy boots barely showing. Jim led him to a table laden with fruits, flowers, tequila, whisky, sodas, and cookies, before awkwardly moving toward an older couple that had just sat down on one of the leather couches. One of the women seemed extremely bereft.

She looks like Jack's wife, maybe one of her sisters?

Can we get away from her, Tone? She's affecting me too much.

After pouring himself a glass of sparkling water with a lime slice, Tony spotted José through the open French doors. He was surrounded by a few people, animatedly talking in the courtyard. Feeling isolated in the big room full of older cops he did not know, and at his sister's prompt, Antonio moved toward him.

"Hi José. I am sorry for everything taking so long before we found Jack."

"Hola, Tony. You were the one who found him so fast, once you got hired. Thank you. We both knew our job was dangerous when we took it. We just did not think that it would follow us after retirement."

José turned to his friends, and in rapid border Spanish, explained how Tony and his sister had helped find Jack. After a few more concerned comments from his entourage, José motioned for Antonio to follow him to the far side of the courtyard.

A few potted plants, mostly cacti, stood up in a corner. Without a word, José pulled out a tall, leafy ocotillo, still sporting bright-orange flowers at the top of its thorny, green branches. His eyes were moist as he explained, "I potted a single stem many years ago and two trunks came up the following year. I don't know if they have a common root or if they are separated below the soil line. Usually, at first only one branch comes out, then later they multiply like a shrub. Ocotillos don't like to be bothered, so I did not look at their roots. When I met Antonia, I knew that plant belonged to the two of you." He handed Tony the tall plant.

Antonio thanked him and jokingly said, "Tall, thorny

stems, covered in small leaves with beautiful, pointy, orange flowers. That's us all right." It was all he could do to not let tears of gratitude flow from his eyes.

Get back, Sis. You're gonna make me cry!

You need to get us out of here, can't hold back my tears much longer. José is the most affected here.

As Tony got ready to leave, the older man instructed him on how to take care of the ocotillo and helped him secure it in the bed of his pickup. Sunny showed up at this time, and, before going into the house told Tony that he had gotten in touch with his cousin in Kingsburg, who would call him Monday, mid-morning.

Before Antonio got into his truck, José held his arm, measuring his words before talking. "If you need help finding someone around here, I am very familiar with the whole southwestern part of this state. Besides a little gardening, I don't have much to do here anymore. I'm old and slow, but if you need a hand, I'd like to help, pro bono, of course." He smiled, and watched Antonio smile back at him.

"Thank you. Actually José, we could use your help right now. We're working on two difficult cases. Can you come to the office tomorrow, late afternoon? That is, if you're available on Sundays?"

The old man's eyes twinkled as he smiled. "No problem, all days are the same for me since retirement. But don't you take a break now and then?"

"We do when things are quiet, but all this past week,

it has not been quiet."

As Tony opened the door of his truck, he shook hands with José. But José pulled his arm down and reaching up, gave him a hug. "Thank you, Antonia. Thank you for being such a dedicated person," he whispered into Tony's ear.

He knows.

Add one more to the list.

Right, but one who won't give us away.

~~~

Chapter 15
Snooping on Friends.

It SEEMED THAT MORA WAS WAITING FOR THEM at seven o'clock the next morning. She answered right away. "Hi, Tiger. Hi, Tonia. Hi, Rosa. I looked at the mountains this morning and the sun was shining on them, and a little bit of the shadow of the mountains was on the left side. Does that help?"

"It certainly does. Are the two peaks the same size or is one smaller than the other?"

As the girl took a minute to answer, they were afraid they had lost her already.

"I think they are about the same size. But there are more mountains far away, behind them."

"Thanks, that helps me a lot. I met your friend Omar. He's very nice, very polite. He said that he misses you."

"If you see him, tell him I miss him, too. I hope nobody is bullying him. Imelda said that the faster I learn all this stuff, the faster I'll be out of here. So I'm trying really hard to learn everything."

"Omar seemed to be doing well. I also met Mrs Castillo, from the school. She said she talks to you a lot?"

"Yeah! More like she asks me questions all the time. She's so nosy. She always wants to know what I'm doing.

What Mom is doing? I don't like her, but Mom said I should be polite and answer her."

As abruptly as she had answered earlier, Mora was gone in a flash.

Rosetta asked, "Anything else you'd like to work on today? My first client won't be in until ten."

"Do you have any idea how we could find the blond girl's last name?"

After handing them a sweet cup of coffee and chicory, the seer took out an old deck of hand-painted cards and started shuffling them. She spread them out and asked them to pick one. Flipped over, the card showed a wide face, with exaggerated features, especially big eyes, over a tiny body, arms and legs spread out.

"You have already run across her name. I see new, fresh eyes. Let someone else look for her in what you've already looked at."

"We've just asked a friend to look at the files we've researched already." Antonia murmured, not wanting to break the older woman's concentration.

She moved three cards to the bottom of the pack and flipped the next one over, placing it to the right of the first one. It showed a dog digging in the dirt, while an old, bearded man, leaning on a shovel, looked on.

"You will be very close to what you seek, when you help someone find a lost treasure."

Antonio blurted out, "You can tell all that by looking at this strange Tarot deck?"

"These cards were drawn by my great-grandmother.

She painted them on goat hides. This was the only belonging she brought with her when she came across the ocean. They are a wonderful tool to help my guides tell me what I must see."

The next card pictured a narrow footbridge, hanging high between two cliffs; on it, walking in single file, were people carrying heavy burdens on their head, while a river snaked below. Rosetta frowned. She turned a final card and placed it next to the hanging bridge. On this one, a tall dark shadow was emerging from behind a large rock, a crescent moon partly hidden by clouds high above it. "The woman and the girl are linked by the greed of two nefarious men, a father and his son. The closer you get to these two men, the more cautious you must be. There is a dark, veiled purpose above all of it. That is all I see." She put away her cards in a colorful woven bag.

"Thank you Rosetta. You are amazing."

"You're welcome. Coffee early tomorrow morning again?" She asked as her old, black, dial phone started ringing. She ignored the call. "They'll call later, if it's important."

Tony told her. "Yes, coffee please. But hold the sugar for our cup, if you don't mind."

They hugged her and called for Tiger, who came bounding out of the back room, followed by the well-licked kitten. The Tonys inhaled the last swallow of their cup of sweet coffee before going home.

~~~

At eight o'clock sharp that same morning, Nicole had let herself in and moved to the large desk. A handwritten note and a picture were waiting for her next to the large computer screen.

Dear Nicole,

Please research all available media for a woman whose first name is Danielle or Danny, missing for the last two to four weeks. Look first in New Mexico and in western Texas. If you cannot find anything, then try the nearby southern states.

Then if you have time, also look at the UTEP rosters of the students and faculty and staff for the last twelve years. We have looked but may have missed her. Thanks.

Here is a picture of Danny today. Her face is very swollen, but it may help if you find someone resembling her.

Lunch is in the fridge. Needs warming up.

Nuestra casa es su casa.

The Tonys

Nicole went right to work. It was just like doing research for the law firm, searching through file after file. It made her feel useful and essential. She craved being wanted and knew she had a knack for fact-finding. But she could not discover anything the twins had not already found. She kept looking throughout both states of Texas and New Mexico, and, after a couple of hours, she had compiled a list of twenty-seven names and last known addresses of missing persons whose first or last name started with the letter D. All of these had disappeared in the last two months. She printed the list and left it near the computer.

Before eating her lunch, Nicole thought about the twins. Why had she never seen them together? Why had she always felt that they were hiding a big secret? Her curiosity was insatiable. At the law office, they called her the Bulldog. They told her it was really one of her assets, that she would grab hold of any subject the firm gave her and keep on searching until she found the answer.

After looking outside the front windows, she went from the office to the residential part of the house. After all, she reasoned to herself, they had said *mi casa, su casa*. With strong feelings of guilt and unease, she started down the hallway, opened the first door, found a bedroom. A king-sized bed, a big night table with a Tiffany lamp on it, a brown, leather chest, an opulent, red, brown and tan Middle Eastern rug, Turkish maybe. In a corner near the window, looking into the backyard, stood a comfortable tan leather armchair, a small table next to it. Of the two doors on the far wall, one led to a bathroom, the other to a large closet. Inside the walk-in closet, cowboy boots and loafers were tidily arranged on the floor, facing the back wall. Above these, men's clothing hung neatly next to shelves filled with perfectly folded clothes.

She went into the bathroom, which connected to

another bedroom. Both men's and women's toiletries were under and above the double sinks. Two toothbrushes, one tube of toothpaste. So, they liked the same toothpaste. A citrus-scented liquid soap, an aftershave, an eau de Cologne, a hair brush, and a comb. She felt that she was just an unscrupulous snoop, but now her interest had gotten the best of her and she had to keep looking into the next room.

The same arrangement in reverse. A cream-and-dark blue oriental rug by a large bed, a birchwood chest at its foot, a stained glass Tiffany lamp on the night table, a small tan leather couch by the side of the window, soft-green and blue watercolors on the wall. Unlike the other tidy room, the quilt on this bed was wrinkled, the pillows tossed, as if someone had left in a hurry. This closet contained women's clothing and footwear, but not as neatly arranged as in the other closet.

Nicole quickly returned to the office, feeling ashamed for having violated their private space. She ate the lunch they had prepared her, wrote them a note saying that she'd be back in the morning for another four hours of research, and left, anxious to be away from their home after her unforgivable foray into her friends' affairs.

~~~

On their way home, the Tonys stopped at their favorite fish market. The owner of the small store, hidden in the middle of a strip mall, always told them exactly how fresh his seafood was. In this landlocked state, it was a feat to keep recently caught fish arriving twice a week, but his reputation for telling the truth about his fare kept him in business. Anything a couple of days old went into his Mediterranean fish stew, which was also a successful treat for his regular customers.

Arriving home, their arms still full of groceries, the Tonys read the list Nicole had left for them. She had worked hard and fast. They would have to follow up on it and see if anyone fit Danny's profile.

After our lunch with Claire.

Yes, everything can wait until after Claire!

Can't wait to see her.

Antonio wanted to marinate the halibut in lemon juice, warm up the marinara, start the water boiling for the pasta, and prepare the fresh-greens salad. They made their way to the kitchen at the end of the hallway, putting away the food.

Then they stopped first in their private bathroom.

Can smell Nicole in here.

Yeah, Sis, she may have used our bathroom instead of the one next to the office.

No, Tone, she was also in both bedrooms.

What? You think she was snooping?

Know so, but what did she find?

Nothing! I hope two perfectly arranged bedrooms, showing two people of different sex.

Hope so too. Would be nice to stay on the same level with Lou, who may not take it well. Let's see how she acts next time she sees us.

Once they had returned to the kitchen, their attention was focused on preparing the meal for Claire, someone they really wanted to impress, someone they liked dearly, and also one of their few true friends who knew of their dual nature.

~~~

Sirena had told her children years before that they could act as if they were home when they visited Doctor Carrel. They did not have to pretend to be either male or female. When still very young, they played with Claire, who was six months younger. They rarely saw Henry, four years older than his sister, and already serious and mature. Losing his mother at a young age had taken its toll and robbed him of parts of his childhood. As a toddler, his sister had adapted better to their loss.

While the Tonys were going through puberty, they went to the doctor's office every four weeks. Sometimes they would see Claire when she came to her father's practice after school. She would do her homework in the waiting room. The doctor performed many tests to find out why they had such debilitating monthly cramps. Eventually, he found out that, while their hormones were waging internal wars, Antonia's womb was atrophied and Antonio's sperm was not viable. They would not be able to reproduce. At the time, the twins' mature answer to that verdict had been that it would be easier that way, as the world was not ready for people like them. The cramps lessened each passing month and eventually ceased.

Sirena worked hard at keeping them healthy during their adolescence, eventually bringing them to the doctor only for yearly check-ups.

The last time they saw Claire and Henry in person was two years ago, when they had attended the good doctor's funeral. Both of his children looked so sad, though very professional, when they started what would become a long stream of eulogies for their father, as his many friends and clients also wanted to honor this exceptional man. The Tonys were so choked up about their loss, they could not speak, but Sirena did, without revealing any family secrets. She mentioned how lucky she was that Dr. Carrel had been available when she had first needed him. How he had always clearly explained her options on any medical matters regarding her family; how he let her make her own informed decisions. She emphasized that she was deeply thankful for his compassion and knowledge.

~~~

Chapter 16

Meeting Claire

THE SMELL OF THE MUSHROOM-AND-RED-WINE
marinara Antonio had prepared earlier permeated the
whole house. Claire showed up shortly after one that afternoon, a tall, ponytailed brunette, looking stunning in a
coffee-colored pantsuit partly hiding a shimmery, blue silk
shirt. Matching the color of her blouse, her light-blue eyes
lit up as she hugged Tony.

No perfume. She smells nice!

"Hum! Smells nice in here. It's seems like eons since
we played together," Claire said.

Am in love, Tone.

Me, too. Let's play together again.

"Hey, we missed you bossing us around when we were
kids."

They reminisced about the childhood games they
played. They talked about Henry, whose practice was
booming and who had started a family. They talked about
Sirena, sharing with Claire that she was still working, but
thinking about going back to school. She was only missing
a few credits toward a teaching degree, if twenty-year-old
academic credits were still honored.

"Lunch is ready. Are you hungry?"

"Starved!"

They moved toward the kitchen, and carried the dishes to the dining room

"You two haven't changed. You look great! I need to tell you, Henry spilled the beans about your dual nature, but I had already figured it out," Claire said.

"What gave us away?"

"For one, there is your long skull that neither Sirena nor you hid from our family when you visited us at home. Back then, only one of you visited us at a time. Your mother was so protective of you; I could not understand how she could leave one twin behind. And your eyes give you away. Hazel, but one greenish, the other bluer. I've often seen it in dogs, one blue, one brown, but it is so rare in humans. I had also noticed that you are ambidextrous, perfectly ambidextrous. With most people, one side usually will be weaker than the other, but both your hands are equally agile. Oh! And also, I remember you having these strange, fast conversations, as if questioning and answering yourself at the same time, like twins do. I once saw you fight over a board game, playing both sides by yourself, yet arguing back and forth over the better moves. Do you still talk to yourselves like that?"

Antonio grinned. "We always have, and still do, but inwardly now. More discreet that way."

Antonia quickly added, as if annoyed by the revelation, "Tell us what you've been up to in Santa Fe?"

"I'm working with an investigation team. We handle old and difficult, unsolved crimes. We have access to all kinds of new technologies, some not even on the market. And we keep coming up with new testing methods right in our labs. I just finished working on a thirty-year-old case. Most fingers, all the toes and part of the face were missing. No fingerprints or DNA on record. Pig teeth marks and blood on what was left of his extremities. Great lunch topic!"

They all laughed.

"No problem, it stimulates the appetite."

"You asked for it! For the last year, I have been doing some research on hereditary bone and tissue characteristics. That's how we solved our last case. They had kept some of his DNA. He was second-generation African American, which made it easier for us to figure out who he was. He was managing a pig farm that was suspected of being a money laundering-business for a large company. The unlucky bastard must have been ready to spill the beans. We think they tried to feed him to the pigs. No pork on the menu today, right?"

"No, we don't eat mammals, only fish and eggs."

After lunch, Claire showed them the pictures she had put together. She asked if she could go with them to see JD.

"Sure! She's expecting Antonia at three."

Claire explained how she had studied forensic anthropometry with a couple of blind scientists who deciphered genealogy by palpating skull shapes. They helped her develop new techniques with their tactile methods. The first time she met them, they asked her for permission to touch her head. It was an amazing learning experience.

They showed her how to proceed, what to look for. They also said that now they would be able to recognize her among millions of others.

"I'd love to palpate your skull, not that it will give me any insight about your genetic background, we already know what it is, but I'm so curious about how the two brains are melded."

"We'll need to leave soon to meet Danny, but we can be your guinea pigs!"

And more, anytime, be our guest.

They called ahead to see if Danny would be willing to have her skull checked.

"I'd love to meet your friend, I'm not going anywhere." She had replied.

~~~

The pictures Claire showed Danny looked like a variation on a theme; wider to narrower nose, lower and higher cheekbones, different lips, mostly thin upper and thick lower, and various tapering of the eye shapes. The woman kept staring at a single one within the dozen splayed out on the cover of the motel bed.

"This one looks familiar. Let me look at it in the mirror."

After a couple of minutes followed by a short, bark-like laugh, she said, "That used to be me! But I don't recognize myself in the mirror, and I still can't remember my name, or what I was doing before."

Antonia chimed in. "Your memories are starting to come back. You recognized your first name, your face, and the university you attended. Did you find anything about that used book store you were looking at yesterday?"

"Yes. Present to Past, that's the name. I called, but the owner does not ask the names of his clients. He told me to come by, see if he could recognize me. But I'm not ready to go out yet."

Her left eye was still bloodshot and puffy, showing some marbled, dark-brown color around it, and then there was the problem of the missing front teeth.

Sis, did you notice the perp was right handed, according to her bruises?

Like eighty-seven percent of the population!

"I'll take your picture to that book store, see if the owner's remembers anything."

With her eyes closed, Claire gently palpated Danny's head, avoiding the places where deep bruises still showed. She spoke in a soft, humming tone. "You definitely have Nordic roots, with a small amount of Asian characteristics."

"I'm impressed you can tell all this by just feeling my head."

"Not just your head, but I see the rest of your body, too. You are slim-boned, yet not too tall, with a narrow face, especially around the temples. Your face shows a slight flattening of the cheeks. Your forehead is also very flat, but your chin is sharp. Your hair is thin but straight, dark-blond, probably getting darker as you age. Your eyes are dark-blue yet slightly almond shaped, with very small eyelids. Your lips are thin. The picture you chose as your face also shows all these specific traits. Are you familiar with the Sami tribes of Finland, Norway, and Sweden?"

"It doesn't ring a bell. But I'm sure I was born in the States."

"You're sure? What makes you so sure?" Claire asked sharply with the tone of a practiced interrogator.

"I can't tell you. I just know." Danny replied with exasperation.

Antonia interjected, trying to be positive, "Good! More progress. I know you're frustrated by the slow speed of your recovery, but we're just trying to find out who you are. And you've just confirmed that you are an American. This will tremendously help our search."

~~~

Claire had to go back home that afternoon. She asked that they drive back soon to their house so she could pick up her car. She had an appointment to attend early the next morning in Santa Fe. On the way to the office, Antonia thanked her for all the work she had done, and for being so positive toward JD. How could they repay her?

"There is one thing. Let me palpate your skull! I'm fascinated. Please, just satisfy my curiosity. I won't publish anything about it."

Fifteen minutes later, they were in the living room. Tony was sitting on the edge of the sofa, with Claire standing up behind. She started slowly, very gently, with the back of their neck. She went up on each side of the ears, following plate lines, searching their scull for indents, contours, creases, running both hands on the long part of their skull. Still holding on to the top of their head with one hand, she came around to the front of the couch. With her eyes still closed, her hands tenderly followed the sides of their head. She caressed their forehead, their brows, their eye sockets.

Oh, Tone, I want her!

Me, too. I'll make my move when she's done.

While she worked she was humming to herself. She felt their cheekbones, pushed softly on their sinuses, moved down to their mouth, their chin, their jawline. Once in a while she would let out a *"Wow!"* or an *"Amazing!"* The Tonys were on fire. Opening her eyes and looking at them for a reaction, she went back to their skull. "I'm sure you know about the Mangbetu, the African tribe in old Congo, which practiced elongating the heads of female babies by binding their skull."

They warbled back, something they did when both were talking aloud at the same time. "When we were in high school, we would get called Mangbetu by some of the other kids. We told them it was a sign that we were intelligent and powerful, and that would squelch some of the taunts. Mostly we became pretty good at ignoring the negative remarks."

Claire finally ran both hands under their ears back to their cervical vertebras and stopped, waiting for them to open their eyes. With her hands still on the back of their neck, her mouth next to their right ear, she whispered,

"Can I kiss you now?"

In a quavering voice, almost an echo, they turned their head toward her and answered, "We wish you would."

The kiss lasted a few minutes, before Claire disentangled herself from their embrace. "I have to leave, I'm sorry to say."

"We wish you could stay, too."

They made a date for the following weekend. Claire had heard there was going to be a Bluesy-Jazz band coming to a venue near the university.

In unison, the Tonys warbled, "We have a guest room. You can stay here."

"Perfect! I'll bring my dancing shoes."

~~~

Chapter 17
Present to Past

MORA ANSWERED RIGHT AWAY AS SOON AS
Antonia called on her. "Hi, Tiger. Hi, Tonia and Rosa.
How's my beautiful Tiger doing today?"

The dog whined her happy song.

"She is doing fine. She can hear you, but I don't think
you can hear her, right?"

"No, I can't hear her, only you, I hear you inside my
head. Tell her I miss her, please."

"I did! You did! Tell me, what are you doing this
weekend?"

"Same thing as the other days. We've got classes
everyday. Some dancing classes, some music classes, some
beauty classes. And also some boring proper manners
classes. Really boring!"

"Tell me about your teachers. Who are they? Do you
know their names?"

Mora took a few seconds before answering. "There is
only one, if you don't count Josette. She's the cook. She
shows us how to put make-up on, and pluck our eyebrows,
and put on perfume on the best places on our bodies, and
things like that. The other is the art teacher, Miss Manners
— that's what she wants us to call her. I don't think that's

her real name. So Miss Manners, she teaches all the other classes. She says, she is an artist and that we won't be successful unless we do everything properly, that's why we have to take proper-manner classes. Only the dancing is kind of fun." Mora stopped talking.

Antonia waited. "Can you still hear me?"

"Yes! But something moved, so I got worried. I don't want Lobo to hear me."

Antonia waited another minute before quietly resuming. "Are you OK?"

"Yes, it was just one of the girls turning in her bed."

"So, there are Josette, Miss Manners, Papa Patron, and Imelda, and the seven girls, plus you. Who else is in the compound?"

"There is Raul. He helps Miss Manners teach us how to dance. We dance with him, he leads us like a man, you know, when we dance. But I don't like him. He's not very nice, and he smells really strong, and one time, I saw him outside with a big gun. He doesn't bring his gun in when we dance. Oh, and sometimes there are two other guys with guns in the courtyard. They come out and smoke cigarettes and talk with Papa Patron."

"Thanks. That helps a lot." But now Antonia knew that she was talking to herself. Mora was gone again.

Antonio spoke aloud. "Guns! That will make her rescue really difficult."

"Yes, and it shows that this Papa Patron is definitely running a very illegal operation." Antonia replied.

Seeing their distress at the new findings, Rosetta

drew her divination cards. The first one she pulled out of the deck depicted a giant grinning face on a small body. The teeth were pointy. Both hands and feet sported huge claws. Below his face, the body was covered in black fur. Two birds, one blue, one red, flew on each side of his head, while two black and white lizards slithered away from his big feet.

"Is that the devil?" Antonio could not help blurt out.

"No! This shows that a very powerful man is in control. He is a fierce enemy, feared by his underlings, but ambivalent about his conquests. He is strict and powerful but can also be generous at times."

The next card showed a dark woman in a plain, white shift, standing up to her knees in water, looking up at the sky. A few small fish seem to be nibbling at the tip of her fingers. Above the woman, hung a sad-eyed blue moon with icicles dangling from its sides, opposite a laughing sun whose mouth was spitting flames. "This one can also go either way. The girl understands the danger but has not made up her mind which way she should go. She can choose the hot, fast and exciting path or the cold and slow one. She is being pushed to make a decision, but looks to others to lead her. There is a sense of urgency to the whole venture, as the warmth is very tempting."

Rosetta held out her cards. "One more. Antonia, you pick one for her."

Tony closed her eyes and slowly her left hand approached the deck. Still without looking, her index finger touched one of the cards. Rosetta drew that one, stared at it, and finally placed it face up next to the other two cards. It looked like a very busy picture. A feast of colorful foods, fish, birds, small mammals, fruits, roots and flowers were piled up on a large white hide on one side of a stream, towering cliffs lined both sides. Guarding the feast, a big lion with a monstrous raised paw, clawed at the lower cliffs. In front of the food, many swords and spears crisscrossed. Again a small sun and a moon adorned each upper corner.

Rosetta explained "Her reward is in sight, but the way to it is dangerous all around. Again she has to make a choice between two opposites. If she decides to follow her mother, she must come in through the longer path; the river is the only safe solution. Her father's path is riddled with dangers but close by and very attractive." Rosetta stopped and seemed to be asleep on her high stool. The Tonys waited.

"Antonia, I think you must try to steer her to the light. She is looking at two sides: the loyal female or the dominant male. You need to reach into her unselfish side, letting her know of the attractive dangers ahead. She is first a rebellious one. It may not be easy to steer her as she gets deeper into all sorts of forms of entertainments."

Antonia nodded while contemplating her dilemma. "I'll think of a way to guide her."

Will help when can, Sis. We can plan how to reach her tomorrow.

Then Rosetta told them that she would not be available the next day. Her friend Woody was driving her tonight to Kingsburg where she would meet a young man the following morning for a consultation. She did not have a car, nor had she ever learned to drive. Every time she needed a ride, she would call on Woody who had been living in Deming for the last ten years.

A few months back, the Tonys had met Woody Slim Dubois. Rosetta had introduced him as, "My special friend, another Louisiana expat, and my favorite bongo drum player in all of New Orleans." Then she had introduced Antonio to Woody as, "My favorite and most unusual New Mexican friend."

Woody's bony hand was strong when he shook Antonio's. He was very tall and thin. His once fair-skinned face had been tanned and wrinkled by too many years in the sun. But when he smiled, his face radiated so much exuberance, that it was impossible not to smile back at him. The Tonys had immediately liked him and thought him a perfect match for Rosetta.

~~~

The twins had most of the afternoon to themselves, and Antonio wanted to check out Present to Past. He took a copy of Danny's picture and drove to the little used-book store on the eastern edge of El Paso.

A low-pitched buzzer rang when he opened the door. The whole place smelled vaguely of East Indian incense but mostly of old paper dust. Bookshelves were packed tight on both sides of narrow aisles. The front desk was covered with uneven stacks of paperbacks, the titles on their spines facing the customers. Half hidden behind these sat a bearded, older man.

"Hello, what can I help you find?"

"Hi! I was hoping you would remember my friend," Tony started as he pulled out the picture Danny had said was to her liking.

"Is she really your friend or are you a cop?"

"Yes to both," said Antonio, opting to stay close to the truth. "My friend is out of town. She called you yesterday. She thought you might remember her, as she has suffered a head injury and couldn't remember when or why she was in your store."

The old man put on a pair of old tortoise shell glasses and took the picture. He hissed a few noisy breaths through clenched teeth, then finally smiled and looked up. "I remember her. Such a nice young lady! All she bought were treatises on how to dissect animals, antiquated human-anatomy books, and embalming manuals. Actually I've saved a book for her I think she might be interested in. It's been a while since I've seen her. Let me see where I put it."

He trailed off, disappearing into the back of the shop. He soon returned with an old, leather-bound book. He blew off the accumulated dust from its spine and head before handing it to Tony.

"It's the second edition of *The History of Embalming and Preparations in Anatomy, Pathology and Natural History*. Its first edition was printed in 1838, in England. I've been holding it for her for about a year," he said proudly.

"How much do you want for it?"

"It's in good shape for its age. I don't remember what I paid for it. If you will give it to her, twenty dollars should do."

"So you have not seen her in a year? Nice of you to hold on to it this long," he replied, handing him a crisp bill.

"I do like to make my customers happy."

"What else do you remember about her?"

He looked suspiciously at him for a second, pulled down a few times on his long beard, then grinned and added, "I don't believe she'd do anything illegal. She is such a sweet girl. A little bit on the sexy side, if you know what I mean. She must be a medical student. Right?"

"You got it!" He thanked the old man and left with the book under his arm.

~~~

After the forty minutes drive back, Antonio went straight home, changed, and shortly after, Antonia drove to the Road Runner motel. She handed Danny the book without saying a word.

"Wow! I looked for this book for a while. It's the old bible for us medical examiners." Danny said, carefully turning the pages.

Bingo!

Antonia smiled. "You do realize what you just said.

You are a medical examiner."

Danny looked confused for a minute. "I don't know. It just came out! Isn't that weird to dissect dead people for a living?"

"There are no weird jobs. All jobs have a purpose. Where do you practice?"

"I don't know. I don't know. In a big city, I guess."

"Try to visualize what the building looks like, inside and outside."

She closed her eyes, while shaking her head and rubbing her hands. "I can't see anything. Why did I choose this job? Maybe I'm insane, and that's why I can't remember anything."

Trying to ease the accrued tension, Antonia said, "Sure! I can just see you. A dark lab, the light is flickering on an off. You're wearing a long blood-stained lab coat while hacking away at a blue corpse with an axe, licking your lips and cackling in a sinister way."

They both laughed.

She continued, "I'm sure you've helped relatives deal with the loss of loved ones." She let that sink in for a minute. "The old man at Present to Past said that you were on the sexy side. Does that mean anything to you?"

"Not really, but it might explain why I got raped."

"You were not raped because you are sexy. Someone committed a violent act against you for his own justification, not because of the way you look."

They both sat still for a while, digesting the new findings.

After a bit, Tony added, "Look at the book. See if it brings back anything else. Call me if it does. Meanwhile, save yourself some money and try to research who graduated with a bachelors degree in your field at UTEP: forensic science, criminology, pathology, or even just general medicine. See if you recognize anyone. You should be easy to find, now that we know your profession. There are not that many people in your field. I'll be back tomorrow night, if not before. My brother and I are going to follow your alleged brother's car, if he shows up during the night."

~ ~ ~

As they drove home, a myriad of questions were firing inside their head.

Never would have guessed her for a medical examiner!

More women go into forensics now, since it's such a rat race to become a doctor.

Claire, too!

Miss her already, Tone.

That was quite a kiss!

Don't be worried that she's just curious about us! Am sure that she cares for us, not like our last fling.

That's why it only lasted a week!

He was only intrigued after he figured out we were linked.

And we've known Claire since we were toddlers.

Think we're in love.

Sis, what's with Danny's sexy side?

Maybe that's how she relaxes after looking at dead bodies?

Couldn't do it. Would have to crawl out of my skin after each one I saw.

After a small dinner, they spent the evening researching medical examiners and coroners in New Mexico and western Texas. The field was now dominated by younger women. They did not find Danielle in the listings of the American Society of Crime Laboratory directory, either. She was young enough that she could have just entered the field, and thus may not have shown up on anyone's radar. Of course there were no pictures or descriptions of the alumni, just names, and they only knew her first name. There were photographs in the high school and university yearbooks. They quickly tired of looking at pictures of graduates after an hour. They would ask Nicole to expand the search.

~~~

Chapter 18
Stakeout

FIRST THING THE NEXT MORNING, THEY CALLED
José to see if he wanted to go for a ride with them, over
dirt roads to areas south and west of town.

"Sure, what are we looking for?"

"A square hacienda, with a courtyard, a fountain, and
a razor-wire topped fence. All of it set on flat land but for
a couple of twin peaks in the distance. We'll tell you more
about it when we pick you up."

José was waiting for them at the end of the driveway.
Antonio unlocked the truck's passenger door and explained
that they were searching for a young person.

"What should I call you, if I don't know which side of
you I'm talking to?"

"Tony will do. Thanks for keeping this to yourself,
José."

As they started moving toward the west side of town,
Antonia's voice took over,

"What we are really looking for is Mora, this young
girl who's been missing for almost two weeks. Since you
understand unconventional techniques, let me explain
how we get in touch with the girl."

She proceeded to tell him how, with the help of

Rosetta, they had been able to reach Mora and find out about the building where she is being held. Antonio, not wanting to be left out, would interject his opinion now and then.

José was impressed. "Too bad I didn't have your help, or Miss Rosetta's help, when I was working for the narcotic squad, or when Jack went missing for a couple of weeks, years ago. I'd love to meet Miss Rosetta."

After they had told him most of what they knew about Mora and her captors, José said, "I think this Papa Patron could be the elusive Patron de los Lobos that ICE and Homeland Security are looking for. A very dangerous guy, with no scruples. He's been dealing on both sides of the border, mostly drugs and prostitutes, but hasn't been caught yet. Rumor has it, his son is trying to take over the business in El Paso. By the way, I'm carrying a concealed weapon. But it looks like you two will need some serious help, some federal help. I may be too old for the job!"

"We're sure you're not, but anytime you want to go back home, please let us know. There are many other ways you can help. And by the way, we also have a concealed-carry permit."

"If you still want my help, I will not let you go by yourself to look for this treacherous perp. But let's be ready to ask for the big guns when we need them."

"Definitely! That's the only way we work. We do the research, then we call in the cavalry." The Tonys agreed.

They looked over topo maps and decided to keep the search area to a triangle southwest of Las Cruces.

José had many questions. "Did she hear trains, or planes, or semis, or any kind of traffic?"

"She did not mention any of these. The place sounds remote and quiet. I'll ask her about trains and planes next time I talk to her," Antonia replied.

"I love how your voice switches over from male to female. Do you ever make mistakes?"

Antonio responded. "Never, because you see, once we are inside one of our genders, we do not switch over without a conscious effort. Although Antonia is always trying to interfere, trying to tell me what to do inside my head. She's a control freak!"

To which she retorted. "We are always fighting about this, but internally. The nature of this dual beast is that we both want to control the other."

José laughed at this, knowing he had touched a sensitive topic. "Does the girl remember anything about her abduction?"

"Very little. She was blinded by the fact that they told her she was going to be a movie star. She did not pay attention to where she was going."

"What about flight patterns of birds, types of vegetation, sonic booms, anything else that would give us a clue as to her whereabouts?"

"Being early summer now, means the birds have arrived at their destinations a while back and she's only been at that place for two weeks. The only type of vegetation she has mentioned, are dried weeds inside the courtyard and dark-green bushes outside. Next time, Antonia can ask her about what else she can see outside. But their conversations are usually very short and tenuous. She can't always reach Mora. Personally, I don't think the girl understands that she is in danger."

Antonia did not reply. She was thinking of ways to coax Mora to get more information about her whereabouts. She also had a hunch that today's search would bear no fruits. This did not feel like the right place.

They took a frontage road by the interstate going west for a dozen miles, then turned off on a small county road towards Aden. A couple of dirt roads led to the south. José interjected, "We should look at these on the way back. That's the Torres's cattle ranch. Not much there beside cattle and water tanks. Let's go to where we can get a better look at the country."

They kept going toward a small set of hills. Two large dump trucks traveling the opposite way sprayed dirt and gravel all over their pickup. They turned off on a narrow dirt road leading to the center of the Aden Hills, a low complex of mounds. Passing a few buildings at the foothills, then a couple of large, metal sheds, they continued on up. The road ran for another quarter mile to the top and ended abruptly at the highest point. A four-wheeler's dream path. Barely a couple of hundred feet above the county road, the view was limited. Scanning through their binoculars, the area around them looked deserted, but for a large hacienda, some small storage buildings, a huge barn and an extensive set of corrals.

"That's the Torres ranch headquarters, over there.

Good, honest people. Very religious. They adopted half a dozen boys since they could not have any kids on their own," said the old man, pointing to the east side.

Down the other side of the rise they had just climbed, smaller hillocks pock-marked a gentle slope before distant flats. Red and black flecks that most likely were cattle dotted the land among the olive-green shrubs. On the west side, more hillocks in the distance behind railroad tracks. North of them, mostly mesquite and creosote bushes covered the whole area.

As they were surveying their surroundings, José talked in a hushed tone. "After you came to us, I looked you up with one of my past contacts in the force, a young man I trained just before retiring. It took him a while to find out about your birth and childhood. Nothing on record about your medical condition, if you don't mind my using that term. That is how I found out that your birth certificate has both your names on it, but just one certificate altogether. Antonio Antonia Urbani. Then I did some research on my own, about conjoined twins and chimeras. I hope you will forgive my curiosity." He finished in an apologetic tone.

"Thank you for letting us know how you found out." Half choking on his words, it was all Antonio could reply.

There are no secrets anymore with the internet, Tone.

José stared at them for a second. Antonia said:

"Could you feel us thinking?"

"No. I was just thinking about the way of the internet and its lack of privacy, and thought you had said something about it. But I did not see your mouth moving."

See, Sis, some people do sense our ruminations.

Back on the county road, they continued for a few miles before turning south onto a straight dirt road. Signs warning about buried pipelines flagged both sides of the road. A few miles more and another dirt road led east. They passed a couple of rusty signs asking to watch out for livestock, then a two-track jeep road beckoned to them on the left side of a fork. The rusty-pipe cattle-guard rumbled as they crossed it. Tony put the truck in four-wheel drive again. Cattle came, trotting toward them, thinking feed had arrived. Besides a few bunches of cows with young calves at their side, a running coyote, some dry arroyos, and a water tank here and there, they could not see any signs of habitation. At the end of the road, a large, dried-up dirt tank sat in front of a barbed-wire fence covered with No Trespassing signs. Time to turn around, and try the other side of the fork.

Just more ranch land, with an occasional worker's shack. Not much happening there. They were getting close to the border and the area seemed barren. José called Alex Torres and asked him if there were any haciendas near his ranch house.

"Nothing but flat land between here and the border. Just the ranch hands' shacks, but I would not call them haciendas. My men work hard and I like to provide them with a roof. But I just provide the basics, you know. No swimming pools!" he laughed, before hanging up.

The Tonys returned José to his home after asking him

if he would be interested in helping them with a stakeout later on that night, for a different case. He agreed and they arranged to pick him up later.

~~~

Nicole had not left by the time they came home. She seemed very excited to see Antonio. "I expanded the search as you asked, and I think I found her. There is a woman named Danielle D. Jorgensen who attended the University of Texas in El Paso thirteen years ago. Using that name, I was able to follow her to the University of Texas in Austin, where she graduated with a degree in pathology a couple of years later. Here is her graduation picture."

On the screen, a younger version of the picture the Tonys had handed her was staring back at them.

"Nice work, Nicole!"

The young woman beamed. "Wait! There is more. There is a D. D. Jorgensen who has been practicing as a medical examiner for the city of Austin for the last six years. No pictures. I followed up on it and the twenty-four hour number referred me to an on-call coroner who complained that Dr. Jorgensen quit without any notice last month. He's had to cover her shift all of last week until they can hire someone new."

"You did great, Nicole. She will be so relieved to find out her name. Thank you."

As soon as Nicole had left, Antonia called Danny. "Is your last name Jorgensen?"

"Wow, Tony, you are good! Yes, yes that is my name."

"You went to UT in El Paso and in Austin, studied pathology, and practiced in Austin, for the city?"

"Yes, yes! That's right! All of it is correct. Let me digest this for a minute."

Tony could hear her inhale sharply while they waited.

"Wow. You are fantastic!"

"Thanks, I had some help. But let me warn you that the city is thinking you quit them without notice. You better call them if you want to keep your job."

"I will. But I don't know who to call. I'll look up names, maybe that will further my memories."

"Do look it up, please. Would you like to get a psychologist, or at least a victim support group, to help you with the new findings?"

"No, thanks. I'll do this on my own. The police did not help me. The shrink at the hospital did not help me. You did. You found out more than all of them put together. But actually, I also want you to find out who harmed me and why. Can you still help, please?"

"We will, of course. As a matter of fact, we were planning on following the man who drops off the money tonight, if he shows up, that is."

Danny answered in a lighter tone of voice. "Be careful, then. And thanks again. You have no idea how much better I feel already."

"My pleasure. Call us if you remember anything else."

JD — DJ, Danny Jorgensen! Still not a coincidence, Sis?

No! Only subconscious recollections.

~~~

After a light lunch, the Tonys took a nap, to rest before the night task awaiting them.

At eleven o'clock, Antonio went to pick up José in his pick-up.

Wouldn't the dark Subaru be more discreet, Tone?

Nah, Sis, every third vehicle in New Mexico is a white pickup. Besides, this is a man's job!

Chauvinist pig!

José was waiting for them outside the gates, a thermos bottle and two cups in his hand. He was smiling as he got in. "I haven't gone on a stakeout in over twenty years. This is exciting."

They drove to the motel, talked to the manager for a minute, and parked a couple of doors from Danny's room, but across the lot. Tony shared the new findings about Dr. Jorgensen, and sipping on some very dark coffee, they talked like two colleagues sharing past adventures.

Shortly after one, when they were thinking he would not show, a low vehicle turned into the motel, shutting off its lights at the entrance.

"Amateur," José quietly said, as they both sank into their seats. The sporty car cruised slowly past them, turned around the U-shaped parking area, and finally stopped right across from them. The driver stayed in the car, no lights showing.

José pulled out a pair of night goggles. After donning them, he asked Tony to write down the license number as he spelled it out. Sinking farther down in his seat, he speed-dialed a number on his phone.

"Hi, Herman. You're ready? OK: on a light-colored Audi R8 Coupe, Utah plates, here is the number." He read the numbers Tony had written down, by the light of his phone.

His phone vibrated a few minutes later. The man across from them was still in his car. Under the dashboard, José wrote down a few lines on a pad of paper.

"OK. The car has been leased from a company in Salt Lake City for over a year by a Gunter Levi Schmidt from El Paso. I have his address, phone numbers, date of birth, and occupation."

"That was fast and easy! So glad we're doing this together. You don't have his social security number, too?" joked Tony.

"I do, but you should not need it." He whispered back.

Just then, a short, stocky man emerged from the Audi, looked left and right, then at the few cars parked in the lot, before walking to Danny's room door. He slipped an envelope under the door and turned around, almost running back to his car.

"You want to apprehend him?"

Tony answered, "No, we have no authority. We only needed his name and address. We'll do a little research on his background tomorrow and see what else Danny wants to know. Thank you so much for all your help."

"My pleasure! It's a lot more entertaining when you're working on the sideline. No pressure from the boss!"

They waited until the man left, before Tony took José back home.

~~~

Sleep did not come easy that night. Too much coffee. Confirming the identity of the covert donor was opening pathways that needed to be examined. They researched Schmidt on the internet. A professor at UTEP for the last eighteen years, he had been teaching genetics and paleoanthropology. He wrote a book on the sexual similarities of apes and men, *Greater and Lesser Simian Carnal Behaviors*. The Tonys read a couple of dozen pages throughout the book. It was a dry dissertation about the typical comportment of primates, comparing humans' and greater apes' physical and social contacts, especially through erotic and aggressive behavior.

Did he rape and beat Danny?

Then repented and is trying to repair his violent acts?

Does he want to be discovered? He did use part of his name to register her.

And then be punished for what he did? He keeps coming back on a predictable day. We should meet him.

Confront him!

But first let's find out more about him.

He would not have a criminal record and still be teaching!

Probably not.

Attend one of his classes? Follow him around?

Maybe Danny will have answers.

Tomorrow! Let's try to sleep.

~ ~ ~

Chapter 19

A Strong Connection

THE TONYS KEPT YAWNING ON THE WAY TO
Rosetta.

Too much info, not enough time, not enough sleep.

Good info. You know we prefer the fast pace!

After greeting Tiger, who immediately made a beeline
for the kitten, Rosetta handed them a cup of steaming,
black coffee.

"Hum! Dark Ethiopian, no sugar. Delicious. Thank
you, Rosetta," Antonia said as she sank into the enveloping
armchair.

"*Ohayou gozaimasu,* Tiger, Tonia and Rosa. My name is
Sachiko," was the first thing Mora said.

"Hello, Mora. What was that you said?"

"I said 'Ohayou gozaimasu'. That means good morning
in Japanese. My new name, Sachiko, means happiness. I'm
going to be the black geisha in this movie they are going
to make. So I have to learn a lot of Japanese fast. It's fun!"

"Good morning to you, Mora — I mean, Sachiko. I
need a favor from you, can you help me?"

"Sure, what is it?"

Calculating her words, Antonia continued, "First, let me tell you that I am a professional detective."

"Cool!"

"But please, keep it to yourself. What I need from you is that you be my assistant detective. Can you help me find out some things I need to know?"

"I'll help you. That sounds like fun."

"Do you hear sometimes trains in the distance or planes overhead?'

The child took a minute to answer. "No, but sometimes I hear helicopters. Then the ladies here want us to stay away from the windows when they fly over."

"Tell me about the ladies?"

"I already told you about Josette. She's the cook and the cleaner and the beauty teacher."

"What does she look like?"

"She is medium size. She's very old, like fifty or something. She looks like a mouse with brown hair and brown eyes and a pointy nose. She puts on a lot of makeup, blue eye shadow and really red lipstick, and she smells like lemon. Does that help?"

"It does. Thank you. Is she Hispanic?" Antonia rapidly continued.

"You mean like Mexican?"

"Yes. What color is her skin, and does she have a Mexican accent?"

"Oh, no! She has very white skin with freckles. She's not Mexican, but Miss Manners is."

"Tell me about Miss Manners. What does she look like?"

"She is petite, very small for a grown-up; she likes to be called petite. She's just a little taller than me. And she has really black hair. She says she doesn't color it, she only curls it. She also wears a lot of makeup, and pointy heels, and fancy clothes, and she puts on really strong, flower perfume. And bye! *Sayonara.*"

They discussed their findings with Rosetta. It would be harder to change Mora's opinion about her situation, now that she was immersed in what she thought was her new role as an actress. All three concluded that Papa Patron was making kiddy porn flicks, and may be using Mora soon. She had not mentioned any filming yet. There was also a possibility that the man had other nefarious plans for her. They needed to find the place where they were holding her and the other girls, before anything happened to them. They needed to get more help, fast.

~~~

After their session, Rosetta asked them if they would have time to help her with a difficult situation she was in the middle of.

"Of course! How can we help, Rosetta?"

The kitten jumped on her lap. Taking her time, sipping on another cup of coffee, she started talking about the Kingsburg boy she had gone to see with Woody the day before. "This young man's name is Leo. In the cards, I saw a strong connection between Leo and Mora. A very strong connection."

She saw that she had their full attention. She took

a deep breath and continued, "Leo is a thirteen-year-old child who was adopted by his aunt after both of his parents had died. When he was four years old, two years after his father had passed, his mother had given him a protective medal. She had the medallion made especially for him. One side shows Nicholas, patron saint of children, and on the other side there is Ganesh, the Hindu elephant deity, protector of everyone and everything. Leo's mother passed away two years after giving him that pendant. This is the only thing he has left from her. It is very precious to him. Alas, at school, in Kingsburg, the bigger kids are always picking on him. During a fight last week, just outside the schoolyard, the medal was yanked off his neck, broke off its small chain, and thrown into the dirt. He was not able to find it and has asked for my help through one of his cousins. Woody and I met him yesterday. He is a sweet child, polite but insecure. I looked for the pendant with a pendulum and with my divining rod. The crystal remained fixed, meaning the medal was not nearby. The rod, however, pulled me a distance to the east. As you know, I cannot walk very far with my bad leg, and we had to drop it at that time. I told the child that I would be back in a couple of days. I was hoping you would be able to help me. It would be without pay, I am afraid."

Tomorrow, midday, Sis?

Of course!

Antonio quickly responded, "You have helped us so much already, Rosetta. We'll be glad to help Leo. We owe you much, my friend. How is tomorrow, after our session with Mora? Would you have time then?"

Antonia got up and moved toward Rosetta, reinforcing her brother's words. "Would it be easier to do this earlier in the morning?"

"Mid-morning would be perfect. You see, Woody does not wake up as early as I do, and he likes to take his time. I don't want to rush him. Leo told me he is staying home, as he is afraid he will be picked on again at school. He thinks he is in grave danger without his medallion. Also, he does not want his aunt to know that he lost her sister's medal. He said that she gets mad easy. He is pretending to be sick. Besides, you have a date with Mora in the early morning."

The woman got off her stool and gave them a generous hug. They could feel her warm kindness through that embrace, as she thanked them repeatedly.

As they made for the door, Antonio turned around and said, "I'm curious. Could you share what the card looked like that showed the link between Mora and Leo?"

"I can. Two paths are coming forward to a Y. A man carrying a bow and arrows on one path and a woman with a pitcher of water on her head on the other, both still in the distance, but coming to the fork in the road at the front of the card. There are birds above and fish below. This is a card I often draw when people want to know if they should marry each other. In this case, it showed me that the two children will nurture each other in the future. But right after that, I drew another card that showed there could be delays and perils. On it, vultures are circling above a few fish caught in a circle of rocks on the edge of a big waterfall. You should be careful, too. I will see you both tomorrow morning." Rosetta added, dismissing them.

~~~

On their way home, their phone was busy. First a call from Lou, with excitement in his voice. "Hey, Tony. I found your mystery woman! According to the prints, she is Danielle Diana Jorgensen, a medical examiner for the city of Austin, Texas. Lives in Austin. I've got her address, social security, and phone numbers. She has been missing for almost three weeks, according to that city's finest. They even said they miss her. She is their best coroner."

"Thank you, Lou. That helps us a lot." Antonio did not have the heart to tell him his daughter Nicole had already reached that conclusion, but it also confirmed that they had the right name for Danny.

Next, at nine o'clock sharp, Sunny's cousin called. "Hello. May I speak with Antonio Urbani, please. This is Carlos Garcia with Customs and Border Protection."

"Hello, Carlos. This is Tony. Sunny said you'd call. Thank you"

"No problem! My cousin said you need my help finding someone missing near the border. Is that correct?"

"Yes, sir. Can we meet? Do you ever come to Las Cruces?"

"I'm posted in Kingsburg. Do you ever come to our lovely city?"

"When would be a good time to meet you in lovely Kingsburg?"

"Today or tomorrow at noon. I have an hour off for lunch."

"Today, then. I'm half an hour east of Deming right now. I can be there in a couple of hours."

Carlos gave him directions to a small motel no longer in use as such, that used to be called The King's Rest, and was now their main office, on the west side of town.

Let me go. Talk to him man to man!

Sure, Tone! But let him know we're a set of twins, in case he asks for me. Am the one in contact with Mora.

Afraid to be left in the dark?

Can't! Am sticking to you like glue.

~~~

They turned around and stopped at the first gas station to change clothes. As Antonio got back in the car, in cowboy boots and hat, blue jean jacket over a striped red-and-white Western shirt with pearl snaps, one of their two phones' caller ID showed the Road Runner motel.

Antonia answered in her melodious voice. "Hi, Danny. How are you today?"

"Hey, Tony. I'm well. Thanks to you. Memories are flooding back. It's almost overwhelming. They're all jumbled. One moment I see my mom holding my hand on the way to the dentist, the next I'm dissecting a human chest and removing a still heart. But I wanted to let you know that I studied genetics under professor Gunter Schmidt. Actually, we became friends, just friends, you understand. And I would go to El Paso occasionally, to

221

hang out with him. He would have these wild parties. Lots of booze and sex. Safe sex, but unsafe amounts of booze. Lots of his old students would come to them. So I wondered if that's when this mess happened to me."

"Let's talk about that in person. I may be able to stop by this afternoon, if that works for you?" Antonia said soothingly.

"You know me, out and about all day long! Do come by, please. I'm still not going anywhere. I'm waiting for my financial records. I contacted the main bank in Austin, and they were able to tell me who my credit-card provider is, thanks to you finding out my social security number and birth date. I'm waiting for all that in the mail. I gave them your address, by the way. They did not want a post office box or a motel address. If I made any purchase in El Paso before the incident, that may open more doors."

The Tonys were relieved that she was recalling her past so quickly.

Am worried that she may not be able to deal with the trauma very well, when it surfaces.

She's a coroner, Sis. She can handle it!

She's a woman, she's more emotional than you, man!

~~~

Chapter 20
Help at the Border

THE BLACKTOP WAS ALREADY HOT AND SHIMMERY by the time they passed through Deming again. They made their way to middle-of-nowhere Kingsburg, a place fast on its way to becoming a ghost town, if not for being right off the interstate and having a train stop and a couple of fuel stations. The Customs and Border Protection office was hiding in an old, shabby motel near the railroad tracks.

Inconspicuous up front, except for a six-foot fence complete with razor wire on top, the building had been slightly renovated, a mostly-cosmetic paint job over repaired cracks and an asphalt-covered parking lot. Next to the faded letters that once proclaimed the place to be the King's Rest on the placard above what must have been the reception lobby, three large, green initials — CBP — showed them they had the right place. A dozen green-and-white trucks could be seen behind the building. The place looked deserted. After parking the truck on the south side as instructed, Antonio went to what must have once been the reception lobby and knocked on the door.

"Come in!" a deep voice answered.

Two men wearing dark-green uniforms sat behind two desks on each side of the room, which stank of cigarette smoke, combined with faint odors of wet dog and stale coffee.

The taller and slimmer of the two agents stood up. "Tony Urbani? I'm Carlos Garcia."

"Nice to meet you, and thanks for seeing me so quickly."

"This is my partner, Mando Hernandez. Hope you don't mind if he sticks around."

"Not at all. Protocol, I guess?"

"That, and Mando here brought his own lunch. He can't miss a meal," Carlos said with a smile, as his portly partner grimaced, but seemed to take it well.

Tony handed him one of his business cards and took out his electronic notepad.

Carlos was handsome, with dark hair and dark eyes, in his early thirties. He looked like someone who was happy all the time. After glancing at the card and the fancy notepad, he picked up a pen and an old-fashioned yellow paper pad with a derisive shrug, and cast his inquisitive black eyes toward Tony.

"We have been hired to look into the disappearance of a young girl, who has been missing for more than two weeks now. We have reasons to believe she has been abducted to a place somewhere between Interstate-10 and the Mexican border, probably in a sparsely populated area. We have a tentative description of the building and its surroundings."

Carlos interrupted. "How did you get that information?"

"My sister has been getting small notes, presumably from the girl, although we have never met her."

"How do you know it's not a hoax?"

"The girl's mother has hired us to find her."

"Why is the girl contacting your sister, and not her mother?"

"My sister, Antonia is sitting the girl's dog. Mora, the girl, has a habit of running away now and then, but she always takes care of her dog. In the past she has never been gone longer than a couple of days, usually staying at a friend's nearby. Her mother is strict and will probably punish her."

Not!

Right, but how else do you explain your empathic abilities?

Carlos tilted his head and stared at him, raising one eyebrow. "OK! What else have you got?"

"She is being held in a large, square building, encircling a courtyard with a fountain in the middle. Bars on the windows. Tall fence with razor wire all around. Have you seen such a place in your travels?"

"Sure! About a hundred of them between Carlsbad and Bisbee. Many people have protected their haciendas from looting illegals. What else have you got?"

"The landscape is just desert. Mountains in the distance. There are two peaks on one side, not too far away, probably on the west side of the building. Wolves roam the area."

"You're gonna have to do better than that! That barely eliminates a few of the places. How do the notes get to your sister?"

"They are slipped under our door during the night."

Right! You go, Bro.

"Could you bring these to me? We might be able to

collect fingerprints, or even DNA."

Antonio realized that his lie would not work. He'd have to tell them the truth if they were to believe him.

Let me handle it, Tone. Even if I look the fool.

"My sister will bring you the documentation."

"Any names or description of the people holding the girl?"

We're here now, Tone! Tell him about the patron, tell him about the wolf!

Carlos again tilted his head while staring at Antonio's face with a concerned look. "Are you OK, Tony? Looked like you had gone somewhere else there for a second."

"Just thinking. My sister can probably explain everything better. There is also this guy by the name of Papa Patron whom Mora talks about."

"So Mora talked to your sister?"

Sharp guy!

"That's just a figure of speech. The note said this Papa Patron has a pet wolf with a shock collar."

"OK. Now you may have something. Let me check on 'El Patron de los Lobos'. Could be the same guy. How old is the girl?"

"She's young, only eleven years old."

"Pretty?"

"Yes, her mother showed us a recent picture. She is very pretty."

A worried look came over Carlos's features. He talked rapidly to his co-worker, asking him to get some maps from the storage room. The stocky man left with a resigned sigh.

"OK, I'm not supposed to share this info, but you're a good friend of Sunny's. This guy we have heard of for the last few years has been kidnapping young girls, mostly Mexican, and he brings them back to somewhere on this side. He teaches them English, gives them fake papers, and then he has them work the streets of El Paso. Rumor has it, he is expanding his business. He also goes by the name of Papa Lobo, but we still haven't found out where his operation is."

His companion came back with an armful of waterproof topo maps.

"Let me do a little research. Can your sister get messages to Mora, probably not, right?" Carlos said, watching Tony shake his head back and forth. Then almost sarcastically, as if not certain he believed him, he added. "It would be nice to find out a little more about the terrain. You know, what else is around the hacienda. What kind of plants grow there. If there is a dirt or paved road going to it? Call me if you get another note. I'd like to talk to your sister. Have her come with you, next time. Here is my direct number."

As Tony lingered by the closed door on his way out, through the large tinted-glass window, he could hear Carlos saying, "Hey Mando, it sure looks like el Patron de los Lobos is at it again! We gotta find the bastard."

Then he heard: "Sunny says his sister is quite the looker. I hope she comes in next time."

Carlos heard us, heard our internal voice.

Right, when he asked me if I had gone somewhere else.

We need to be more vigilant.

Right, and you need to shut up and let me do the thinking and talking

Easy, Tone. No need to bite our head off!

Am just worried about her. It's taking us too long.

Got any new ideas to speed it up?

We could get Lou involved in this.

You heard Maria, she has ran away too many times. They won't look for her. Besides how do we explain to our big friend how we get in touch with her?

When we know where she's at, we can try to get county and CBP to work together.

If they don't botch up the job trying to outdo each other.

Give them more credit, Sis. They do work together, even if they don't like it.

~~~

Tony called Janos to see if he would pose as a student while he checked out a professor in El Paso.

"Sure, man. I even look the part now. I'm all cleaned up. I cut my dreads, got a straight haircut. I just got a job as a courier on that bike you got me. Got some panniers I can lock up, and I deliver shit to this or that company in the city. I start at seven and I'm done by noon, most of the time. I get great tips, too. Neat, hey! So what, when, and where?"

"If you want to come by the house around four, we'll take off for El Paso. The guy's last class finishes at five today."

"I'll see you at four, man. Thanks for the job opportunity."

Sounds like Janos is taking the straight path!

Yeah, Sis. Most of them grow up, eventually.

Janos is a good kid. He just got lost once.

~~~

Chapter 21
Greater Apes

AFTER ANOTHER QUICK GENDER CHANGE, Antonia went to the Road Runner motel. Danny looked radiant. A big grin appeared on her face when she saw the detective.

"Antonia. You're great! Thank you for everything."

"Hey, Danny. You're welcome. We just found out your cell number. Of course you may want to get a new phone."

"I don't know. I may just use the number associated with this tablet and forgo an actual phone. I'm also thinking of joining the local forensic team and moving out of Texas."

"Why don't you wait until you recover all your memories? You're already well on your way. It's not that we don't want you here, but I'm sure there was a good reason for you to be in Austin."

"I don't know. All these flashbacks are making me very tired. I can barely function, as it is."

"Give it time. Look at what you've accomplished in the last couple of days."

Danny grimaced and replied, "Yes, with your help. Thanks again."

"Do you remember anyone in your family? Someone

who could help you recover faster? You mentioned your mother. Could she come and get you?"

Her eyes tearing up, she said, "No. I do remember going to my mom's funeral, a while back. Only a few people attended her service. I don't think I have many relatives, if any."

"What about close friends, or lovers? Did you stay in touch with anyone from the year you were in El Paso?"

Danny shook her head, back and forth. "If I have any friends, they must not be close. No names come to mind. I think I'm a loner."

"So, tell me about your interaction with Gunter. Off the record, of course. I won't take any notes."

Danny took a deep breath and started. "I've always liked sex. It keeps me sane, I guess, especially after cutting up dead bodies. I need an outlet, a way to cope with what I've seen. But even before I started in Austin, Gunter had these parties, nerd parties, the whole school talked about them. You had to have read his book on greater apes to be invited. I read his book during that year I was at UTEP. It was almost mandatory reading, if you took his class. Most of his students had read it. Then one day, when I told him I was switching to UT-Austin, he asked if I wanted to come to one of his parties after the end of that school year. That was a privilege at the time. I guess it still is. Few people got invited. They had to be out of UTEP and preferably have a job. I went and ended up going often. He had parties usually every three months. We'd talk and eat and drink and some of us took a partner to one of his guest rooms. It was thought-provoking, and wild, and fun. We all thought we were on the edge of making history, like the Beatniks of the sixties." She took another deep breath. Her cheeks were red, as if ashamed.

"Thank you for sharing, Danny. Alcohol and sex are still legal," Antonia added with a smile. "Tell me about Gunter himself. Could he have been the one who hurt you?"

"Oh, no! He's always been a gentleman toward me."

"Have you ever seen him lose his temper or drink too much, become violent or belligerent?"

"No, never. During his parties, he barely drinks. He presents us with a different theme each time, sometimes it's fantastic or surreal or even absurd. He shares his ideas with us, although not at first, not until at least half of us have expressed our opinions, but mostly he watches all his guests. I've always felt that he was researching his next book with us. It seemed like a game for him, a little like his own private show."

"Has he made advances toward you?"

"Never! And I'm sure, I've never slept with him. You are really bringing back a lot to the surface." They sat still for a while.

"Tell me about the last party you attended."

"I... it... it must have been recently. Or what else would I have been doing in El Paso? But I can't remember it. Hold on... What I can remember is reading about it. Maybe it was in an email or on a postcard. Yes, it was a postcard. That's how I get the invitations. Just a postcard.

On one side, his initials GLS in big italic letters, and on the other side just the date and time. Nothing else, but my address, of course. I remember thinking that I could go this time. It fell on my days off. I work four days on and four days off. But… but I can't remember packing or leaving home or arriving here, arriving in El Paso, I mean." Danny was getting upset. She kept rubbing her hands, in a washing gesture. Angry tears were jutting from the corner of her eyes.

"You've accomplished a lot today. Don't torture yourself. It's all coming back, and coming back fast. I'm sure you are still very frustrated about not having total recall, but I think you will regain the rest of it soon, although these memories may be the most painful. I'll let you relax. We can follow up tomorrow."

Danny stopped rubbing her hands. Looking into Antonia's eyes, she said, "Thanks. I'm sorry I'm such a mess. I hate not being in control. Let's keep going, get this over with."

Don't do it, Sis. She's at the end of her rope. She just started washing her hands again. You're pushing her too hard!

Antonia took a deep breath and asked, "One last question, then. An easy one, I hope. Where do you usually stay when you come to town?"

Danny relaxed her hands and sat upright. "I usually try different hotels. The Double Tree, the Radisson, the Hilton. I like my comfort when I'm on vacation."

"Great. You've given me something new to work with.

I'll get someone to go check these. See if we can find your belongings. I have to go, but I'll see you tomorrow. Call me anytime if you need to talk."

~~~

As soon as she got in the car, she told her brother to call Lou.

"Hey, Lou. I need another favor."

"Tony, you're gonna owe me big! What's going on?"

"It's about Danielle. Once she knew her name, thanks to you, she started remembering a bunch of stuff, but not all of it. One thing she remembered was staying in a four-star hotel, like the Hilton, the Radisson or the Double Tree. But she can't remember which one, and she still doesn't want to venture outside. Her luggage could still be in one of these."

"You know El Paso is outside my jurisdiction, but I can ask the city chief if he can send one of his uniformed officers to the fancy hotels." Lou preempted him.

"Thanks, Lou. You're the best!" Tony could feel the sheriff beaming on the other end of the line. "You know Lou, if she gets her stuff back, her wallet, her phone, her clothes and whatever else she left in one of these hotels, she'll probably regain all of her memories. Then you can bust the perp who did it."

"Yeah, right! Most likely it will be the El Paso cops who'll get all the glory! I'll let you know what they find," he said as he hung up.

The Tonys rushed home so they could change before going with Janos to El Paso. They were tired, yet elated by everything they had accomplished so far in one day. And the workday was not over yet.

~~~

Chapter 22
The Professor

TAKING A BIG THERMOS OF COFFEE WITH THEM, Antonio and Janos took off for the short, hour ride to El Paso. Janos had really cleaned up his act. Clean clothes, good haircut, yet not too short, freshly shaved, he could easily pass for a university student. Most of his tattoos were hidden under a long-sleeved T-shirt.

Tony complimented him on his appearance, then got down to business. "We're going to attend the end of this professor's class, or at least wait outside his classroom door. He teaches genetics. This particular course is called "Evolution and the Human Condition." When he is not teaching, this man may be involved in sexual activities, one of which did not end well. My sister and I think he is trying to make amends for an incident that happened some weeks ago with one of his former students. We are working for that ex-student, a woman named Danny. As far as we know, he is not violent, but we're not certain. We're trying to figure out what happened to her. We need to find out about these parties he throws a few times a year. Sex and booze, but allegedly no drugs."

"So, what do you need me to do?"

"We'll play it as we go. I'll use you as my sounding board. Maybe you can ask if he knows of any parties in the area? I've seen him at a distance but he has never seen me. I don't know yet how we'll approach it."

~~~

It was almost five by the time they found which classroom Gunter Schmidt was teaching in that day. Tony spotted his car in the parking lot, not too far from the hall. He gave Janos a few more pointers before they went in.

The amphitheater seated about one hundred people, and more than half of the seats were occupied. They stayed by the door and watched the students firing questions at the short man on the podium. The lecturer knew his subject well, held his head high, and answered questions in a soft baritone voice, clearly and concisely. Tony thought that despite the assertive manner, the man hid a somewhat demure and mild manner. He had a thick mane of dark hair, a sharp, curved nose, and dark eyes over a well-dressed body that probably never saw the inside of a gym.

"He doesn't look too threatening to me," murmured Janos, as they retreated from the door to let the students exit. They blended in with the crowd and climbed into the pickup, keeping an eye on the professor's cream-colored Audi.

Twenty minutes passed before Schmidt came out by a side door and stepped into his car. For a while it looked as if he was looking at papers or books, with his head bent over the passenger seat, and it seemed he might not drive away anytime soon.

Did he spot us?

Don't think so. Probably just sorting things after his last class.

Seeing the parking area starting to empty, Tony was worried that the two vehicles would be the very last to leave. He decided to drive ahead of the professor's and wait in the main street heading toward the west side of town.

"Here he comes," said Janos, looking in the vanity mirror above his head.

"We'll let him get ahead. If he goes home, I know where that is," replied Tony.

Following him, after a couple of red lights, it became obvious that he was not going home.

"Maybe he's going shopping or to a restaurant," volunteered Janos.

The Audi coupe finally turned into a small strip mall and parked by a bar called the "Rusty Nail", its facade covered by weathered barn planks complete with old nail heads, black streaks running beneath them.

The two men waited five minutes before walking in. It was fairly dark inside but for two large screens showing the same basketball game. As luck would have it, there were a few empty stools at the long bar on the professor's left side. They sat next to him. Never glancing toward him, they ordered drinks. A draft beer for Janos and a Rusty Nail, the house special, for Tony. Janos started talking about some of the women he had seen in the amphitheater, without giving away where they had been, as Tony had advised.

"Remember that tall brunette with the big knockers?"

"Yeah, kind of." Raising an eyebrow, Tony was going to let him run with it. He had advised him not to sound too stereotypical or sexist. They were dealing with an intelligent man; they could not let him see through their scheme.

"Man, she was asking all the right questions. Smart! I like smart women, 'specially when they look that good."

Quickly glancing around, as if to see if anyone was listening to their conversation, Tony noticed a smile on the professor's lips, although he was staring ahead at the mirror behind the bartender.

Good, you have his attention, Tone!

Antonio slightly nodded at Janos to begin phase two of the plan they had concocted before walking in.

"Hey, barkeep, you got a minute?" Janos said.

"Yes, sir. Need another beer?"

"Not yet, not yet. Soon. Hey, would you know about any parties around here? Like, tonight maybe?"

The young bartender shook his head. "Not this early in the week." He watched Janos slip a fiver in the tip jar. "You know, actually I heard that Friday, there is supposed to be a big shindig near Sunland Park. No band, but cool DJs." He raised a questioning eyebrow, then looked toward the professor as if caught giving trade secrets.

Tony followed his gaze and stared at the professor. "Hi, do I know you? Oh! Wait. I know you. You're that guy on the back cover of that book. I read that. About the sexual behavior of men and apes being pretty much the same. Is that you?"

"You got me! I'm Gunter Schmidt. I wrote *Greater and Lesser Simian Carnal Behaviors*," he said, as Antonio shook his head up and down in agreement.

"My name's Tony. Pleased to meet you. I like your book. I like how you explain how when the males don't get sexual favors from the females, they get aggressive. That is just like people. Your book reveals a lot about today's behavior of some males in our society. We're really not so different from those wild, big apes, are we?"

They went on talking about the book for a few minutes. Tony paid for another round, including one for the professor, careful to slowly sip on his drink while munching on the spicy jalapeño nachos the bartender had brought them.

Gunter was curious now and started asking questions. "You two going to UTEP?"

Janos took the lead. "Not yet. Name's Janos. Nice meeting you. I just finished my undergrad in psychology at UNM and I'm looking at maybe continuing in El Paso. I hear they have a pretty good program here. Lots of new technology."

Tony had briefed him well, and Gunter seemed to believe him. He let them know about the master's program in experimental psychology and mentioned that he taught some of the classes. Then he turned to Tony. "What about you?"

Antonio took a few seconds before answering.

He asked for it Tone. Let him have it!

Pensively, Tony looked into his drink, then, raising his eyes to Gunter, he replied, "I graduated in criminal justice at U of A, more than seven years ago. My sister and I have our own practice now. We run a detective agency in Las Cruces."

"I see. You didn't want to go into a state or federal agency?"

"No. You see, my sister and I are twins, and we like to work together." With the mention of twins, Tony could tell he now had his full attention.

"Are you staying busy? Las Cruces seems a pretty tame town."

"We stay busy. We've had to put people on a waiting list at times, but we have a good reputation, and people will even wait for availability."

"What are you working on right now — if you can talk about it, that is?"

Go get him, Tone!

"We're working on a difficult case right now. We're searching for a young woman's two front teeth." He paused, while the professor stared at him with a surprised and dubious look. Tony continued, "...and also for her memories!"

Suddenly understanding, Gunter's face fell. He panicked, he got up quickly almost knocking over his drink, and moved toward the door. Janos moved faster. Catching up to him, he grabbed the professor's forearm while steering him away from the exit and said, "Tony knows where you live, where you work, about the parties you have on a regular basis and a lot more. Why don't you come back to the bar with me, and we'll chat, civilized like."

Understanding his predicament, the professor walked back, looking down at the floor, and sat down again next to Antonio. An uneasy silence ensued.

Once the bartender had gone to help customers on the other side of the bar, Gunter asked, "What do you want from me?"

"Not for me, Gunter, rather for Danny. She needs a couple of new front teeth, to start with, and a nose job, too. But mostly she needs the last of her memories back."

Gunter nodded his head, then lowered it again as if in shame. "I'll pay for her dental work."

Tony did not let up. "Most of her memories have come back. It's only a matter of time before she figures out the whole story. But she still needs to remember the actual traumatic part. As of yesterday, she could not recall what happened at your last party. She knows she attended it, flew in from Austin, went to her motel, but what happened afterwards is still a blur. Can you help her?"

"Look, I just put these parties together. They are, in truth, just meetings of the mind, intelligent minds, mainly with some of my older students. We talk about various topics, usually about the conflicts humans encounter today, the changes we have to deal with in this new world, and how it differs from what we experienced one hundred years ago. At times, it gets a little political."

Tony, a little irritation in his voice, cut him short. "I don't need a lecture from you right now, Gunter. I need to know exactly what happened to her at the last party you had two weeks ago."

You go, Tone!

The man hesitated. He ordered another beer before looking toward the door as if ready to bolt again. Janos gave him a look: *just try it again, see what I'll do to you.* It worked.

"I'm... I'm really sorry. Please tell her that I'm really sorry. I introduced her to this new student, Angel. I don't know much about him. He seemed smart, but there was something different about him. I guess I noticed him because he seemed...intelligent but wild, very intense. He partook in the talks but it felt feigned with him, like he was trying to fit in. You know what I mean?"

"No! What do you mean?"

Tone, this man does not vet all the people who attend his parties. Parties are often crashed.

But he prizes himself on having special and limited attendance for his intellectual parties, therefore he is responsible for the outcome.

Not getting a response from the man, Tony continued in an icy tone, "Tell me about this Angel."

"He came with one of the women I invited. Invitees may bring one guest to my parties. She said Angel had attended a few of my classes and was interested in learning more. I don't usually let current students in. It's really my fault I let him in." He gulped the last sip of his draft beer and asked the bartender for another round. Janos accepted one more, but Tony kept on nursing his second drink.

"After a while, Angel and Danny were acting like they had known each other forever. I did not pay much attention to them, until they left together. At that time the party was winding down, and I just thought they were getting along and the rest was none of my business. John, another one of my older students, went along with them. They said they were going to get plastered somewhere else, as it was getting boring at my place." Gunter downed his beer and called for another.

"You're riding your bike tonight, professor?" the bartender asked.

"No! But these young men will give me a ride!"

Tony acquiesced and a new draft beer was soon standing in front of the professor.

"The three of them left. The next day I got a call at four in the morning. John said that Angel had gotten very drunk, and it made him crazy, and Danny was hurt. He said they were going to take her to the hospital emergency room. When I got there, they had already dropped her off and left. I did not dare go in, as police officers were standing by the emergency door. I should have gone in, but I was afraid of what Angel might have done. I'm a coward. Tell her I'm sorry. I never wished her any harm." Gunter was sniffling. He pulled out a handkerchief from his pants pocket and blew his nose. He kept apologizing for all the harm Danny had suffered.

"It's my fault. I'm so sorry. I did not know what Angel was going to do. I'm sorry. Please, let Danny know I never meant her any harm!"

After giving Gunter's car keys to the bartender, Tony drove him to his house, only a few blocks away.

~~~

Still snuffling a little, Gunter fumbled to unlock the door of an attractive, low adobe house tucked in the back of a well-manicured yard near the edge of the city. Janos and Antonio were invited in. In the ample living room, covering much of the walls and some of the furniture, were many African artworks: carvings, paintings, masks, and textiles. Overwhelming the whole room and facing the couch they were asked to sit on, hung a large canvas depicting a black gorilla hunched on his knuckles in the middle of a green, leafy jungle. Gunter disappeared for a few minutes into the kitchen, followed by Janos, who was not going to leave him alone until they had all the answers they needed. While Antonio was checking the room, trying to imagine the kind of parties that happened regularly in it, the two men came back with a platter of assorted cheeses and crackers, and a few bottles of beer and ginger ale. Tony opted for a non-alcoholic ginger brew and noticed that the professor was doing the same.

Although he had been silent on the ride back, Gunter, slightly slurring his words, started talking again, as if releasing a pent-up dam. "I went to see Danny in the hospital the next day, but she did not recognize me. I realized then that she could not recall any of what had happened to her. She must have trusted me somewhat, because she asked me to get her out of the hospital. I lied and told the hospital workers that she was my sister and filled out a bunch of paperwork. The doctors wanted to do more tests and said she would be ready to be released the next day. I went back, picked her up, and took her away from the city, so she would not be in any more danger. I really like her. She has always been one of my favorite students, and I don't want any more harm to come to her."

Tony got the last names and phone numbers of John and of Amber, the woman who had invited Angel to the party. Gunter again told them he would pay Danny's medical bills. By that time however, he was sprawled on another couch, barely able to keep his eyes open or to construct a full sentence. The drinks had taken their toll.

Tony and Janos left, confident they had some of the answers they were seeking. The phone call to John proved to be useless, as his answering machine said he was out of the country for the next few weeks. Amber, on the other hand, was home and said she would meet them at the twenty-four-hour laundromat next to her place.

~~~

The only person in the laundromat was a tall, slender, somber-looking young woman with limp, brown hair, grayish skin, thin lips, and sunken eyes, sitting on a chair facing a spinning washing machine. She stood up when they came in.

"Hi. I'm Amber. You called me? I don't know how much I can help. You said you are looking for Angel?" She spoke fast, as if in a hurry.

"Yes, we are. Thank you for meeting with us."

"No problem. I needed to catch up on my laundry. What do you need to know?"

Calmly, Tony answered, "As a start, how well do you know Angel?"

The woman did not slow down, her words still flowing fast, as if she had no time to waste. "I met him last month in one of Gunter's classes. After the class, he started talking and flirting with me. He is so handsome. Silly me, I was flattered. Most men don't even notice me. I thought he liked my mind. We talked. He seemed intelligent. That also attracts me in a man. Then a couple of weeks ago, I met him in a shop near the school. He invited me for a drink. Then he wanted to know what I was doing during the weekend. I said that I was going to a special party, one where we exchanged ideas rather than listening to loud music, dancing, and looking for one-night stands. He acted really interested and said he would love to watch me discuss any topic. Again, he flattered me. I fell for it. I invited him to Gunter's. The next day I met him outside the school, and we went to the party together. As soon as we got there, he ignored me, and before I knew it, he was flirting with Sophia and Danny, the two prettiest women in the room."

Antonio was worried that the trail had cooled down again. This woman did not really know the perp. "So, you had never seen him before you met him that first time?"

"No. I would have noticed him. He is really good-looking."

"When Angel left the party, did you go with him?"

"No. He did not even look at me once the whole time during the party. John and Danny left with him. I don't know why John went with them. Maybe because he's a friend of Danny's, I guess."

"Do you have any information about Angel? His last name, address, phone number?"

Amber looked upset. She would not look at Tony but kept staring at the washing machine, although it had stopped its cycle. "He introduced himself as Angel Villalobos. He did give me his cell number, but when I tried it the next day to tell him I changed my mind, and that he should not come to Gunter's, all I dialed was a disconnected number. I thought I had entered his number incorrectly. Now, I don't know. Maybe he never meant to give me his number. I tutor students on Saturday afternoons. He was waiting for me outside the school, the day of the party. Before we walked to Gunther', we went and had a drink at a bar. I should have dismissed him then, but I didn't."

She took a deep breath, and faced Tony. "That's all I know. I don't know where he lives. I don't remember seeing him inside the school, other than the one time. I don't know. Maybe Danny and John have his real number."

"Thank you, Amber. If you see him again, would you

give me a call right away, please," Tony said, as he handed her his business card.

~~~

Chapter 23

Car Chase

THE TWINS WERE GETTING READY TO GO TO
Rosetta's early the next morning, when they heard Tiger
barking loudly outside. Looking out the front window,
they spotted a brown van.

Is that the same van she was abducted in?

Let's follow it!

Tony quickly got into the Subaru, which was parked
outside the office. Tiger jumped in the front as soon as
the door was opened, and they followed the van. It slowed
down as it went past Mora's high school. Antonia could
see the school secretary getting out of a brand-new red
Mustang, turning around and squeezing her remote to
lock its door. But after slowing down to a crawl, the van
sped up past the fenced-in building, then turned left, and
left again, and again a third time around the block. The
Tonys tried to stay back until the van would turn the next
corner, so as not to be seen. Finally the driver went slowly
by the school again without stopping.

He spotted us!

No, don't think so. How could he, we just got started!

On her red stilettos, still standing by her car, the

secretary stared at the van going by.

She was waiting for him!

After going across the city, the van turned north onto the Interstate. They followed a safe distance back. Its license plate was not the same color they remembered. This one was black, with red and green chiles. They called it in to José, to see if he could come up with a name.

He called back a few minutes later. "I'm sorry, but it looks like this license plate was stolen from a Dodge sedan."

Another stolen plate!

As they hung up after thanking José for the information, they saw that the van had exited the highway for a smaller road parallel to the interstate.

José called back shortly after. "I'm worried that you could be in danger. Call me every fifteen minutes, with your whereabouts, please."

The brown van was slowing down and at once made a sharp turn to the left, onto a bridge crossing the interstate. The bridge was empty, but just before it, a big, dark-gray truck sat idling at the intersection. Inside, the driver was making a phone call. The tires on the truck were huge. One of those monster trucks, as seen in the big cities. A strange place for one of these, in the middle of farmland.

As soon as they passed the big truck, it started moving, following them onto the bridge, above the highway. At once, the truck sped up and quickly gained on them.

Don't like this, Tone.

It stinks of a set-up!

The brown van spotted us when we went by the school.

Right again, Sis.

She swerved all over the bridge, surprising the truck driver. He slowed down before gunning it again and, passing them on the left, he squeezed them against the small curb, hitting, then rubbing the side of the little car, obviously intending to run them off the overpass. She sped up, driving partly on the curb.

He missed us!

No, he's coming back!

He's gonna plow into us.

Antonia cleared the bridge, but the brown van was blocking the middle of the road in front of them. She jerked the wheel to pass the van on its right, just as the big truck hit the left side of her back bumper, less than ten feet past the bridge. Her Subaru had enough ground clearance as it jumped over the concrete edge, before knocking over the barbed wires between two fence posts, luckily not setting off the airbag.

Let me drive, Sis!

No, got it under control.

Am scared.

Me too! So help me make the right choice instead of trying to take over.

The truck had passed her sudden turn, skidded to a stop, backed up, then followed her off-road on a narrow ridge overlooking the interstate. Now it was gaining on them again, less than twenty feet behind. Then it rammed the smaller car again, this time hitting the back of it, pushing them further onto the dirt. Their neck snapped back.

That hurt!

We're alive!

And in danger!

Tiger had jumped to the floor of the back seat when the monster truck first scraped them. The smell of partially digested dog niblets invaded the car as the poor, frightened animal threw up her recent breakfast. The dirt ridge they were on was very narrow. A barbed-wire fence penned them in on their left; on their right, a perilously steep slope with scattered shrubs restricted them to the higher ground. They sped up, as best they could, well above the two lanes of the interstate, going the opposite way,

Hearing a loud pop behind them, they saw that the truck's front driver-side tire had blown up. He slowed down, and seemed to struggle to control the steering. Undeterred he soon was right back on their tail. She hoped the truck was all show but with not much horsepower.

All looks, half brain, like you, Tone.

Not now, Sis, you'll get us both killed!

He was too close. The grass was tall, never mowed, and the slope had many mesquite shrubs in the way. It was so steep, they would roll the car if they tried to go down it. She had to slalom through the brush and stay on the crest of the ridge as best she could.

No ruts, no holes, please!

Tiger whimpered.

"Be a good girl, stay down," she told her, in a wavering voice.

The truck was keeping pace with them, swerving as it went with its blown tire, and most of the time too wide to fit between the scrubby shrubs, just crushing them as it went, but not slowing down. Choosing the path of least resistance, their engines roaring in low gears, the two vehicles weaved through the mesquite, hoping their hard thorns would not puncture their tires. The ridge crest climbed up away from the highway. But suddenly, the hilltop neared its end and it angled downward again.

If I remember right, Sis, there is a big arroyo coming up.

Will slow down when getting down from this ridge and let him be right on our tail. Then will make my move onto the highway at the last second.

The truck was now only ten yards behind them, weaving like a snake, barely under control. In her rear-view mirror she could see the driver grinning. Good, maybe he would not anticipate her next move.

Don't let him get too close!

Moving away from the fence, she sped up as they headed downhill, the tires ripping up two new trails on the sand, still well above the highway. He sped up, too, and again was less than ten feet away. Was he going to try to ram them again? The large arroyo was looming on their left side. The slope was getting shallower.

Still going sideways downhill, the top-heavy truck almost flipped over, but the driver gunned it again to try to catch up and straightened his vehicle upright again. The arroyo, coming closer, was very deep. The guard rail suddenly loomed right in front of the Tonys. She jerked the wheel to the right and climbed out of the sand and grass onto the pavement. The car caught some air as she jerked her body and the wheel to the left, violently landing on the break-down part of the asphalt on all four tires, scraping the railing while facing the wrong side of traffic. Angrily honking, a big semi coming at them moved to the other lane, while they hugged the side of the brake-down lane to the middle of the bridge. They laughed nervously, shaking off the rush of the chase and the narrow escape. Antonio sent his sister a mental high-five.

Great job! Glad we took those extreme defensive driving classes, Sis.

Me, too, and thanks, could not have done it without you.

Looking in the rear-view mirror they saw that the monster truck had not fared so well and had climbed over the ramp-like beginning of the guardrail. Metal on metal, sparks flew. Tilting one way, then the other, still riding the rail, its wheels spun but could not grip any ground. They watched it listing too far on the driver's side, until its heavy weight toppled it into the arroyo.

They stopped just past the bridge, with the engine still running, to take a look. Over the edge, they saw that the truck had flipped over, three of its four wheels spinning up in the air, the cab partly crushed on the passenger side.

Then, astonished that anyone could survive that forty-foot fall, they saw a pistol smash the crumpled windshield. A hand came out and the gun started weaving back and forth, as if seeking a target. They ran back to their vehicle.

Both lanes on the highway were clear as they pulled a U-turn to make their way back to Las Cruces. But as they gathered a little speed, they realized that the Subaru was badly damaged. Something was screaming underneath the rear, the steering wheel was shaking so hard they could barely hold on to it, and the whole car pulled hard to the left. It was definitely not going to make it back home in that shape. The next town going back the other way was only a mile or two.

You probably destroyed the suspension after that last jump, Sis.

Sure, it was my fault, I was driving, not you!

Sorry! You did good, Sis.

They found a spot where emergency vehicles turned around, crossed over to the other side, and going north, they limped to Truth or Consequences, the nearest town.

As they neared the fatal arroyo on the other side of the highway, they noticed two cars had stopped and were looking over the edge.

Good! Someone besides us will call it in. Our name won't be mentioned on any form.

That bastard won't find out who we are that way.

With the hazard lights on, they slowly drove on the break-down lane.

They first called José, and explained what had happened.

"You'll have to report it!" was the first thing he said.

"Can we wait a little while, so the perps don't find out who we are?"

With hesitation in his voice, José continued, "Did you suffer a concussion? A head injury that could make you forget to call it in right away?"

"We did! Thank you, José."

"I'll keep you posted on what I find out about the driver. I'm going to call a friend in State Police. I'll tell him that I saw a truck upside down in an arroyo on the west side of I-25, see if he can give me any info. That should help us find the trail to Mora. And I'll look a little more into the school secretary. You said Lou already looked into her past. My sources don't always follow the letter of the rule. They may find something else."

They left a message for Rosetta, telling her that they would not be able to make it that day. Their last call was to a friend who managed a small, out-of-the-way motel, with amazing, steaming hot baths oozing right out the ground. T or C used to be called Hot Springs, and the many springs there are very soothing to aching muscles. There was also a massage therapist they had used before that would be helpful. Their neck and left arm were very sore.

By the time they got to town, the oil gage was blinking nonstop and smoke was oozing from under the hood.

Just killed my little car.

257

Yeah, but we're alive to talk about it.

Tiger was miserable. She was crouched on the floor, making herself as small as possible.

She won't even look at us.

No, but she's alive, too.

~ ~ ~

After a long, hot soak and a relaxing massage, they called a friend who had a garage in town. "Hey, Johnny. I was just chased by a lunatic who rammed me off the road into some mesquites and destroyed the car. Can you check it and hide it from sight. I sure don't want him to find me," whined Antonia.

Johnny, sounding worried, asked, "Is he local? You know who he is?"

"No idea! Maybe he does not like foreign cars. Anyway, I don't think I know him."

"Bring it by. I'll take a look at it."

After napping for a couple of hours, with Tiger on the foot of the bed, they felt much better and decided to take the Subaru to Johnny's shop. As the car would not start, Johnny came over to pick it up. Antonia and Tiger climbed beside him in the tow truck.

At his shop, he raised it off the floor and inspected the car with an incredulous look on his face. He wiped his hands on his pants legs before telling them, "I'm surprised you made it to town. You drove a few miles after the accident, you said?"

Shaking his head, he continued. "It looks like the engine is blown, there is a long crack in the oil pan, which let all of the oil seep out. Most of the suspension is gone. The dent on the backside will not let the hatchback open. The doors on the driver's side look like someone used a can opener on them. Sorry, but I think it's ready for the trash heap."

At once understanding her predicament, Antonia asked. "If you can work out an estimate, I'll call my insurance. And would you have a loaner car for a day or two?"

"I can do that, but I don't have a loaner. I'll take you to Manuel, he usually has a few rentals available. There is no way I'm gonna let you use my car, not the way you drive," he added with a big grin.

~~~

Chapter 24
José the Knight

DRIVING THE DODGE SUV THEY RENTED FROM Manuel, they got home in time to call both the insurance and the car leasing company, despite having to stop every fifteen minutes for a panting Tiger, who needed to get her land legs back. They decided to keep a small bottle of her potion in each of the vehicles in the future. Both the car insurance and the leasing companies wanted a police report, especially as the Tonys had told them that they had to escape to save their lives. They would obtain another vehicle as soon as the leasing company received the paperwork.

Then they called Sunny, asking him to contact the Sierra County Sheriff or the T or C police, as Antonia had not been thinking clearly earlier, and only wanted to get as far as possible from the maniac who had rammed her car over and over again.

The T or C police chief called her a few minutes later. "Hi, Ms. Urbani. This is Lieutenant Morales from the Truth or Consequences City Police. I understand you were in a vehicle accident earlier today, is that correct?"

"Yes, sir. I was chased and rammed by a madman in a large truck on my way to Williamsburg this morning."

"Ma'am, I do wish you had stopped at our station. We could have helped you, and we would have been able to get a full report from you. Can you come by right now? I can keep the office open until you get here."

"Thank you. But I am currently at home in Las Cruces, and not feeling up to traveling at the moment."

"Did you get hurt during that accident?"

"Well, sir, I did suffer a slight head concussion, just a bump, but my left arm is quite bruised. My seat belt saved me from further injuries although the air bag never went off. At the time, I was afraid for my life and only wanted to get away and be back home as soon as possible."

"I understand, ma'am. Can you come by the station tomorrow so we can have a complete report? Oh, by any chance, was the offending vehicle a large, gray truck with oversized tires?" Lt. Morales continued.

Sis, they're going to find the Subaru's matching paint on his truck. Be careful!

"I'm afraid I did not look in my rear-view mirror until I was well away from the truck. I was shaking so much from the impact. I thought the driver was trying to kill me. I just wanted to get away. However, I do remember that it seemed like a tall, dark truck with tinted windows, but I never saw the driver."

"Can you give me the make and color of your vehicle? We've impounded a truck involved in an accident, and there are some serious scrapes of a different color on the outside of the front and passenger sides."

Might as well let him know now, Sis.

"My car is, or I should say was, a dark-green Subaru

261

station wagon. It is currently in a garage on Cook Street, just off Broadway Street." Hoping to be done with the interrogation, she gave him the name and phone number of the garage. But the T or C chief was not finished. "Did you go to the hospital after the accident?"

"I did not, but I went to see a therapist I know in T or C. She was a nurse for many years. She assessed me and thought that I should get a CAT scan if I get dizzy or if I have any headaches tomorrow. She also palpated my arm and told me it was just bruised, not broken."

"Do you have any open or bleeding wounds?"

"No, sir. Just bruises."

Antonia gave the police chief the name and the number of her massage therapist and promised to come by to see him the next afternoon.

Their next call was to José.

"Tony, you'd better call Lou. He's got wind of what happened to you and has already put the two incidents together. He's very worried, but I think he's also angry that you didn't call him for help."

"Thanks, José. We'll give him a call. Did you find out anything about the gunman or the truck?"

"Some. The truck was stolen from a college kid in Tucson last year and had another vehicle's stolen plates on. You sure keep strange company. You always get in trouble with car thieves?"

"We don't look for trouble, José. It finds us without any problems. I guess that's the nature of the business."

"If you say so! You know you can ask for my help

anytime. How's your head?"

"We'll be OK. We'll see how we feel tomorrow and take it from there. We're sure tired, but we were told to stay awake until this evening and go to bed at our normal time."

"Would you like me to come over. I've had some medical emergency training in my working days."

"We're all right. It's just a couple of bruises. Besides, we called our mother and she's coming over to spend the night."

"I know Chief Morales. I helped him years ago, when he was just a rookie. He's a good guy, very thorough. He already took fingerprints from the truck, the nine-millimeter bullets and their cardboard case, which were scattered all over the cab. He'll let me know as soon as he finds something out."

Antonia was quiet for a while, reliving the chase, seeing the gun pointing out through the broken windshield.

Sensing her torment through the phone line, José continued, "You know, it's amazing that the perp walked out of that smashed truck. It must have had some substantial roll bars. Can I ride along with you for the next few days?"

"All right, José. Let's try tomorrow if we feel good enough to work. We're used to working alone, but this has shaken us up. We'll be glad to have your company, as well as an extra pair of ears and eyes."

"I only want to see you safe. My wife died a few years after the birth of our only child. And...when my son was nineteen years old, he was in a car accident. A head-on collision. He died instantly. I still miss him. I will always miss him. I wish I could have protected him better. It's been...I guess, you fill that gap. I won't go in when you see your clients. I'll wait in the car, but I'd like to at least accompany you while this maniac is out there."

"Very well, our knight in shining armor." Antonia laughed. "We're planning on going to Deming early in the morning, barring any headaches. We'll call you and you can come to the house for breakfast at six."

José replied, "I'll be there at six, even if you decide not to go. And no breakfast, just a cup of coffee. I usually eat my first meal at five."

Next, Antonia called Lou, and left a voice mail to let him know that she had been in an accident, that she was fine, although a little bruised, and that she wanted to get some sleep before talking anymore about it.

Sirena came by to check on them. She had kept up with basic emergency training and wanted to be sure they were OK. She prepared them dinner and ate with them before taking Tiger for a walk. As they retired to bed, they told her, "Thanks for coming over. You know we're never too old to be mothered." Mother and children had tears in their eyes as they said good night.

~~~

The next morning, at a quarter to six, José was at the

door with two empty thermos cups in his hand, which the twins promptly filed with strong black coffee. Sirena had left for work, a couple of hours earlier. Just as they were getting ready to leave to go see Rosetta, Lou called back and immediately asked Antonia how she was feeling.

"I'm doing much better, thanks, Lou. I do have a huge bruise on my arm, but no headaches, no dizziness, no cuts. Still shaken by it all, though."

"Good! I've been working with Chief Morales, from T or C. I put in a good word for you and your brother. We should have the fingerprint report later this morning. The guy also left some blood behind. We'll have his DNA on hand, too, in a couple of days."

"Thanks again, Lou. Please, let me know as soon as you get any findings."

"I will, but only if you tell me what you're working on. Do you think you know this guy?"

"No, I have no idea who it was, but I think he is connected to a case we're working on. Remember that fancy secretary at the high school, the one with a shady past?"

"I sure do! Is she connected to the driver of the truck?"

"We have reasons to think she might be."

"When are you going to let me fully in the loop? After another accident? This is a police matter, you know."

"We'll talk, Lou. As soon as I can spare a few minutes. I promise."

She had barely hung up when Sunny called. He, too, wanted to know how she was doing. She explained that she was fine, but had to leave right away to go see someone in Deming.

"You want an escort? I don't have anything pressing at the moment."

"Thanks, but I'll be fine. I'm going to see someone who may not be receptive to talking with a lawman by my side."

"I'll stay in the background. But I'll have you in my sight that way! I'm worried about you."

"I know you are. I've noticed the city patrol car passing by every half hour since last night. I'll be fine. You remember José? He or my brother will be with me all day. No worries, OK?"

Then the Tonys, José, and Tiger rushed out and jumped into Antonio's white pickup to go see Rosetta, hoping to get there in time to talk to Mora. They were anxious to hear from her after missing their customary rendezvous the previous day.

~~~

While José waited in the pickup with his phone, a thermos of coffee, and a mystery paperback, Antonia went inside Rosetta's cave.

Mora answered her right away. "Hi, Tiger. Hi, Tonia. Hi, Rosa. I waited for you yesterday. I thought something bad happened to you. Are you OK?"

"I'm fine! Although I was just in a car accident, that's why I could not talk to you yesterday morning."

"But you did not get hurt, right? I don't want you to stop talking to me."

"I'll try not to miss anymore of our talks. Let me ask you, do you know a boy named Leo?"

"Leo, that's lion, right? No, I don't know him."

"It doesn't matter. Tell me what's happening on your side."

The young girl explained how she was learning more Japanese, mostly greeting forms, and also learning how to serve tea.

"It's difficult to do it right, you know. It's like a ceremony. Miss Manners says it's an art. You have to do it just right. There is a big difference between serving tea the American way or the Japanese way."

Still trying to find out her whereabouts, Antonia continued, "Can you get outside in the courtyard?"

"I don't think so. Papa Patron does not want us to go outside. And I'm scared of his wolf!"

"Can you ask him if he would make an exception? Tell him you're getting pale, that you need some sunlight?"

"Papa Patron doesn't come to see us very often. Only when somebody does something he doesn't like. I don't want to make him mad. I'll have to ask Imelda and Josette and Miss Manners."

Mora was gone again. Not much learned that day, but that Miss Manners had knowledge of the complex Japanese tea ceremony.

She may have been to Japan?

Or have Japanese ancestry?

If properly taught, that could take days.

They hoped they had a few more days before Mora would be filmed or moved out of her prison. Time to see if they could help Leo find his medallion.

~~~

Chapter 25
El Descanso

AFTER THE SESSION WITH MORA, ANTONIO donned his garb, getting ready for Rosetta's search. Woody drove up just as everyone was leaving the Cave. He and Mrs. LaFleur were introduced to the patient José, who had been stretching his legs while waiting outside. Rosetta got in the passenger seat of Tony's truck, Tiger hopped in the back, and Woody invited José to join him in his turquoise-colored, vintage Ford pickup.

The two trucks drove in tandem to an area a dozen miles east of Kingsburg. Rosetta held a rectangular wooden box on her lap, that she insisted on keeping with her. She explained that her divining tools were in the box, she had freshly energized them that morning. They could not be far away from her until she found the medallion or they could lose some of their properties.

A small cluster of mobile homes, half a mile from the highway, huddled together in a long hollow. With Woody leading, they pulled up to the last trailer in the lane. A raked dirt yard, with only a couple of pots of marigold on each side of the door, made the place look almost deserted. On a chain, a scrawny, brown mutt, part Rottweiler, mostly

Heinz-57, got out of his little dog house and barked at them.

A frail-looking child about twelve years old opened the door. The worried look on his face transformed to a smile when he saw the kind woman and he let them in. After petting Tiger on the head, he told them that the dog could not come in. His auntie did not allow animals in the house. José went with Tiger, past the barking dog, to wait in Tony's truck.

The child's auburn hair was neatly combed and his suntanned, freckled skin was scrubbed almost raw. His clothes, obvious hand-me-downs, were frayed but clean, creased, and ironed. He shook hands with Woody. Then Rosetta introduced Antonio.

Leo told them that he was home alone. He had been feeling sick ever since the day he lost his lucky medallion. The living room of the older mobile home showed a lot of wear and tear but was impeccably clean. They sat down on a clear-plastic covered sofa, while Leo almost disappeared inside a large armchair across from them.

Rosetta asked him to tell Tony his story from the beginning. Tentatively at first, but then mustering up his courage, he started a long rambling story. "Some of the kids at school don't like me. They're always picking on me, 'cause I'm the only one with red hair at school, and 'cause I don't have a mom and a dad anymore. They call me 'Red Orphan', but my auntie is my new mom now.

She's my real mama's sister. She takes care of me, with my cousin Nina. My other cousins are older, and they don't live here 'cause there's no jobs here. My cousin Nina is almost eighteen, and she doesn't go to school anymore. She got a job in Kingsburg, at the supermarket, and she brings food back, and she's here a few minutes after the school bus drops me off — when I go to school. But I don't want to go to school without my mom's medal, 'cause I'm afraid something bad is gonna happen to me. My auntie doesn't know that's the real reason. I told her that I was feeling sick to my stomach, and she said that if I did my homework and the chores, then I could stay home. Excuse me."

He got out of the big chair, walked to the kitchen, and soon came back with a pitcher, some glasses, and folded paper towels. He offered them some water before returning to his story. After exchanging an appreciative glance, they all solemnly took the water they were offered.

"Sam is this big bully at school. So, last week, Sam and Joey and Fat and Teddy did not let me get on the bus after school. They were all around me, and they told the bus driver that my cousin was going to pick me up, so he could leave. Then after the bus left, they kicked me and punched me in the stomach, and Joey grabbed my medallion, and broke the chain and tossed it behind him in the sand. I looked for it, but I couldn't find it. I don't know if they took it or if they kicked it in the dirt. So I cried, 'cause my mama gave me that medallion and I don't have anything else from her. They called me a crybaby and they left. Then

I called Nina and she picked me up on her way home. Nina had heard about you, Madame Rosetta, and she said you had special talents and you could help me find my medallion." His lower lip began to tremble. As he lost his composure, he turned to the big woman, who invited him with open arms. He buried himself in her ample bosom, his shoulders racked by big sobs.

Rosetta, patting his back, took the story over. "There, there! We'll find it. That's why I brought my friends with me today. So, after Nina called me, I came with Woody to see you, and we looked all around the school, but we could not find it. I drew my cards, and they told me that your talisman had flown to another place. I did not have the right tools with me then to find out where that was, but today I do, and with Woody and Tony and his dog Tiger, we are going to find it. Then, I turned over one more card on that day. It showed two children, a boy and a girl, holding hands, walking on a trail in the distance. They are following a large, dark bird, while a full moon lights up the way. Below them are daggers threatening to cut them off from the rest of the world. So I knew we had to work fast, and that Tony here, and Tiger, the dog outside, had to be involved, as they are both looking for a young girl who has something to do with you, somehow. I think that's the girl next to you in the picture."

Self-assured once more, the boy straightened out, rubbed his eyes, and went back to the big chair. "What's her name?"

Tony answered his question. "Her name is Mora. She told us that she does not know you. But Madame Rosetta thinks you will meet her, eventually. Is there anything else you want to tell us that would help us in finding your medallion?"

"Can I tell you about Mama and Papa? Would that help you find my medal and this girl?"

"Yes." Gently, Tony answered, sensing that Leo needed to tell them more. The poor child had so much grief written on his face. "Yes, tell me about your parents, please."

Looking down at the floor, while trying very hard not to cry, he spoke in a faint voice, "Mama said that Papa got sick when he worked for the road department. He got sick after he was cleaning up some yellow dirt with his front-end loader. A big semi truck was in an accident one day and some big barrels filled with yellow powder fell off the truck. Then Papa buried all the powder and the big barrels in a big hole on the side of the road and returned the loader to town. The next day some people wearing white suits with white helmets and white masks and white shoes came and dug up everything my dad had done. They even closed the road and dug it up, too. Then they put some new dirt and some new road stuff over the hole. And then they stole his front-end loader, so he did not have a job anymore."

Leo had started silently crying again and Rosetta got up and held one of his hands, while combing his hair with her fingers. The boy stopped crying and seemed more confident as he continued. "He got very sick. He was throwing up all the time. Mama said that was because they took his front-end loader. Then he got warts all over and they got bigger and bigger. And his hair fell off, and he could not eat, and he could not get out of bed, and... and the ambulance took him to the hospital. And then, he died."

Don't remember hearing about a nuclear-waste accident around here.

That doesn't mean it didn't happen.

Could be some other toxins.

The boy sniffled for a while, before Rosetta gently asked him, "Tell us about your mother."

He grabbed a paper towel and wiped his nose, but his tears started flowing again. "Mama had a little baby before Papa died. But my baby sister Carmencita died when she was born and went to see Papa in heaven. Then Mama also went to be with Papa and Carmencita. And then I went to live with my aunty and my cousins." Rosetta hugged him tight, as he buried his head into her chest again and cried.

"So, how did you get that medal?" asked Antonio, trying to change the subject when Leo's shoulders quit heaving.

The boy sat up straight in the armchair. "After Papa and my baby sister died, Mama had it made special. It came in the mail. On one side there is a skinny man with a beard. On the other side there is a fat man with a head like an elephant. But it's a good elephant. He protects people. Mama told me that the two saints would look after me if she had to go live in heaven, too. That's why I have to find it. That's the only thing I have of my mama. And I want the two saints to look after me." He nodded once, stood up, and facing the three of them on the couch, he placed his fists on his hips as if to tell them to do something.

"All right, let's go look for it," Antonio told him, guiding him to the outside, his hand on his shoulder. Everyone got in the two trucks, and soon were traveling toward Kingsburg, on a road adjacent to the superhighway.

~~~

As they started their journey, Rosetta, once again in the passenger seat, had asked her divining wands for help with a direction of travel. In her hands, she held loosely two thin, copper bars, both bent at a right angle. The rods, seeming to move on their own, drew parallel, and pointed to the west. She had also brought a map and a pendulum, among the array of gris-gris in her wooden suitcase. Besides her set of old cards and the dowsing rods, Tony had no idea as to what the rest of her stuff was for. She lit a chunk of incense inside a small porcelain bowl. Despite the windows being rolled partly down, the burning myrrh smoke rose straight up. Before buckling her seat belt, she held her pendulum over the map. It was turning in tight circles, counter-clockwise. Leo was in the back seat with Tiger, holding her tightly by the neck, while trying to look over Rosetta's shoulders, fascinated by her activities.

Every quarter-mile, Rosetta would ask Tony to pull over while she consulted her pendulum and her rods. Finally, when they stopped once more, about ten miles from Kingsburg, the pendulum did not spin, but started pulling to the left, oddly moving sideways, its straight cord defying gravity. She raised her rods; these also veered to the left. All they could see was a narrow dirt road taking off toward the south, and a large patch of ground completely barren but for a couple of scrubby, leafless trees on one side of the lane. Above them a large raven circled clockwise, over and over.

Woody and José stopped behind them, and seeing it was taking longer this time, the two men stepped out of the antique truck. On the freeway that ran parallel to the small county road, the big trucks roared north of them.

At once getting caught up in the excitement, Leo almost jumped out of his seat. Pointing his finger back toward the highway, he shouted, "Look! Look here. See that cross with all the flowers and the little yellow toy backhoe? See it?"

Following his finger, half way between the small road and the interstate, they saw the *descanso*, a large white cross covered with red plastic flowers, buffeted back and forth by the turbulent winds of the passing semis. A fatal accident shrine, like so many dotting the New Mexican highways.

Catching his breath with a big sigh, Leo continued, "Me and Mama, we put up that altar for Papa, so whenever we see it we know that he is in heaven. This is where he buried the yellow powder. Mama said this is where he started dying, that's why we put it there."

They let the child settle down. Two more ravens joined the first one and lazily circled overhead. Woody and José jumped in the bed of Tony's truck, and Antonio drove slowly on the dirt path for a couple of hundred yards, directly opposite Leo's father's memorial. Rosetta had Tony stop the truck by the second of the wind-blown trees, as her rods were practically leaping out of her hands. The thin wisp of smoke from the incense wafted outside her window, then wrapped itself high around the barren plant. She asked Tony and Woody to look inside an old nest made of strings, feathers, and dead branches at the top of the tree.

Woody knit his hands together and told Tony to step into them. Then he lifted him high so Tony could look up into the nest. It was empty, abandoned, and full of bird droppings, but there was something shiny at the bottom of the nest: a medallion showing its Asian elephant face.

After wiping the medal on his shirtsleeve, Tony handed it to the boy. "Is this what you've been missing?"

Leo was crying and laughing at the same time, then he was screaming to the wind: "Mama, I found you. Mama, come back. Please, come back Mama! I don't wanna stay with Auntie Josette. I wanna go back to our home with you."

Tony asked Leo to repeat the name of his aunt, not sure he had heard correctly.

"Auntie Josette."

Josette, Sis.

That's the link!

Hot tears were now pouring out of the boy. Woody grabbed him around his shoulders, then held him tight against his chest, saying, "Now, boy. My parents disappeared when I was a baby and gave me nothing to hold on to. I did not even know their faces. My grandma took care of me. I thought she was mean at first, but she was just old, old and tired, and trying to raise me the right way. When she had the money, she bought me a set of drums and told me to take my anger out by banging on them. So I did, and it helped me deal with my parents being gone. And later, it helped me with my grandma being gone. Music is the healer, boy. Are there any musical instruments in your aunt's house?"

The boy stopped crying but did not answer.

As they returned Leo to his home, Tony asked him what his aunt did for a job.

"She cleans this place in the middle of nowhere. She leaves early in the morning, at six, that's when she wakes me up for school, and then she comes back at the same time as the school bus."

Definitely her! Tone, we're going to find Mora!

"Do you know where that place is?"

"No. She can't take kids there, she said. It's not a place for kids."

"Does she drive or does someone pick her up?"

"She drives! Even on Sundays. Me and Nina, we have to go to church by ourselves."

Tony asked Leo if he had a picture of Josette. Above some shelves, there was a color photograph of a couple showing, on one side, a narrow-faced brunette wearing a lot of makeup.

She does look like a mouse!

They found out the make of her car.

Maybe one of our official friends can tag her car?

Leo went into a corner of the living room, turned on a cheap electric piano, and banged on the keyboard.

"Good! Get it out of your system, boy!" Woody sat on the bench next to him, and started playing a soft melody on the low range of the keyboard. Leo stopped and asked him if he could teach him how to play.

"I can, boy. But I don't know much about pianos. I'm really a drummer. I like to play the bongo drums."

Rosetta interjected, "And he is really good, too. Maybe if you come to Deming once a week, he can teach you the piano!" She winked at Woody and raising one eyebrow and one shoulder, she looked at him questioningly. He looked back, nodded in acquiescence, and smiled at her. As they left, they could hear the child slowly tapping one note after the other.

~~~

The tied-up mutt outside barked a goodbye after them, all the way to the trucks.

"You were right again, Rosetta. Those cards of yours are miraculous. We're going to have the cops or the border guys track Josette to where she works. We know we are right on this," Antonio said, as they all stood by his truck. Rosetta opened her suitcase on the front seat. She grabbed her deck of cards, shuffled it, and asked Tony to pick a card.

"The top one," he said reverently. She nodded and flipped it over.

"Full circle, with much danger," she said, looking at a snake biting its own tail. Above the encircling serpent, lightning bolts shot out of dark clouds. Below it, two alligators were fighting, their toothy mouths squarely engaged.

After giving Tony a hug and telling him again to be careful, Rosetta rode back with Woody. On their way to Las Cruces, the twins and José talked about all the possible avenues available to them. Antonia explained that it was only with the help of Rosetta and Tiger that she had been able to reach the missing girl.

"I've never worked with a psychic dog before!" José said with a grin. "But Madame Rosetta is quite a resource. What a woman! I wish I had known her when I was working for narcotics!" he continued. "What does she mean, full circle?"

"She does not tell us everything, only what she sees. Sometimes it is murky. But I read this as everything will get resolved," Antonio answered.

Antonia's voice chimed in, "Tony is the perpetual optimist, while I fear for the girl. So much could go wrong, especially as they are armed and not new at this disgusting game. I also fear for Leo. He is a sweet child who has suffered enough, and does not need to lose yet another parent."

They explored a few strategies to rescue Mora safely.

José suggested. "Between the two, I mean the three of us, we have access to many legal resources. Maybe they can all be involved and work together."

"Yes, but we need to be careful not to let CBP or the FBI take over the whole operation. They may only want to bust the perps, and could incarcerate the children for a while. We both fear for Mora's life. We also need to know if Josette is in on it. My sister is right. Leo can't afford to be orphaned again, but what if the woman is guilty...," Antonio trailed off.

José replied, "We must contact all available resources and urge them to work together. But as you know, in cases involving kidnapping over state lines, the feds are in charge. I don't know if they will let any other police agencies work with them."

~~~

Chapter 26

A Dark Angel

THERE WERE A FEW STOPS TO MAKE BEFORE THEY could relax that day. In Deming, they grabbed a quick bite at El Otro Taco, a new-age Mexican restaurant offering tuna tacos and beer-batter rellenos. Before leaving, Antonio went for a quick change of clothes in the bathroom, which brought a knowing smile on José's face when Antonia came out. She drove to Las Cruces to visit Danny. When she stopped, José took Tiger to the back of the motel for a short walk.

After knocking softly on the door, seeing the smile on the woman's almost-restored face, Antonia queried, "Hi, Danny. Anything new today?"

The young woman was dressed with some of her own clothes from the bag that one of Lou's deputies had dropped off. "Thanks so much for getting my travel bag back to me. My calendar has helped me recover even more of my past. When I called the lab in Austin, the director was very understanding. He told me that my job was still waiting for me. After I said I liked the Southwest, he replied I was the most thorough coroner he had ever had. I may even get a raise."

"That's great news! And a good recommendation if you're still interested in coming out here. I, too, have information for you. My brother and one of his friends went to see Gunter Schmidt. They met him at a bar he frequents after classes. Once he knew that you were remembering most of what happened to you, he told them that he would pay for your dental work. He feels responsible for what happened. He is willing to meet with you, if that would help you recover faster."

"I guess Gunter is all right, but I don't want to see him until I am fully recovered. Also, I've got dental insurance and it should pay for most of the work. He can pay for the deductible. I don't know yet if I'm going to have it done here or in Texas. Did he say anything else?" she asked with a worried look on her face.

"He did. He told my brother that you left his party early. Yes, you were there that weekend. He said that you left with two men while it was still going strong."

Danny looked puzzled, she obviously did not remember that point in time.

Antonia's phone vibrated in her pocket. Excusing herself, she looked at the caller's number, 'Lou'. She decided to ignore it. As she was getting ready to tell Danny the names of the two men, her phone buzzed again. Lou again. She put the phone back in her pocket. "So, Gunter said you left with two men named John and Angel." Danny's face blanched, and she started rubbing her hands.

The phone vibrated again and this time Antonia

answered it. "Yes, Lou. I'm working with a client right now. Is this urgent?"

"Hi, Antonia. You never showed up at the precinct. Not only am I worried, but Sunny is worried, and Lieutenant Morales is worried too."

"I'm fine, Lou. Just real busy!" She said with a tone of annoyance in her voice.

Sitting on her bed, still dry-washing her hands, Danny interjected, "Go ahead, I can wait. This sounds urgent."

"Thanks, Danny!"

She moved to the far side of the room. "So, Lou, what cannot wait for me to come see you in an hour or two?"

"Antonia, look! You may be in a lot of danger. Morales said that they found fresh blood on the front fender of the truck. Since you don't have any open wounds, we both think it could belong to someone else the driver may have ran over, unless it belongs to him when he got out of the truck through the destroyed windshield. We've matched the fingerprints inside the truck to a dangerous perp. We're talking drugs, gun running, prostitution, and a whole lot more."

She opened her tablet ready to take notes. "Look, Sunny's got surveillance going by my place every half hour. I've got a friend who's an ex-cop staying with me all day long. Quit worrying, please."

Lou interrupted. "An ex-cop? I'm jealous! Who is he?"

"Oh, stop it! You know him: ex-narc, packs a gun. It's José. OK!"

"Why didn't you say earlier it was José? I heard he helped your brother with Jack Overmyer. Morales told me he worked with him years ago. Actually, José is the one who called me about your accident."

"He did?" she said innocently. "OK. So now, you're gonna tell me the perp's name?"

"Slow down, will you? José is a good man. He was just worried about you. That's why he called me. So anyhow, the guy's name is Angelo Villalobos Sanchez."

She repeated the name aloud, entering it in her tablet. "Angelo Villalobos Sanchez, is that right?"

Danny leaned back on the bed, then turned on her side away from Tony and started sobbing, her hands now furiously rubbing each other.

"I've got to go. Thanks, Lou. I'll be there in a while." She hung up and turned to the woman quivering on the bed. "Danny! Danny, talk to me. Is this the same Angel that harmed you?"

Don't even start, Tone!

Didn't say a thing!

Sensing you fine! Remember Rosetta and her full circle. Should have been wolves at the bottom of that card, not African crocodiles!

How can this incident be related to Mora?

Don't know yet. Let's help this woman first!

Danny was shaking her head back and forth, unable to talk. Tony went to get a wet towel in the bathroom and placed it on her forehead. The cold helped the woman calm down. Gopal, the hotel manager, knocked on the door, asking if everything was all right. Cracking open the door, with the chain latch on, Antonia replied that they were fine, but could he fix them a couple of cups of soothing herbal tea. Gopal told her he'd be back soon.

"See, Danny. Even Gopal is watching over you."

Danny stopped her tears. Then she sat up, briskly rubbing her hands again. Antonia wiped her face with the towel, then wrapped her arm around the woman's shoulders. They both sat still quietly, side by side, waiting until the motel owner came back with two steaming cups of Chamomile tea. When she opened the door, she saw José, just behind Gopal. She nodded to him with a smile, to let him know that everything was under control.

Danny told her what she remembered. After they left the party, she thought Angel had laced her drink with some drug, maybe a date-rape drug. She'd ask for the toxicology report from the hospital when she felt better, as they had not given it to her, not knowing her name or background. She told Antonia that they drove to a motel. She vaguely remembered going into the room while John waited outside in the car. Angel looked menacing as he demanded that she get undressed. When she did not want to have sex with him, he smashed his fist into her right eye. Then he continued to hit her face over and over again. She recalled screaming, but the head blows or the drugs, or both, must have made her lose consciousness. When she woke up, she was in the hospital. She was glad now that John or someone else had helped her. Without help, she could have died in that motel room.

After another quiet pause, tears still running down her cheeks, she declared that she was ready to make a deposition and a formal complaint against Angel Villalobos. While she took a shower, Antonia briefed José on the latest. He told her that while she was inside the room with Danny, he also had just found out the perp's name, from Morales.

"But I thought Villalobos-Sanchez attacked you because you were on the trail to find Mora's abductors?"

"I think the two are connected. Remember Rosetta's 'full circle fraught with dangers?' Somehow the two are connected."

"You're spooking me now, *mi hija!*" He said, calling her his daughter.

~ ~ ~

After notifying Lou that the three of them were coming to the station, they piled in the truck. Tiger was tired of being driven around after having to stay in the truck most of the day, so they dropped her off at the agency on the way. A few minutes later, they walked into Lou's office. Lt. Morales was waiting with him. He stood up and shook hands with José. Then lifting his hat, he nodded toward the two women. José asked him to come with him to an adjacent room. They had business to talk about, he said.

Danny gave Lou her deposition, with as many of the gruesome details as she could remember, naming Angel Villalobos as her attacker. He had not used his second last name with her, but she clearly identified him among the many pictures the sheriff showed her, although these were mostly school pictures from El Paso. The most recent photo they had of him came from an old Texas driver's license. It showed a dark-haired, dark-eyed adolescent, sixteen at the time, wearing an arrogant smile. A computer image aging him artificially, part of their pending files, was brought up. Danny had the police's virtual artist change a few details: smooth the hair back, sink both cheeks a little, add a small scar splitting one of his eyebrows in two, and a thin mustache above his lips.

Looking at the final sketch, Danny pronounced Angelo Villalobos Sanchez the definite culprit. A warrant for his arrest was issued. Lou advised her that there were already many warrants out for the man, but that so far, he had always managed to slip under the radar. He also thought the man was most likely using assumed names and fake IDs. She declined pressing charges against John and Gunter, saying that both had probably saved her life. Lou told her that he wanted to get a deposition from them, to further his investigation.

Morales and José walked into Lou's office when Danny walked out. Antonia gave the lieutenant her deposition, this time explaining the whole story, including the run around the high school, the chase, the attacking truck, and how it was all connected to looking for a runaway child as part of her job.

"My! Miss Urbani, you do keep busy! A runaway and a rape victim! Anytime you want to come work for me in T or C...," Morales trailed off. He had her sign his paperwork and, satisfied that he had gotten to the bottom of the story, he left.

~~~

Lou had a deputy take Danny back to her motel. He could not wait to talk to Antonia. "José, I'm sure glad you're keeping an eye on our friend, here. If you don't mind, I have a few more questions for her."

Antonia interrupted him. "José is working for us at the moment. I'd prefer if he stayed. If something confidential comes up, I will let him know and he can wait outside."

The older man nodded with a smile and said, "I'm still your bodyguard, but I prefer to stay outside the room."

"Thanks, José. Antonia, you're sure you don't have a concussion?"

She shook her head sideways.

Turning to José, Lou continued. "You see, the Tonys and I go back quite a few years. We have helped each other on various matters. We have no secrets."

José lifted an eyebrow but said nothing as he turned around and walked out of the room.

"Show me that bruise on your arm. You're sure it's not fractured?"

Pulling up her left sleeve, Antonia showed him a huge, purplish bruise on the side of her arm. Lou winced at the sight.

"Don't faint on me now. I'm fine. It's just a bone

bruise. But we do need to talk. Seriously talk. I need help from the sheriff's department, the city police, namely Sunny, the Border Patrol, maybe the State Police, and who knows what other local agencies with SWAT teams. It is imperative that not a word gets out before these teams move in, or the life of a few young girls may be at risk."

"Who made you commander in chief?" Lou said brisling at the biting remark.

"Sorry, Lou! But I really fear for this young girl. I do not wish any more harm done to her."

"If this is a kidnapping, we'll have to involve the FBI, Antonia."

She scowled at him. "Let me get José back in. He knows more about how the feds work than you or I."

The old man walked in as Antonia was adding, "And I'm afraid if we involve the FBI, they will take over and will not care for the life of a young Hispanic runaway."

"If this is a kidnapping, we have no choice but to involve the FBI, Antonia."

She stared at Lou. "Right now, she is a runaway!"

"Woman, you are so strong-headed!" Turning to José, who had watched the two spar, Lou asked, "What do you think?"

"Unless one of us can informally discuss the problem with an FBI agent, I think she may be right. But with Sanchez in the picture, we will have to involve CBP or ICE. From my past experiences with Border Patrol, I know if they take over the whole operation, the girl could be in danger! They may even move her to a holding facility, thinking she is a Mexican national, if she doesn't have her papers with her."

Lou slammed his fist onto the table. He stared at Antonia, with narrowed eyes. He opened a yellow notepad, grabbed a pen and with a frustrated sight, told her,

"Hell! Woman! I want to know everything that is going on with this young girl, right now. I will not let you out of this office until you have told me the whole truth!"

She relented, too tired to fight any longer. "All right. Could you call in Sunny? Ask him to come over. He can help with Customs and Border Protection. Then I won't have to tell my story twice."

Calming down after his outburst, Lou agreed.

You know he is only afraid for your life.

Right! It has to come out if we're going to get their help. It might as well be now.

~~~

Fifteen minutes later, Sunny walked in with a big grin. He sobered up immediately after seeing Lou, José, and Antonia's long faces.

Antonia started at the beginning, about her interest in the dog, about finding and then talking with the girl's mother and others who knew the girl. Finally, watching closely for Lou's and Sunny's reactions, she talked about Rosetta's help and involvement. Lou just listened, frowning now and then, while Sunny only nodded his head at the mention of the clairvoyant. She continued, explaining how most days she was able to learn a little more about the girl's predicament through the medium's help, until they found the cook and maid who worked at the place the girl is being held. Finding that woman meant that they had been right all along.

Seeing that now they were riveted to her every word, Antonia continued, "So this is where we stand at the moment. We have a probable person partially involved in what could be a child porn business. Possible multiple abductions of young girls with promises of movie fame. A madman with the name of Villalobos who tried to kill me when I followed one of his henchmen, and who could be related to an older bossman who calls himself Papa Patron and may have a pet wolf. CBP and ICE are currently looking for someone who calls himself El Patron de los Lobos. Too many probables! Of course, I mostly know all this through a clairvoyant. But I think we have real criminals on our hands and we finally know where they are operating. How do you think we should rescue these young girls without creating additional harm to them?"

Sunny and Lou were silent, digesting what she had just told them.

José took the lead. "I've been there for some of these uncanny events. I believe every word Antonia has told us. I can personally vouch for the authenticity of what happened in the last two days — including that of this amazing medium. I know we are told to ignore ninety-nine percent of the crazies that come up with visions and whatnot. But Madame LaFleur, I mean Mrs. Rosetta LaFleur, is the genuine thing. I have seen her in action, and I am really impressed with her aptitude. I also think that the criminals may now be wary, after Antonia followed one of theirs. It will only make the problem more difficult and more urgent to resolve."

Sunny took a moment before adding, "I've heard of LaFleur. She's helped one of my uncles find a suicide victim up north. He works with state police, in Ops. I'll give him a call."

They were quiet for a while longer, feeling overwhelmed by the tasks ahead. The only one obviously not fully convinced was Lou. "Hell! We'll be working on hearsay and voodoo. No one is going to take us seriously. No offense, Antonia! But this is a little too weird even for me."

José and Sunny almost in unison said, "I believe her!"

Lou continued, "I'm going to call Sheriff Muñoz, Edward Muñoz, in Hidalgo County. He may have heard something. Maybe we can get his help too."

José interjected. "I don't know, Lou. I don't like it. The Josette woman's last name is Muñoz, if I remember correctly. What do you think, Antonia?"

She replied without hesitation. "You're right. I remember Leo telling us about his aunt's last name being Muñoz. All the people in that small village must talk to each other. Maybe half a dozen mobile homes, total. We don't want the word to get out, and have someone talk to the wrong person. I think they would all disappear, move their whole operation somewhere else, and then we would loose sight of all those kids."

Lou was quick to the point. "Kids! I thought there were only two. A boy and a girl. How many are we talking about here?"

Seeing Tony's distress, José took over. "The boy Leo is not involved. He's only a ward of the Josette woman. The girl Mora, talks about another six or seven young girls her age in the whole building."

Antonia chimed in, staring at Lou. "If I'm correct, from all this voodoo thing, there are seven girls, eleven or twelve years old, and one older girl, maybe eighteen. All are in danger of being used as prostitutes, or sold as slaves, or used in kiddy-porn flicks. We cannot wait on this. I may know someone in the FBI. I don't know if she can help. I don't even know if I have the right agency for her, but I can feel it out and see. Let me talk to that person and get back to you. Sunny, maybe you could have your cousin, Carlos, in Kingsburg, tag the Josette woman's car, without giving him too much information. We haven't talked to him since last week, before the accident."

José said gently, "Antonia, your brother talked to him a couple of mornings ago."

"You're right! He did. It feels like a week ago. I think I need some sleep."

Lou could not help himself. "Why don't you ask your brother to take over?"

"I was the one involved in the accident, but I'll talk to him. Thanks for everything Lou. Thanks for all your help. Do you think we could meet tomorrow, late morning?"

Lou, glad to be in charge again, seemed to have made his decision. "Yeah! You call your mysterious agency friend. Sunny, can you get in touch with your cousin with CBP and tag the Josette woman's car? We need that exact location. I think La Migra will be the least noticeable out that way. And also get in touch with your uncle with State Police. Have him find out more about LaFleur and see if he can help, too. José, I know you have kept your data sources — they're even better than mine. See what you can find out on the Muñoz family in Kingsburg, please. I'll wait to hear from you before I talk to the sheriff down there. Also, could you look up Villalobos Sanchez? I can't get much on him, just trickles from offenses here and there. I know his name has come up before, for all kinds of illegal dealings. Drug running across the border mostly. That's your area of expertise. Someone is covering his tracks. Or maybe, his info is locked up in some feds' network. Shall we reconvene tomorrow at eleven?"

They all agreed and shook hands before leaving.

As he locked up the station, Lou gave Antonia a hug, whispering in her ear, "It's not that I don't believe you, you understand. It's just too unusual. I don't usually follow that kind of hunch. I gotta be sure it's all genuine before I call the amount of resources we're going to need. We're using the taxpayer's money, remember?"

She hugged him back, smiled, thanked him again and left.

~~~

Once back in the truck, José told her, "Thanks for including me. If you can drop me off at my place, will you be all right for a couple of hours? And do you have a comfortable sofa I can use?"

"José, I could not have done it without you. Don't worry about me. Sunny still has patrol cars coming by our place. And we have a couple of spare bedrooms. I truly appreciate your protection right now. I'm pooped! I just want to sleep. Here is a key to the house. And here is a dollar. Your full pay for a year! Now you're officially a detective with our agency."

She handed him the single bill with a big grin. The old man was smiling back gratefully as they arrived at his home. Turning back, and giving her an exaggerated wink, he said he would be back as soon as possible, especially now that he was on the payroll.

~~~

Chapter 27

Coincidence or Not

JOSÉ ARRIVED JUST IN TIME FOR A LATE DINNER. After a small bite of black olives, fresh goat cheese over toasted and buttered sour dough bread, and a couple of glasses of Pinot Noir to wash it down, Antonio went into one of their bedrooms to talk to Claire.

She answered right away. "Hey, you two. I miss you. What's up?"

"Claire, we have a problem. A runaway is our affair, right?"

"Right. And?"

"A kidnapping is a federal problem, right?"

"Yes. Especially if state lines are crossed. Get to the point?"

Antonio proceeded to tell her what he knew, leaving out the parts about the guns in the courtyard, the other children, and of course the methods they had used to find out about the girl. He then mentioned that they had found one person who could lead them to that girl.

Claire was upset. "You're leaving out some important facts, aren't you? This is a case of abduction, multiple abductions, maybe? You need to report this to the FBI right away. Are you using me? Or trying to get me to lose my job?"

"No, Claire. I care, we care too much about you for that. We just have a serious problem on our hands. Someone tried to kill us yesterday, he ran us off the road. Antonia's little car is totaled. We're only afraid that the wrong move could catapult the whole thing into possible harm for this young runaway. I'm just asking for your opinion, without trying to put you in jeopardy."

That seemed to placate her. After a few seconds, she replied, "I'll talk to my boss. I'll try to get down there as soon as possible. If I do come, it won't be as a federal employee, it will be as a friend."

~~~

That night their dreams were filled with chases. In the last one, they remembered big dogs turning into wolves, nipping at their heels, all four of their heels. Although their subconscious mind shared the same dreams, while living them, they would be two separate entities, twins, man and woman, going through the same motions, moving side-by-side. The wolves soon turned into two large horses coming from both sides, who knocked them down with their front hooves. Soon the horses were fighting each other, their mouths locked, teeth against teeth, copious amounts of spit flying all around them. The animals reared up above the twins, no longer paying attention to them, giving them the opportunity to run away from their violently prancing hooves. Together, they ran for their lives, into a narrow strip of land fenced with barbed wire, which eventually funneled them into a dark alley. They slowed down. In the dim light, they came across young prostitutes wearing Hindu saris, who started soliciting them. The girls were all lined up, waving their arms up and down in a slow-motion dance, but soon the colors all turned dark, everything shifting to high speed again. The girls melded into a winged demon, a giant dragon with the head of an elephant. Its raised trunk had a forked tongue lashing toward them; its long, leathery tail ended in a scorpion's stinger, slashing the air back and forth. It was flying fast at them, with four clawed arms swinging toward their eyes.

They woke up screaming.

Should we keep going, Tone?

We have no choice!

Right. Full circle, full speed ahead.

José was on the other side of their door, knocking and asking, "Are you OK in there?"

"Thanks, just a nightmare. Too much wine last night, not enough cheese. Sorry about waking you up."

~~~

Early the next morning found them at Rosetta's door once more. Antonia had invited José to come in with her that morning, since he had already met Rosetta and was aware of her gifts.

After a Japanese greeting, Mora plunged in right away, speaking fast, as if afraid she would not be able to convey much that day, "Imelda told me that to make my skin darker, I just need to put more make-up on. Mrs. Josette said she cannot ask anything of Papa Patron. He could fire her, and she would no longer be able to feed the two kids she has at home. Then Ms. Manners said that she will teach me how to put on dark make-up. So I don't think I can go outside.

"All right. I don't want to put you in harm's way. I want you to be very careful all the time. Anything new?"

"I have a new friend. She just got here yesterday. She cries a lot, but that's because she's scared. She doesn't want to be an actress. She wants to have a band and be the lead singer. The people that brought her here, told her they would help her have a singing career. That's why she went with them. But she thinks these people are really bad, and that they are going to ask her dad for lots of money. But her dad doesn't have a lot of money, so she's afraid they're gonna kill her."

"How old is she?"

"Cindy's eleven, like me."

"What's Cindy's last name?"

"I don't know. I'll ask her later."

"Did she go to your school?"

"No, I never saw her before. She said they just moved to Deming, but she doesn't like it there. It's always windy, and dirt is flying around all the time. She doesn't like her stepmom, who always picks on her. She tried to run away."

At once, Antonia felt it was becoming dangerous for Mora to ask too many questions. The woman Josette was still an unknown quantity. She took care of Leo, but did she understand what the operation was about? She had to suspect something was not right. "Mora, I would not share what we are doing together with Cindy or with anyone else, not until you know her better. You have a lot of intuition. Think before you ask anyone for anything. Don't put yourself in danger by asking too many questions. OK?"

"OK! *Arigatou*, Tania. That's thank you in Japanese. I'm starting to learn a lot of Japanese words. Oh! And I forgot to tell you," she whispered, "There is a fat, scary guy here now, with a gun. He is not here now, right now, but he'll be here after we have breakfast. His face has lots of holes. He just sits on a chair all day long and watches us in a nasty way. So, I'll be careful, but you be careful too. Watch out when you're driving. I miss you when we don't connect. Sayonara!"

She was gone again.

~ ~ ~

After watching the interaction between the two women and the young girl, José seemed in awe of the mystical woman. "Madame Rosetta, you have an amazing gift. In my past line of work, the department never trusted psychics. But, then again, most of them were quacks. You, on the other hand, are certainly the genuine thing. I am hoping that others will accept your talent to help all of us in finding these girls. Is there any way for you to tell us how to proceed?"

"Señor José, I can only work with what living beings and charged objects can offer me. I am only a conduit."

"Madame Rosetta, you are too modest. Your skills are invaluable. The many people now involved in this affair need your services."

"Señor José, whenever I have worked with law agencies, I have been ridiculed, threatened with complicity and jail, forcefully taken away from people that have asked me for my help. Why should it be different this time?"

"Madame Rosetta. If I may explain. The life of a little girl, maybe the lives of seven or eight young girls, are in danger. Antonia has let it be known to her policemen friends that she has been receiving these messages through you. I'm sure the many law officers that Tony and I know will provide you with protection, safety, and respect. Hopefully your help will only be needed for a day, the day we put everything in motion. Thanks to you, we will soon know their location."

"Señor José, if I were to agree to help the police, do you really think they would accept a channeling dog and an old, clairvoyant woman?"

"Madame Rosetta, the various law enforcement agencies in our little corner of New Mexico are desperate to find out about certain criminals, particularly the man who tried to kill Antonia and one of her clients, but also one of this man's likely family members, one who is probably behind the kidnappings. They also want to find out more details about the disappearances of the runaways. Did I mention that the man who ran Antonia off the road is also a rapist?"

Getting up too quickly from her stool, she sent it flying behind her. Both the dog and the cat scrambled through the partially open door of the adjacent room. Rosetta now had a worried look on her face. She closed her eyes for a minute. Then she took her cards and, with a questioning look, turned toward the old man.

"Señor José. Can you tell me the name of this desecrating wolf?"

"You see, Madame Rosetta, you are already ahead of us. His name is Villalobos, Angelo Villalobos Sanchez."

Rosetta's mouth was moving, silently weaving protective spells. Then she took a mouthful from a tequila bottle on one shelf and spat it on the floor. She did this four times, one for each corner of the room. She lit three blue candles, and kissed a little statue of a black Madonna, which she then tucked between her breasts. After shuffling her cards and calling her kitten, who promptly returned to the living room with Tiger in tow, she asked, "Ma petite Layla, could you pick a card for me?"

Tony and José watched in amazement as the kitten jumped on the table in front of Rosetta, and, moving a few cards to one side, placed her paw on one. Once flipped over, the card revealed a picture of two hyenas with the torn body of an antelope on its back between them. The larger of the two predators is ripping its prey's throat and the smaller one, its belly. In the background, two more hyenas await their turns. All around them, vultures circle, waiting for them to be done with the best morsels.

Rosetta shivered, then watched as her cat pawed at another card. It showed a white-winged woman with indigo-blue skin, dressed in a light-blue shift, her kinky hair a giant black halo around her head. She is standing on a cloud, looking down at a multitude of small animals. These appear to be guinea pigs or short-eared rabbits with long tails. A crow flies by her left shoulder, a black panther sits behind the blue woman, its head showing on her right side, its long black tail on the other.

Rosetta petted her kitten with her eyes closed, sighing now and then. Finally, still siting on her stool, she turned around toward her guests. "The young wolf is the son or the nephew of the man who has Mora. He has not learned proper manners from his parents, but has chosen a fast and vile path to profit from helpless people. Both men are very dangerous and fearless. I will help the authorities with this situation, but only if I can stay at home. And I do not want to be mentioned in any report. Go now. I have some cleansing to do."

Antonia and José thanked her profusely before getting in the truck. The leasing company was supposed to deliver a new car at the agency later that morning, so they needed to get back to Las Cruces. On the way, they wondered how they could include Rosetta in the operations without moving her from her cave.

"We'll need Tiger with her, too, as I don't think I'll be able to reach Mora without her. That will be interesting: introducing a dog as part of a criminal investigation."

José joked; "In narcotics, we used dogs all the time: sniffing dogs, tracking dogs, protection dogs."

Antonio could not help himself and said aloud.

"Psychic dogs?"

"That dog is incredible! Why do you think she's the link to Mora?"

Antonio continued, "Since we first saw her, we've been attracted to her. She used to wait for Mora across the street. That's how we started looking for her. How about that for a coincidence!"

Antonia immediately replied. "No! Not a coincidence. This is an old feud Tone and I have, José. He believes in coincidences. I believe in cosmic consciousness. We are given directions, situations, happenings at certain times, and all these are linked together in infinite space and time. Everything, even a tiny event or a simple thought, amasses energy, multiple forms of energy. Receptive beings sense these ethereal vibrations when they cross paths. When a focal point is defined, it all gets concentrated and many things happen at once. Did you ever notice how some inventions are made simultaneously by different people in different parts of the world?"

As usual, speaking too fast, she did not wait for a response. "Anyway, we had just lost our Border Collie and were looking for another intelligent dog. Then we saw Tiger across the street. With Rosetta's help, the dog linked us to the girl. You know, this wonder of a woman used to assist the New Orleans police when she lived back there, undercover of course."

Antonio voiced his opinion in a slower timbre: "Actually, my sister is the one who is in contact with Mora. I'm just barely beginning to understand how this sixth sense works."

José kept looking at the Tonys. It never stopped amazing him how such a complex being existed inside a single body.

~~~

Chapter 28

Sorting it Out

ON THE WAY HOME, JOSÉ AND THE TONYS KEPT thinking about the problem at hand. The old man said, "I hope Border Protection can get some info through this Josette woman. They can question her about her whereabouts, and what she does for a living."

"We don't know if she's involved in this mess or if she is just genuinely working at that place only as a cook, a house cleaner, and a beauty teacher. Although it seems that she should suspect something is not right if the girls have to move away from the windows when a helicopter flies by. But another of our major worries is that we don't want Leo to lose another parent."

"How about giving more reins to Sunny?" José continued. "He has good judgment and is up to date on how the various agencies in the area work together."

"Sunny is obligated to serve the city. You know that if he gets out of his jurisdiction, lawfully, he has no authority."

"My point exactly! Without state or federal authority, he will know how the various agencies work together, and won't try to take over. But I'm out of touch, been retired too long." José continued, "You said that your mother, Sirena, understands you. Is that also a psychic connection?"

"You could say that. I think I got it from her. Tone is more like our dad!"

Thanks a lot, Sis.

Only meant on the psychic side.

"Could your mother also help us?"

"I don't know. Sirena is connected to us, but not to Mora."

The phone vibrated in the truck's console.

"Hi, Mom! We were just talking about you."

"Do you have a minute?"

"We do, Mom. What's up?"

"This morning I received a call from a lawyer in New Iberia. You were right: Tonino passed away last week. A boat accident. His first mate, Chucky, and I are to inherit his fishing enterprise. I will have to go to Louisiana soon, to settle this."

"We're so glad he remembered you. When will you be going?"

"That's why I'm calling. I'm not sure what to do. I'm afraid for your safety while this pervert killer is still out there."

Antonio cut in, with a smile in his voice and a nod to José. "We are well protected with José — he's become our personal body guard. But we are also near closing one of our cases, the one with Mora. We may need your help with this."

"What can I do?"

"Mom, we don't know yet how it's going to turn

out. We're meeting with Lou and other law agencies this afternoon. We'll let you know as soon as we know ourselves. What are you going to do with your half of his business?"

"I talked with Chucky, and he would like to buy my share at fair market value. I think he deserves it, maybe I should give him the whole thing for taking care of Tonino all these years."

The Tonys took a minute to answer.

She deserves it, too, Tone. She worked so hard raising us without his help.

She sure does. Then she can retire.

You believe that?

No, she'll find something else to do.

"Mom, you should sell him your half. Besides, we're sure, the man is too proud to take a handout. We know you can put that money to good use. Retire maybe? And you could probably take care of the whole deal through phone and internet. You should not have to go to New Iberia. Let Chucky and the lawyer deal with it. Tell them what you want. We would trust Chucky."

"OK. I'll keep you posted. It sounds like you're on the road. By the way, I gave my two-weeks notice to the bed and breakfast, when I found out that Tonino had died. They understood, and because the inn will stay quiet until kids are out of school, they said I could take my vacation time right now. I'll come over to see how I can help with Mora. Say hello to José for me."

~~~

In front of the office sat a brand-new, gray Subaru Outback. The petite Japanese woman working for the car lease company mentioned that she knew they had insisted on a discreet exterior and no black seats inside. "Light-metallic-gray body, with rich, tan leather seats! A 3.6 engine. Exactly what you asked for! I think you will be happy with this model!"

Antonia signed the new lease and received the keys from the woman. As she escorted the small woman to the front door, she saw two vehicles slowing down and parking right across the street. The dark-blue lead car, with white letters on its sides, was city police and the other a CBP truck, all white but for one wide, green stripe.

Sunny and Carlos?

Yes, and someone else with Carlos.

She invited the three men in. José came into the office when he heard the new voices.

Sunny introduced Antonia and José to the two border agents. "And this is Ruben Medina, Mission Support Manager, from his El Paso office, and your brother has already met Carlos Garcia. Both are with Customs and Border Protection. We would like to talk to you before we meet with Lou, if you have time."

Over some freshly made coffee, Ruben started, "My cousin tells me you have received information about El Patron de los Lobos in a very unusual way. Your brother has told Carlos that this information was coming through messages. We understood at the time that it was a paper trail. Can you elaborate on this?"

Antonia was shifting on her seat, worried that CBP would take over the whole operation, to concentrate only on busting the Patron. "First, let me apprise you of a very important situation regarding this matter. The lives of many young girls are at stake. I understand that you have been seeking the whereabouts of this Lobos Patron. It is quite possible that this is the same man I have indirectly heard about. Part of this man's last name may even be Villalobos, but ..."

His arms crossed over his chest, the fifty-or-so-year-old man, dark haired, squat but fit, interrupted. "You have contacted us before you contacted the police. We will take over this matter now. Could you, please, explain your means of contact with the girl or girls?"

"Actually, we have been in touch with the police for a long time."

Liar!

White liar! We've known and worked with Lou, Sunny, and others for many years.

After taking a deep breath, Antonia continued, "And currently the FBI is also involved."

Ruben smiled smugly and said, "Good! Then we will work with them. Your explanation, please."

"As I'm sure you have been told, I have been working with a medium, a clairvoyant. She has helped me reach this young girl through uncommon means, while we were looking for the ownership of a dog that turned out to belong to the kidnapped girl."

There, used the word kidnapped, equaling FBI!

She continued, "The medium put me under hypnosis and guided me to the girl. The girl, her name is Mora, has been talking to me during those sessions. I've tried to reach her most mornings around seven. Our discussions are very brief, as the child is being watched constantly and has to pretend to talk to herself when we do communicate. This is how I learned about the man in charge of this alarming operation. He is known to her as Papa Patron and has a pet wolf with a radio collar. The children are not allowed to leave the premises, nor make phone calls, nor use the internet or any other means to reach their parents or the outside. I believe this is the reason this child has reached out to me. She must have enhanced telepathic aptitude, and with the help of her dog and Rosetta LaFleur, the medium, we've made the connection." She sighed heavily, unsure whether this federal officer would believe her or if he would even care about the children.

Ruben uncrossed his arms and glanced at Sunny and Carlos, as if confirming his suspicions. "All right, Ms. Urbani. I will choose to believe you until proven otherwise. What else have you found out during these exchanges?"

Although relieved the man was going to listen to what she had to say, she still felt that he did not believe her, due to the unusual sources of her findings. "I am extremely afraid the man will use these children for his own profit. It could be a child-porn movie enterprise. Or he may be an underage prostitute procurer, or he may sell them as slaves. We have not yet found out what he does with them. These girls are learning how to apply make-up, how to serve food and drinks, how to play musical instruments, and how to speak foreign languages. All on the pretext and incentive of becoming a movie star. These young girls may also be credulous runaways looking for a better life. But first they are victims."

The CBP chief seemed to soften for a minute. Crossing his arms again, leaning toward her, staring into her eyes, he said, "Ms. Urbani, I can assure you that we will do everything in our power to help and protect these young girls. Thank you for your information."

"Mr Medina, my brother and I have been investigating this matter for the child's mother. Would you have any information you would want to share with us to further our search, should this operation be delayed?"

"If you are coming to the meeting at the sheriff's department later this morning, we will share what we know so far with all the parties involved."

Frustrated at the coldness of the officer, Antonia blurted to the men's backs as they departed, "My brother will be there."

Sunny turned around and gave her a thumbs-up and a nod, as if to let her know that all would be fine.

Tony told José that she was going to change, and that they should leave in fifteen minutes. Without saying a word, the old man reached out to her and gave her a hug.

~~~

Chapter 29

Meeting with the Law

ARRIVING AT THE MEETING EXACTLY AT ELEVEN, Antonio felt the tension in the sheriff's office. Only men were present. Everyone was extremely serious. Antonia was glad that her brother represented them that day. Clearly that morning, Lou was the man in charge.

After everyone had introduced themselves, he recapped the whole affair. Not to be left out, Sunny pointed out that it was thanks to the twins, who had done all the preliminary research, that the girl was found. Then Antonio quickly outlined how he and his sister operated a detective agency which had been looking into the girl's disappearance, and that they had asked for help from the legal authorities after an incident meant as a threat to his sister's life. José spoke next. He told everyone that he was working with Tony and his sister, and that he was their field agent and bodyguard.

Cute! He's great!

Careful, Sis. You know Carlos can sense when we talk to each other.

A tall man in a black uniform, with tanned skin, short, dark, curly hair and dark, penetrating eyes, had earlier introduced himself as Captain J.R. Brown with State

Police Special Ops. He proceeded to tell them that all this was news to him, but that his chief had asked him to participate, as the State Police SWAT team may need to be activated for this mission.

Yes! Now there is hope to get her out safely.

And the others, too.

And Leo may be out of the picture.

Ten minutes after they had started, Lou's deputy let another man into the meeting room. Handsome, with short, gray hair, clear glasses over blue eyes, looking to be in his fifties, he was dressed in a three-piece suit with a striped, blue tie. He walked rigidly to an empty chair toward the end of the long table. Clearly he was someone high up in whatever agency he belonged to. He introduced himself only as: "Smith, Agent in charge, FBI." Without sharing any more personal information, he said, "I'm only here as this case seems like possible multiple abductions. Go ahead. I'm all ears."

Undaunted, Brown, the State Police officer, asked him, "Which division, please?"

"I'm with the Abduction Branch, Children's Division." He answered, as if reluctantly.

Once everyone had introduced themselves again to the FBI man, Lou started by giving a concise but detailed rundown of all that he knew, mainly what Antonia had told him the day before, and other information he had discovered earlier this morning. "I believe that we already know about two of the people involved in this matter. One is Angelo Villalobos Sanchez, the man who tried to run over Tony's sister, Antonia. She was following a van that could have been the same one that abducted the Mora girl. When she went by the girl's school, the school secretary was there, by her vehicle, early, as if waiting for someone. Her name is Hope Esperanza Castillo. I suspect her to be the one handing out the names and whereabouts of local girls who may have been abducted. As that may be, shortly after passing the Castillo woman, the van led Antonia to the Sanchez man, who then tried to run her off the road. At the moment, our department is monitoring the whereabouts of Castillo."

Lou drew a deep breath and seemed to hesitate. He wondered how these conventional law officers would react to Antonia's telepathic abilities. All eyes upon him, they waited.

He took another deep breath and continued. "Antonia receives messages from the girl through the intervention of a fortune-teller. Although this seems totally unprofessional, it looks like the psychic, LaFleur, is genuine. She led us to Josette Muñoz, who possibly works at the place where the girl is being held."

Us? Don't remember seeing you.

Shut up!

Relaxing now that the peculiar means of discovery was out in the open, Lou spoke again, "We are not able to find much on the Sanchez man, nor on the Castillo woman. It seems that both their records are not available to us. This is all I have so far." Then he asked if anyone had any other new information.

Ruben Medina immediately took over. "As my cousin Sunny requested, early this morning, we set up three immigration checkpoints, five miles each way, from the Josette Muñoz residence. No one notices a surprise immigration check so close to the border. Just CBP earning their government checks! We tagged a magnetic GPS transmitter on the woman's car while she was stopped at one of our checkpoints and we had a drone with a camera trail her. She took the southern route, toward Playas and then Animas, then to a spot fifteen miles south of Animas. Mostly dirt roads from there. We have the vehicle's coordinates. Unfortunately the drone was only programed to follow the transmitter. It came back to us before it ran out of power. The car is still sitting there, along with another one. I had agents take a look at it at o-nine hundred, but there was no one in it. There is another car, a Ford sedan, parked next to hers, license number: New Mexico MFD 334. Both cars are near a locked gate. Two sets of foot tracks led to a vehicle on the other side of that gate — small ones, probably women or children. Larger footprints opened the gate and let them through, then walked to a large vehicle's driver's side. All four wheels of the vehicle on the other side of the gate are similar: wide, four-wheel-drive tires. According to the multiple tracks, it looks like that vehicle drives to the locked gate on a regular basis. As per your instructions, we did not apprehend anyone involved." He stopped, seemingly upset for not having more to tell.

As soon as he mentioned the license plate of the other

vehicle there, Lou had researched it on his computer. "That Ford sedan belongs to an Anita Manzano, from Hachita. Her driver's license says she is forty-nine years old, four foot nine, one hundred and ten pounds, black hair, brown eyes."

Miss Manners?

Carlos was looking at Antonio. "Do you know this person, Tony?"

"No. I was just thinking my sister mentioned a Miss Manners, a petite hispanic woman who allegedly teaches there too. Dark hair, dark eyes. I was just thinking that both women may get a ride to the place where the girls are being held up."

Lou said, "That would make sense! Anita Manzano is very petite and her license picture shows Hispanic features."

Smith, quiet until now, finally opened up. "So far, it seems to me, we only have coincidences, a couple of vehicles parked in the middle of nowhere — not unusual for this part of the state — and psychic connections, for whatever those are worth. I really would like to see something concrete."

José, who had also been quiet all this time, ventured in. "Mr. Smith, do you have any information on this Villalobos Sanchez you would be willing to share?"

Smith seemed to hesitate, but after looking at all their faces, he finally decided to participate. "All right. This cannot get out of this room. Do all of you understand?"

Everyone nodded their heads in agreement.

Smith continued, "We have been trying to connect Angelo Villalobos Sanchez with an international crime committed on this side of the border about five years ago. A drug lord from Mexico was killed right after crossing into the States, in El Paso, and the Sanchez name came up. Actually his fingerprints did. After years of research, ATF was about ready to bust this major dealer and his whole organization, until he turned up dead. Back to ground zero, thanks to Sanchez. That man is slippery. So far, we know he is partnering with his uncle Ernesto Villalobos Jimenez, a Mexican national, who runs a big whorehouse on the other side of the border. Every time we get close to Sanchez, he disappears." Smith had a smirk on his face as he was looking around for comments. None came his way, but for a worried look on Antonio's face.

Standing up without showing any emotions, Sunny tried to defuse the accrued tension. "Yeah! I heard about it. So what else do you know about Villalobos Sanchez?"

"We suspect him of trading guns with the drug cartels of Mexico. We know he ran a prostitution ring in El Paso. Just your basic, run-of-the-mill criminal this side of the border," said Smith, another smirk coating his face.

Let it go, Bro. It's just his sick sense of humor!

Changing the subject, Lou interjected, "What do you know about the Castillo woman?"

"Nothing. I just found out about her a minute ago. But Sanchez is supposed to be quite the ladies' man. Is she pretty? Do you know if they are seeing each other?"

Lou replied, "Pretty, yes. Other than that, we don't

know. Just that the two are most likely in contact with each other. It could be that the Castillo woman is the one procuring the children, identifying the ones that are attractive but vulnerable. José, you told me you found out some info about Castillo?"

José was ready with his answer. "Earlier, I could not find anything about her while she was in juvie. But one of the guards that watched over Castillo while she was in, told me that she would brag about having strangled her adoptive mother with her bare hands. She was fourteen at the time. Two years later, she was the instigator in bringing in drugs for the other juvies. They could not prove it, but they were certain she was the ringleader. This gives you an idea about her potential for wrongdoing."

Lou continued, "Thank you, José. And thank you, Ruben, for being discreet this morning." Lou nodded at the beaming, chunky man and added, "I want to stress the importance of not making contact with other officials in the area. The hamlet where Josette Muñoz lives has a total of five homes in it. Each house contains at least one relative of Ernesto Muñoz, Josette's deceased husband. So we cannot approach the woman at her home without it being known throughout the village.

The sheriff of Kingsburg, I mean Hidalgo County, is also a Muñoz. We have not contacted him, either. If any of the Muñoz clan is actually involved in this racket, we risk endangering the whole operation. Anyone else have more information?" he asked looking around the room.

Antonio slightly raised his hand, then put it down. "I

do. My sister contacted the girl again early this morning. A new girl was just brought in. Her first name is Cindy, from Deming. Unknown last name. She's another runaway. Mora also said, and I quote: 'There is a fat scary guy here now, with a gun. He just sits on a chair all day long and watches us in a nasty way.' Now, this man is new, and there are at least two, maybe three, other armed guards in the compound, with big guns, as Mora puts it, besides the patron. And there is also a wolf with an electronic collar; it could be a guard animal, or it could be trained to attack."

Tone, you just gave that wolf a death sentence.

He is no longer wild.

Carlos tilted his head as he stared at Antonio.

Sorry, Tone!

Lou said, "Thank you, Tony. Now, if there is nothing else, that wraps it up for all the primary details. Do you all want to grab some lunch? We could walk over next door, catch a bite at the Cocina del Sol. Their burritos are fresh and fantastic. They see cops all the time, and they have a back room."

All eight of them agreed and went outside. Two of them, Ruben and Smith, took advantage of the short walk to smoke a cigarette.

~~~

Chapter 30
Revelation to a Friend

As soon as they were seated in the restaurant's special-event room, and everyone had ordered food and drinks, JR took the lead. "Since there are five agencies involved — city, county, state and two federals — if no one minds, I would like to coordinate this mission. I have more than ten years of experience as Incident Commander for State Police. I have been the head of Special Ops for the last three years. Our agency has a SWAT team here in Las Cruces, that can be deployed in one-hour's time."

All the other officers agreed, but for Smith who was furiously typing on his cell phone.

Finally, after receiving the information he needed, the FBI man also agreed, "JR, you were just on that mission at La Ciénega near Santa Fe, last week. Congratulations for rescuing those hostages so quickly."

"Yes, that was a difficult one. But we were already working on it, after your agency's forewarning, as a matter of fact."

When the two men were done praising each other, JR turned to Tony and José. "Although both of you are civilians, I would like you to join our team, with the understanding

322

that not a word about this mission can escape to the public, the media, or anyone else, without my knowledge and permission. That includes family members and friends."

"Of course, that was understood. My twin sister will be helping us, too. I will share our findings with her and only with her. While I have your undivided attention, I want to thank all of you for your help, past, present, and future, on behalf of these young girls," Tony said, scanning the room.

José turned to JR and replied in turn, "As an ex-narc agent I, too, understand the importance of confidentiality, and will be glad to help in any way I can. Antonio and his sister have been working on this case for the last two-and-a-half weeks. I can vouch for their reliability."

While the two civilians were talking, Smith was again working his cell phone, glancing at both of them occasionally. Finally he returned the phone to his pocket and nodded positively to Ruben.

JR continued, "We have a state-of-the-art incident-management room, here in town. It's brand new. It's even better than the one in Santa Fe. Down here, they call it the War Room. Let's use it as our main operation center. We'll reconvene there at fourteen hundred hours. I'll have badges made for all of you." He took their names and affiliations.

They finished their meal, some of them recounting recent assignments, but only the ones with comic aspects; while pointing a gun at a convenience-store clerk, a perp tripped over his shoe laces and shot himself in the leg; another guy called his girlfriend's home on the hotel phone, to let her know he had just robbed their safe. In no time, the whole room was roaring with laughter.

~~~

Most of them had already set off for the new Incident Command Base south-east of Las Cruces, but for Lou, Antonio and José who were left savoring their last cups of coffee. The coffee was excellent at the Cocina del Sol, a dark-roast Columbian Arabica, freshly brewed with spring water, one that kept the neighborhood cops coming back for more.

Seeing Tony's worried look, Lou moved over and sat down by him. "What's bothering you, Tony? Are you worried about the girl getting hurt in the process?"

As he said this, his hand shot out and grabbed Antonio's left arm in a gesture of comfort, right where the bone bruise was. Antonio winced and slightly recoiled from the touch. Lou did a double take. Staring at him, he reached for the bruised arm again. Antonio tried not to flinch, not to move a muscle, but closed his eyes for a second.

He knows! Let's see how he reacts.

Lou asked Tony to stay behind for a minute. José told them he'd wait outside.

"What's going on, Tony? Show me your arm!"

He's figured it out. Show him, Tone.

Antonio peeled his shirtsleeve back. The bruise was a ripe deep purple now.

Lou's face fell. "Hell, man! Tony! What's going on? You... You and your sister! Who are you? Why didn't you tell me? How long have you played this game?"

"Lou, listen. We are a one-of-a-kind. A freak of nature. We are what is called a chimera and a hermaphrodite. While growing up, we were treated as freaks. Scorned. Rejected by our peers, for our long head and our wide chest. Our mother gave us strength and love and care. She protected us by homeschooling us and by teaching us to present either as one or the other, male or female, in order to be accepted by society. She also taught us that we were no different but better off than someone with a slight handicap."

How can we show him that we trust him, Tone?

Afraid they were going to lose his friendship, Antonio continued, choking up on the words. "Lou, we're alive. Few conjoined twins survive. But we survived! For us, the only way we could carry on was to pretend to be two people. Don't look at us as if we are a monster. Chimeras were originally believed to be mythical beings made of many different animals. Then it was discovered that now and then, a mutation can occur during ordinary cell division. It happens in plants, animals, and humans. We are two people in one." He watched Lou shaking his head, still not understanding what Tony was telling him.

After a minute, in a soothing tone, Antonia's voice took over. "Now that you know what we are, we want you to realize that we both are your friend. That will never change." She stopped and watched Lou staring at them through tears rolling down the big man's face.

He feels betrayed, Sis.

We have lied to him all this time.

We had no choice!

He quickly wiped his tears with the back of his hand and said, "Am I your friend? If I am, could you not have shared with me what you...who you are?"

"Lou, we care for you as a friend, as someone we trust. I remember when we first met you, I, Antonio, first met you. Then later, you saw us as Antonia. After that, we could not change. It was too late. Even you act different when you're with me or with my sister. Remember?"

Lou swallowed hard and regained his composure. "But how do you do it? How can you switch from one to the other? What kind of a detective am I, not to have seen it before?"

It was Antonia's turn to put her hand on Lou's arm. At the touch, he flinched.

This is not going well, Sis.

I know. We need to give him time to absorb it all.

In her melodious voice, she said. "But you figured it out. On your own. Very few people have. Lou, you still have two friends who care very much for your understanding. Two friends in one body. Please, don't reject us."

The big man stared at them with a confused look for a minute.

"I'm sorry, Lou. We wish we could have shared this earlier." The twins stood up, and gave him a hug.

Awkwardly, the sheriff untangled himself from the hug, unable yet to assimilate what he had just learned. "I don't know Antonio. Tony! I don't know what to think. I guess it's gonna take me a while to d-d-digest this." Lou stammered as they exited the restaurant.

~ ~ ~

Chapter 31
The Plan

THE WAR ROOM WAS AN IMPRESSIVE WORKING space. Located beneath the state police building, the main room was enormous, four times the size of the sheriff's department's meeting room, with soundproof, bulletproof, even bombproof walls and doors. No windows. Soft lights radiated from the ceiling. Slightly tilted down toward the back wall, cushioned, rubbery floors helped anyone standing up for too long. Refrigerated air quietly blew in from all four corners. Comfortable, padded chairs. Large desks loaded with shimmering computers and electric outlets, neatly arranged in a half-circle facing the wall opposite the large, double-entrance door. A massive protective womb, where only a faint but constant heartbeat could be heard from the electronics, softly humming. If not for the size of the place, the cocooned atmosphere would have been claustrophobic.

Shortly after they had all filed in, another state police officer joined them. JR introduced the small, blond woman with a flattop haircut as Deputy Chief Lindsey Simon of Las Cruces. "Lieutenant Simon will be our Communication Officer. She has been briefed on what we know so far."

One by one, they shook her hand, introducing themselves. Antonio was last to meet her. She commented, "I've heard a lot about your agency, all of it good of course. Your sister is quite famous in our precinct. I heard she recently had an encounter with the Sanchez wolf. Is she all right?"

Tony answered, "She suffered minor injuries and was quite shaken up from the violence of the man. Her car was totaled. She will be helping us with this operation, but mostly from home. I will brief her and give her your call sign and the frequency you will be using. We were approved for radio communication with state police a few years back, and have kept up with the newest Las Cruces wavebands."

"Let her know I look forward to working with her," she replied.

On the long back wall, five giant screens were arranged in a slight arc. The one on the left displayed an aerial map of Hidalgo County, with a large, red dot where the two female suspects had left their car during the day, and a smaller yellow dot, west of Separ, where the Muñoz woman lived. Highlighted were the names of the small towns of Rodeo, Animas, Playas and Hachita, as well as two small villages by the border with the names of Bramlett and Antelope Wells, two possible escape routes into Mexico. Just north of Hachita, another yellow dot indicated the home of Anita Manzano. A light-gray area highlighted four townships at the center of the map.

Once they had settled down by the central desks sporting their names and studied the screens, JR explained, "We're looking at roughly three thousand square miles for the total area you see here. Until we have better intel, and according to what we have learned so far, we will be concentrating on the highlighted, one hundred and forty-four square miles in the middle of this map, centered around where the two women left their cars."

Below that was a topo map that spanned the whole southern part of New Mexico, from the Arizona border to the Texas border, with a blue line for Interstate-10 near the top, and a red line for the border of Mexico below.

The next screen to the right showed names and pictures of the known people involved. The Villalobos clan was in there. They had pictures for some of them, including Sanchez's uncle, Jimenez, and his wife and kids, all five of them Mexican nationals. Only an old driver's license and more recent police sketches existed for Angelo but nothing for his relative, the elusive El Patron, both of whom were thought to be US citizens. A dozen possible associates of the Villalobos were included, as were known names and faces of people who may have been underlings of the two men. One of them, Joe Turner, was fat and short, with a pockmarked face.

Tone, that could be the fat scary guy!

Below these, were pictures and bios of many of the Muñoz family, the largest one of Josette. Next to her photo were images of two current driver's licenses, one for Anita Manzano and the other for Hope Castillo.

The middle screen showed the organization of the team. The mission title was "Operation City of Wolves". JR's name was at the top, as Incident Commander. An arrow on the left had a tag with the NMSP SWAT team logo and two pictures of state police helicopters. Below JR's position, six more arrows pointed down to six rectangular boxes, arranged horizontally, with names and titles.

Sunny and José were Logistics. Arrows below their names pointed to black-clothed military-like people with helmets and guns; pictures of motels, foods and drinks; red-crossed ambulances and medical facilities, and pictures of various vehicles, buses, planes, and helicopters.

Lt. Simon was to be Communication, as they had already learned. Below her tag, Carlos would handle communication with CBP.

Ed Smith, as Planning Chief, was in charge of maps, research and scenarios. In a smug tone, he pointed out that he had entered the current maps on the first screen.

Lou and Ruben were to run Operations. They would prepare task assignments with the various agencies and their respective SWAT teams and transportation, as soon as the Incident Commander provided everyone's details.

Lou would also be the principal Liaison Officer, for the five official agencies that were involved, plus the Technical Advisors, which were named as Antonio and Antonia Urbani, José, as well as Rosetta LaFleur. Three arrows below them were labeled Mission Initiator, Intel and Subject's Contact.

Along with several blank grey squares, the next screen

had first a large picture of Mora in one corner, the same picture Maria had given the Tonys. With Antonio's help, Mora's data was also displayed in one of the gray boxes.

Smith had personally met the girl's mother to obtain more information about her child. He explained that this was the reason he had been late for the morning meeting. Eventually all the blanks were filled in, including Mora's parents' full names and drivers' license pictures, her date of birth, her school records, her friend Omar's full name.

JR asked Smith if he had found anything new after talking to the mother. In a condescending tone, Smith said, "Can we trust the mother? She does not seem wealthy. She may have sold her child."

Antonio impulsively replied, "Maria is very trustworthy, she is a hard-working woman. I have met her and talked to her on multiple occasions in the last two weeks. Neither she, nor her husband, would want to profit from their daughter's life or place her in any kind of danger."

Relax, Tone. He's only just met her.

Right, but he is so prejudiced.

Agreed!

"I'll need to talk to the father, then. Tomorrow morning," Smith said in a voice that cut the room like a cold, sharp blade.

Sunny spoke up as if to vindicate himself. "I feel that I have failed in my duties to serve and protect. The mayor had asked me if we should continue looking for this child, who runs away on a regular basis. I knew that each time, she would return home after being gone for a couple of days. So we stopped looking for her and just waited for her to reappear. I dealt with both parents the first three times she ran away. I know, we always look at the parents as possible offenders, but in this case I can vouch for both of them. And actually, Andrés Aguirre is not her natural father. He married Maria when she was six months pregnant. He is a good man, he cares about the girl. The girl's genetic father was a previous boyfriend of the mother, a soldier on furlough, who died shortly after returning to duty in the Middle East. Andrés adopted Mora when she was born."

JR thanked Sunny and Tony for the information and asked if anyone had more to add to the screen displays.

José spoke up. "I could be wrong, but during this morning's interaction with the young girl, she mentioned to Antonia that there was a man with a gun watching her. She said he was short, fat, with a face full of holes." Pointing to the second screen at the man with the old chicken-pox scars, he added. "I think this Joe Turner fits the profile. And let's not forget about one or more wolves, the four-legged kind, which could be part-wolves even, possibly trained to attack."

See Tone, José has a lot of intuition.

The last screen's title was Assignments. A dozen lines already filled a small part of it. Everyone took notes and printed pictures of the faces on the screens, while drinking mediocre coffee and eating overly sweet cinnamon rolls.

JR and Smith went to a far corner of the room and, for

a few minutes, the two seemed to be arguing more than planning.

They both want to run the show.

JR has more training and is a better diplomat. He'll stay at the top.

Hope so. Smith is creepy.

Shush! Carlos is staring at us again.

The CBP officer seemed to be scrutinizing them, his head tilted to the side, until the twins quit their internal dialogue.

~~~

Standing at the podium in front of the screens, JR started the briefing. "This operation will involve nearly one hundred persons altogether, including four different agencies' SWAT teams." Everyone turned to him, and listened attentively.

"The area is mostly farming and ranching lands, surrounded by mountains, the Animas range on the east and the Peloncillo range on the west. The girl Mora remembers a ride that took a few hours, maybe three, to get there from Las Cruces. She has also said that the land is level around the building, with a couple of peaks in the distance, which would place her in the Animas Valley, as confirmed by the location of the two working women's last car-pooling vehicle. Tony, thank your sister for taking notes since the beginning."

At least, he believes me.

Antonio nodded his head in acquiescence, and JR continued. "In order to narrow our search, Ruben and

Carlos, can you tag the transport vehicle and follow it from above?"

Ruben, not giving Carlos time to reply, said, "I have already given orders for a drone to drop a small GPS transmitter on top of that vehicle when the driver returns the women to their cars this afternoon. Then the same drone will follow, well above the vehicle, to its final destination. Carlos will obtain its GPS reading, and plot coordinates. With luck, we should know the Wolves' location this evening."

After thanking the CBP Mission Support Manager, JR started typing on his laptop, but Ruben was not finished. "I will also contact the two women later today, and see if either one will cooperate."

"You may not!" JR firmly replied. "Ed Smith will contact the Muñoz woman later today. Ed is our highest-ranking federal officer here. He wants to interview her and offer her prosecutorial immunity in exchange for help and information." Still staring at Ruben, he continued, "Josette Muñoz takes care of two teenagers at home, she has a lot to lose if put in jail. We don't know enough about the Manzano woman. She seems to live by herself. She may be very involved in their operation. She does a lot more than clean and feed the girls. She is not teaching them your average school curriculum. She has to know what her teachings are leading to. And no one is to deal with the Castillo woman, yet. If we cannot net all the perps at once, we'll arrest her and find out where the rest of them hide, if she is involved."

Turning to Carlos, he added, "Agent Garcia, you are the liaison between your organization and this command post, the War Room. But if you can, I would like you to stop Josette Muñoz before she gets home, and take her to a location not too far from there, where agent Smith can interview her. Preferably today."

Ruben quickly cut in. "We have a safe house in Separ, just a few miles from Lonnie's Landing, where she lives. I can fly there and apprehend the woman this afternoon."

Smith nodded in approval, before JR continued, "Thank you, Ruben, but I still need you here at the moment. Carlos, can you get there in time to apprehend her this afternoon?"

The border agent looked toward his boss and got a nod of approval. Glancing at the large map, he said. "I will contact my unit in Kingsburg and have them put a roadblock between Playas and her home. They can detain her until I get there. I'll take the CBP helicopter, the one Agent Medina came in on this morning. Then I can take her to the safe house and the chopper can come back to pick up Agent Smith after we get her in."

JR agreed to the plan. "Good. There should only be CBP helicopters flying in the area at the moment. I'd rather keep our state police bird here until we launch the final attack."

Carlos left walking tall, unable to hide the large grin on his face.

When he was done typing, the commander finished entering his results and the assignment screen lit up:

CW-0021- RM to record whereabouts of transport

vehicle, with GPS transmitter and drone.

CW-0022- CG to direct J. Muñoz to CBP safe house in Separ

CW-0023- ES to interrogate J. Muñoz in Separ, to see if she will cooperate.

The list, which was started in the morning, went on filling half of the screen. The commander then turned toward Sunny and asked him, "Since this is in your jurisdiction, can you monitor the whereabouts of Ms. Hope Castillo? She may try to contact Villalobos Sanchez or decide to go south on us. All puns intended!"

Everyone smiled. Sunny agreed before JR, facing the whole team, continued, "Sunny and José, as the logistics team, I would like you to secure lodging in Rodeo, Kingsburg, and Animas. Enough for twenty people in each town, for the next two days. In order to stay as discreet as possible, let's offer a rumor to the motel managers that there is going to be a big bust on I-10. Tell them you heard about a convoy of three Winnebagos, loaded with drugs, on their way to Arizona. You should also try to obtain as many transport helicopters, planes, or other vehicles as feasible, to move the teams rapidly once we have an exact location. I can talk to National Guard and see if they'll help with large-scale transport." The two men agreed.

Ruben interjected, "We have a concealed station just north of the border, actually just about twenty miles from the transport vehicle's last known point. Our SWAT team will be housed there. We also have buses, Humvees, and helicopters at that station."

"Thanks, Ruben. Which brings me to readying the

other SWAT teams. Smith?"

The FBI man quickly answered. "I will have four units from Albuquerque arriving tomorrow, early in the morning. Is that soon enough, Commander?"

"Perfect. Thank you." Turning to the sheriff, he continued, "Lou, how many and how fast can you commandeer your SWAT team?"

"I have twelve officers highly trained and ready to go within sixty minutes, more or less two hours from the perps' probable location. I'll need a three-hour advance notice."

"Good. Thanks, Lou. Our SWAT team here will be housed in the state police dorm starting tomorrow morning, o-seven hundred. If everything goes according to plan, we can move on this thing fast. Barring retaliations from Murphy's law, of course."

The fifth screen lit up again, as JR added more assignments: CW-0035-SV to maintain surveillance on H.E. Castillo: CW-0036-SV/JO to secure lodging and transport for incoming teams (60 units).

He continued with the activation of the various SWAT teams and their responsible parties. After taking a long drink of water from a stainless-steel bottle on his desk, JR turned to the FBI agent. "Ed, in your spare time, I would like you to follow up on missing young girls in the southern part of our state. I have contacted Chief Mike Sanders in Deming. He is looking into the recent disappearance of a youth named Cindy. Not having a last name for her certainly does not make his job easier. Sunny and Lou can help you with any missing female youths in the last two years."

Finally he looked at Tony. "Antonio, I will need José to continue with logistics today and tomorrow morning. It's a big job. Can you protect your sister tomorrow?" Tony hesitated, not knowing where this was leading. "Sir, could I trade with José and finish with logistics, and have him protect Antonia?"

JR replied, "I would like to be present during your sister's conversation with the girl. This is not about disbelieving the medium or your sister. You understand? I've done my research on Ms. LaFleur, and it seems that she has helped the Louisiana NOP on many occasions, with good results. I'm just curious and need to confirm that she is actually in contact with the girl before I move mountains to save what may be obscured or misinterpreted details. This operation already has and will cost a lot more of taxpayers' money."

"I understand, sir. What do you want me to do?" conceded Tony.

Tone, how are we going to manage that?

Lou intervened. "JR, I can come and help tomorrow morning. I will call my SWAT team tonight. I've already filled out most of the task assignments for today. I can be liaison on my cell phone and on the radio tomorrow. We will have cell coverage all the way to Deming. The District Four frequency covers all the way to the Arizona border, including the bottom of the boot-heel. Tony has told me that he will be busy on another project at that time. This is the Urbani's means of living, you see. So may I suggest we give Tony a little leeway, and besides Antonia is the one who is in touch with the Mora girl. I'll introduce you to Antonia in the morning."

Whoah! Thanks, Lou.

Tony gave Lou a grateful nod.

Slightly miffed that he had not been assigned to that task, José told the commander that he had been the one protecting Antonia since the Sanchez man had attacked her. Most of his logistics assignments could be done by phone. "Sir, if I may. Sunny said that in the morning, he would go to Kingsburg and Rodeo to secure lodging and spread false rumors. We have already divided the assignments and can do all of the transport, medic, and victuals research on the phone in the morning. I will take care of Animas, after Antonia is done with the seer. But, if I remember correctly, as of three years ago, there were no motels in Animas. It's just a little farming village. I may be able to get a room at the fire station, but it will be without amenities. "

JR took his time before saying. "All right. Lou, then you can come with me in the morning. Tony, whatever you need to do, go ahead. I fully support what you and your sister do. Actually you have made us look good on a couple of occasions. José, you have been protecting Ms. Urbani for a few days, so please continue to do so. You know this area better than I. Go ahead and do your thing."

Relieved that they could keep their own schedules, Tony and José thanked the commander.

Lindsey Simon walked in and whispered into JR's ear. "You can share this with everybody, Lindsey. We are all in this together."

"OK. I just heard from Agent Carlos Garcia with CBP. After one of the women was dropped off at her car, the drone followed the white transport van to a small building, about three hundred square feet, only five hundred yards from the pickup spot. The building did not look like a hacienda. More like a small shack. Once the driver went in the house, the drone dropped off a magnetic tracker on the vehicle's roof. After thirty minutes, the drone had to come back to base before its battery went dead. Carlos also said he is taking the Muñoz woman and her car to Separ and the CPB pilot is flying the helicopter back to us. ETA to Las Cruces NMSP helipad, ten minutes."

After thanking the communications officer before she left the room, JR noticed Ruben, looking at the floor. He seemed disengaged. JR urged everyone in the room: "We need to find the Wolf's building. Soon! The Manzano woman did not take her car. She may still be there. Agent Smith, Ed, please, see if you can get directions to the perps' house from the Muñoz woman. Any other suggestions, anyone?"

Antonio ventured, "If the Manzano woman works there till the girls turn in for the night, she will go home in a couple of hours. The van will pick her up at the Wolf's and take her to her car. If the transmitter still emits its signal and the means to capture that signal are still available, are there any assets nearby you could use to track that signal?"

JR was quick to reply. "Thanks, Tony. I believe the FBI can call for satellite surveillance if CBP can't. I'll call my chief and see if we can get it going."

Ruben still looked upset, and looked at Smith, as if for approval. "We can also get satellite surveillance as needed. And we might have three more choppers available, if they're not in use at the moment. But do we really need to continue with this charade, put all this in motion solely on a palm-reader's word?"

Ignoring that last comment, JR raised one hand to ask everyone to be quiet. He covered his earbud with his other hand, and then reached for the microphone on his lapel, tilting it toward his mouth and said, "Thanks, Lindsey. I'll let him know." Releasing the mike, turning to the FBI man, he continued, "Ed, the CBP helicopter is landing. You need to get on board for your meeting in Separ. Call me as soon as you're done with the woman."

Smith nodded, gave everyone a thumb's up, and left the room through the side door. During the few seconds the door was open, the spinning rotor blades on the pad above them cut the air loudly.

"Ruben, how fast can you get something up to track the van? Preferably within an hour."

Smoothing the skin of his forehead, the man looked worried as he retired to a corner of the room to make some phone calls.

"OK, folks. I think we've covered all the bases until we have more data. Keep me posted or call Lou. And just remember: no other Muñozes are to be contacted or informed in any way of what is happening in their county.

And until we have all the intel, we are not moving in. I repeat, we are not moving in. We'll reconvene here at eleven hundred hours tomorrow. Does that give everyone enough time to finish their assignments?" He paused and looked around the room. "Remember stealth and speed are the keys to success in this operation," JR told them as they filed out.

Getting off his cell phone with a satisfied smile, Ruben approached the commander and said, "I've got a chopper on its way to the white van. ETA ten minutes max. The transmitter should have enough batteries for another two or three days."

"Let's hope they don't see the helicopter. Have it stay at three thousand feet AGL, and a little behind the van. They may not be able to spot it at that altitude. Your pilot should be able to fly that high without any problems in those quads. And CBP is less noticeable in that area rather than one of ours. Thanks for obtaining it so quickly."

Ruben beamed at the praise. "You're welcome, sir. No problem, here. That pilot flew missions in the Middle East before joining us. She'll have no problems. She is the toughest cookie we've got in the agency. A little like your Lieutenant Simon. Man, where did all these tough women come from?"

Ignoring his comments, JR turned off the monitors and the screens.

"We're all starting early tomorrow. I hope you can get a little rest. Are you flying back to El Paso tonight?" he asked Ruben.

"No, sir." He rambled on, as he snapped up a couple of radios, a satchel and his garment bag. "My ride is in Separ right now, transporting Smith. I'll just spend the next few nights in town. My cousin has invited me to stay at his place. We haven't seen each other in over a year and we have a lot of catching up to do. Besides, I wouldn't want to miss a minute of this operation. I may get Sunny to take me to Separ. This is the most exciting thing that's happened to me since last year. Much more entertaining than catching illegals crossing over. They dig tunnels, they get dropped off in make-do parachutes..."

But JR was no longer listening and had reached the main door in a few quick steps, keeping the door open for Ruben to get out.

~~~

Chapter 32
The Details

"DO YOU HAVE ANY AVOCADOS AND TOMATOES?" asked José, as he walked in Tony's house.

"Avocados, yes. I have a couple of perfectly ripe ones. No tomatoes. I won't refrigerate them into mealy cardboard. With this heat so early in the season, they don't keep very long, unless you pick them straight from the garden," Antonio said.

"Avocados will be fine. I brought some blue-corn tortillas, made by one of my neighbors. She also makes a delicious asadero cheese. I had some green chile sauce and some Anasazi beans in the freezer. My turn to cook. I hope you like your cheese enchiladas hot."

"I do. Do you have enough for a third person?"

At once, José looked embarrassed. "I'm sorry. I didn't know you had someone over. I can come back in the morning."

Antonio replied quickly, "Oh no, you don't! I forbid you to deprive us of your enchiladas. Besides, it's about time you met our mother. She wants to make sure we're safe, too. The two of you should be enough protection for the two of us! And she will be staying in the other spare bedroom. She should be here any moment."

After sitting down to a traditional stacked enchilada dinner, no raw onions for Tony, they could not help talking about the day's mission. Antonio started by saying that their mother was well aware of Mora's plight, but that they could not share anything with her about the operation itself. "I think JR is really sharp. I like him. Do you think the girls will be safe, when the teams descend upon them?"

José looked once toward Sirena and said, "Yes, our Incident Commander is quite the hero up north. He always seems to be available when there is a big crisis. He can read people with precision, and has a reputation for getting the job done right every time."

"And I saw that he doesn't let anyone step on his toes!"

The old man continued, in an amused tone. "I was glad to see him disregard the short pipsqueak's comments. That man has no respect for anyone."

Knowing fully well that their mother would never divulge any secrets, Antonio still took the old cop's hint and stopped using names. "Right. And the boss also knows how to work with the stiff suit, giving him plenty to do, but not the reins. He recognizes the abilities of each and every one of us, and respects the opinion of us bystanders! We're impressed."

José took a minute before saying, "Lou did not know until recently about you two, right?"

"Yes. As recently as today, after lunch. We've been

good friends for a long time. I'm glad he handled it so well, this afternoon. Covering up for me. We were afraid he was going to be very upset."

He's still upset.

Sure, but he is also a man of honor.

Need to apologize to him, Tone. Don't want any awkwardness between us.

Sirena was staring at them, with a slight frown.

The old cop continued, "I've followed his career for a long time. He is another good man, and one with a heart of gold. I can tell he really cares for the both of you."

Antonia was silent. She did not dare think again inside her brother's head while her mother was there. She also knew that José was able to sense their internal musings. Actually, he had found out about them right away.

But Sirena was very sentient. To dissipate the sudden uneasiness, she turned toward José and said, "José, it was a pleasure to finally meet you. The kids have told me so many good things about you. Thank you for such a delicious, authentic meal. But I'm sure you all still have much to talk about tonight, and I did wake up early this morning. I think I'll turn in now."

With a smile, she held her hand out to shake his. Instead, he gently turned it over and kissed it. "It was my pleasure, ma'am. I really admire a woman who flawlessly raises twins by herself and stays as beautiful and energetic as you are."

"Thank you. You are as chivalrous as the twins told me. It sounds as if there will be enough people around Antonia tomorrow morning, so I think that I'll stay home, and get a few things done around here. Good night."

The Tonys kissed their mother and bid her good night.

~~~

The following morning returning from a relaxing, pre-dawn walk with Tiger, Sirena had just reached the front door as Lou and JR arrived. After a handshake for the state police officer, and a hug for Lou, she let them in the house. As they walked in, they inhaled the fragrance of medium-dark-roasted Ethiopian coffee. Lou did a quick introduction of Antonia to JR, which brought in the usual comments about the uncanny resemblance of the non-identical twins. Lou, standing behind JR, just grinned, before stepping up and giving her a hug. Then they sat at the dining table for a quick breakfast of huevos rancheros over toasted onion bagels.

Sirena said to the two policemen, "If there is anything I could do, I'd be glad to help."

JR thought for a minute before saying. "Actually ma'am, as of this morning, I was asked to find a police woman to help receive the children after we have rescued them. To no avail. The children will need a mother figure to comfort them, to ease them away from their plight, before a certain federal agency takes them away for debriefing. I have a feeling you would be perfect for the job. I can deputize you right now, for the duration of the operation. I will make sure that there is an armed law officer with you at all times. It could still be dangerous, you understand.

We know so little about most of the hostages. Maybe your son can fill you in about the operation, if he has not done so already."

"Sir, you can count on me. These last few days, my daughter has shared some of her quandaries regarding Mora. I am glad my children have finally contacted the authorities regarding this awful situation. I will talk to Antonio later today to get the details," Sirena answered before she left them to finish their breakfast.

~~~

JR was following the new Subaru in an unmarked car as they all headed to Rosetta's. They had just reached the entrance to the interstate, when a text message from JR appeared on Antonia's cell phone: 'Conference call at 0620. Dial the following number, then the accompanying code.'

Five minutes later, the call started with Sunny, Ruben, and Carlos joining in.

"JR here. Good morning, everyone. I have Lou with me. Tony's sister, Antonia, José, and one dog are leading the way to Mrs. LaFleur on the southwest side of Deming. Antonio is not available today. Carlos, can you tell us how your operation went yesterday?"

"Yes, sir. Yesterday CBP Team C-4 held the Muñoz woman at sixteen-ten, five miles north of Animas, for about fifteen minutes before I arrived. I directed her to get in her vehicle and follow me and one of my agents to our safe house in Separ. As soon as Agent Ed Smith arrived, at seventeen-forty-three, I turned the operation over to him. I then returned to our Charlie Base to observe the tracking of the number-two Wolf vehicle. At eighteen-five-o, from location W-2, — that's the shack of Wolf 2, the transport man — Wolf 2 moved east, then south, then east again before arriving at location W-3 at eighteen-fifty-seven. Just past nineteen hundred hours, Wolf 2 drove back past W-2 to W-1, the location where the Muñoz and the Manzano women's vehicles were parked. I strongly believe that the W-3 location is where the main operation is, sir. I have sent the coordinates of W-1, W-2, and W-3 to Lieutenant Simon at the War Room."

"JR here. Carlos, what was the Muñoz woman's reaction when you took her to the safe house?"

"Carlos here. Sir, the woman seemed relieved. She said that she thought she would be apprehended sooner. When I asked her what she meant, she said she would only talk to my superior."

"JR here. Thank you, Carlos, for this detailed information. Agent Smith is unavailable at the moment. Ruben, you went to Separ last night. Tell us what you found, please."

"Yes, sir. Ruben here. I drove to the Separ CBP safe house and met with Agent Smith shortly after the Muñoz woman arrived. I had been told that she was fearful when first apprehended. But when I saw her, she did not seem so worried. She asked to see my credentials and kept looking out toward the door and the windows. She is worried that the Patron will find out that she is talking to us, and that he will hurt her children, or that she will lose her job or be killed. Her words, sir. When Agent Smith offered her the FBI deal of partial immunity from prosecution, she asked for full immunity in return for her full cooperation. He told her that if she can confirm she had no previous knowledge of the nature of the operation before commencing her employment and will fully collaborate, she may get full immunity. But she will have to disclose everything about any past, present, and future activities regarding this business and must comply with all of our requests."

"JR here. What have you learned about her possible cooperation?"

"Ruben here. She has given us directions to the hacienda. Smith and I confirmed the coordinates after she left, and W-3 is definitely the Wolves' hacienda and their main place of operation. She thinks the Patron is there most of the time. In the last three years, she noticed that he has been slowing down. Maybe he is ready to retire. She has given us a full description of the man. If we have time to get her to a profiling computer, she can give us a good rendering of him. He is between sixty-five and seventy years old. He has curly, gray hair, a graying goatee, thick eyebrows, brown eyes. He is about five foot nine, has a limp, and walks with a cane. She also mentioned that she will not be able to carry any electronic surveillance systems. When boarding the transport van, the driver's name is Renaldo — I guess that's Wolf 2 — anyway he searches everyone for cell phones or electronic gadgets. She said that lately security has been increased. In the last two days, Wolf 2 has used a wand on both women before he takes them into his van. Yesterday morning, he even asked them if they were wearing any metal wires. She also said that there is now an armed guard watching over the girls during the day. This is new. In the five years she has worked there, this is the first time an armed guard has come inside the girls' part of the hacienda. There are usually two armed men outside. El Patron had told her that it was for the security of the girls, as they are so close to the border, and he is only protecting them from being kidnaped. When she first got the job, he told her that the girls were under his protection from harm from their own family members. He pays her very well to keep her mouth shut. She had to sign a release that she cannot talk to anyone about where she works or what she does, again with the postulation of protecting the children. There are seven young girls there at the moment, in their early teens, plus an older girl named Imelda, in her late teens, who was already there when Josette Muñoz started five years ago. She noticed that the girls are moved out of the hacienda when they start their — huh, huh — their women's menstruations. She has never seen any of these girls return. When one or two disappear, they are quickly replaced. This was what first made her think that something was not right about what she had been told." He then stopped for emphasis.

The commander replied, "JR here. One: do you think that she can pretend ignorance and go about her business as usual, now that we have contacted her? And two: did you get anything else relevant to our operation?"

"Ruben again, sir. She's very scared of being found out

but thinks she can act as if nothing happened yesterday. She admitted to pretending not knowing what was really going on. She is sorry she failed to contact the authorities, when she had doubts about what the boss had told her. She hopes she will not have to deal directly with El Patron. She is afraid he might retaliate and injure her children if found out. She asked that her youngest daughter and her nephew, who both currently live with her, be placed into protective custody from now until all this is resolved."

Ruben took a deep breath and continued, "She also mentioned that she thinks Anita, she does not know her last name — that must be the Manzano woman — she thinks Anita is related to one of the armed guards, someone named Raul. There is a Raul Manzano on the bulletin board."

A family relationship, Tone, not a coincidence!

Sis, did not even begin. You're right this time.

"The Muñoz woman was returned to her vehicle at nineteen-forty-five. She followed my instructions to drive first to Kingsburg, before returning to her home, in order to foil anyone possibly following her."

"JR here. Thank you, Ruben. You have discreetly acquired quite a lot of very useful information in a couple of hours' time. Anyone else?"

"This is Lou, in the same car with JR. I will place the Muñoz children under protective custody in Las Cruces this afternoon."

"Sunny here. If I may, I can take the kids to my sister. She already has about six adopted kids at her home. Will that work for you, Lou?"

"Thanks, Sunny. Lou, again. After our meeting, I'll pick up the kids in an unmarked car and bring them to you myself."

At once all the phones beeped, signaling a new incoming speaker.

"Ed Smith here. Sorry I'm late. In the light of what Ruben and I shared last night, I have asked for one of our best child hostage negotiators from the Bureau. She's flying in from Texas. Should be at our meeting later today. Also I have pulled up the files on Raul Manzano. He was a small-time arms dealer in El Paso who was on the ATF radar, until a few years ago. After that he seems to have disappeared from circulation, right about the time Sanchez disappeared, too."

After a minute of silence, JR continued, "Moving right along, folks. I'll see you all at eleven hundred hours in the War Room."

~~~

Chapter 33
Clairvoyance for All

"GOOD MORNING, ROSETTA. I HAVE SOME GOOD news and some bad news!" Antonia started, while grabbing a steaming cup of coffee from the woman's hand.

"Hello, Señor José, Antonia. But this is not Grand Central Station. Who are all these people, child?" the big woman exclaimed, as Tiger and Layla ran off to the back room.

"Rosetta, we are about to rescue Mora from her jailers. We finally went to the authorities, and they are going to help us! The bad news is that some people do not believe in your power of clairvoyance. They want proof. I've told you about Lou, and this is Captain JR Brown, with State Police."

It was all Rosetta could do to contain herself. As she took deep breaths, her opulent chest stuck out and back down, like a lizard doing push-ups to intimidate another. Her eyes were glowering at the uniformed officer. "Mister, I don't care who you are, or what or whom you believe. There are too many people in this small room for my comfort. You may all leave! You can stay, Antonia!"

The three men filed out.

Tony apologized, "Rosetta, it's my fault for bringing these men in without any warning. I got too excited about finding Mora and hoping we could bring her back home. I am truly sorry."

The big woman seemed to calm down a little. She moved to hug Antonia, and quietly said to her. "All right! Which one needs the most convincing? The tall, bleached, African king?"

Antonia exhaled loudly and said, "I did not see that. But yes, he is the one that needs it the most. He is also the main commander for this operation. And we probably need to hurry, if we are going to contact the girl this morning."

She went outside to talk to the men, asked JR to come in, and for the other two to wait in the car. Looking downward, without meeting the seer's eyes, the tall man apologized. Rosetta told him, "Never come into my home again without announcing your arrival beforehand. Now sit in that corner and be quiet. We have work to do, and I hope we're not too late."

~~~

Hearing Rosetta starting her routine to reach Antonia's subconscious in a gentler voice, Tiger and Layla came back in the front room.

"Mora? Mora, can you talk?"

She took a minute before answering in her little girl voice. "Hi, Tania. Hi, Tiger. Hi, Rosa. Something is weird. Imelda is in a really bad mood all the time, now. Fatso stares at me and at Cindy with a weird look. I'm getting scared again, 'specially when he looks at me and licks his lips. Gross!"

Antonia gently said, "I want you to be very aware

of anything new and different during the next few days, please. You told me before that you're supposed to hide when there are helicopters flying by. Remember?"

Mora was rapidly whispering. "Yeah! But I have not heard any lately. Do you think there will be some coming? Is that why they are all in a bad mood?"

"Look, Mora. Are there places you and the other girls can hide? A closet, under a sink, under a bed? I think another helicopter will be coming, and when it does, you will need to hide. You understand?"

Mora was sobbing now. "Are you coming to get me? Uh, oh! Here come Fatso and Imelda. She's crying. Sayonara!"

In a whisper, JR asked, "Can you ask her for Cindy's last name?"

Antonia let out a sharp cry. Then her whole body shook as a loud crack resonated through the room.

Glaring at the man for his interruption, in a sharp tone, Rosetta told him, "Mister! Never barge in during a session. Never. You understand?"

Sheepishly, like a child scolded by his mother, JR answered. "Yes ma'am. Forgive me, please. This is the first time I've ever witnessed anything this peculiar."

Rosetta then approached Antonia, touching her shoulder, saying in a softer tone, "Five. You did good. You have learned a lot in a short time, yet were able to warn her of possible new events. Four. You will feel rested and invigorated when you wake up. Three..."

Antonia looked very worried as she came out of her trance. "No, JR, I cannot ask any more of Mora today. She said good bye, and has left for the day." Then, turning to

Rosetta who was again staring with disdain at JR, she said, "Rosetta, do you think the man Fatso is raping Imelda?"

"I fear you may be right. Imelda is a lost child, she may never grow to be an adult. Let's try to reach the young girl much earlier tomorrow morning. You may bring your mother, but no one else inside the cave."

Rosetta left the room to brew another pot of coffee. JR walked over to Antonia and sat next to her. "I apologize for having broken the connection. Forgive me. This was an amazing experience. I've never come across anything like it."

"Mora cannot talk once other people enter her space. It is a very fragile connection we have worked on, practically every day, since she first contacted me. I always fear that I may put her in danger when I reach her."

Looking uncomfortable, the man said, "Thank you for sharing. I can see this is exhausting for you. Are we done here?"

"Hold on, sir. I don't think Rosetta is done."

~~~

The big woman came back in the room with three steaming cups of coffee.

Looking down at the seated man, she handed him a cup of dark brew and asked, "You had a question for me when you first came in?"

His teeth clenched as he tasted the overly sweet coffee. Tentatively, he said, "I did. May I ask it?"

"In a minute," she replied.

Antonia was still sitting in the soft armchair with her back straight, her eyes closed, both thumbs and indexes forming a circle, meditating upon the recent conversation with Mora, impervious to her surroundings. Sensing that she needed to give Rosetta and JR some space, she asked the seer if she could go into her chambers.

Between her little sculptures and a few lit candles, Rosetta picked out four small, crystalline rocks from her crowded table: a red, a black, a yellow and a white one. She shook them inside her closed hands and tossed them on a small linen mat on the table. "You want to know why your wife does not want to have any more to do with you?" she said after looking at the crystals.

"Yes ma'am. That's correct! You've guessed it!"

Still looking at the crystals, she took a deep breath and continued, "When you met your wife, you omitted to tell her about a very important part of your past. One you seemed ashamed of. She needs to know what you have kept hidden from her all these years."

At once the man crumbled. He turned a questioning look toward the seer. "She comes from a very aristocratic, white family. I have never told her about my black African ancestor who was brought here as a young slave. He later married a white woman, and all their offspring looked white. My father told me about it when I became a cop."

Scowling at him, the dark-skinned woman said, "Are you ashamed of who you are today?"

"No ma'am. I am only afraid of my wife's reaction. I

have lied by omission to her for many years. I did not even speak up when one of our children was born with a darker skin. And that is when our estrangement started."

Rosetta gathered the four stones and tossed them again. She stared at them and finally turned to him. "Your ancestor also came from an aristocratic family. Before he was caught and brought overseas, he lived with his father who was the king of his tribe. If your wife loves you, she will honor your apologies. She is worried that there is no longer any trust between the two of you. You may go now."

"Thank you, Mrs. LaFleur. What do I owe you?"

"You owe Mora and her roommates their freedom. You owe respect to all sides of your family. And you owe respect to Antonia and to myself," she replied in a quiet voice, before she knocked on her bedroom door.

Tony woke up from her reverie and came back into the front room. "Thank you again, Rosetta. I have a feeling the next few days may prove dangerous. My mother will also be helping with the girls' rescue. Could you share some of your protective spells for her and me, please?"

JR bowed deeply in a Japanese fashion to Rosetta and then to Tony. Both women bowed back to him in return, although not as deeply. Before leaving the cave, he told them that he was going to wait outside until they were done.

Rosetta lit up some sweet-smelling, braided grasses and waved their thin smoke over Antonia. Then she brushed the top of Tony's head, her shoulders, her front and back with feathers of what looked like a hawk wing tip, while she singsonged some words that did not sound English at all. Finally she took four sips from her tequila bottle which she successively spat on the floor in the four cardinal directions.

After rummaging around her backroom for a couple of minutes, she returned holding two small leather pouches. Followed by her kitten, she walked three times around Antonia.

"Keep one of these bags next to your skin for a day. Do not open it. Then try to always keep it close to you. Give the other bag to your mother. Also, during this undertaking, do not bring the Red Bull, the fed who thinks he is in charge, to the cave. I do not want to be on any more files. Now bring in your big baby friend, so I can meet him."

After giving her a hug, Antonia stepped outside to fetch Lou.

~ ~ ~

While shuffling his feet side to side, the big man could hardly look at Rosetta, as if ashamed or afraid.

As soon as Tony had left, the seer asked Lou to sit down. "Now, I feel better having you at eye level. My neck gets stiff looking up at you. Would you like to tell me what is bothering you?" She moved to her cluttered table and picked up her crystals, shook them inside her hands and threw them onto the counter.

Clearing his throat, Lou started, "You see, it's — it's the twins. I don't know — I — I just don't know what..."

He stopped, unable to hatch a full sentence.

Rosetta took over. "You have not really digested what you have learned. You miss the past, the way things were before you knew. You also feel like a fool for not seeing their subterfuge. You do not understand what they had and still have to go through to protect themselves, to be accepted, and to function with some degree of normalcy in our society. I think they have succeeded in their endeavors. Don't you?"

A large tear rolled down his right cheek. Rosetta softened her stance and again shook the four stones in her cupped hands as she waited for his response.

"Yeah! Yes, you're right. I should just let them be. I just need to be their friend, right?"

The woman did not answer immediately, waiting for him to acknowledge his emotional feelings. Another tear came down from his right eye. "I guess I want us to be like we were — I mean, before I knew. Can it still be that way?"

"You have strong feelings for them, especially one of the two. Now you have discovered that what one knows, the other does, too. Your problem is that you know you have been found out, but the affection they have for you will remain the same as before, if you don't ostracize them. You need to accept who they are, for they have not changed. You have."

"Mrs. Rosetta, what can I do now for our friendship to remain intact?"

"They know and care for you, or they would not have brought you to me. Try to maintain the relationship you had with them as if nothing happened. But, I personally fear for Antonia, after what happened with the young wolf. If you are their friend, please protect them in the best way you can."

Lou shook his head in accordance. After a minute, he looked up at her as if a weight had been lifted from his shoulders, his usual good cheer resurfacing. "I've always supported their endeavors, but I will be more diligent now. Let me reassure you that Antonia, I mean, both of them will be under my protection at all times."

"I know that, Lou. But remember not to smother them, as they would not stand for it."

As Lou left, he stuck a large bill into the canister right by the front door labeled "Donation Box for Cat Food."

~~~

Chapter 34
Plotting the Approach

Bᴀᴄᴋ ɪɴ ᴛʜᴇ ᴡᴀʀ ʀᴏᴏᴍ, ᴇᴠᴇʀʏᴏɴᴇ ᴡᴀs ᴀʙᴜᴢᴢ with excited comments. When JR walked in, they quieted down. He first introduced Antonia and her mother, explaining that the two women would be helping from Deming and Separ during the actual operation. Then he turned to Agent Smith and asked him to present the person by his side, a soft-looking, small, plump, and unassuming woman of Asian lineage. In her fifties, wearing low, brown shoes, shapeless, brown slacks and a loose tunic covered with large pink roses, her appearance was in direct contrast to the sharply-dressed Smith.

"This is Isabel Aquino. She is the best in our Hostage Division. She has dealt with the worst criminals in the Philippines and in New York. Fluent in seven languages, she has also worked overseas in the middle of Mafiosi negotiations. She's just flown in on the red-eye and can probably use a cup of coffee right now."

Stern-faced, the woman only acknowledged the room with a curt nod, and sat down on one side, away from Smith and the rest of the crowd, as her dark eyes scanned everyone. Bringing her a cup of coffee, Sirena sat next to her and thanked her for coming so fast to help out. A beautiful smile immediately lit up the woman's face.

That one will be hard to predict.

But she doesn't kowtow to the Red Bull. She could be a great asset.

Antonia sat on the opposite side of the room.

To balance the male-female energy. Too much testosterone in here!

Feel it too, Sis!

Soon they were all sitting down, looking attentively at JR as he started giving a short briefing on the new developments since the previous afternoon. He recounted the CBP detainment of the Muñoz woman at the Separ safe house, the woman's interrogation, and her willingness to cooperate if granted immunity from prosecution. "The woman fears for her life and for the two children in her care, if she is found out. Her two wards will be relocated this afternoon. As for the authenticity of the medium, it certainly seems real. I was impressed by Ms. LaFleur and by Ms. Antonia's ability to reach the child. Now, all of it has been proven genuine with the contributions of the Muñoz woman. Due to the increased security and the addition of another armed man in the Wolf den, I believe we need to move fast."

While talking about the discovery of the location of the W-3 building, which matched Mora's description, the commander highlighted the three known locations for the Wolves on the mapping screen. "All are within one-mile's distance of each other. Considering the locked gate and the dirt roads, I think it will be best if the incoming teams stay off and away from the roads. Two teams can come in at once or drop in from the air. The safety of these girls relies upon our stealth, speed, and coordination."

After a brief pause, he continued, "The Wolves monitor all incoming electronics, therefore they probably monitor the local radios. I'm surprised they did not discover the tracking magnet on the van. We will be using codes, as if we are looking for a shipment of drugs transported by Winnebagos on Interstate-10."

Ruben had his hand raised, but JR was not ready to hand him the floor yet. He resumed, "As for body counts: There are the two women who care for the children. One of the two may be related to one of the guards. Three to five armed guards plus the Patron, mostly outside the children's compound but for one on the inside during the day. Their security was increased two days ago, right after Ms. Antonia was run off the road. Not to forget, there is at least one four-legged wolf. As for the victims, we're looking at seven girls, eleven to thirteen. There is also one older girl, who may have been sexually assaulted by one or more of the guards. That girl may also be related to one of the perps, as she is able to get in and out of the locked compound, unlike the younger ones. We do not know whose side she's with."

While holding one finger up toward Ruben for him to wait, he took a sip of water from a silver sport bottle on his desk, and continued, "If you check the satellite picture on the left screen, it shows the hacienda, with the location of the girls in that green, rectangular building on the west side. Opposite the courtyard, in the red building, is where the Manzano woman delivers the food Muñoz has prepared for the kidnappers. This is also where the guards and El Patron spend most of their daytime. The central building opposite the entrance, in yellow, is probably for sleeping quarters and storage." He turned to Ruben who had lowered his hand. "Agent Medina, you have something to add?"

"No — no, sir." Ruben stammered, then, recovering his composure, he said, "I have the elevations for the area if you need them."

"Thanks. We'll get to that in a short while."

We sure know who's the boss here!

JR went on with his briefing. "Sunny, you told me that Ms. Hope Castillo has not had any dealings so far with anyone besides the people at the school."

Sunny answered, "Yes, sir. She is laying very low at the moment, except for having meals by herself at a local restaurant. I did find out that she just bought a brand-new car, a Mustang, last month. Cash! Quite a feat on a school secretary's salary! Although last year, she did inherit some money from her elderly husband. Also, José told me he has heard about Angelo Sanchez."

José, not liking to be in the limelight without a warning, fidgeted in his seat. "Sir, I still have access to my past informants, here and across the border. It seems that Mr. Villalobos Sanchez was hanging out at his uncle's in Juarez for the last couple of days and has just bought a ticket to Acapulco on Aeroméxico, due to leave at noon today. The Mexican passport used is registered under the name Carlos Villalobos."

"Thank you, José, that one is hopefully out of the way for a few days. Any other data on the lead players?"

Smith stood up and said, "Once we have the children safe, I will contact Interpol to have Sanchez arrested. Regarding your Rosetta LaFleur, other than having been an informant for the New Orleans Police, she has surprisingly clean records."

JR took over. "Thank you, Agent Smith. This morning, I observed Ms. LaFleur in action with Ms. Antonia Urbani and the young girl's dog. I was told that the dog is a part of the equation in this matter. What I saw and heard certainly made me a believer. Ms. Antonia, would you tell us in a few words your take on the matter?"

"Yes, sir. During a difficult case, when my brother and I need information we cannot retrieve in a conventional manner, we ask Ms. Rosetta for help. She places me under hypnosis. Of the two of us, I am the most receptive, therefore I am the one she uses. The dog, Tiger, belongs to the abducted girl Mora. She is definitely linked to her owner. I have felt a kinship for that dog from day one. I needed to find out why the dog was waiting outside our agency. I took Tiger with me when I visited Ms. Rosetta, and the dog seemed to help me contact Mora. I am convinced that Mora senses when Tiger, Ms. Rosetta, and myself are together. It was quite uncanny at first. A little-girl's voice was coming out of my mouth. Even the dog recognizes her voice and starts licking my hand when she hears her.

I know it may sound strange to most of you, but I did believe that we — that I was on the right track. Still do! I do trust all that Mora has told me. As we progressed with our almost daily conversations, they've become much easier, like a sort of ritual. I can hear her now so clearly, as if she is in the next room. I was able to piece together more and more information. Unfortunately, we cannot communicate but for a short time in the early morning. Finally, all of it was confirmed when my brother learned about Josette Muñoz and her work connected to the girls. This morning the older girl, Imelda was crying. Although I did not hear it from Mora, my feeling is that this girl is being raped by one of the guards. She is one of the victims too." As she finished, she turned toward the hostage handler, who nodded once with just a thin smile of acknowledgment.

"Thank you, Ms. Antonia," said JR. "Again, I would have had a hard time believing you, if I had not witnessed your conversation with the girl this morning. All right. Now, if there are no more reports, let's move on to assets, locations, and transport."

He took a sip of water. Then, from his laptop, he highlighted a blue rectangle on the map on the large screen as he spoke. "The Wolves' hacienda is at forty-nine-hundred feet of elevation. There are two peaks nine miles away to the west, at sixty-four-hundred and sixty-five-hundred feet elevation. Animas Creek is two miles due west from

W-3. There is farmland on the east side of the creek. It offers low-lying, flat terrain. I particularly like this area."

He moved the arrow to a level spot on the map, near the creek. "Highway 338 is just one point five miles west-north-west from it, and over one-hundred feet elevation below the house, from that point."

He took another sip of water, before continuing. "I think this may be one of our best points of entry from the ground. It will be fairly level but there will not be much cover besides the occasional arroyo. On the plus side, at the moment, the moon is no longer in our sky after midnight. It will be very dark until first light at o-five thirty tomorrow morning. If we can reach the compound by o-four hundred, I think we have a good chance of catching them still in bed. We can parachute people in from the north. I've got a trained team which is raring to do that. Another point of entry could be on the south side, coming in cross-country with two or three Humvees. We can bring in troops and retrieve the children with them, too. It will not be a very discreet approach, but we can get right to the building that way. This station has one Hummer available. Ruben, how is your supply of all-terrain vehicles down in your corner?"

For the next hour, they plotted their approach and came up with a general plan, filled with possible contingencies. They unanimously decided that they should be ready to invade the Wolf den at o-four thirty, the next morning. That evening, all the team leaders were able to confirm to JR exactly what kind and how many assets would be available.

~~~

On her way home, Antonia called Danny. She sounded upbeat. "Hey, I nearly have total recall now. Actually, I'm remembering things I probably would be better off having forgotten. There are still a couple of little details missing: somebody's last name, someone else's birthday, but nothing really important. So I'm glad to say I will no longer need your help, but I'm sorry that I won't see you for a while. I'll be back if the cops find Angel, but from what they've said, I doubt he will be easy to find. So, I'm flying back to Austin. They're waiting for me to resume cutting up dead bodies."

Antonia replied, "As long as you enjoy it, that's the important part. It's been a pleasure helping you, Danny. I'm sure you're looking forward to your life going back to normal."

"I sure am. I think I'll apply for the job in El Paso or in Las Cruces. Maybe they can use me here in Las Cruces. Anyway, I just wanted to say thanks, and that I'd like to stay in touch. Oh, by the way, the check is in the mail."

Antonia smiled. "Thanks, Danny. We always knew you were good for it."

When Tony and José arrived at the house, they spotted a shiny, white Lexus parked across the road.

That's Claire's car!

Tiger was waiting for them in the front yard, her long tail waving back and forth. Claire and Sirena were talking and cooking in the kitchen. The Tonys shared a long hug with their friend before they sat down around the central island.

~~~

Chapter 35

The Operation

CARRYING A LARGE BOX, JR ARRIVED JUST AS THE four of them were starting dinner.

"Sorry to intrude. I just wanted to meet with Agent Claire Carrel for a minute. Agent Smith said she came in this afternoon."

Antonia invited him to the dining room and introduced Claire to JR. Then bringing a plate, a glass, and some silverware and placing these in front of him on the table, she said, "Please, sit down. Have you eaten yet? We have plenty of grilled scallops in a ponzu dressing, udon buckwheat noodles, and a cilantro-cucumber salad."

He slid onto the bench and sat down. "That sounds delicious. Thank you."

After dinner, JR grabbed the large box he had left by the entrance and joined them in the living room. "I brought everyone bullet-proof vests. I hope I guessed the right size for each of you."

He opened the box and distributed four black vests, three for the women and one for José. "Ms. Claire, I've asked Agent Smith to let you protect Ms. Sirena, while you are down in our corner of the state. Ms. Sirena will help care for the children after their recovery. I would like you to go with her to the Separ safe-house tonight. You will get closer to the incident base as we move on, but you both should stay at least two miles away from the actual operation. We are planning on being operative in the morning at o-four hundred hours."

He proceeded to give her a short run down of the particulars. Then added, as he got up to leave, "I would like everyone to keep a log of all their actions for our records, please. We have a difficult task ahead of us in the morning. You all be safe, and I'll see you at the debrief in a day or two, if not before."

~~~

Sirena and Claire left for Separ right after the meal, leaving José and Tony behind. The twins were disappointed not to have more time to visit with their renewed friend. As she was leaving, reading the chagrin on their face, Claire promised: "I'm staying till Sunday night. We'll have time to spend together, if everything goes according to plan."

~~~

In the dark of that night, José, Tony, and Tiger arrived and parked outside of the clairvoyant's place. They noticed a light coming on. Immediately thereafter, Rosetta, clothed in a zebra-striped velvet robe, opened the front door.

"How did you know we were coming in so early?" asked Antonia.

"Layla woke me up an hour ago and told me her pet dog was coming in," she laughed, as she invited them in and went to get coffee.

They had just bitten into warm chocolate-glazed crois-
sants, when they heard the radio crackle.

JR's voice came on. "This is Black Hawk. My team is
currently incoming and will be on time. Are we all ready
to approach Winnebago Three? Leader of Packrat, please
confirm."

Lou answered, "Packrat leader here. Ready and willing. In position at assigned location."

Smith spoke next. "Black Hawk, this is the leader of
the Bulls. Four units incoming on time, sir."

Ruben followed. "This is Golden Eagle leader. We are
moving in on target. We will arrive early and wait for further instructions."

"Black Hawk to Eagle. Do not, I repeat, do not approach
Winnebago Three until your assigned time. Stay at least
three miles away from target, until you hear from me."

"Roger that, Black Hawk. We will fold back and wait
for your orders."

Even through the slightly muddled radio, JR's tone of
voice showed some irritation. "Black Hawk to Eagle. How
far are you from target, at the moment?"

"Golden Eagle to Black Hawk. All ground supports are
folding back to the three-mile point. They had only ad-
vanced another half-mile toward target. Magpie five-nine-
four flew over the compound once already, but I have just
instructed them to go back to base, and keep their engines
running, sir."

JR cut him off, "Black Hawk to Support Team One."

"Black Hawk, sir. Support Team One here. We are just leaving for our assigned position. Twenty minutes, ETA," Claire answered.

The radio went silent again.

~~~

"Mora. Mora. Can you hear me? I need you to wake up."

"Hi, Tania. I couldn't sleep. It's like something woke me up a while back. Why are you calling me so early?"

"Mora, remember I told you that you may have to hide?"

"Yes. Are you coming to get me?"

"I hope to see you later today. I want you to go to the best hiding spot and wait."

"Can I take Cindy to hide with me?"

"You can. Be careful."

"OK. I'll try to talk to you after I hide."

"OK. But only if you feel safe."

Antonia was worried. What would happen to the other girls, if everything did not work out as planned?

Rosetta threw her four crystals on a light-blue embroidered linen circle. She frowned and told her, "One of the girls may be in grave danger. I'm sorry, but I cannot tell which one it is."

~~~

Ruben was at the CBP Charlie Base, just fifteen miles south of the Wolves' compound, running his team's operations. He could not wait to get his Special Ops Eagle Star team moving. Safe in his office by the border, he felt that his agency could handle the whole mission. They had the training and the technology. He craved the respect from all the agencies involved, especially the FBI, and also the adrenaline of the catch and the glory of a mission accomplished. "Golden Eagle to Black Hawk. It is o-four twenty. Shall we move on to Winnebago Three?"

"Black Hawk to Golden Eagle. You are to be the last one to come in to the mission location, as planned. Your vehicles are noisy and may warn the perps ahead of time. If your team cannot wait until I give you the go, I will ask you to stand down."

"Yes sir. I understand, sir. I'll wait for your orders."

"Black Hawk to four-o-five. What is the Bats' status."

"Four-o-five to Black Hawk. All Bats have departed the craft."

The next communication came in a muffled voice. "Big Bat to Black Hawk. I'm on the ground, north side. Three Bats are inside. Sixteen outside with me. Waiting on the main door to open. One canine has been neutralized. No sounds coming from inside."

"Black Hawk to Packrat. What is your position?"

"Packrat to Black Hawk. We are moving in on the west side, about one hundred yards from the Bats."

"Big Bat to Black Hawk. Packrats have joined us. We are waiting by the front door. Still no movement from the inside."

"Black Hawk to Golden Eagle. Move ground vehicles

to outside perimeter. Magpie five-nine-four is to hover five hundred yards to the south. No spotlights. Bats and Rats have night vision."

The first three State Police SWAT team members to land were the most skilled. Two men and a woman in their early forties, ex-military, the three of them trained together once a week. They were first to jump out of the transport plane and had arrived twenty seconds apart inside the courtyard, detaching their parachutes as soon as they landed. Andy, the first one in, had his pistol in his hand when he hit the ground. The tranquilizer dart hit the wolf instantly. As the animal softly fell to the side, without a sound, his two partners were also ready for anything else moving inside the yard.

Everything was quiet, but for the slight swishing sound of the parachutes being dragged to a corner. Still using her night goggles, the woman ran to the gate. Her specialty was opening safes. This gate was easy, no electronic alarms, just three simple deadbolts on the heavy steel doors. She pulled a small, lithium grease gun out of her belt and sprayed the locks and hinges. The doors swung open quietly, as the three of them raised their thumbs up. Andy clicked on his radio twice, the signal that the front gate was open and the way in was clear.

~~~

Faintly, Antonia heard a whisper from Mora. "Tania,

Rosa, we are hiding inside the bathroom closet. It's hot in here. I heard a helicopter a little while ago. But I don't hear it any more. What do we do?"

"Stay where you are. Don't move. Don't talk. Help is on the way."

She could feel the young girl's fear, giving her arms goose bumps in the warmth and safety of Rosetta's house. Tiger licked her hand, as if aware of what Antonia was experiencing, before lying down by her feet. "I'm listening, if you need to talk. But what I'd like you to do for your safety, is to not move at all, and to try to stay as quiet as possible."

Her response was an even fainter, "OK."

~~~

Lights came on inside one of the rooms, then went off right away. A man's voice called out, "Lobo. Lobo? Come."

Then a moment of silence. The Bats were spread out inside the courtyard. At once, a volley of automatic bullets flared in an arc from inside the east wing's windows. Only one silent shot was returned to the shooter. Then all was quiet again, waiting for either side's next move.

A short woman in a white shift opened a door on the southern end and ran, screaming, toward the girls' wing. She unlocked a side door and went in. A few bullets flew again randomly from inside the building as soon as she was out of sight. Inside the yard, the men dressed in black were scattered, crouching to offer a smaller target, and firing only when they saw someone aiming a weapon at them. Their guns had silencers and laser sights. But for the tiny red dot of the laser once on its target, nothing could be seen until the gun fired, a quick orange flash at its business end.

The young woman in the white negligee came back out and ran back to the other side, while a couple of loud bullets aimed at the entrance gate exploded. She stopped and screamed at the top of her lungs. "They're gone! They took the girls! They're all gone!"

Lights came on in another room in the south side, silhouetting a short, half-naked man, who stepped out of the building screaming. "Bitch. You let them out!"

He shot her six times with an automatic rifle. Her body writhed, her shift seemed to flail with her, until the rapidly fired bullets stopped and she fell to the ground.

The man who had just killed her, immediately received one single shot in the back of his head delivered by a tall gray-haired man, who had stepped out of the dark east wing. A dozen small red dots immediately centered on the tall man's heart. After looking down at his chest, he slowly put his rifle on the ground and raised his arms.

An eery silence ensued, finally punctuated by the tall man's words. "Joe. You idiot. Imelda never did any wrong. She was a simple child. I hope you rot in hell. *¡Hijo de puta!*"

Two more men came out of the sleeping quarters with their hands up and were quickly subdued by the police teams. Some of the Bats went inside to check for more people, while four men from the sheriff's team ran to the girls quarter. They called Mora and Cindy's names, but got no answers.

"Packrat leader to Black Hawk. All Wolves are re-strained. My team cannot find the girls. They're gone."

"Stand-by, Packrat," JR said as he started dialing the Bat leader on his cell phone.

After hearing Lou's and JR's voices on the radio, Antonia asked, "Mora, are you still inside the closet? Mora, talk to me."

Sobbing, the girl answered in the tiniest of voices, "They shot Imelda. Are they going to shoot us, too?"

"No. Some people are coming to rescue you. I don't think there will be anymore shooting. But stay where you are. A woman named Isabel is going to come get you. Make sure you don't talk to anyone else until she talks to you. OK, Mora?"

Sniffling, the girl's voice wavered, "OK, but tell her to hurry. I'm scared."

Antonia tried to reach her mother telepathically, but was interrupted by the ringing of her phone. It was Sirena. "Tony, do you know where the girls are? The place has been secured."

"Mom, get Isabel to go into the girls' wing. They are hiding in the bathroom closet."

"Black Hawk, this is Support Team One. Could you get

Isabel to go into the bathroom and have her clearly say her name. The girls are in there."

A female voice with a strong foreign accent took over. "Black Hawk, this is the Bulls' hostage negotiator. I copied and am on my way to the closet. ETA one minute to the west wing."

Isabel walked into the children's wing with her pistol drawn. She was dressed in black, too, her cargo pants tucked into leather hiking boots. Two of the Packrats were standing on each side of the door, their weapons drawn. They nodded to her, before pointing to an open door on the other side of what seemed to be a large dining room. The woman nodded back at them and removed her infrared goggles, sticking them into a large pocket on the sleeve of her shirt, making it bulge out next to her thick vest.

Walking silently, she went through the next door. Faint night-lights were lined up, eight feet apart along the walls. A long hallway on one side, with a row of open doors, then another open door just in front of her. She walked into the next room. Again, two more SWAT team men were waiting on each side of that door. She slowly scanned the room.

A large dorm with unmade beds lined one side. A row of dressers on the other side. No closet here. The room was empty. She backtracked to the hallway, turning on lights above her. Behind each of four open doors, she saw a bathroom with a toilet, a sink, and an open shower.

She stood at the end of the corridor, facing two closets. A humming sound came from the last one. The water heater, she surmised. The large, bifold doors next to it were also shut. With her back up against the wall opposite the bigger closet, she motioned to the two men who had followed her in to step back into the dining hall. She removed her helmet, holstered her pistol, but kept her hand on its stock. Facing the closet, in a gentle voice, she started, "Mora and Cindy, my name is Isabel. Can you hear me?"

No answers.

"Mora and Cindy, this is Isabel. I am a friend of Antonia. She has asked me to come and take you to her place. Are you here?" She waited, facing the closet doors.

A whisper came out through the slatted doors. "What's my dog's name?"

"Her name is Tiger. She is a very smart dog who wants to see you."

"Are you alone?" the child continued in a stronger voice.

"In this room, I am. In the yard, there are two dozen people dressed in black who just arrested all the bad guys. Outside the building, there are more good people waiting to take you to Antonia, Tiger, and your mom and dad. Would you like to ride in a Humvee?"

Mora opened the door a crack and looked at Isabel. The closet's folding doors, once fully opened, revealed five girls lying on shelves of linen and towels and two more crouching on the floor among the cleaning tools and bleach bottles.

~~~

Isabel asked Ruben to let her transport the seven girls in two of the CBP Humvees for the first couple of miles, as planned, where they would pick up Sirena. During a private conference call between JR, Smith, and Lou, all three agreed to give the still-frightened girls more time to recuperate until they felt far enough to be safe from their previous jailers, all the way to Deming. Once there, Antonia could ride along with Mora, who kept asking for her and for Tiger, and with Cindy and another girl. Sirena could ride with the other four in the following armored car.

Meanwhile the three perps that were still standing, Papa Patron included, were being driven by Ruben in another Humvee, to a federal jail in Deming. Agent Smith thought that the CBP Humvee would be more discreet than a prison wagon. He feared retaliation from El Patron's family and retinue. A fourth man, who had suffered a chest wound at the beginning of the altercation, was transported by a waiting ambulance to the Deming Hospital, accompanied by a state police officer.

While all the transport vehicles were gathering for the trips to their respective holding facilities, the girls were met by Sirena and Claire with chocolate milk and cookies. Sipping her warm drink, Mora looked straight at the twins' mother and asked her if she knew Tania.

"Of course I do. Antonia is my daughter."

"Does she look like you?"

"Yes, she does. Do you look like your mother?"

"Yes, I suppose I do. I don't look like my adopted

father. Where is Tiger?"

"I'm not sure, but I think she's riding along with someone else."

"Is Rosa coming, too?"

"I don't think so. Ms. Rosetta is a very private person," replied Sirena.

Right away they were back on the road, Sirena sitting next to Mora and Cindy, with Claire following in her car right behind them. It was a peculiar convoy, on that still-dark, early morning. Two helicopters flew above. The State Police Able four-o-five led the way, while the CBP Magpie five-nine-four secured the rear, a quarter mile behind. On the ground, six black Humvees, with highly tinted windows, about two hundred yards apart, interspersed with three private vehicles, followed a state police SUV that led the way. The ambulance brought up the rear. No lights or sirens. Everyone was maintaining radio silence for fear of divulging any information to the wrong listening ears. Any necessary communications were made by cell phone through JR, who rode in the lead car.

On the way Ruben, who had billed himself as the Mission Manager, was sure to tell everyone in his vehicle that the wounded perp was going to a four-star hospital, but that they were going to a four-star detention center. He was the only one to laugh at his own joke. Behind the center grille, El Patron de los Lobos did not utter a word during the whole trip. When one of his underlings started talking back to Ruben, he got a glance from his boss that froze him in place. No chit-chat. Ruben was disappointed that he would not be able to give JR any juicy tidbits. He wanted to have done more than be the transport. He should have been the one in charge of the whole operation.

While going through Animas, one of the Humvees transporting a state police officer, an FBI agent and a CBP agent, picked up Anita Manzano. She had just gotten up and was putting on her make-up, getting ready for work. She acted the ingénue, as if she had no idea why she was picked up but kept asking for a lawyer. Hands cuffed behind her back, she was put in the prison van, which had just arrived. Then they were on the way to Josette Muñoz's house.

Josette had been advised to maintain her cover as long as possible, especially while she was near the Manzano woman. She knew she would be transferred to a new location and to a new life with her two wards, as soon as her final depositions were made. Until then, she, too, rode in the prison van, in hand cuffs. The women were quiet during the ride, occasionally glancing at each other. Anita's cold dark eyes gave Josette the chills; she wondered what the woman knew. She was afraid of retaliation, of being outed as an informant. She was afraid for her daughter and for her sister's son. Perspiring heavily in the still-cool back of the van, she worried that her voice would betray her if she said anything to this angry woman sitting next to her.

~~~

Sunlight was just starting to peep out when they reached Deming. The convoy splintered from there. A new black Humvee carrying El Patron went north, to an unrevealed location. His two accomplices were dropped off at the Deming Federal Penitentiary. The two women in the prison van were taken north to the women's federal prison in Grant.

Antonia met with Mora in Deming. While she was getting in the Humvee, José, who was driving the Subaru, lowered the windows so the girl could see her dog. Tiger was waving her whole body, as she whined a happy song when Mora called out her name. Antonia rode with the girls to Las Cruces.

A Winnebago, which had been wrecked when its driver had a heart attack a few months before, was being towed to Las Cruces at the back of the reorganized convoy. In order to protect the children, the cover story for the media was that a big drug bust had just happened. The reporters were told the drugs were hidden and transported inside a travel trailer on Interstate-10.

~~~

Chapter 36
Tying up Loose Ends

CLAIRE AND THE TWINS SPENT THE NEXT twenty-four hours together. As if trying to outdo each other, they took turns cooking elaborate meals, from breakfast to dinner. They talked on and off about past personal matters, avoiding the recent events. They did not want to color their facts before the debrief. They went for a leisurely hike up in the Organ Mountains, looking at the native flowers that were blooming profusely after the last shower that had cooled and healed the parched earth. Early in the evening, they walked to a small pub, where they drank locally crafted beer and listened to cheerful Mariachi music.

Back at the house, they prepared another delicious meal: miso soup, vegetable sushi rolls, fresh, fatty tuna sashimi, and a cucumber salad. During dinner, over small glasses of saké, they talked about cases in their respective occupations, never mentioning names or locations. Finally, they spent half the night in one of the twins' king-sized beds, exploring each other's beauty, until exhausted, but satiated, they fell into a deep sleep.

~~~

The debrief was pushed back a few days. While the mission had gone smoother than anticipated, there were still a few loose ends to tie up. Only two fatalities, the innocent and abused Imelda and the man who killed her, and one casualty, a severe chest injury to the eager gunman on the Wolves side, who was shot at the beginning of the assault.

A state police officer had stayed behind with the girl's and the henchman's bodies, until the Hidalgo County Sheriff, Henri Muñoz, and a coroner from the same county had arrived to pick up the remains the first morning of the mission. The caged wolf was tranquilized again, picked up by a local Game and Fish officer to be sent to a wolf management facility. Being a beautiful specimen, he would probably be used for breeding. When everyone was out, the sheriff sealed the compound and placed deputies to guard it, until the FBI came back to finish its investigation.

Agent Smith had taken El Patron up north, to unknown parts. JR was the only one to join him in interrogating the big boss. It cost him a day to get there and a day to get back to Las Cruces. Meanwhile, Lou and Sunny returned to work after a day of rest, eager for the run-of-the-mill dealings after a stressful endeavor. Ruben went back to El Paso, reported to his superiors, and told them how he had practically managed the whole thing. Carlos got a promotion, but had to stay in Kingsburg. José went home and asked the Tonys to be sure to call him for their next assignment. Sirena went home, too, saying she would be back after Claire left.

Five of the young girls were returned to their grateful

families, each promising to never run away again. Mora and Tiger stayed home, and would not venture outside but for Tiger's morning walk, and only when accompanied by Maria, who decided to take a couple of weeks off work in order to be with her daughter. Sirena offered to homeschool her, but to her surprise, Maria told her she would do it herself in the morning, and work at the salon in the afternoon. She mentioned that she had studied for two years at the community college for a degree in education, but quit school when she had Mora.

The news media plastered the air and the papers about a Winnebago from New Jersey that had been seized by multiple agencies on Interstate-10, in New Mexico, near the Arizona border. State Police Deputy Chief Lindsey Simon of Las Cruces reported how they had been looking for this particular operation's boss for many years, how the Customs Border Protection, Doña Ana Sheriff Department and New Mexico State Police agencies had been working together, culminating in the arrest of three American men and one Mexican national. Her report was followed by that of a young sergeant, who mentioned that ten kilograms of pure heroine had been confiscated, without indicating when or where.

A picture of a partially wrecked motorhome decorated with much graffiti made the top news nationally for a couple of days, before becoming old news, heard and seen too many times.

~~~

The following morning, the Tonys were listening to the many messages left on their voice mail, when there was a knock on the front door. As they opened the door, Tiger bounded in, singing loudly her high-pitched song, her tail waving her whole body side to side. Maria and Andrés were holding Mora's hands on each side. The girl's hair was French-braided. She was wearing new stylish clothes and new shoes. She ran to Antonio and gave him a long heartfelt hug. Not missing a beat, she said, "This is really for Antonia, but you can share it too, 'cause it doesn't make any difference who gets it."

Another one who knows, Tone.

Not the last one, I'm sure.

Then she gave him a handwritten poem, with the name: Mora Aguirre, signed at the bottom.

The Tiger and the Angel

Tiger has a tail,
Always on the right trail.
An angel and a tiger
I will love no other.
Sometimes she is a monkey,
To my heart she holds the key.
An angel and a tiger
I will love no other.
She brings an angel to me
When monsters surround me.
An angel and a tiger
I will love no other.

The Tonys were deeply touched by her poem and gave her another hug, promising that they would try to spend time together often.

As he shook Antonio's hand, Andrés spoke with a thick, Hispanic accent. "Her mother is going to teach her school every morning, and she will be with me every afternoon. This way, no one can steal her from us. Thank you for finding my daughter."

Mora added, "And Papa has moved back in with Mama. We're a family again." As an afterthought she added, "Oh, and I have a job for you. I would like you to find a good Australian Shepherd boy dog for Tiger to have babies with. I will pay you with the pick of the litter."

"It's a deal," Antonio answered, as they shook hands.

~~~

JR called everyone for a debrief a couple of days later. They met in the War Room at ten in the morning. Only one man, an investigator by the name of Agent Bill Jones, came from the FBI. CBP was represented by Carlos and Ruben. Everyone else involved showed up, including Antonia and Sirena.

Starting the meeting, JR introduced Vincente Duran, a man whose eyes seemed to always be twinkling. He had a large dimple on his chin, and a thick mustache.

"Mr. Duran is with the PFM, la Policía Federal Ministerial, the Mexican equivalent of the FBI. He was contacted by Interpol, while they were looking for the

Sanchez man. I have invited him here today to share his research of the crimes committed by the Villalobos family, and also, so he can fill us in on the other side of the border's investigations."

JR then proceeded to give a short history of the Wolf's operation, a description of the events that occurred in the boot heel part of the state, followed by the results of the last three days. He praised all the agencies for working so well together, mentioning especially the SWAT teams of Las Cruces State Police and Doña Ana County Sheriff. He praised the non-officials that helped accomplish the mission, referring to the intensive preliminary help of the Two Tony's Search Engine agency, but omitting Rosetta's involvement.

"It is quite an accomplishment to have realized our goals without any injuries suffered by our teams. Thank you, all." He raised his water bottle to all present. "Now some follow-up news for the last few days. El Patron is awaiting trial in a federal prison up north. He denies any charges of wrongdoing. The Manzano woman and one of El Patron's accomplices are willing to talk for reduced sentences. They have indicated already that the girls were being primed for underage prostitution somewhere in El Paso. The man that was wounded during the operation is still in critical condition and may not recover. Josette Muñoz and her nephew Leo are being relocated to another state. The Muñoz daughter chose to go back to school in the fall, au pair, somewhere in Europe. She has left the country already. In a couple of months, she will contact the rest of her family and tell them that her mother is with her. As for the Hidalgo sheriff, Henri Muñoz, he was not aware of the problem in his county, but mentioned two young schoolgirls who disappeared with no trace, eight years ago. The FBI is looking into it. Hope Castillo was picked up for interrogation and ordered to stay put. Unfortunately, as soon as she was released, she disappeared. She traded in her car at a Ford dealership for a much older Ford Escort sedan, and I guess, quite a bit of cash back. We are currently looking for the used car in our state and in Texas."

He paused and sipped some water. Everyone in the room was quiet, revisiting internally the events of a few days before.

"Of the seven girls, five were reunited with their parents. One was abducted from western Texas, another from Arizona. Three others are New Mexican. The two Guatemalan girls are currently under the protection of Immigration and Customs Enforcement, but they are about to be transferred to the Department of Health and Human Services. Both ICE and DHHS are trying to find their families, but this could prove a difficult task, as they seemed to have come from a farming community that was completely destroyed by insurgents two years ago. As unaccompanied alien children and victims of severe forms of trafficking, they may qualify for permanent T visas. But this can be a very time-consuming process that would not solve all of their problems."

Maybe we should look into this. Would like to help them.

Sis, doubt if ICE will let us non-feds have any say so in the matter.

Carlos was staring at them again. Antonia stared back with a polite smile.

Think Carlos can help us?

Not now, Sis! Let's talk later.

JR continued, "Regarding the girl Imelda, it turns out that she was a distant relative of El Patron. The mother was a great niece of his, who died of a drug overdose years ago, and left the handicapped child behind. Villalobos, I mean El Patron, said he always took care of the girl and made sure she was safe, fed, and clothed. As a matter of fact, he has just wired some money to our facility to arrange a Catholic funeral for her, as soon as the body is released."

He took another sip of water, looking around the room, as if assessing their attention. Everyone's eyes were still glued to his mouth. "On the plus side, the FBI cleaned up the Wolves' den with a fine-tooth comb. In the process, they found a ledger, started two years ago, with dates, dollar numbers and sets of initials. I was shown only one page of the ledger, but I believe some of these initials stand for Angelo Villalobos Sanchez. The large sums of money could indicate the sale of young girls. This ledger may very well be the evidence we need to bust the Sanchez son for running a youth prostitution ring in El Paso. If we can ever catch him, that is."

Another pause, another drink of water. "Mr. Duran, would you like to elaborate on your findings, if you can?"

In perfect English, with barely a trace of an accent and a slow enunciation, Agent Duran took over. "Certainly, sir. Everyone understands that this is confidential. We have been following the Villalobos family for many years. We know that Angelo Emilio Villalobos Sanchez was born in Mexico City, to American parents. Unfortunately, the mother died during childbirth. The father, Emilio Ernesto Villalobos Sanchez, took him back to the US and raised him as an American. We think he procured a fake passport for the child, as well as a fake Social Security number. We found out from Interpol that his Social Security number originally belonged to an American child who died a month after he was born. Sanchez should be about twenty-eight-years old, give or take a month. Our organization has tried to pick him up for questioning a few times, to no avail. We have tried to contact him by phone many times. Every time we think we are getting closer to him, he disappears. We have his fingerprints on a gun that killed Manuel Enrique Mendoza, a big drug lord in Juarez, and also on a vial of barbiturates belonging to Mendoza's wife before she died of an overdose of sleeping pills. That happened five years ago. One year later, two American tourists, also with the last name of Mendoza, disappeared. They were never found but for the woman's purse with, we think, a photo of her and Sanchez swimming naked in a lake. That one is still under investigation."

He paused long enough to look at everyone and

continued in the same, concise diction. "Interpol asked me to look for Villalobos Sanchez in Acapulco a few days ago. I found traces of a man who fits his profile, who recently boarded a flight from Acapulco to Mexico City with an American passport, under the name of Ernest Sanchez. Both these men had their left arm in a cast, which helped us make the connection. We have been watching two of his uncles, on our side. One lives in Juarez, the other in Mexico City. In the past, Sanchez has spent a lot of time with one or the other. Neither uncle was available. His uncle Villalobos Jimenez, is suspected of running a prostitution ring in Juarez. Sanchez's only aunt lives in Oaxaca City. Her husband and she run a small hotel. They do not want to be associated with any of the Villalobos. She will call if Sanchez ever comes to see her."

He looked around the room with emphasis marking his last words. "I came here today for two reasons. First, to warn you: this man is very dangerous and has no scruples. I urge you to be extremely careful. And second: if you have any information about Sanchez, please get in touch with me."

"Thank you, Agent Duran. José, you have a little bit of information from Lieutenant Morales, T or C's chief."

"Yes, sir. Just a small detail. The blood found on the front fender of the truck Sanchez was driving was actually canine blood. It was not human."

Antonia let out an audible sigh. Lou smiled at her, while JR continued, "All right. Agent Duran, please, keep me posted of any new development, and I will do the same. Thank you for coming to meet with us. And everyone, please, be patient five more minutes or so, for something else coming in."

At that moment they heard a knock on the door. An officer brought in a rolling, stainless-steel table filled with plates of hot burritos and steaming coffee pots from the Cocina del Sol.

"A small thank you for everyone's hard work." JR said, as they all gathered around the food.

Lou sat down to eat next to Antonia. After gulping down a mouthful of hot coffee, he said, "How are you holding up?"

Turning toward him, she smiled and replied. "I'm all right. Hey, Lou, Antonio wants you to stop by the house for dinner tomorrow. Grilled catfish, Cajun style, and heirloom-tomato salad with cilantro dressing. Maybe an apple pie, if he has time to make one. Can you come?"

"Some of my favorites. I'd like to see him. Tell him I'll be there."

~ ~ ~

In the evening, Sirena brought a large bowl of spaghetti marinara, a tossed arugula, pear, and radicchio salad, with a sweet Meyer-lemon dressing and an inverted peach tart tatin. Antonia was glad her brother would not have to cook; they were exhausted from all the emotions of the bust, for fully realizing the young girls' danger, for dealing with Lou's mixed-up feelings, and also for fearing another possible attack from the dreadful Angelo, who may still want to vindicate his family.

Seeing the worry in her children's eyes, Sirena started talking about her future, to get their minds off the recent events. "Your father's remains were buried the day before we helped rescue the girls. His friend Chucky took care of the whole thing. I'm sorry I couldn't attend his funeral. I followed your advice and talked with Chucky about selling him my half of your dad's business. He seems like such a nice man. Very polite. He is willing to buy the whole fishing shack. He said he had been managing it for the last four years and had made a few improvements already. He would like to buy my half at fair market price. He is ready to send me the paperwork and the money. Your dad's lawyer said it was a very reasonable settlement."

She took a very small sip of the cabernet sauvignon they had opened to go with the marinara. "Here is what I'd like to do with that money. I would like to create a home for damaged, single, young women. I would also like to open, adjacent to it, a small school for gifted and handicapped children. It will be called Angel Imelda's Retreat. It would offer the basic curriculum required by the national school system, plus additional courses that the children themselves would choose. When I was with the girls in the Humvee, on our way to meet you in Deming, I listened to them. They had some very interesting ideas. Mora wanted to learn from Rosetta 'how to feel the real motives of people' — her words — and she also wants to learn foreign languages, other than Spanish. Cindy mentioned that music lessons should be available early in school. I hope I can find the right people to offer classes like these. I would like to help the children with special needs from Kingsburg, Deming, and Las Cruces. "

The twins almost started their internal dialogue, but voiced it out loud instead, rapidly one after the other.

"Mom, we might already know two people with these criteria. Rosetta and Woody."

"Mom, this doesn't sound like retirement."

Sirena continued, "Antonia, yes, Rosetta and Woody would be great teachers, if they are both willing to do it. But Antonio, retirement? Would you rather I crawled under a dark rock, waiting for you to come visit? You know me better than that."

She took another sip of wine, then after a long, deep breath, she continued, "I have been given this great opportunity to do a good deed with my life. There is a need for this kind of venture, here and now. So, in order to accomplish this soon, the other thing I would like to do is to hire a detective agency to: one, find the proper buildings outside and west of Las Cruces; two, find monetary grants from local and state agencies; and three, find dedicated teachers who will not give up as soon as one student asks a challenging question."

"Mom, you know there are not too many agencies that would accept this job," Antonio replied jokingly, already knowing where his mother was going with her inquiry.

"I know, that's why I thought you two would be best suited for this research."

After thinking about it for a few seconds, they responded, warbling their pitch alternately with every sentence, "We'll do it, Mom. With a few conditions: You cook us three meals a week until we find you the perfect location. And you have to eat these meals with us, so we can discuss our findings. Regarding the grants, we'll get Nicole to help. She's really good at it. You can pay her for her time. After we find the locale and have sent for the grants, we'll run ads for teachers. We'll do the interviews. You can help with the interviews, but understand, you need to let us do the primary investigation. We'll keep you posted when we dine together."

They smiled broadly and asked, "Meanwhile, how do you plan to find the kids?"

Beaming back with a glint in her eyes, she raised her eyebrows and replied, "When everything is ready, I think they will find us."

~~~